THE MESSENGER

Claire Bamford

First published 2025
by Rowanvale Books Ltd
The Gate
Keppoch Street
Roath
Cardiff
CF24 3JW
www.rowanvalebooks.com

A CIP catalogue record for this book is available from the British Library.
ISBN: 978-1-83584-093-1
eBook ISBN: 978-1-83584-094-8

For Mum and Dad

PROLOGUE

Elizabeth had been staring out of the study window for fifteen minutes with the note clasped in her hand. Standing for so long was making her ache, but she felt disinclined to move despite the discomfort.

A spring shower had poured itself out onto the garden. The bright sunlight that now took its place was making the grass glisten. A blackbird bounced down the stone steps that led to the paved path in front of the study window. Elizabeth watched it curiously eye a puddle where some of the slabs had sunk into the ground beneath. It hopped in, splashing and dipping its head. Beads of water slid down its pitch feathers.

Elizabeth sighed deeply.

'These old bones are nearly ready for their final rest, I think, Mr Blackbird,' she said, turning away from the window and shuffling slowly back to her writing desk. She eased herself into the chair, her back and legs glad for the relief.

Her jewellery box lay upside down, exposing the secret, empty compartment within. The interior was plain, not as ornate as the exterior with its patterns of roses and leaves. The piece of wood that should have been its base sat separately, next to a blue leather notebook.

Elizabeth opened the note and read it again.

'No more I can say than that.' She signed and dated it like she did with all her correspondence. *'18th April 1972'*

She went to place the note inside the upturned box but was unable to let it go. 'How will I know if what I do is for the best?' The note remained just between her fingers, as if it were dangling from a great height and letting it go would allow it to fall into an endless chasm.

'Better I leave an explanation than nothing at all,' Elizabeth resolved. Talking to herself had become a habit, having never married or had children. 'I cannot leave someone to navigate this blindly if it happens again.' She let the piece of paper slip from her fingertips and placed the book alongside it. 'And last of all.' She picked up a small, black, velvet box and ran her thumb over the material one final time. Then, it took its place inside amongst the other items.

She picked up a paintbrush and dipped it into some wood glue, with which she edged the base of the box then the piece of wood that would seal the tiny tomb. She noticed a sizeable chip on one of the edges and tutted. 'I should have used a better tool than a letter opener to prise this off.'

After carefully positioning the base back in its rightful place, she sat silently, waiting for the glue to set before lifting her hands away to inspect her work.

Leaving the box on the desk with a letter addressed to her niece Violet, Elizabeth raised herself up from the chair to ascend the stairs to bed.

She looked back at the scene for the last time. 'There's no more to be done. I hope you know what to do, Violet. My time is more or less over. I wonder if Agnes will be waiting for me when I get there.'

CHAPTER 1

The scent of the border wafted gently despite the cooling late-autumnal air. The hours had romped away, and it was beginning to get dark.

Jen's movements gave her away to the security light above the garage door and it cast its bright white light over the brick driveway, making her squint. 'That's the last of it, Mum,' she shouted up to the open bedroom window, locking the car and, with some effort, picking up the final box, labelled *'Photos'*.

Jen popped the box down on the front step of the semi-detached house and waited for her eyes to adjust. The lavender and rosemary had grown to waist height, and she could reach them without bending. She had always loved their aroma; it felt like coming home. Jen lifted the box again and hooked the front door with her foot on the way in, closing it behind her.

Glancing at the windowsill on her way up the stairs, she noticed a letter addressed to her parents, *'Mark and Jacqueline Hattley'*, with a postmark dated *'12th November 2022'*.

Been a while since they needed anything addressed to the both of them, Jen thought to herself, heaving the box up the next steps.

Jacqui was contentedly hanging clothes in the fitted wardrobes in Jen's old room when Jen dropped the box and collapsed onto her bed. She'd started moving out of her own house two days earlier, dodging the times that her ex-husband was going to be there. Her dad had helped the first day with a hire van and a mate from work who had skills in the heavy-lifting department. Her mum was helping today with the lighter loads, although it turned out some of the boxes were a lot more weighty than Jen had anticipated. She would be aching the rest of the week, she was sure of it.

'You don't have to do that, Mum, we've been at it all day. Time for a takeaway and a sit down, I reckon.'

Jacqui slid a hanger into a turquoise hoodie and slotted it into its designated place amongst the other greens and blues already at home on the rail. 'You know I like doing this. Let me have my fun.' Jacqui smiled. 'Do you really wear all of this? I'm sure some of it could be moved on.'

Jen rolled her eyes and took her phone out of her back pocket. Her mum was the declutter queen—if it hadn't been used or thought about in the last six months, it was time for it to go.

Ignoring the comment, Jen perused some food options. 'What do you fancy? Pizza? Chinese? Ooh, what about that Lebanese place you like? I bet they deliver here.'

Jacqui carried on arranging the clothes while Jen ordered their dinner and caught up on her emails. She would steal a look at her daughter each time she picked up another bit of clothing and couldn't help smiling; having Jen back home, lying on her bed in her old room, made her heart full again. Not that she had been feeling particularly without purpose or sad lately—having Jen near just made her feel complete.

Jacqui stepped round one of the wardrobe doors to hang a coat on another rail and glimpsed herself in the mirror. The last time she had spent so much time in this room was when she helped Jen move out. She was greying now, but not as much as others she knew; some dark brown still filtered through. Her hair was shorter, too, making her 'go to' gold earrings more noticeable, and she'd lost a little weight since then, mainly due to taking up walking with her friend twice a week.

This is all lovely, but you're going to have to tell her sooner than you hoped, Jacqui's inner voice reminded her. *She's going to ask questions when she starts noticing.*

The voice was promptly shushed.

After another twenty minutes, and with a 'Ta da!', Jacqui presented her finished work.

Jen got up from the bed and ran her hand over all her clothes. Tops, jumpers and cardigans in a cascade of colour across the rail, left to right. A rainbow in a cupboard. Her mum loved to organise.

'I have to admit,' Jen said, 'it does look impressive. Thanks so much.' Jacqui had turned to tidy the vase of dried lavender, which she'd placed on one of Jen's side tables. 'Seriously, Mum, thank you. Letting me move back in, helping me with it all, I really appreciate it.'

'I'm always here for you, no matter what's happening, you know that,' Jacqui replied, turning round to give her daughter a hug. 'Now, where's that food? I am starving.'

'It's on its way! Best get the table laid.'

Both women made their way down the stairs. Jen headed to the kitchen, while Jacqui went towards the dining room.

'Just getting the placemats out,' Jacqui said. 'That takeaway grease never comes out if you get it on the table.' She stopped in her tracks as she passed through the doorway. 'Oh, come on now,' she said quietly, as if reprimanding the room. 'You know we can't have this. Not yet.'

Every chair was askew from the table, as if six people had upped and left in a rush. Jacqui quickly circumnavigated the table, pushing all the chairs back into their places.

'Everything okay?' Jen asked, bringing the plates and cutlery in.

'Yes, yes, just having a tidy, like I do. Glasses for wine? There's a decent red in the rack.'

Jen smiled as she placed everything on the table, then went back to the kitchen for water and wine.

Jacqui made sure she had left before continuing her rebuttal. 'Now, behave yourself. Seriously. Not on the first night. Give me a chance.'

The doorbell rang, signalling the arrival of dinner.

***

Both women leant back in their chairs with satisfied appetites and empty plates.

Jen poured the last of the red wine into her mum's glass. 'I'm in the office tomorrow, so you can finish this.'

Jacqui motioned 'cheers' to Jen and took a sip. 'Are you sure you're not going back too quickly? You've had a lot to deal with over the last few weeks.'

'It's all pretty much over now, and I need to get back to normality. I'm working from home the rest of the week anyway. Worst case, I'll book some extra days off. I'll be fine, I promise.'

Jen gathered the plates and cutlery to take out to the kitchen.

Jacqui's mobile started to ring.

It was Mark. 'Hey, how did the rest of the moving in go? Jen settled in okay?'

'Yes, I have her doing the dishes already.' Jacqui laughed as Jen turned and pretended to scowl.

'Ha, great. If anything heavy needs moving around, I'll be over at the weekend, so just leave it till then.'

'Thanks, we already have a list of jobs for you, don't worry. Did you want to speak to Jen?'

'Yes, but… can she hear you right now?'

Jacqui grabbed her wine glass and got up from the table. She moved into the hallway and sat on the bottom stair. 'I'm in the hallway. What's the matter?'

'What if she starts noticing? Things ramped up somewhat after she moved out.'

Jacqui breathed in deeply. 'She's not even been here one night yet, but, so far, there's been nothing to notice.'

She could hear her husband thinking. Thinking before he spoke was a quality she admired in him.

'Just, with the split—I know it was a while back, but—it would be a lot for her to take in right now. I know you planned to tell her soon, but maybe now isn't the right time.'

Jacqui, conversely, took no time to think. 'There's never a right time to tell someone this kind of thing. I don't plan to send her over the edge; give me some credit! Anyway, she's a lot stronger than we both realise. I hope to keep a lid on it as long as I can, then I'll find the right moment to explain it all to her. It's not something I want to put off for much longer; she needs to know and ask me questions while she can.'

'I get it, sorry, you know how I am about it. You have it all under control, like you usually do. Well, enjoy your first night having our daughter back at home. What's it been, over ten years since she moved out? I am a bit jealous.'

'It is lovely to have her here, even if it's only for a little while.' Jacqui drank the last of her wine and looked at Jen through the dining room door as she tidied the table. 'There'll be plenty of times you can enjoy this with me. She might fancy staying with you for a few nights. Anyway, I'll pass you over. Speak later.'

Jacqui walked back into the dining room, passed the phone to Jen and took over the rest of the tidying up.

***

'Let's make a rule not to watch the ten o'clock news again. The anniversary segment for that woman that went missing—how awful was that? Her family is stuck with having no answers every single day. Does my head in.'

Jacqui was having a look out into the back garden, peeking through the long, heavy curtains that covered the bifold doors. Jen couldn't see, but she had a pensive look on her face.

'I remember when she went missing. You must have been coming up for six years old and I was around the same age as her. She had kids, too, and I remember thinking how horrible it was that her little ones had their mum vanish into thin air.'

Jen shook her head and turned off the TV. 'Just winds me up. The poor woman; someone obviously killed her and they're just getting away with it.' She stretched her arms above her head. 'I don't want to think about it anymore. I am done in. I'll try not to wake you up in the morning.'

'I'm usually awake early these days anyway, so pop your head in to say goodbye before you go.'

'Will do. Night, Mum, love you.' Jen rose from the sofa, gave her mum a kiss on the cheek and headed to bed.

'Love you, too.'

Ascending the stairs, Jen stopped to look at the familiar photographs adorning the wall: her mum and dad holding hands with her at a theme park—probably in the nineties, judging by her neon clothes; Jen on the lap of her nan, Violet, both with Christmas cracker hats on. Jen leant in, taking in her nan's kind eyes and contented smile. Then, Jen, her mum and her nan sitting on the sofa, which had teddies sitting along the back, all together at her nan's old flat, not long before she died. That one was at a bit of an angle compared to the rest, so Jen righted it gently.

There were numerous other pictures with family and friends at life's milestones. Then, of course, in pride of place was their beloved dog Bailey, so named due to Jacqui's love for the drink. His soppy brown eyes framed by his golden fur stared back at her, as they had when he was alive.

Jen kissed her fingers and planted one on Bailey's face and one on her nan's. 'Still miss you.'

Jacqui came away from the curtains, listening for Jen ascending the stairs. There was a creak, which meant she had made it to the second-to-last step at the top. Moments afterwards, the whirr of the bathroom extractor fan came on. Jacqui stood still, waiting for Jen to pad her way along the landing and close her bedroom door.

It was like déjà vu, but this was no trick of her memory. Jacqui remembered performing the same routine, on evenings when Jen and her husband would stay over for Christmas or New Year.

Jen's bedroom door clicked shut. Jacqui stood in the living room, listening intently to the house. She could hear her own breath: *inhale, exhale.*

After what seemed like several minutes, Jacqui wondered if tonight was going to be a quiet one, but almost immediately following the thought, a cupboard door slammed in the kitchen.

Jacqui breathed in deeply, and the hairs on her arms stood up. She felt her heartbeat quicken; her adrenaline had kicked in.

She listened for any movement upstairs, hoping Jen had not heard. Silence again.

Then another cupboard slammed.

'At least they waited for her to go to bed,' Jacqui muttered.

She took her laptop out of the cupboard by the TV and strode into the kitchen, closing the door gently behind her.

Jen was already half asleep by the time she got under the duvet, but she thought she could hear her mum's muffled voice downstairs. *Maybe she's on the phone*, she surmised, before sleep fully took over.

CHAPTER 2

Jen awoke to her alarm going off and the faint smell of lavender in her nostrils. She'd slept so deeply it had taken over a minute for the annoying sound to permeate her unconsciousness. She couldn't remember the last time she'd had such a good night's sleep.

Sitting herself up, she looked round her old bedroom expecting to feel out of sorts. The wallpaper and carpet had changed, as had the curtains, from when she'd lived there before, but her wardrobes were the same and the light coming in through the window felt familiar. As it was, she was feeling the most comfortable she'd been for a while—almost as if coming back home was allowing her to hit the reset button.

The last couple of weeks had been draining, physically and mentally. Three months before they separated, she and Tom had tried marriage counselling. She had described the overwhelming sense of not feeling at ease in her own house, as if she didn't fit in there or the house itself didn't want her there—which had sounded mad when she said it out loud to the counsellor. She'd had stomach aches every morning for what seemed like ages; the counsellor helped her realise these were stress related.

The more Jen had talked about her feelings, the more she realised what was inevitable. The sessions weren't helping them fix their marriage, they were confirming what she already knew: she and Tom used to be good together but now they weren't. She had no idea why. They just didn't fit together like before.

When it eventually came, the split itself was relatively amicable. But tensions started to show, mainly on Tom's side. It was Jen who had stood in their kitchen on a Sunday morning and told him that their marriage needed to be over, citing their different ways of looking at life, that she was no longer in love with him. Tom hadn't disagreed with any of her reasons—he also felt their relationship wasn't as it used to be—but he hadn't wanted her to be the one to initiate the ending of it all. It was Jen leaving him, Jen taking control of the situation, Jen saying out loud that it was over, and with that came some resentment, a few self-pitying comments here and there about being 'left nearly forty and childless' and 'How could she do this to him?'

All this just made her feel even more sure that her decision had been the right one. She'd been the brave one, the one who had decided that living the rest of her life like that wasn't okay. They both deserved to be happier; she was just the one who'd called it.

She wondered now where the future was going to take her and wasn't scared by the fact that she didn't yet know. She was excited.

After a quick shower, Jen popped her head into her mum's room to see her reading in bed. 'I'm off. See you when I get back.'

Jacqui looked up from her book. 'Have a good day! Let me know if you're home for dinner.'

'Will do. Love you!' Jen hollered as she headed down the stairs.

'Love you too, dear,' Jacqui called after her.

Midway down the stairs, Jen noticed the picture of her, her mum, her nan and the teddies was at a jaunty angle again. She stopped, straightened it up and gave it a smile.

**

Jen found herself on her usual platform, queuing for the train between the familiar faces she saw every Wednesday morning—the lady with the stylish mustard scarf and the teenager in his black private school uniform. They all stood in the same places to get on the same train. They'd never spoken; a courteous smile—or in the case of the teenager, a look up from his phone—being enough of an acknowledgement. As the train pulled in, the three of them edged forward, ready to claim their space, whether standing or sitting, for the twenty-five-minute journey.

Jen counted herself lucky as she found a seat and squeezed herself into place, making sure she had her phone in her hand and her earbuds in. There was no room for shuffling about in her bag once the train pulled off.

The man next to her was already into some series on his tablet; the one opposite tried to subtly spread open his paper without encroaching on the personal space of a young woman sitting next to him. He clearly failed, based on the eye roll he unknowingly received as the corner of the paper brushed her arm. Jen studied her look, having not seen her before: blonde hair, black-rimmed glasses and a camel-coloured coat; she had her earbuds in and was intently tapping away on her phone. Jen expected the infringement from 'newspaper man' was being broadcast to her friends on various social media in real time.

All were in their own little worlds, and Jen settled into hers for the journey. She was still getting used to being back on the train; Covid had ushered in a new era of company policy, which saw her employer ditch its larger London Bridge office in favour of a smaller, shared, Victoria-based one, and they encouraged their employees to embrace working from home.

Although Jen was more than happy with the new culture, when the opportunity had come up to run weekly face-to-face training sessions, she'd welcomed it and quickly volunteered. Forcing herself out of the house was a welcome distraction from everything happening with Tom, and luckily, she could still use the same station from her mum's house. It was too easy to stay indoors, embedded in her routine of pyjamas and cereal to start the day's tasks. This gave her a chance to air out the clothes designed to be worn outdoors and remember how to apply some mascara.

Jen opened her emails on her phone to see who her delegates were for the day. As she skimmed the names—some familiar, some not—a voice message popped up from her best friend, Laura.

'Hey! So, I didn't want to message yesterday as I know you had the move to do—hope that went okay and it was a good first night at your mum's—but I know you're in London today and wondered if you wanted to go out after work? Krish is working from home so can look after Olivia. Let me know! I can head in and meet you wherever. Bye!'

Jen's face lit up. A girls' night sounded excellent, and with Laura, even better. Jen and Laura had been friends since they were in their late teens, having met working part-time at a telesales company whilst doing their A-levels. They'd stuck together ever since, keeping their friendship alive while Laura was at university and Jen started her first job. Laura was there when Jen first met Tom, and both were bridesmaids at each other's weddings. There was nothing Jen didn't tell Laura, unless it just fell into the category of mundane, and she felt this was reciprocated.

Not wanting to voice message Laura back on the packed train, Jen sent a quick reply confirming she was up for it and a suggestion of where they could meet.

Maybe I'll have time today to nip to the shops for a quick costume change, she thought.

She sent a text to her mum. *'Hi. Is it okay if I go out after work with Laura? I feel a bit rude considering this would have been our first proper night at home. Hope it's okay?'*

Jacqui replied quickly with two thumbs up emojis.

Jen switched to some music and saw out the rest of the journey quite happy with how her day was panning out so far.

***

Jacqui had been finishing up in the bathroom when Jen's text came through. As much as she wanted to spend more time with her, it was a blessing for Jen to be out most of the evening; it would give her time to work out how best to explain the current situation and what was going to happen later.

Checking the time, Jacqui headed downstairs to have breakfast before driving to work. She aligned the photograph of her, her mum and Jen, which was slightly askew, as she descended.

CHAPTER 3

Most of Jen's day consisted of colleagues asking how she was. Some already knew about her divorce, and some just noticed she was no longer wearing her wedding ring; the latter tried to find subtle ways of working out if she wanted to talk about it or not. Most people were being kind and wanted to check she was okay, but she knew a few were just after the latest gossip.

Her boss had called her around lunchtime to check in.

'Glad you're back in the office, let's get some time together tomorrow to properly catch up,' he had said, before they went through some of the new training material for the next few weeks.

As Jen was contemplating her options for lunch, a message popped up from Laura.

'Hey, so looking forward to tonight!!' Various food and drink emojis were sprinkled in.

Jen was equally excited. It had been a hectic year, so she hadn't sat down with Laura completely on her own for what seemed like ages. She loved Laura's daughter Olivia very much—thirteen years old and still wanting to spend time with her 'Auntie' Jen whenever she visited—but sometimes the friends just needed some freedom to chat away from little ears.

Laura had been a pillar of strength and support for Jen during the marriage break-up. She and Krish had welcomed Jen into their home during the initial days, providing her and Tom with space during some of the bitterest moments. Jen hadn't wanted to move back in with her mum straight away, seeing it as a bit of a step back, but after speaking with her parents it seemed the most sensible solution to enable her to get back on her feet.

After taking a brief look at her emails and seeing there wasn't a great deal going on, Jen grabbed her coat and headed out to the shops. As she came out the office doors, she noticed a hairdresser's window opposite displaying 'Wednesday Flash Sale', with various cuts and colours at a discounted price. They probably had their 'flash sale' every Wednesday, but Jen had never noticed before.

She ran her fingers through her hair. *I can't remember the last time I paid you any attention*, she thought.

All of her time over the last year had been spent on the separation; focusing on her hair or any element of her appearance had fallen by the wayside.

Jen made a quick check of the road and dashed across, thoughts of a new outfit forgotten.

The receptionist smiled as Jen walked in. 'How can I help you today?'

Pointing at her mousy brown hair, Jen said, 'What can you do with this?'

***

It was about 4pm when Jacqui arrived back home from her job at the local primary school. As a teaching assistant, she covered three days a week opposite another lady and very much enjoyed it. She'd originally trained just to fill her time when Jen became a teenager and no longer needed her at home so much. It was something just for herself, but she had found she got immense satisfaction from being involved with the classes. Jacqui had been at the same school ever since and had no plans to leave.

After unlocking the front door, she immediately headed for the thermostat in the hallway and knocked it up a few degrees. The temperature had started to fall the past week or so, but the house felt extra cold.

She took her phone out of her bag, shivering a little as she shrugged her coat off. She had a couple of text messages from Mark about the weekend and one from her friend about their pub lunch on Friday. She sat on the bottom step of the stairs and went to the messages from Jen first, with photos of her new hairdo.

Good for her, Jacqui thought, replying that the new cut suited her.

Jacqui stared past her phone for a few moments, remembering how upset she'd been when Jen first told her about the break-up. Not for the fact that the marriage was over, but that neither she nor Mark had really noticed anything was wrong. She felt guilty; as Jen's mum, surely she should have seen some signs of her daughter's unhappiness. But then, not everyone advertises what goes on behind closed doors, even to those closest to them. Jacqui knew how easy it could be to hide something so significant. She and Jen were clearly similar in their ability to do that.

After popping the kettle on in the kitchen, Jacqui went upstairs to her room. Opening one of her wardrobes, she reached up on tiptoes and shuffled a large, floral sewing box from a shelf.

'You've been in this cupboard longer than I thought. Look at all this,' Jacqui said to the box, surprised at the thick layer of dust on top.

She took it over to the windowsill and, despite the cold, opened the window latch and gave the box's lid a good thwack with her hand. A puff of dust sprang upwards and out into the late afternoon air.

She fixed the window shut again and opened the box. Inside were four notebooks. One was much more aged than the rest, its maroon fabric cover faded and its corners worn. The next two were in a better condition, both blue leather with a gold embossed flower on their spines. The last was more modern—a hardback spiral notebook with a black cover—but equally as well used as its predecessors.

Lifting the notebooks out carefully, Jacqui saw the familiar pile of photographs lying underneath. She smelled the faint aroma of lavender and rosemary emanating from some dried sprigs tied together with care, the faded green ribbon also showing its age.

Hearing the click of the kettle, she placed everything back in the box. It was time for a cup of tea and some revision.

***

Jen stepped through the door of the bar and had a quick scan for Laura. She spotted her waving from a table.

'Oh my God, look at your hair! It's gorgeous!' Laura exclaimed, wrapping her arms round her friend.

'Thanks! No time to go shopping in the end, thought the hair needed more attention,' Jen said as she took her coat off.

The women sat down. Jen raised the glass of wine in front of her and noticed the bottle chilling in a bucket. 'Good work, as always.' She smiled at Laura as she took a sip.

Laura waited for the wine to be savoured before jumping straight in. 'So, how was the move? Did you have any problems with Tom?'

Jen took another sip. 'To be fair, he pretty much stayed out of the way. He did hang about a bit on the first day, trying to chat to my dad, which got frustrating. It was as if by showing that my dad still liked him then maybe I would too… It was all a bit awkward, but luckily he left us to it after half an hour.'

'How has the rest of the divorce stuff been? Everything done and dusted?'

'Still some admin to do, but nearly there. I didn't want it dragging on. Tom was not impressed when the emails started coming through, but I did give him a heads up before it started. It took me long enough to make a decision. I just felt I needed to get on with my life and get back to being me, you know?'

'Amen to that,' Laura replied, chinking her glass to Jen's. 'I have to say, these last few weeks, it's like my old Jen has come back—when I hadn't even realised you'd been gone. As if the Jen I've known the last few years was a black-and-white version and you've just burst back in full colour. It's great, I'm so glad you are feeling yourself again.'

'Me too! Changing my name back to Hattley brought it home really. I was definitely missing somewhere but now I am back.' Jen laughed, giving her hair a dramatic toss.

'Is it odd being back at your mum's without your dad there? He moved out after you, didn't he?'

Jen tapped her nails on her glass, pondering the question. Her dad had moved out not too long after she had. Her parents had seemed really happy together, so it was a shock when they told her they needed some time apart. She remembered them being very stressed; her dad, particularly, looked unlike himself. Jen had wondered if they'd just been hanging on until she left the house before splitting up, but as time passed, they evidently got on fine; there was no talk of divorce. They still spent lots of time together and hadn't really gone into detail about what had driven them apart. In fact, now Jen had time to think about it, she began to wonder why her dad had not moved back in.

'It's not odd, he's actually there loads. I think because I've been used to visiting Mum while he's been there anyway, I've not really noticed much difference. Come to think of it, I'll probably only notice it in the evenings, as he never stays.'

'It's a weird one. When you told me your dad had his own place all that time ago, I thought one of them must have had an affair or something. But that idea sounds daft now, seeing how they are together.'

Jen and Laura moved on quickly, exploring every corner of their lives, from how both their jobs were going to Laura's daughter Olivia. They talked about Tom, they talked about Krish, they talked about the old days in their telesales jobs and they talked about what they wanted to do together over the rest of the year.

Before long, one bottle of wine turned into two, which then turned into a number of G&Ts. When they finally realised the time, and that their train didn't run for much longer, Jen and Laura journeyed home together, parting with hugs at the station into their own taxis.

After taking three attempts to open the front door, Jen stumbled into the hallway and locked the door behind her. Her mum had left the landing light on for her upstairs, so it wasn't pitch black. She put her phone and keys on the side cabinet and, holding on to the banister, kicked her shoes off.

She was about to head up to bed when she heard a noise from the dining room.

Putting it down to the drinks, Jen put one foot onto the bottom step. She then heard what sounded like a dining chair scraping on the wooden floor.

Clarity cut through her drunken haze. *Mum is likely in bed, so who is making the noise?*

Stepping off the stair, Jen walked quietly towards the dining room, her heart beginning to race. *What if it's a burglar?* she thought, kicking herself that her phone was back by the door and too scared to go back for it.

Hearing another chair move, she took a deep breath. Suddenly, a shiver ran across her arms, and she felt sure that something had brushed her leg, giving her a light shove on the way past. She turned back to look up the stairs and heard what she thought was the creaky second-to-last step.

Feeling utterly puzzled and like the evening's drinks were making her imagine things, Jen shook off her fear, walked into the dining room and turned the main light on. Four of the six dining room chairs were out from underneath the table, as if untidy guests had been round for dinner and not put their seats back where they found them. Two were at such an odd angle it was hard to see how anyone could have left them like that without feeling impolite.

Jen walked toward the chairs, then stopped. Her mum would never have left the room like this before going to bed. And not just that, the chairs, the way they were pushed out, it all looked so familiar. Bailey had loved lying under the table, especially when he was waiting for the last person to come home of a night—usually Jen or her dad, as her mum was never one for going out late on her own.

Jen slowly went round the table, pushing the chairs back under.

Being a golden retriever, Bailey had taken up most of the space under the table, and when he stretched, his big paws and long legs would shove the chairs left and right until he had enough room, making a racket on the wooden floor. When the last person came through the front door, the chairs would move again as he made his way out from under the table to greet them, then he'd take himself up to his regular sleeping spot on the landing between Jen's room and her parents'. If Jen was last in, she always stopped on the landing to give Bailey a good fuss and say goodnight; she was pretty sure her dad had done the same.

She walked towards the light switch, took a bemused look back into the dining room and turned the light off.

She grabbed her phone from the side cabinet as she went up the stairs, pausing again halfway up to straighten the picture. She stopped on the landing and looked down at the spot where Bailey had always slept. She felt her eyes fill with tears, looking at the empty space; it had been such a long time, but she still really missed him.

Too much booze, she thought, shaking her head and flicking the landing light off. She entered her room and closed the door.

After ten or so seconds, she opened it again and poked her head out. 'Night, Bailey.'

***

Jacqui hadn't heard Jen come in; she was fast asleep.

Earlier, she'd been sitting at the dining table, notebooks and pictures spread out in front of her, and a cup of tea and a half-eaten toasted sandwich to one side. The late afternoon and evening had been spent reading the notebooks, reminding herself of their contents. Occasionally, she lifted the aged sprig of lavender and rosemary to her nose and inhale their perfume—she knew they couldn't possibly still hold their aroma after all these years, but it comforted her to smell the plants, her senses remembering what was no longer there.

The notebooks were familiar reads. Jacqui was particularly fond of the blue ones; she loved to trace her fingers over the light sketches of flowers and ornate patterns on the inside back covers. She wondered what the woman might have been thinking as she drew them, how she'd been able to make sense of her world and put it all down on paper.

She'd tried to stay up long enough to be awake when Jen got in, but reading all those words and absorbing all those thoughts had drained her. Her eyes felt heavy, and she'd had to go to bed.

She had gathered the notebooks to place back in their box, lingering on the spiral-bound black one. She opened it again and pressed her hand to the first page, where her own mother's handwriting flowed across the paper, her name spelt out in full at the top with the date: *'Violet Elizabeth Morley, 10th February 1975'*. Her mother always had beautiful handwriting; Jacqui, not so much, which was why her 'notebook' was on her laptop. Jen would never have been able to read it herself otherwise.

With the notebooks and photographs carefully stored, Jacqui ascended the stairs. The picture of the three of them was straight for a change, not out of place. She stroked the frame.

As she got to the landing, she stood still to listen.

Silence.

She waited another minute, but no noises could be heard anywhere in the house.

No visitors tonight, she thought to herself.

In her room, she placed the box on her dresser, but on second thoughts put it back in its place in the cupboard. The thought of Jen finding it and going through it on her own didn't feel right.

Jacqui felt so exhausted she could barely get undressed. Her eyes felt like they were closing before her head touched the pillow.

CHAPTER 4

Jen awoke slowly the next morning, her mum's hairdryer providing an unobtrusive background noise. Her alarm had sounded as usual, but she had turned it off and gone back to sleep. Her first waking thought was of Bailey and the dining room chairs, but this was quickly overtaken by a headache, which was gathering pace.

Jacqui turned her hairdryer off and could hear Jen groaning as she shuffled towards the bathroom. 'Good night, was it? How was Laura?'

'Yeah, it was great,' she replied. 'But I'll be paying for it this morning, I think. Laura is fine. Krish's started a new business, seems to be doing well.'

Jen looked at herself in the bathroom mirror. The smudged mascara round her eyes was a real look, but she smiled, remembering her new haircut and running her fingers through it. She doused a cotton pad with makeup remover and, rubbing her eyes, mulled over what had happened when she arrived home.

She wandered down the landing, still wiping the mascara off, to her mum's room, where Jacqui was sitting on the end of her bed brushing her hair.

'Mum,' Jen began, 'last night, did you have anyone over?'

Jacqui stopped and turned away from the mirror to face Jen. 'No. Why?'

'It's just that, when I came in, the dining room chairs were all pushed out and I could have sworn I heard noises, like the chairs were moving across the floor… May well have been the wine. It was the strangest thing, just felt like the way Bailey used to leave it… Anyway, I tidied the chairs up.'

Jacqui gripped her hairbrush tightly. 'I didn't hear anything, so you're probably right about the wine.' She smiled. 'Maybe I just forgot to tidy before bed; I was using the table last night.'

Jen shrugged her shoulders and walked back to the bathroom.

After a splash of water to her face, she headed down to the kitchen to hunt out some paracetamol but had to stop in front of the same picture of her, her mum and her nan. It was off-centre again. This time, she took the picture off the wall and inspected the back of it. She wiggled the hook that it hung from; it was fixed well and the hanging wire in the back of the picture seemed secure.

She placed the picture back carefully. 'And this picture of you, me and Nan at her flat,' Jen shouted up to her mum. 'Think Dad will need to check the fixing; it keeps sliding off the hook. It seems like every time I walk up or down these stairs, it needs straightening up.'

'I'll add it to his list!' Jacqui replied.

Jacqui stood up, brushing herself down. Walking out onto the landing, she looked down at Bailey's sleeping spot. 'Behave yourself, just for a bit longer, eh? That's a good boy.'

She made her way down the stairs and could hear Jen filling the kettle. She turned to the aforementioned picture and said, as if she were whispering in someone's ear, 'I'm going to tell her soon; you saw I had the box out last night. I've got plenty of time. Just leave the picture alone. I promise I am onto it.'

Having found the paracetamol for Jen, Jacqui left for work at the school. As she picked up her keys and stepped out the front door, it dawned on her that this would be the first day Jen had been alone in the house since moving back in.

Sitting in the car with the engine running, Jacqui wondered if that was a good idea. But what could she do? She wasn't going to call in sick, and Jen would wonder why she hadn't gone into work; she had looked perfectly fine before leaving.

'It'll be okay,' she said out loud to herself as she turned out of the driveway.

***

Jen spent her morning between meetings, emails and messages to Laura about who'd got away with the better hangover.

Feeling a bit fresher by lunchtime, she walked to the local shops, having decided to cook dinner that evening; a few supplies were needed and it also meant she didn't have to make herself lunch, which she hated doing when working from home.

The afternoon consisted of more meetings and preparation of slides for an upcoming training course.

Jen tried to break the time up by looking for jobs to do around the house. She emptied the bins, put the contents of the dishwasher away and tidied away the bits on the draining board.

Later, the tumble dryer clicked to announce it had finished its latest task. Jen unloaded the clothes, folding a pile for her and her mum. She wanted to help; she didn't want her mum running round for her like she was a teenager again.

Jen popped the neat piles into the basket and headed upstairs. Looking at the picture with her nan, she was surprised to find it straight and in its place.

After leaving the wash basket in her room, Jen took Jacqui's clothes and headed into her mum's room to place the piles neatly on her bed. She didn't want to intrude, so refrained from putting them away completely.

She sat on her mum's bed for a moment. Like in her bedroom, some things had changed but some had stayed the same. There was different paint on the walls, different curtains, different carpet, but the same comforting smell of her mum was there. The same trinket boxes and bunch of dried lavender in an ornate vase were on her dresser.

That's when she noticed it. Sitting in the middle of the dressing table was her nan's floral sewing box. The fabric was very seventies, with browns and pinks, but now well back in trend. Jen hadn't seen it for years, probably not since she was eleven or twelve. It had always been in the living room cupboard at her nan's bigger house. Jen used to ask to take it out and open its cushioned lid, like a treasure chest. But instead of gold coins and jewels, this one was filled with threads and buttons of every colour.

Jen remembered how she would sit on the floor, spending ages arranging everything into size order or colour order, or both, muttering away to herself as she organised them all by the minutest difference in shade. She'd only stop when her nan came in with lunch, arranged on the small coffee table, just for her: a small china bowl with cucumber, the skin peeled off and cut into chunks, how Jen liked it; Marmite sandwiches in neat squares on white bread; ready-salted crisps, not Jen's favourite but she never told her nan. Lunch was always made with love; that's how it felt. When that was finished, a slice of angel cake or pink wafer biscuits— often it was both, as Jen's nan adored her granddaughter and wouldn't deny her two desserts.

Jen gazed at the sewing box, fondly remembering her nan; those lunches and teas at her house had been special times—something she didn't realise when they were happening but very much understood now. The memories made Jen catch her breath for a moment, a pang of grief bubbling to the surface.

Jen felt compelled to pick the box up.

She sat back on the bed with it placed on her lap and ran her fingers over the fabric lid. She popped the clasp on the front, anticipating the buttons and threads she remembered, but in their place were old photographs—black-and-white ones of people Jen had never seen before. She lifted out one after the other, looking closely at the faces and the clothes and placing each picture on her mum's duvet.

The final picture was of a toddler and a woman laughing at the camera and sitting on a chequered blanket on an immaculate lawn. Despite not being in colour, Jen recognised the blanket and knew it was blue and red, as it now permanently resided in her mum's car boot. She could see her mother's eyes beaming out from the toddler's face, a look of sheer joy on her nan's.

When the pile of photographs came to an end, Jen noticed the notebooks. One maroon with a faded fabric cover, two blue leather ones with gold embossed flowers on the spines and a spiral-bound, black hardback. She placed these on the duvet also.

Finally, she noticed the sprig of lavender and rosemary, tied with an old green ribbon, at the bottom of the box amongst bits of leaves that had fallen off and gathered in the corners. Jen held it up for a closer look. It looked like it had been in the box for a long time, so how could she possibly be smelling its scent so strongly? She felt light-headed; the bouquet emanating from the plants was almost overwhelming.

Jen had not heard the front door click shut. She had not heard footsteps ascending the stairs or the creaking of the second-to-last step at the top. She had not noticed the bedroom door push open.

But she did hear her mother's gasp, causing her to turn round suddenly. 'Mum, I am so sorry, I shouldn't have been nosing around in here.' Her face flushed with embarrassment and she started placing the items back in the box.

Jacqui stood motionless for a few seconds, taking in what was before her. She then perched on the bed and placed her hand on Jen's. 'No need to tidy them up.' She reached over to take the sprigs from Jen's hand, raised them to her nose and inhaled. 'Where did you find the box?'

Jen pointed to the dresser.

Jacqui sighed, shaking her head. 'You just couldn't wait could you, Mum? Well, no time like the present, I suppose.'

CHAPTER 5

Jen didn't know what to make of everything. She picked the box up and followed her mum downstairs. She set the box down on the dining room table and waited for Jacqui, who had gone into the lounge.

Jacqui returned with her laptop and a bottle of wine. She took two glasses and two coasters from the cabinet and poured a generous measure for each of them.

'I was going to cook for us,' Jen said, not really knowing what was going on.

'Come sit with me. We'll worry about dinner later,' her mum replied, patting one of the chairs.

Jen sat down and Jacqui opened the box. Jacqui carefully took the four pictures out and laid them in a line, placing a notebook near each. Her laptop was at the end of the line along with the picture set in the garden on the blanket. She took a sip of wine and placed her glass gently back onto its coaster.

Then, she took Jen's hands in hers and looked directly into her daughter's eyes. 'Jen, I am going to tell you a true story about three remarkable women. Just try to listen to me for as long as possible before firing too many questions at me. Is that okay?'

Jen was confused. This whole situation was strange. Why was her mum holding her hands in this odd way? What was so important it needed this kind of build-up, and what did it have to do with the contents of the sewing box? Whatever was going on, she decided she needed to give her mum her full attention.

Jen squeezed her mum's hands. 'I'm listening, and I'll hold my questions in as long as I can. Promise.'

'Okay, let's begin.' Jacqui turned to the photographs. 'I expect you recognise me and your nan, Violet.' She pointed to the picture in the garden. 'But the others you probably haven't heard much about. So, we'll start at the beginning with Harriet Macey.'

Jacqui picked up a black-and-white photo that was placed above the maroon notebook. Turning it over, she showed Jen the year written on the back: *'1886'*. Turning it back, she passed it to her daughter.

'That there is Harriet,' Jacqui said, pointing to a lady sitting at an ornate wooden table alongside two other ladies and two men. They all had their arms spread out, their hands resting on the table, their fingers and thumbs touching, forming a circle. Behind them, on the right, was a decorative cabinet displaying glass and china, and to their left was a bookcase. Harriet wore a dark-coloured, long, thick-looking skirt, which covered her feet, and a white, long-sleeved top, which was done up to the neck. Her voluminous sleeves brushed the lady and gentleman sitting either side of her. Her face was calm, almost blank—no smile. She looked like she belonged there, but equally, looked out of place; the clothes of the other four people looked much finer and more expensive.

'Harriet was a seamstress by trade,' said Jacqui. 'In between birthing and looking after her ten children.'

Jen coughed on her wine. 'Ten!'

'Yes. You know, in those days it was a numbers game due to how many children sadly died in early age, plus, well, no family planning, I suppose! Anyway, I expect you are wondering how a low-paid seamstress from the local village ended up in a photo with this well-to-do bunch?'

Jen didn't answer.

'That lady there'—Jacqui pointed to the lady sitting to the right of Harriet—'is Mrs Annabelle Fitzroy-Lawson. She was the head of the Fitzroy-Lawsons who lived in the large estate just outside the village.'

Jen looked closely at Annabelle. She was dressed fully in black, and her light-coloured hair was tied tightly back with a middle parting. Her well-tailored dress had long sleeves embellished with lace that continued across the bodice. At her neck, clasped to the dress' collar, was an oval brooch, presumably edged in silver or gold, which looked like a soulless, dark eye. Her skirt took up most of the space underneath the table, and her hands were partially covered by lace gloves. She was the most striking person at the table, her beautiful face holding a solemn gaze into the camera.

Jen noticed that Annabelle was holding Harriet's right hand, whereas the other people forming the circle simply had their hands next to each other.

'Annabelle is in mourning, I presume?' Jen asked. 'Sorry, that's a question.'

Jacqui smiled. 'I'll let a few slide. Yes, Mr Fitzroy-Lawson had died that year, and she, by all accounts, adored him. This was mainly why Harriet was there and in this photo.' She went on to explain that the other people in the photograph were one of Annabelle's sons (she wasn't sure which one), her only daughter, Eleanor, and Eleanor's husband.

The men were dressed very plainly: dark suits, white shirts and thin, dark neckties. Eleanor wore a lighter-coloured dress with the same dark, oval brooch as her mother's. Both the men and Eleanor were looking into the camera, expressionless.

'The story goes,' Jacqui continued, 'that Annabelle had been looking for a seamstress to help alter some dresses bought for a dinner party being held at the house. She probably tried a few who did not meet her standards when one of the servants mentioned that Harriet Macey, who lived in the village, was the best seamstress for miles around. So, she asked Harriet to come to the house the next day.

'Harriet proved to be a skilled seamstress, and Annabelle was impressed by her work—this was a few years before Mr Fitzroy-Lawson passed. By all accounts, the ladies got on very well. Harriet continued to work for the family for quite a while.

'I know all this because it's written in here.' Jacqui held up the maroon fabric-covered notebook and opened it.

Words in ornate writing on the inside cover read:
'*To Harriet,*
May you use this to chronicle your wonderful gift.
Yours faithfully,
Annabelle Fitzroy-Lawson,
1889.'

Jacqui gave the book to Jen, leant back in her chair and took a slow sip from her glass. Then, she said, 'I can only assume Annabelle taught, or at least helped, Harriet to read and write, considering her poorer background. This notebook contains Harriet's notes about her gift. I am guessing you want to know what her gift was…'

Jen looked at the notebook, taken aback by how old it was. She looked at the photograph again, the table, the hands in a circle. 'Don't tell me she was talking to the dead!'

Both women sat silent for a moment.

'Harriet could talk to dead people, yes,' Jacqui said, trying to work out what her daughter was making of it all.

Jen now leant back in her chair, placing both the notebook and photograph on the table.

'It seems Harriet was able to contact spirits after her mother died,' Jacqui continued. 'She would have been about thirty-two. I imagine she didn't go round advertising it; they would have chucked her in a lunatic asylum.' Jacqui opened the book to a couple of pages in. 'She mentions her own mother a few times in her entries, so it seems her own mother also spoke to spirits.'

Jacqui's manicured nail traced under a couple of entries. The writing was less elegant than Annabelle's, the entries dated and short.

Jen managed to glance at one while the book was open.

'*12th June 1895*

Boy spirit John Oaks wanted me to speak to his sister. Reminds me of my Will when he was young. I did not tell him I could not find his sister; Mother had taught me not to upset the spirits. I promised to pass on his message, and he went away happy.'

Jacqui continued. 'Annabelle and her husband had been part of the upcoming Spiritualist movement, so they were very open to Harriet's abilities. They believed in ghosts and the paranormal. When Annabelle was desperately missing her husband, knowing what Harriet could do, she asked her to try and contact him. One seance turned into two—Annabelle ended up hosting a number of them at the estate house. It really was quite a fashionable thing to do back then.' Jacqui leant forward and closed the maroon notebook. 'All of Harriet's experiences are here for you to read when you are ready. Shall I carry on to the next one?'

Jen's interest was piqued. She hadn't a clue what more her mum was going to tell her next, but the story of this woman was fascinating. Did she believe that Harriet could really talk to dead people? She wasn't sure. But her mum seemed convinced.

'I'm good; carry on.'

Jacqui picked up another black-and-white photo, this time of a group of people outside a church, and placed it in front of Jen.

This group didn't look as prim and proper as the Fitzroy-Lawsons; it was a welcome contrast to the sombre mood of the seance picture. Everyone looked happy. The bride and groom stood beaming in the middle surrounded by various relatives young and old. The groom proudly wore his uniform; Jen wasn't sure what part of the military he was in but thought he looked very handsome and smart. His arm was interlocked with the bride's and he leant slightly into her. The bride had a pretty, long-sleeved tea dress ending at her calves, with white stockings and pointed white shoes. Her bouquet of lilies cascaded past the hem of her dress.

Just behind the bride's left shoulder was a woman, older but clearly a sister, as they looked so similar. The woman wore a smart hat and glasses. She was equally as happy as the bride, a large smile on her face. Her fur stole was perched on her shoulders, and Jen spotted the familiar oval brooch pinned to it.

'The brooch, it's the same as Annabelle's… and these two look like sisters.'

Jacqui was impressed by Jen's intuition. 'Yes, you're right. The bride is Agnes Macey, soon to be Laycock, and the lady on her shoulder is her sister—her favourite sister, Elizabeth Mary Macey. These are two of Harriet's daughters. And these are Elizabeth's notebooks.' Jacqui picked up one of the blue leather notebooks and opened it to the inside cover, as she had done with the maroon one, so Jen could read the inscription.

'*To Elizabeth,*

May these notebooks help you make sense of the wondrous gift your mother has given you.

Yours faithfully,

Annabelle Fitzroy-Lawson,

1908.'

Jen took the notebook from her mum's hands and ran her hand over the writing. 'Annabelle must have been fond of Elizabeth, as she was of Harriet. I presume Annabelle believed that Harriet's ability to talk to spirits passed to her daughter?'

Jacqui leant in to look more closely at the photograph. 'Correct. Annabelle continued her relationship with Harriet pretty much up until Harriet died in 1907. Elizabeth had occasionally worked alongside her mother, so had also formed quite a bond with the lady of the house. It seems that when Harriet died, her eldest daughter inherited her gift and began to see the spirits for herself. Elizabeth continued conducting seances for Annabelle's spiritualist friends until the First World War changed everything for everyone.' Jacqui let out a sigh and reached for her glass, which she realised was empty.

Jen leant over and poured what was left from the bottle.

'The war devastated all families, the rich and the poor. Annabelle lost her eldest and youngest sons within a year of each other on the front, leaving Eleanor, from the photo, and her second eldest son. From what Elizabeth describes, the loss to the family was too much and grief finally took its toll on Annabelle.

'On her passing, the brooch you saw in the seance photo was passed to Elizabeth as a thank you to her and her mother. They provided Mrs Fitzroy-Lawson with a lot of comfort over the years, which she obviously appreciated deeply.

'The brooch came with a sum of money, allowing Elizabeth to live very comfortably. It's no wonder she never married; she didn't need a man for a secure income like other women her age did. She was a free agent—unusual for her time. Also, she had built a reputation with those in higher society as a medium, so despite the passing of Annabelle, she was still invited to a number of dinners and events. You have to realise, the country was suffering collective grief; more than ever, people wanted to know if they could really talk to their loved ones beyond the grave.'

Jen was absolutely captivated. Whether these women could talk with ghosts or not she didn't know, and part of her was still concerned as to why her mum had been so serious at the beginning, but she held all that to one side, not wanting to spoil her enjoyment.

'Do you remember the surname Laycock?' Jacqui asked. 'Mean anything to you?'

Jen pondered. It did sound familiar, but she could not work out why. Looking back at the wedding photo, there was also something familiar about Agnes.

'Agnes married James Laycock,' Jacqui said, pointing at the bride and groom in the picture. 'Agnes was your nan's mother, so Laycock was your nan's maiden name, making Agnes your great-grandmother. Harriet is therefore your great-great-grandmother. Elizabeth is your great-great-aunt.'

Jen's brain whirred; she felt like she needed to draw it all out on a piece of paper to get perspective. Also, her stomach was rumbling.

The meal she had planned could wait until tomorrow; she knew the freezer could sustain them this evening. 'Hold fire, Mum. Let me get some pizzas in the oven.'

Whilst Jen rustled around in the freezer and got the oven on, Jacqui messaged Mark.

'I'm telling Jen everything at the moment. Going okay so far, I think.' She added a crossed-fingers emoji and sent it.

She could see Mark start to type, then he stopped.

'Do you want veggie or pepperoni, Mum?' Jen shouted.

'You pick for me, Jen,' Jacqui replied, still looking at her phone. Mark hadn't started typing again. She wondered if he was struggling with what to say—it wasn't really your normal family situation they were dealing with, after all.

Jen came back in with some plates, a pen and paper. 'Say that to me again about how I am related to them all.'

Jen drew a quick family tree, starting with Harriet and ending with herself. She took it back into the kitchen to look at as she prepared a salad to go with the pizzas, glancing over at the family lines while she chopped a cucumber.

Jacqui joined her in the kitchen, and they stood by the oven as the timer ticked down.

'Who did you learn this all from?' Jen asked. 'Is all this information in the notebooks?'

Jacqui pinched a cherry tomato from the salad bowl. 'We could only assume certain things from the notebooks, your nan and I. Nan actually heard a lot of the story first-hand from Elizabeth, or Auntie Betty as Nan used to call her.'

The oven pinged to announce the pizzas were ready, and the two women headed back into the dining room.

'Mind your fingers,' Jacqui said. 'I don't want greasy cheese prints on these notebooks!'

Jen had started eating with her hands, as was usual, while her mum had opted for some cutlery. Jen nodded compliantly, her mouth full of pizza crust.

After making a dent in their dinner, Jacqui eagerly returned to her story. 'Okay, where did we get to…? Yes, Elizabeth and Agnes.

'The age gap between Elizabeth and Agnes was eight years, I think, but they were extremely close. Elizabeth made no secret of how Agnes was her favourite of all her siblings.'

Jacqui slid her plate to one side and brought both blue notebooks towards her. 'Elizabeth was financially independent for a lot of her adult life, thanks to Annabelle. She took full advantage of the generous amount left to her and used it wisely. She travelled; she gave some to her family. She explored her abilities in a way her mother was not able to, or maybe didn't want to—

to be fair, Harriet might not have had time with ten children!

'Elizabeth's notes are not only about visitations or seances that she had personally; she talks about the diverse people she met, people she came across by chance and people she sought out herself. She didn't just stick with talking to ghosts, she wanted to understand as much as she could about the supernatural. Spiritualism was still around but was becoming a bit less popular; you can imagine how people thought they could make a few quid by claiming to be able to talk to "old Aunt Gladys" or a long-lost son from the war—stories of fraudsters made it into the local and national press. But Elizabeth managed to keep in with a few like-minded circles. She wanted to speak to believers and sceptics. She'd go to Spiritualist meetings and psychic dinners specifically to see if she could spot a fraud or to see something that defied explanation. She really wanted to learn as much as she could. She even joined a group that investigated hauntings. She was like an investigator, I suppose.'

Jacqui opened the second book and flicked through a few pages.

'*9th December 1931,*

Appointment to see Mrs A. on Monday next week. Claims she can produce objects from thin air. On the face of it she seems trustworthy, but we will see.'

Jacqui turned more pages.

'*2nd February 1932,*

Attended a gathering with our group. I found the whole sitting rather boring; clearly theatrics at play.'

Jen motioned to her mum to pause. She ran out to the kitchen to wash her hands and returned, holding them up for her mum to check before picking up the notebooks. She leafed through the first one's pages with dates, people and places, the occasional sketch.

'Why just initials for some people?'

'I suppose she didn't want anyone to be embarrassed if her notebooks were read by someone else. Ghosts and ghoulies were still very much laughed about; most people passed paranormal activity off as being made up or a trick.'

'Fair enough.' Jen thumbed through the second book, then paused to look back at the family tree she had drawn. 'So, Harriet has this ability passed to her by her mum, then it goes to Elizabeth. Where does Nan come into it?'

Jen watched her mum take in a deep breath. Jacqui had been relatively relaxed whilst telling Harriet's and Elizabeth's tales but had now tensed up a bit.

Jacqui held her wine glass in both hands as if it might provide some guidance, thinking carefully about her next words. 'Nan was born in 1921, and Elizabeth doted on her. She visited Agnes and your nan often, telling stories; she was a great storyteller by all accounts. Your nan had vivid memories of her time with Auntie Betty, and even stayed with her a few times in the school holidays. She remembered all the wonderful books her aunt had on subjects she had never heard of at school: witches, poltergeists, hauntings—some fiction, some not. She even had a spell book!

'In 1940, your nan tragically lost her mum to cancer, as you know. Both she and Elizabeth were bereft. Nan was nineteen and considered old enough to look after herself; her brother was only eighteen months younger. Auntie Betty had promised Agnes to look out for both of her sister's children, and a very special bond continued to grow between Nan and Auntie Betty.'

Jen refilled her own wine glass, noticing that her mum had barely touched hers for a while. She'd known her nan's mum had died young but had no idea about the relationship between Violet and her aunt.

'Nan must have missed her mum a lot,' Jen said. 'Not sure how I would have coped if I'd lost you at nineteen.'

Jacqui met her daughter's eyes and raised a little smile. 'I know your nan missed her mum a lot, but Elizabeth did her best to make sure both children had every opportunity they needed to be happy. She never had children of her own. Your nan told me she and her brother basically felt like they were her kids, that's how deep their relationship was in the end.

'I met Elizabeth, but I was very small, so I don't remember. Mum was so happy and proud to be able to show me off to her. Elizabeth died when I was just starting school, I think. Made it to ninety-two.'

Jacqui paused, contemplating what she was about to say next.

Jen sensed a shift in the atmosphere. The story was reaching an important moment; she could feel it coming. She unconsciously leant forward in her chair, listening intently.

Jacqui piled the maroon notebook on top of the blue ones and rested one hand on them. 'When Elizabeth died, she wanted these notebooks to go to the next person who would need them. She was a smart woman; she had studied her abilities thoroughly and understood clearly how they impacted her life, how they affected the way she saw the world around her. She poured all that knowledge and experience into these notebooks. She knew the next recipient of her "gifts" would need help understanding them too.

'Jen, your nan was the next person to receive the notebooks.'

CHAPTER 6

Jen looked at the notebooks and back at her mum, who was now taking an unusually large gulp from her wine glass.

'Well, that makes sense, they felt like mother and daughter, so of course Elizabeth would leave something so precious to Nan,' Jen said, not really understanding the dramatic pause Jacqui had taken.

Jacqui sat there silently, straining as if she might hear the cogs turning in her daughter's head.

Jen shot her mum a puzzled look and something compelled her to look at the tree she had drawn. She looked down at the names: Harriet Maccy, Elizabeth Maccy, Violet Laycock, and underneath them, her mum and herself. She looked back at Elizabeth's name and imagined a line connecting her to Violet, a line purely made of love. Her eyes moved to Harriet's and Elizabeth's notebooks on the table, which her mum had explained, then to the black spiral-bound one and her mum's laptop.

Without realising, her hand moved to the black notebook, and she was opening it, her eyes widening as she took in the writing—the writing she knew from so many Christmas and birthday cards. There were dates and names, similar to how Elizabeth's book was set out, all in her nan's hand.

'Elizabeth knew that, despite people's efforts to investigate the supernatural and bring order to it, it just didn't work by any real rules. Her group spent years visiting many people claiming to have this gift or that gift: some ghosts appeared as if they were flesh and blood, some were fainter than the smoke from a cigarette end, some could speak at length, some were mute, some could only move things, some didn't even know their own names anymore, supernatural things happened in the day as well as the night.

'Do I think Elizabeth believed everything she saw? I expect not. But what she adamantly believed was that her gift had been passed to her from her mum. She believed that her gift would pass to someone else in the family—a female, as it seemed to have done through previous generations. The older she got and the more she learned, she knew that she needed to prepare that someone for what would happen when she was gone. She somehow knew that it wasn't going to stop with her just because she had no children. The gift would find a way to its next recipient; exact bloodlines didn't matter. And she was right.'

'Oh my God. Are you trying to tell me that Nan could talk to dead people?!' Jen looked straight at Jacqui.

The reply was very matter-of-fact. 'Yes, Nan spoke with dead people.'

Jen's immediate reaction was to laugh—her mum had just told her that her nan could speak to dead people. Hearing about Harriet and Elizabeth in the distant past was exciting, but it didn't feel real. But her nan? She knew her nan; her nan had been a real person to her. All of it was incredible enough in itself, but it also confirmed, just by default, that ghosts and spirits actually existed to be spoken to. Surely not.

But her gut was telling her otherwise. Her mum was not prone to telling lies. Not even little fibs. She wasn't one to embellish stories or exaggerate. Whenever Jen heard a story recounted by her mum, it was always pretty much to the point. In Jen's mind, there was no reason her mum would be making this up.

Everything felt like it had sped up. The questions began to mount up and felt like they were about to erupt from her mouth. But there was one pressing question above all else, screaming inside her head.

'Ask me. It's okay.' Jacqui knew what was coming. Violet, her own mother, had died thirteen years ago.

Jen breathed out slowly; she couldn't believe what she was about to say. 'Can you talk to ghosts?'

'Yes. And at some point in the future, Jen, so will you.'

'Wow,' was the only word Jen could muster up. She stood up from her chair, not really knowing where she was going to go. 'I mean, wow!'

She walked out into the hallway and then into the kitchen. Was her mum for real? Was this one big joke? Either way, this was mind-blowing: her mum believed she could chat with the departed.

'Are you okay, Jen?' Jacqui had come into the kitchen. 'I know how this sounds. You probably think I have lost my marbles. I do know how you're feeling; your nan sat me down to have the same conversation.'

'Of all the things I expected you to tell me, this really wasn't it. I almost think telling me I'd been adopted might have been easier.'

'Well, based on what happened to Elizabeth and your nan, you'd still be stuck talking to dead people. It would have just used my love for you as a bridge.'

Jacqui smiled and Jen smiled back. The tension eased a little.

'I cannot tell you how much I have wanted to explain all of this to you. With you moving back, it was possible you'd start noticing things, so I knew I had to get on with it. It seems your nan was keen, too. She has really been putting the pressure on me the last few days.'

'What do you mean?'

'The picture on the stairs. It's not a dodgy fixing. Your nan was trying to drop me a hint. She surpassed herself with the sewing box, though. She's never moved things to that extent before.'

Jen looked utterly confused.

Jacqui continued to explain. 'I put that box away in my cupboard last night, yet you found it on my dressing table. Your nan's been trying to move things along. No idea why she's in such a rush about it all.'

Jen shook her head. It all sounded quite unbelievable. First, talking to ghosts, now things being moved by unseen forces in the house. *What on earth am I going to hear about next?* she wondered. Though, she had to admit, the picture moving in the same way nearly every time she traversed the stairs was strange and obviously had nothing to do with how it was fixed to the wall. Had her mum just forgotten to put the sewing box away before she went to bed?

A quietness hung over both women for a few moments.

Jen stood and grabbed a glass from the cupboard and filled it with cold water. 'Go on, you ask me now,' she said to her mum.

Jacqui hesitated for a moment but knew she had to. 'Do you believe me?'

Jen drank half the glass of water before replying. 'It is pretty mad, isn't it? You have to admit. But I have to ask myself why you'd be making it up, unless you really have lost your mind.' After drinking the remainder of the water, Jen placed the glass in the sink. 'I believe you, Mum. If you say you can talk to dead people, then you can talk to dead people.'

Jen felt like she ought to be more shocked, but she truly believed her mum. It was an immense thing to share with her and she didn't want her mum to think she doubted her at all.

Jacqui felt so relieved she thought she might melt into the floor. She hadn't just been waiting to tell Jen about this since she'd moved back in; she'd been building up to telling her since she found out about it herself. The ability moved on to its next recipient after the last one died; it was inevitable. She wanted Jen to be as prepared as possible. This conversation had been rehearsed in Jacqui's mind for years.

'There's so much more to go through,' Jacqui said. 'But it can wait until tomorrow if you're tired. I know you have work.'

'Oh no, we're not stopping here. You've started, so you need to finish. Well, finish as best you can tonight. We'll be talking about this for some time, I think!'

Jacqui and Jen settled down together on the sofa in the lounge, legs scooched up underneath them and the black notebook between them.

'I am pretty sure you will have seen your nan having her chats with ghosts. She used to call it "holding counsel" like it was a therapy session.'

'Err, no… I'd remember seeing Nan talking to ghosts.'

'You remember Joey?'

Jen certainly remembered Joey. Joey was nan's blue and white budgerigar who could say his own name. He'd lived in a cage, as was the way back then, which resided to the right of her nan's kitchen sink during the day. Jen had always loved watching him checking himself out in his little mirror or having a dust bath on the cage floor. Occasionally, he would be let out to fly round the living room, always coming to sit on her nan's shoulder. At night, his cage would be moved to one of the lounge chairs and a little blanket put over it before Violet went up to bed.

Well into her teenage years, Jen thought he had lived to quite a ripe old age for a bird, only to find out that Joey had in fact been many Joeys. Her nan had a succession of blue and white budgies, and Jen had never noticed when one died and a new one arrived.

'Was Joey talking to ghosts too?' Jen giggled.

'He may well have been! Who knows? Seriously though, when your nan was standing in her kitchen, peeling vegetables or washing up, you could hear her talking to Joey, couldn't you? Well, she wasn't talking to Joey; she was talking to whoever had *arrived*.'

As Jen listened, she was back in her nan's kitchen. Baby blue Formica worktops with a matching fold-out kitchen table. The floor was always warm as the hot water pipes ran directly underneath. Jen would sit contentedly at the table, legs dangling, with her colouring or some other craft project as her nan spoke quietly at the other end of the galley kitchen. Her flat house shoes, with a chequered skirt that finished mid-calf and a matching thin, short-sleeved jumper was her outfit of choice. The radio was usually on, placed on the sill with its aerial fully extended. The kitchen sink was in front of the window that looked out onto the driveway bursting with pink and mauve hydrangeas. Her nan's back would be turned to her, so Jen could never really make out fully what she was saying. Joey would chirp in regularly, as if he was replying, so Jen had always assumed her nan was making 'bird talk'.

'Your grandad was not a fan of what Nan could do. He hated it and basically told her she was not to do any of it in the house. But her "visitors" wouldn't just go away or stop coming because he didn't like it. So, she found a way to keep it all out of his way: she kept to the kitchen. She knew he'd rarely go in there—I mean, did you ever see him cook or make his own cup of tea? And it wasn't like a ghost turned up every day; it could be weeks or months between visits. There seemed to be some sort of agreement that if her visitors wanted to talk, they had to go into the kitchen, like it was her office.'

Jen was surprised but not totally shocked that her nan had found a way to carry on regardless of what Grandad had said. She was pleased that she hadn't given up on it.

'So, when did Nan tell you about it all?' she asked.

'After you were born. It really drove home to her what was going to happen, not just to me but also to you. She was probably waiting to see if you were a boy or a girl.

'She came to see me when you were about six months old. It must have been complicated for her, working out when to tell me—being a new mum, she didn't want to burden me with the stress but, equally, she didn't want to leave it too long and then never get the chance. You feel like you have all the time in the world, but really, none of us know when we are going to die, and that is, inevitably, the deadline to tell all, I suppose.'

Jacqui continued to explain how Violet had taken on much of the guidance given to her by Elizabeth. She'd documented every conversation, if only with a few words, in her own notebook. Unlike Elizabeth, she'd had the challenge of trying to integrate her new-found gift into her married life and the raising of two children, Jacqui and her brother, Michael. Instead of exploring and seeking out new experiences, Violet kept a low profile. She never mentioned her abilities to friends; she didn't look for anyone else who might have the same gifts. Only Joey knew what was truly going on until she told Jacqui after Jen was born. After Violet died, all the notebooks and pictures came to Jacqui, who decided to follow the path her mum had taken.

Jacqui's notes were all on her laptop, and she showed Jen how she'd collated them by year and month, as she didn't get that many visitors. She explained that some were easy to talk to and could articulate what they needed, while others were more challenging, coming across jumbled and confused. Some started off completely silent.

Jacqui didn't have a budgie as a sidekick, but she managed to contain her guests to the house, even if she couldn't keep them all to the kitchen.

'One time,' she said, 'I was going into the bathroom to have a shower only to find a new one standing in the middle of the floor. Just waiting for me. That was in the early days—really gave me a fright. Your dad thought it was a spider he needed to come and remove!'

Jen hadn't given a thought to her dad in all of this.

'So, does Dad know?'

'Yes, I told him more or less straight away. I couldn't hide something like that from him, and I needed someone to tell. He was nonchalant about it and didn't seem particularly fussed. He just said, "We'll worry about it when it happens." I'm not sure he really believed it at first, and we'd just had you, so there wasn't time to worry about what my mum had told me.

'We were lucky to have your nan for the years we did. Nothing started happening until she was gone, and by then you had already moved out. It was just your dad and me left to muddle our way through it. He really was brilliant.'

Jen wondered if her parents' separation had anything to do with her mum's abilities. She was about to ask when Jacqui gave out a big yawn.

Jen looked at her phone. Time had raced away; it was gone midnight.

'I have so much more to tell you,' Jacqui said, 'but I think bed is in order. Can you wait for the next instalment?' She rubbed the flat of her hand on her chest. 'I also think that wine and pizza has given me indigestion.'

Jen couldn't wait but had to admit she was shattered. Although, sleeping seemed unlikely; her head was buzzing with questions.

'Are you okay, Jen?' Jacqui asked as they both stood up. 'You seem to be taking this very calmly.'

'It's a lot to take in, but yeah, I'm doing alright. I mean, how did you react when Nan told you?'

'Actually, I was a bit like you really. Just took what she said as being the truth. She'd never lied to me or made things up before. I looked at the notebooks and thought, yes, this all makes sense. Which sounds a bit mad, doesn't it? I never thought it would really happen, but then you think everyone is going to be around for-ever, don't you?'

Jen's mind went to a dark place for just a second; the thought of her mum dying was not one to be dwelled on. 'I'm sure I'll have a ton of questions for you, but I'm not banking on taking over any time soon!'

Jacqui wrapped her arms around her daughter. 'Thank you for being so understanding. I was worried this was going to be a complete disaster, but it's gone better than I could have expected. We'll cover more to-morrow or over the weekend. Whenever you're ready. Love you.'

'Love you too, Mum.'

Jen kissed her mum on the cheek and walked up the stairs, leaving Jacqui to turn the lights off and lock the doors.

As she got to the landing, Jen glanced down at Bai-ley's favourite sleeping spot. She peered back down the stairs to see if her mum was in earshot. 'Was that you moving the chairs when I got in last night, boy? I hope it was. Night night, Bailey.'

She then rolled her eyes at herself. What was she doing? But if she was going to believe in ghosts, she was more than happy to think that Bailey was still around.

Jacqui knew it was a cliché, but she felt a great weight lifted from her. Jen seemed to be taking it all well. Whether she fully believed everything told to her, Jacqui wasn't wholly sure, and maybe when it all hit home there would be some bumps to get over.

With all the doors secure, Jacqui packed the sewing box and notebooks back up and ascended the stairs to get ready for bed. Her indigestion was not subsiding, so she grabbed some tablets from the bathroom on the way.

She could hear Jen moving around in her room as she placed the sewing box back on her dressing table, then a hush came over the house.

After running a brush through her hair, she messaged Mark to explain where they'd got to and suggest he come over at the weekend so he could tell his side of the story. It was finally time to explain why he had moved out; it was an important part of their experience of Jacqui's gift that Jen needed to know about.

A thumbs-up emoji came as a reply.

Jacqui lay down and closed her eyes. She felt lighter, unburdened and happy to have finally been able to share it all with Jen. Everything had turned out okay.

A fulfilled smile spread across her face as she fell into a tranquil sleep.

CHAPTER 7

Jen woke up, having slept undisturbed all night. She couldn't remember waking up once, which was unusual. She had been worried that everything her mum had told her would just churn in her mind all night, but she couldn't even remember laying her head on her pillow. It was as if her brain had decided it needed some serious time out.

It was just beginning to become light outside. Flicking the landing light on, she noticed her mum's bedroom door was still closed. Jen thought it best to leave her to lie in; sharing all of the family secrets must have been exhausting.

Having put the kettle on, Jen powered up her laptop and had a quick scan over her diary; the day was pretty quiet, save one meeting at 10:30am. The kettle signalled that it was time to return to the kitchen. Her thoughts turned to breakfast, so Jen opened the fridge to see what they had, in two minds about what to eat. After grabbing the milk, she shut the door and jumped—her mum was standing less than two feet away, already dressed.

'Blimey! Are you in stealth mode? I didn't hear you come down the stairs.'

Jacqui said nothing.

Jen moved to the cupboard to retrieve two cups and went about making tea for them both. 'I have to say, I slept way better than I thought I would. I don't think

I woke up once.' Jen gave the teabags a shuffle in the steaming mixture before squeezing them.

After popping the bags in the compost bin, she picked up a cup to hand to her mum, then paused. She had the mug in one outstretched hand, waiting for Jacqui to take it from her. But Jacqui didn't move.

'Are you okay, Mum?'

Jacqui was trying to speak, but no noise was coming out of her mouth. She looked like a goldfish breathing underwater, her mouth opening and shutting. She closed her eyes, trying to concentrate, but when she opened them again it was as if she'd lost focus on what was in front of her.

A pang of panic flared in Jen's stomach. Her mum didn't look right, but she couldn't say exactly what it was.

'Sit down, Mum. Are you in pain?'

Still, Jacqui did not move.

'Oh my God, you're not having a stroke or something are you? I'm calling an ambulance. Just try to sit down and I'll be straight back.' Jen threw the cup back on the side without care; brown tea spilt onto the countertop and dribbled down a cupboard door, creating a small pool on the floor.

She moved quickly into the hallway and up the stairs to find her phone in her bedroom. As she started to dial, she turned to find her mum standing at the end of her bed, in front of her cupboards.

Jen's fingers stopped moving on the keypad. 'How did you follow me up here so quickly?'

Jacqui was concentrating as hard as she could; Jen could see it on her face.

'I… I'm so… sorry…'

Jen raised her voice in frustration and worry. 'I don't understand, Mum. What's going on? This is scaring me.' She stepped forward to put her hand on her mum's shoulder—and found herself nose-to-door with her wardrobe. She spun round, utterly bewildered, and dropped her phone.

Primal fear took over. Her heart beat faster; every fibre of her being knew something was wrong. She'd walked straight through her mum. 'I'm still asleep, I must still be asleep.'

'Jen!'

The sound of her mother's voice caused her to turn to her bedroom door.

Jacqui now stood there, blocking the doorway, an intensity having taken over her face. 'Listen to… me. I don't know… how it's… happened. I'm struggling… to… get my words… out. You need to call… your dad.' She stumbled backwards and now was fully under the landing light.

That's when Jen saw it. It hadn't been as clear in the kitchen or in her room, but now, under the glow of the lightbulb—she couldn't believe her eyes—Jacqui looked glasslike. Jen could see the start of the banister and the stairs *through* her.

'Jen… try to stay… calm.'

Jen closed her eyes the tightest she had ever closed them. Cold panic coursed through her body. Tears streamed down her face; her chest was tightening. 'Wake up, wake up, wake up,' she said out loud, terrified, over and over and over. 'Please wake up, wake up; this is not real.'

'Breathe, Jen. Breathe, Jen.'

She could hear her mum's voice as if it was close but not quite near enough. A waft of lavender and rosemary passed her nostrils, and she breathed it in deeply. She felt her chest relax and her breathing slow. Her arms dropped to her side, and the aroma faded.

Against her own better judgement, Jen opened her eyes.

Everything was quiet. Her mum was no longer in the doorway.

She dabbed the tears away from her eyes with the cuffs of her pyjamas, then half sat, half collapsed on the end of the bed and leant her head in her hands. Had she had one of those dreams where everything is so real? Partially sleepwalked her way through it? It wasn't something that had ever happened to her before as far as she knew, but she had absorbed so much information the night before about ghosts and ancestors, maybe it had played on her mind. But the house was silent; there was no noise coming from her mum's room, and by now there normally would be.

Jen stood up and looked at herself in the mirror. Her eyes were puffy and bloodshot. She pinched her cheek really hard and watched her face screw up at the self-inflicted pain. If she had been asleep, she certainly wasn't now. With a new resolve, she walked out onto the landing, placed her hand on Jacqui's bedroom door handle and pushed the door fully open.

The light from the landing gave enough of itself that Jen could see clearly into the dimness. Standing opposite, on the other side of the bed, was Jacqui. Her back was to the window and the curtains were closed. A half-light enveloped the room as the sunshine tried to force its way in through any gap it could find.

Jen hadn't noticed what Jacqui was wearing before, but now she took it in. Jacqui had on her favourite pair of jeans and an emerald-green, long-sleeved top, which had small, grey flowers on it. Jen recognised the top immediately; she had bought it for her mum's last birthday. She knew Jacqui loved that shade of green, and it complemented her grey hair so well. She looked great whenever she wore it.

The shafts of early morning sunlight, which were so desperate to be seen, broke through around the edges and the gap between the two curtains. The beams shone through Jacqui, casting their rays onto the duvet cover.

'Don't look, Jen. Just… call your… dad. Let him… do this… for you. Please.'

Jen maintained Jacqui's pleading stare. A single tear dropped from her eye, hitting her hand on the way down to the carpet. 'It's okay, Mum,' she said solemnly. 'I was going to have to do this one day. I just wasn't expecting it to be today.' She turned her head towards the bed.

Her knees could not hold her up for long, and she collapsed sideways next to her mum on the bed.

'Oh, Mum. What happened?' she whispered, reaching out to touch Jacqui's motionless face.

Jen's head dropped, and the tears flowed uncontrollably.

Jacqui Hattley was dead, and she now found herself standing on the stairs with no idea how she had got there. She wanted to be next to Jen. Her daughter's sobs travelled across the landing.

The picture that wouldn't stay still had been turned completely upside down.

'You were trying to tell me, Mum. I ran out of time.'

CHAPTER 8

Time had lost relevance, and Jen did not know how long she sat in her mum's room before calling her dad. She could barely make sense of her own words; saying it out loud made it completely real. She asked him to drive carefully and not to rush, knowing full well he would take no notice.

Jen waited at the bottom of the stairs, longing to hear her dad's key in the lock. She thought about calling Laura, but the idea of repeating the words was unbearable. Everything felt numb as she stared down at the hallway floor. She supposed this was what shock felt like.

The lock on the door finally turned, and Mark burst in, almost falling over in his hurry to open it. Seeing Jen on the stairs, he knelt down and threw his arms round his daughter tightly.

'Oh, Jen. Are you sure? Did you call an ambulance?'

Jen shook her head. 'She's gone, Dad. She's really gone. I just called you first; I wasn't sure what else to do.'

Mark stood up and wiped the tears from his face. His eyes were red-rimmed and puffy.

'She's in her room, Dad.'

Mark looked reluctantly up the staircase. He didn't want to see Jacqui as she was now; he wanted the pictures in his mind to be of her looking alive and beautiful, not replaced with this final image. In a way, he'd hoped to die first so that he wouldn't have to feel the utter loss he felt at that moment, but in another, he hadn't wanted Jacqui to have to go through it either. Only one of them would escape it, and it was Jacqui. That was to be the order of things.

He slowly took his jacket off and hung it on the end of the banister before looking up the stairs again, filled with trepidation as if he was about to scale the highest peak. Then, he slowly climbed, stopped momentarily at Jacqui's door, and stepped in.

Jen remained on the bottom step. She heard her dad quietly talking to her mum: 'I love you so much', 'What am I going to do without you?'

She felt like she was intruding, so she moved to the kitchen and found herself staring out the window. The sun had risen on a new day, and an unusually heavy autumn frost was melting on the patio. A robin flew down onto the lawn and cocked its head towards the ground, listening for breakfast. Jen could feel her cheeks wet with tears; they just came without warning, she couldn't control them. Her own loss was weighing heavily, but now she felt sad for her dad, too. It was too much.

As she watched the robin wondering if a worm would make its way out of the solid earth, a heady waft of lavender and rosemary breathed itself into her nose.

'I'm not sure I can look at you right now, Mum.'

'I understand, but I need you to listen to me, Jen. I'm struggling… to control this at the moment. I don't know how long this… opportunity will last.'

Jen spun round to see Jacqui standing in front of the fridge. 'Opportunity?! You being dead isn't an opportunity! What do you think this is, some kind of training exercise?'

Jacqui was shocked momentarily by Jen's reaction. She was about to speak, then stopped. Struggling with the reality of being dead was challenging and completely unexpected, but she needed to find the right words for her daughter.

'I am as surprised as you are, Jen. I had no idea that I didn't have any time left. I am sorry, but there's not a lot I can do about it. I mean—sorry, that sounds very blunt, but there really isn't.'

'This is too cruel, Mum. You just died. You're dead upstairs and yet you're down here talking with me like it's perfectly normal.' Jen lowered her voice; she didn't want her dad to hear her. 'Maybe I've engineered this in my own head. After all the stories yesterday about Nan and Elizabeth. Yes, maybe I'm just making this up for myself to cope. I'm still in shock.'

Jacqui felt like taking a deep breath to calm herself but found that wasn't really a thing she needed to do anymore. It was an odd sensation; something else she needed to get used to. She wanted to tell Jen to snap out of it, that what they talked about yesterday weren't just stories, that this was really happening. But she knew that breaking into all that less than an hour after her daughter had found her dead in her bedroom was probably not the best timing. She'd just died. Jacqui knew how it had felt when she'd found her own mum at her flat, but that had been different. Expected. A long life lived. Plus, her mum hadn't been waiting for her when she got there. This was a bolt out of the blue.

'I know this is unbearable, Jen. I wish I could… change it but I can't. All I can tell you is that I have no idea how this side of it works. I've only ever been, well, alive. I'm really here, Jen; you're not… imagining me.

But I don't know how long I will be here for. That's why I am trying to talk to you as quickly as possible.'

Jen rubbed her face with her hands. She knew she wasn't imagining it; she could just tell. It would be far easier if she was. She'd inherited the family gift, and her first ghost was her own mum. That was the truth of it.

It dawned on her that talking to her mum, dead or alive, seemed pretty much the same. 'This is mental. Does this mean others are going to start turning up? I can't deal with more ghosts. Not right now.'

'I honestly have no idea when someone could show up, Jen. There's so much more I need to explain.'

'I'll never be ready for this.' Jen leant back on a cabinet and looked at the ceiling. She turned to say something more, only to find her mum had vanished. 'Oh, this is ridiculous,' she muttered.

Jen heard her dad descend the stairs and head into the lounge.

Mark was sitting leaning back on the sofa and staring at the blank screen of the TV, his hands on his knees. The colour was gone from his cheeks.

He didn't notice Jen come in until she sat next to him.

'I've called the ambulance,' he said. 'They'll be here soon. They'll need to work out what's happened.'

'What, like an autopsy?'

'Yes, they'll let us have a death certificate once they know. Then we'll need to sort out the funeral. I suppose we ought to call some people: your Uncle Mike, her friends Trudie and, who's the other one?'

'Michelle. We'll need to call the school. Oh, the kids will be sad to hear she won't be coming back.'

They both fell quiet.

'You should call Laura first,' her dad said. 'You're going to need her.'

Jen knew he was right. She wanted to call her; in fact, she wanted to go round to her house right now to cry, to just be held. But she knew she couldn't tell Laura everything; she'd have to hold something back, and that didn't sit right with her.

She gave her dad a cuddle, then got up to find her phone on the bottom step where she'd left it. She found Laura's number and waited as it rang.

Laura knew something bad had happened. The time of Jen's call was unusual, plus Jen never called, she always messaged.

Laura cried. She cried out of shock and she cried for the pain her best friend was feeling. A pain she couldn't take away.

'I'm here for whatever you need,' she said, knowing how banal it was to say when someone had died. The one thing the person needed was to have their loved one back, but no one could do that. All she could do was hold Jen's hand for however long she needed it.

They didn't chat for long. It was exhausting for Jen, just saying a few short sentences but not letting on to all the other stuff that was happening. What she really wanted to do was tell Laura how after her mum had died, she'd appeared as a ghost because they hadn't finished going through the family legacy Jen had just found out about, which now stretched for at least five generations, that she was likely to see more ghosts and that her mum was probably going to pop up again, making the whole grieving process way more complicated. But she didn't. How on earth was Laura going to understand any of that, let alone believe it? Why would she? Jen wished she had a budgie to talk to.

After her call to Laura, Jen rang her boss, who insisted she ignore work for at least the next two weeks.

She could hear her dad on the phone to her uncle. She knew how many calls they would both need to make and was dreading it. Friends and family, then all the other people: the bank, the council, the utilities. She wondered if it was crass to record her opening lines so she wouldn't have to keep repeating herself.

Jen realised she really needed the toilet, but she didn't want to go upstairs while her mum's body was still up there. But with no downstairs loo, she had no choice.

She scooted past her mum's room, sprinted down the landing as if she was being chased, and shuddered as she closed the bathroom door.

While washing her hands and drying them on the hand towel, she got the feeling she was not alone. It was strange, as it was a feeling she'd never really had before, but she could tell someone else was in the room with her.

The shower curtain was drawn across the bath. Slowly, she pulled it back to find her mum standing in the bathtub.

'How long have you been there?'

'Long enough,' Jacqui said sheepishly.

Jen shook her head. 'Have you no control where you pop up?'

'I haven't mastered that bit yet. I seem to be following you about.'

'Brilliant. You know Dad is here? He's called an ambulance. They're coming to collect you.' Jen felt weird saying that, like her mum was a parcel that needed returning.

'Oh, I see. Yes, that's how it works. Suppose they need to find out what happened to me. I'm hoping I can avoid your dad. I'm sure he can't see me, but I don't want to scare the living daylights out of him just in case; he's not the biggest fan of all this.'

Jen took a good look at her mum for a moment. The bathroom light was on, and she didn't look as transparent as she had earlier—more opaque, but not quite solid.

'You seem to be becoming more… real. How's that happening?'

Jacqui held her arms out and gave herself a good look.

At the same time, Jen pointed at the mirror. 'Can you see yourself?'

Jacqui leant out of the bath and in front of the mirror to see no reflection looking back. Jen stood behind her mum, looking at herself, bemused that Jacqui's head wasn't blocking her view.

'Wow,' Jen said. 'I was expecting you to have no reflection, but it's actually quite a surprise when you don't see it. I thought that was a vampire thing.'

'Oh, don't be silly, Jen. They're not real,' Jacqui said dismissively.

'Are you kidding? You've been a ghost for a few hours and you're telling me vampires aren't real?'

A giggle escaped from Jacqui, which triggered a smirk on Jen's face. Jen's mind was temporarily halted from its grief, and questions were queuing up.

'If I move to another room, will you be able to follow me?'

'I really don't know, Jen. Let's just stay here as long as we can, otherwise your dad will hear us. Well, he'll hear you talking to yourself. Then he'll have his own questions for you. He knows what's supposed to happen when I die.'

Jen put the toilet seat down and sat. 'Was your first ghost as crazy as this?'

'Ah, no. She was quite normal really. A week after your nan died, an old lady came up to me outside while I was moving some of your nan's things to ours. She just walked straight up to me and said, "Can you let the milkman know to cancel my order, please. I'm at number fifteen." She pointed down the road and promptly vanished. I sat in my car for a bit, thinking, *Is this really how it works?* Before I left, I popped a note in the milk bottle holder at number fifteen, asking to cancel the order. I wasn't worried if it looked silly or not; if that's what she needed, then I was happy to do it. That was where it started.'

Jen wondered what errands she might be asked to run. She wasn't sure if many people had milk delivered these days.

'Where are you when you're not here?' she asked.

'I don't feel like I'm anywhere.' Jacqui paused and looked down at the bathmat she was standing on. Although she couldn't quite tell if she was really on it, she couldn't feel where her feet were, and the surface beneath her just felt like nothing. 'No, maybe that's not quite right. I'm aware of you and where you are but I don't feel like I'm in the house all the time.'

Jen pondered her mum's answer for a moment.

'And why are you wearing that top I got you for your birthday? You were in your pyjamas when you died.'

Jacqui looked down at herself again. She hadn't even noticed what she was wearing. 'I have no idea why I'm in this. I don't think my visitors all came in the clothes they died in, but then, I never asked. Maybe it's more to do with what you need to see.' Jacqui shrugged. 'I was hoping to go through more of Elizabeth's books with you; she researched so much. It's all a bit of a mess, isn't it?'

'That's a polite way of putting it. Let's just get through today, eh?'

Before Jacqui could answer, Jen heard the doorbell. The ambulance had arrived.

'I don't want to be up here, Mum, when they… do whatever they need to do.'

'Of course, you go downstairs with your dad. Try to eat something, the pair of you,' Jacqui said as Jen left the bathroom. 'And make sure you have a drink.'

Jacqui hoped she would disappear; she didn't really want to be upstairs with the ambulance crew either. She had spent hours with herself in her bedroom, looking at her body and trying to process what had happened, before hearing Jen get up. She didn't want to see herself again.

The ambulance team was in the hallway, talking quietly with her dad, as Jen came down. They looked at her with empathetic eyes, gave their condolences, then headed up to Jacqui's room.

Jen and her dad found themselves in the kitchen, not really knowing what to do.

'Shall I put some toast on for us, Dad? Make us some tea? Mum would want us to keep our strength up, I expect.'

Mark nodded, even though both of them knew it was the last thing they really wanted.

CHAPTER 9

After the ambulance team had left with Jacqui, Jen went upstairs to look at her mum's room. The bed had been left tidy, the duvet straightened and pulled up to the pillows. She could hear cars passing by on the road out front, the occasional chirrup of a bird, next door's dog barking as it patrolled its back garden. The world continued on, oblivious to the loss of one life. Yet in those four walls it was all consuming.

Jen's eyes settled on the dressing table and the sewing box. She picked the box up and cradled it in her arms. A warmth spread across her chest; it felt good to hold it.

Sitting down at the dining table, Jen spread the books and pictures out, taking the sprig of lavender and rosemary out last.

'What are you for?' she said, twiddling the stems backwards and forwards between her finger and thumb.

Mark came in and put a hand on her shoulder. Looking over the collection, he said, 'At least you got to hear about some of this from the expert.' He sighed and sat down beside her.

Jen was glad her dad knew about the sewing box, her mum's secret. It would be too much to bear, hiding that from him in these moments.

'I've got no idea what mum's laptop password is to read her own notes,' Jen realised.

Her dad smiled. 'Yeah you do. It's the same as all her passwords. Not very secure, but the most important date.'

Jen smiled back. 'My birthday.'

Mark looked at his daughter. He worried for her. He'd seen how Jacqui had coped with her abilities, the experiences she had gone through. Jen was a different animal from her mother, but he knew how unpredictable the gift could be, what it could bring. It was up to him to help his Jen as much as possible now Jacqui was not there. It was what his now late wife would expect of him, and he was ready to do it.

'It's one of the most profound things I've ever experienced, Jen, losing a parent. When they're older, like your nan Violet, it's sad, but you know it's the natural order of things.'

Jen nodded. She didn't want to interrupt her dad's train of thought.

'It was the same with my dad. It's an inevitability you try not to think about, but you're never really ready. You muddle your way through the process as best you can. Then, at some point you start to realise, with a parent or both parents gone, you've moved up the queue. You'll eventually be next.'

Jen rolled her eyes. 'I hope you're not planning to pop off soon, thanks very much!'

Mark shook his head. 'Certainly not! But losing your mum like this; it's too soon. None of us know how long we have, do we? So, it's important to make the most of it all. Say what needs to be said, do what needs to be done. Your mum taught me that when she would tell me about her visitors and their stories. The opportunities missed, the words never said. It's not going to be like that with us. Nothing will be left unfinished. Do you understand?'

Jen could feel the tears welling up. Her dad had always been a sensitive soul, and it was an enormous comfort to know that he would support her with whatever was going to happen next.

'Let's just get through the rest of today and take it a bit at a time.'

'That's exactly what I said!' Jen replied.

Her dad gave her a quizzical look. 'I've got more calls to make. Did you want to stay at mine tonight? It's no problem at all; you can stay as long as you need to.'

'If it's okay, can we stay here?' Jen didn't want to miss her mum appearing again.

A chill of fear ran through Mark's body, and he tried to ignore it. 'No problem. I'll just need to nip back home for a few things.' He wandered out the dining room in search of his phone.

'It'll be fine,' he repeatedly whispered to himself out of Jen's earshot.

Both Mark and Jen spent the rest of the day fielding calls and messages. Jen felt obliged to speak to both neighbours, expecting they had seen the ambulance earlier in the day. Both said lovely words about her mum and told Jen not to hesitate in asking if there was anything she needed.

By early evening, Jen had had enough and hoped sleep would give her some respite from thinking about it all. She kissed her dad goodnight and could hear the TV on in the lounge as she started to drift off, exhausted.

Mark lay on the sofa with the spare duvet. He was equally exhausted, but sleep was far off. He had reluctantly agreed to stay; he'd had to— he couldn't leave his daughter alone in the house for the first night without her mum. But he was finding it unbearable. He hadn't stayed overnight for years. Not since that night. That was going to take some explaining; he would have to be careful with his words. He didn't want to frighten Jen, but she needed to know all the sides to the abilities she now had.

Leaving the TV on, he closed his eyes and tried to relax. 'Jacqui, if you're here, please just keep it quiet for me. Just for tonight.'

After a quarter of an hour or so, a soft purr emanated from Mark. It was an all-too-familiar sound to Jacqui. She watched him sleep, sitting in the armchair across from him. She was proud of him for staying, knowing how it was hard for him.

'I'll keep watch. Don't you worry, Mark.'

CHAPTER 10

The next week blurred into insignificance. Laura visited at least once each day, bringing food and much-needed hugs.

The call from the bereavement team confirmed Jacqui had suffered a heart attack. This came as a surprise to Mark and Jen as there was no family history indicating it was something they should have seen coming. They recommended that Jen have a check-up with her GP, in case it was something hereditary. Laura made a mental note to remind her once everything had settled into its new routine; she wouldn't let it be forgotten.

Jacqui's best friend arranged to visit, where they discussed funeral plans. No flowers, they agreed. Jacqui had loved flowers but she would have hated them going to waste, decaying on some crematorium lawn. A collection was to be arranged for her favourite charity, and everyone would be asked to wear something bright and colourful, reflecting the kind of person Jacqui had been.

Mark had managed to stay a whole week in the house. He wasn't sleeping great, and it showed on his face. Jen assumed it was due to the couch and decided that he should go home once the funeral was over.

She hadn't seen Jacqui since her appearance in the bathtub, and wondered if it was because her dad was there or all the other people that had been round. She didn't want to accept that she might never see her mum again and pushed it out of her mind. The fact that Jacqui was dead had almost become a bit irrelevant.

To fill the quiet moments, Jen read the notebooks. She began with Harriet's and quickly finished it, as it was mostly filled with short descriptions of people Harriet had spoken to. Harriet hadn't been particularly expressive with her words, taking a very plain approach to her encounters. On occasion, she wrote a few lines about Annabelle and her family, mainly when the seances involved them specifically. There was more feeling to these sections, showing a connection between the two women.

Elizabeth's two notebooks were very different—her words accompanied by sketches, the language more vivid. Elizabeth asked herself questions; her inquisitiveness was very much apparent. Jen found herself fascinated with how Elizabeth wanted to know more about how it all worked, something that didn't come across in Harriet's writing.

***

Jen was thankful that the only visitors she had been getting were living. People were in and out of the house regularly, and having only got halfway through the first of Elizabeth's notebooks, Jen had had to hide the sewing box in a cupboard for a few days.

It was dark outside, and Mark was drawing the curtains. He took a look at the thermostat to see if it needed turning up a notch. The temperature had dropped again in the week, something Jen had barely noticed, having not really been outside. She felt compelled to get the box back out, knowing that they weren't expecting anyone else that day. Laura had already been and was taking Olivia to the cinema that evening; her uncle wasn't planning to pop round until the weekend.

Sitting back at the dining table, she got the books out but stopped once again at the sprig of lavender and rosemary bound together by its green ribbon. How did it still smell so strongly? She knew the plants must be years past their best.

Jen looked up to see Jacqui sitting opposite her, hands on the table.

'Where have you been?' Jen asked, slightly disgruntled by the amount of time Jacqui had been away.

'I've been around. It wouldn't have helped if I'd shown my face while Laura was here, would it? I didn't want to put you in an awkward situation.'

'Fair enough. Must be weird, watching people coming and going, talking about you as if you're not here.'

'Well, to them, Jen, I'm not here anymore, am I? But yes, it's all a bit peculiar.'

Jen was about to speak when she heard her dad step into the room behind her. He sat a space away from Jacqui, putting a beer bottle down on the table, and looked over the books.

Jen saw her mum roll her eyes and got up to fetch a coaster from the cabinet drawer. Placing it under her dad's beer, she glanced back at her mum with a smirk.

'What do you know about this?' Jen asked, addressing both her mum and dad. She was holding up the sprig, and watched as her dad shuffled in his chair.

He regarded it with care. 'I don't know much about it at all, really. Only what your mum told me. I think your nan was given it by her aunt.'

'It's that old? How has it stayed so intact? And can you smell that?' Jen sniffed the sprig again.

'Nope, it's just you I think.' Mark took a swig of beer.

Jacqui had been observing their conversation, and Jen could see she wanted to say something.

'Tell your dad it's time for him to tell you why he moved out,' Jacqui said.

Jen looked at her mum, trying to comprehend what she'd just said. Her cheeks went flush at the thought of admitting that her mum was sitting there with them; she wasn't sure how her dad would take it.

'Dad, does this have something to do with why you moved out?'

Mark breathed in deeply. 'There's a lot your mum didn't get a chance to tell you. Some you'll learn from the notebooks, I think, but some things, I suppose, I'll need to explain to you myself.' He took another swig of his beer. 'I moved out because of something that happened in this house. It was the most terrifying night of my life.'

'And mine,' Jacqui added.

Mark continued. 'You'd been gone a few months, having moved in with Tom. Your mum and I were getting used to it just being the two of us again. We had got to talking about the ghosts, we'd had a bottle of wine—I'm not sure what got into us.'

Jacqui had her head in her hands. 'It was so stupid, looking back. I can't even explain what made me make it.'

'Your mum decided to make one of those boards, a Ouija board. You know, the ones with all the letters of the alphabet on. It had numbers, a yes and a no.'

Jen's eyes widened. She'd watched enough scary films. Whether you believed in the paranormal or not, Ouija boards had a bad reputation. She remembered friends at school suggesting one at a sleepover once. It was something she had never wanted to mess with.

'You made a Ouija board?! Were you out of your mind?' Jen blurted out directly at Jacqui.

Mark looked at the apparently empty seat and back at Jen. Jen knew she'd blown their cover.

'Your mum's sat here, isn't she?' he asked, taking another swig.

There was no point hiding it. 'Yup, she's right there.' Jen pointed.

'I had a feeling it wasn't you on coaster patrol. To be honest, I had thought you were taking this all rather calmly, but then, you would be if she's not really gone. I've been waiting for her to turn up; I couldn't believe she'd just leave you to cope with this all on your own.'

Jacqui looked longingly at Mark, wishing she could say all the things she wanted, just to him.

'She's been here since it happened, for both of us.' Jen replied, rubbing her dad's hand. 'But seriously, the pair of you: a Ouija board?'

'I know, I know. As I said, I don't know what got into us. She got some paper and drew it all out, got a glass from the kitchen, and we sat here at this table. We both placed a finger on the glass, and your mum asked something like, "Is there anybody who wants to talk to us?" Then we waited. I honestly didn't think it was going to work.

'We should have realised something was wrong; Bailey usually sat wherever we were in the evening, but he point-blank refused to come into the dining room once the board was out. I should have taken it more seriously.' Mark now had both hands around his beer bottle.

Jacqui looked pensive. 'We *both* should have taken it more seriously,' she said. 'Your nan, she would have been furious with me for doing it. She made a point of saying to me, "Don't dabble with your gift, it can be a wonder and a danger. You must never call for anyone, just wait for them to come." After that night, I understood exactly why she was so adamant about it.'

'Well, that sounds a bit ominous,' Jen said with raised eyebrows.

Mark was sitting, in what would have been silence to him, watching Jen listening to her mum. Sensing a pause, he shook his head. 'We sat there for ages. Nothing happened. So, I went to remove my finger from the glass. That's when it moved for the first time. Just a tiny fraction, but it moved. I said that it must have moved as I got out of my chair, but your mum told me to sit down, then she asked the question out loud again. This time, the glass moved immediately, straight to "yes". It was like nothing I had ever seen. I knew I hadn't moved the glass myself, and if your mum had moved it, I would have felt it.' Mark stood and walked round Jen's side of the table, anxious just thinking about what happened next.

'I told your dad to stay still, to not remove either of our fingers from the glass. I was excited to see who had come through. I'd spoken to a few ghosts already so I just assumed this would be the same as the others. I was so naïve. I'd forgotten some of what Elizabeth had said in her notebooks, warning of the darker things that can happen.'

Jen felt a cold shiver up her arms. What had her parents gone and done?

Jacqui watched Mark make his way round the table and retake his seat, taking a notably long sip of beer.

'So, your mum asked who it was, and the glass slowly moved to the letter "E", then stopped. That wasn't much to go on, so we asked if it had a message for someone. Slowly, the glass moved to "yes". We asked who the message was for, and it spelt out "Elizabeth"—but it didn't pause after that. It started spelling another name. Your nan's name: Violet. The glass was moving around much faster at this point, I swore it was going to spin off the table. It was spelling out your mum's name: Jacqueline.

'I could see your mum getting agitated; I was agitated! Then, all of sudden, we heard this almighty crash come from the kitchen. Of course, it made us jump and we took our fingers off the glass. Which was a big mistake.' Mark stood up and began pacing round the table. 'We headed straight into the kitchen, and it was carnage. Two cupboard doors were open, and every glass had seemingly been pushed out at the same time. The floor was covered in shards. We made to clean it up, worried that Bailey would cut himself on it all. Then the banging started back in the dining room—it wanted us to go back in there.'

Jen's hands had gone cold. '*What* wanted you to go back in there?'

Mark had got up again, unable to sit still. He stood behind Jacqui, shaking his head. Jacqui was looking up at Mark and could see he was struggling.

He left the room.

'We'd been very stupid, Jen,' Jacqui continued. 'We'd gotten involved with something we shouldn't have. When we came back into the dining room, something was physically banging the table. It was as if a closed fist was just repeatedly thumping, over and over. The glass was vibrating across the paper. All I could think to do was put our fingers back on it and try to send whatever it was away.'

Mark returned from the kitchen with another beer. 'We didn't know what it was, but your mum wanted to get rid of it. We placed our fingers back on the glass, and the banging stopped. Your mum told it to leave, that it was not welcome in the house, but it was not having any of it… That's when I started to feel like I wasn't myself. I could feel the glass moving under my finger, and I could tell I was now moving it, but the word I was spelling out wasn't coming from me; it was coming from someone else. Some*thing* else.' He took a swig.

'Your dad changed; he looked strange. His face wasn't right, as if there was another face overlaying his own. His eyes were blank and he wasn't talking; he just fixated on the glass.'

'I knew what it was spelling out before it finished. "J, E, N, N, I, F, E, R".'

'Then his head turned unnaturally towards me. It wasn't your dad anymore. It was looking at me, grinning.'

Jen just sat in her chair, alarmed by what she was hearing. It hadn't crossed her mind that there could be scary elements to her abilities, that other things could come through. She could feel the fear emanating from her parents.

Mark sat down again. 'I had no control of what was happening. It's so hard to explain. It was like I was still in myself, but my being was suppressed, corrupted. I could feel something so dark inside me. I had no control over my actions, what I was saying; I saw *your* name being spelt out, I heard words come out of my mouth, but I was just spectating.'

'It spoke,' said Jacqui, 'and I have never been so frightened. The voice, low, like a growl from an animal, just said, "FOUND YOU." I had no idea what to do. I was rooted to the spot, finger still on the glass.'

'I knew it was all wrong. It wanted you, Jen. It wanted you there, for me to make you come to the house. It made me walk to the kitchen and pick up a piece of glass from the floor. It wanted me to hurt your mum to make you come.' Mark was no longer drinking his beer, but he began to pick at the label.

'The look on his face was unearthly,' said Jacqui. 'Bailey had followed in behind me and was snarling, foaming at the mouth. I had never seen him so aggressive.'

'I was in a fight with it, Jen. I—*it*—followed your mum and Bailey into the lounge.'

'I shouted your dad's name repeatedly, and for a moment, it was like he was back in the room. But all he could say was "Get away from me!" Then he was gone—and it was back.'

'I tried so hard to stop moving, I was battling every part of myself to stop. But I couldn't. I was going to do something terrible.'

Mark became absorbed by the remaining sticky parts of the label. Jen could see he was battling not to cry.

'I was just in a panic,' Jacqui continued. 'How was I going to get rid of whatever it was? Was I going to have to hurt your dad? What if it tried to hurt Bailey? Then, all of a sudden, I could smell lavender and rosemary. It was pungent; it was so strong it took my breath away. My mind cleared for a few moments, and I felt a warmth along my arm, and a squeeze, like someone was comforting me, telling me they were there with me. That's when I remembered the sprig in the sewing box. I'd held it so many times while reading Elizabeth's books explaining what it's for. It's for protection, Jen. Protection against bad things that might try to come through.

'Your dad was blocking the exit back to the kitchen, so I shot out into the garden through the bifold doors. At the time, I had a small patch of both plants growing at the back of the garden. I grabbed at the stems, pulling as much of both out as I could. I could hear Bailey barking, so I hurried back into the lounge to see your dad—it —had Bailey backed into the corner. I had no idea what to do really, so I just put myself between it and Bailey, and pushed my hands and the plants into your dad's face.'

Jacqui felt like if she had still been alive, she would have been out of breath. The recollection of that night was harrowing. She looked over at Mark, who was white as a sheet, staring at the table. Sensing a pause in the story, he looked up.

'I remember starting to come round as myself and feeling like my face was on fire,' he said. 'It was like I was being scratched to pieces, but more than that, the thing was screaming in my head. Then I was the one screaming. I began to hear your mum clearly, shouting over and over, "Leave this house, you're not welcome here! You have no power here! Leave Mark's body and leave this house!" Then, all of sudden, I was back.

'Your mum and I were kneeling on the floor. I still had the piece of glass in my hand, which had made quite a deep cut, but I had never let go of it. I had not used it to hurt your mum or Bailey—but it had wanted me to. I just collapsed onto the floor; I couldn't move.'

'I could see your dad was back to himself but drained, so I left him and Bailey in the lounge. I had to finish it. I grabbed the board and the glass, found some matches, and took it all out into the garden. I smashed the glass on the ground and took a match to the board until it was nothing but embers. It was done. I felt a calm descend around us. It was like I had managed to push whatever it was back and shut the door it had come through. It was gone.'

Jen looked at both her parents in amazement. It was the stuff of nightmares. Not only had her parents been in harm's way, but whatever it was had spelt names of women throughout her family, including her own. Plus, it had come with an ominous message: 'found you'. What did it mean?

Mark seemed to return a little more to normal, now that the worst of the story was over. 'We made up some story that I'd fallen off a ladder into the bushes in the garden, to explain away the scratches on my face and cut on my hand. And we decided that your mum would take a very low-key approach to her abilities, that she would back away from anything too out of the ordinary when it came to her visitors. No dabbling, no looking for things over and above what arrived of its own accord.

'I tried to forget about what happened but, I don't know, it's like it kept its hold over me.' Mark leant back in his chair and looked at the ceiling, as if for guidance. 'I was having trouble sleeping, which was understandable given what had happened, but it went on for weeks. I began having night terrors. I would wake up petrified, believing I'd killed your mum, and I was terrified, every single time I woke up, that I'd actually done it. Then they started to come during the day. I'd be making dinner or watching TV, and it would all be happening again—I'd be back in the kitchen picking up the piece of glass, chasing your mum. It was almost worse than the night the thing came into the house. It was relentless.'

Jacqui reached across the table to squeeze Mark's hand, only to stop at the last moment and pull her hand back. Jen watched the disappointment on her mum's face; it was sad to see.

'Your dad was breaking down before my eyes. Before we knew it, it had been going on for five months. He was sleep deprived; he looked terrible; he'd lost his appetite and was losing weight.

'One night, he suggested we move. I should have wanted to; I should have put him first, but I didn't want to leave. I know it sounds incredibly selfish, but ever since Mum died, there's been times when I know she's here, keeping an eye on things. I've never seen her, not like you see me. But I felt her. Her trick was always to move the photo frames. Whenever she stayed with us, when she was alive, she would always straighten them on her way up to bed—that's how I knew it was her. Then there was Bailey, how could I possibly leave him behind? Finally, there were my visitors. What if moving disrupted them being able to find me? I had no idea how it worked, and I didn't want to test any theories.

'I liked everything how it was, or at least, how it was before we did the Ouija board. Then me and your dad started arguing. We used to bicker, of course, but this was different. Your dad was angry; he felt like I was choosing the house and my gift over him. Perhaps I was. You didn't see any of it because you weren't here, and we made sure to hide it when you were. In the end, I actually felt like we shouldn't be together; it had gotten that bad. I felt like he didn't understand where I was coming from. So, I reluctantly suggested it would be best if he moved out.'

'So that's why you split up? Because of the Ouija board?' Jen couldn't believe it. All this time, and this is why her parents had separated.

Realising that Jacqui had told Jen why he had moved out, Mark brought himself back into the moment and picked up the baton.

'It's what triggered it, yes, but the whole incident had managed to create a wedge between us. I thought a fresh place would be ideal and that we could get back to normal, but I hadn't counted on how much more tied to the place your mum was. Things are different now, but at the time, I couldn't believe she was choosing the ghosts, the house and her gift over me. And I couldn't physically recover from what had happened either, not here anyway. We actually didn't speak properly for a few weeks after I left. I genuinely thought that was it.'

Jen squeezed her dad's hand for Jacqui. 'So, what did you tell your friends? They must have asked questions as you never got divorced? I was completely confused myself at the time, but you were both so tight-lipped about it, I had to leave it be. Then after a while, it was like you were back to normal, save living together.'

Jacqui looked like she was about to speak, so Jen turned to face her. 'The most plausible thing we could come up with was that we'd drifted apart and needed some time to work things out. We said we hadn't decided on whether we would split up or not. Some of our friends were going through marriage problems too, so luckily, we just blended in with the crowd.

'I got asked if your dad had been through a breakdown, which is probably what it looked like given the physical state he was in. I got other questions like "Did one of us cheat?" or "Was Mark gambling?" I just deflected it all and kept to the story that we needed time.

'After your dad began feeling better, we started talking again and realised that we still very much loved each other. It took time, but we found a way round it all. I realised that I missed your dad very much. Our friends had other things to worry about in their own lives by then, and people just stopped asking and got used to us living separately.'

Jen turned back to her dad.

'We tried once to get back to the old normal. I stayed here one night—but I had another nightmare. It had been nearly a year since the last one, but there it was, clear as day, all over again. Being around your mum was no problem; she stayed at mine and I had no issues. She told me all about who would visit, their stories, and I began to understand why it was all so important to her to be here in this house. But I can't come back here permanently, it seems. I don't know if it's because this is where it happened and it triggers the nightmares in my head. We did wonder if the house just didn't like me or thought I was a threat. Can you believe we thought the house had an opinion, too? It's crazy, isn't it?' Mark let out a sigh that sounded like it had been waiting for years to come out. 'As frightening as all that was to hear, Jen, it's important that you know what happened. There's two sides to this gift you've inherited. It has to be respected, and that night, we didn't respect it. Whatever it was, it seemed to know your mum's family line.'

Jacqui nodded in agreement. 'Jen, you're not saying much. This is a lot for you to take in. I'm sorry, this isn't how I wanted this to go.'

Jen rubbed the fingers of one hand over her eyes. They'd just told her that her dad had been possessed by an evil spirit because her mum had made her own Ouija board, but they'd been saved by somebody reminding her mum about the power of the plants in the garden, then they'd had to separate because the whole thing had caused a rift between them. She was pretty sure no one would have the audacity to make this up, let alone both of them. But it was a lot.

'You put all the lavender and rosemary shrubs in after that, didn't you?' Jen asked Jacqui. 'To strengthen your defences?'

'Yes, I reread everything Elizabeth had researched about protection, and we made a few additions of our own. Your dad came up with this clever idea to drill holes round all the doorways, tuck the plants in them and then fill them in. It stops anything coming in from outside unless it's invited. And there's definitely been no Ouija boards or any other ways of calling on the spirits going on in this house since. It seems to have worked so far.'

Jen nodded. 'Now, seriously, are there any other bombshells I need to know about? Is there anything else you need to tell me about the ghosts, the Ouija board, the notebooks? May as well get it all out now while we're here together.'

Mark and Jacqui shook their heads.

Jen suddenly realised something and felt a pang of guilt. 'Oh, Dad, you've been staying here all this time. I thought you were just looking tired from being on the couch but—have you been having nightmares again? I am so sorry.'

'No, nothing like I did before. I don't really remember having dreamt much at all since being here. You know I'd do anything for you, so no feeling bad about it. I agreed to stay, after all.'

Jacqui had watched Mark sleep every night since he had come back and knew he was lying. He may not have screamed like he used to, but he had woken up several times in sheer panic. She'd hoped her presence calmed him.

'You're right,' Jen said. 'I needed to know all this. And I get why you didn't tell me before—I am not even sure I would have believed you back then. I'm sorry you had to give up what you had because of it. It doesn't seem very fair. I doubt there's many couples who could have gone through something as bizarre as that and basically stayed together.'

Jen tried to sound her most convincing, for the sake of her parents—she knew it had been a tough decision and she didn't want them to feel any more guilty about it than they did already—but she had been upset when they seemingly split up and didn't tell her much. She'd spent all those years thinking one of them had an affair.

Then there was the whole spelling out of her name. She didn't know what to make of that. She felt a bit like she needed to cry. Everything was starting to feel like it was closing in on her and she had taken in as much as she possibly could. Overwhelmed is what she felt, and she needed to go to bed.

Mark got up and gave his daughter a much-needed hug. 'This is from both of us, we're here to protect you as much as we possibly can. From anything.'

Jen looked over to the chair her mum had been sitting in, to see it was now vacant.

CHAPTER 11

Jen hadn't been awake long, and it wasn't particularly early, but she was disinclined to get out of bed. Doing that meant the day had to begin, and she didn't want it to. She didn't want today to happen at all.

No noises were coming from downstairs, so she presumed her dad was either still asleep or thinking exactly the same. *I must let him go back to his house this week*, she thought. As much as she wanted him to stay all the time, she could tell he was uneasy—and he couldn't sleep on the couch anymore.

By her side was the sewing box; she'd brought it up to bed, needing it beside her as she fell asleep. She began reading Elizabeth's notebooks.

About two thirds into her first notebook, Elizabeth had recounted a gathering she had attended with only a small number of close acquaintances:

'It has taken me the best part of a day to recover from last night's circumstances. Save for a few cuts to my hands from the shattered glass, I am well and will recover. I fear it will not be the same for poor Margaret.

I will never forget how her face looked when it had hold of her. For a few moments, my friend was gone, replaced with something I cannot yet describe. It will take some weeks, I expect, for her to get over her ordeal. Some of the group want to try again, but I am not convinced this is wise. Whether Margaret will rejoin us at all, who can say.

The whole experience has only further proved to me that there are more than the voices of the dead that wish to come through to our side. Ghosts are the spirits of human beings, once alive, having experienced life. But there are others. Entities that have never been "alive", but that exist—seemingly in darkness and with their own agendas. We must be more cautious in future.'

Jen placed the book down, considering Elizabeth's words and what her parents had told her. It had been over a week since they had described the Ouija board encounter, and she was still playing some of it over in her head.

Everything had happened at speed: her mum telling her about the family gift, then her mum dying and now the potential dangers of what her gift could do. Jen wondered why she was not feeling more agitated, more upset. Was there still an element of shock within her, preventing things from totally sinking in? She had never been much of a worrier; if something could be changed to make things better, she would do it, but she wouldn't sit there worrying about something she had no control over. And this felt like something she had no control over. She couldn't bring her mum back; the upset and grief were there, but she had no choice. And her new abilities—they were there to stay. She had no choice but to believe her parents, either; the alternative was that she, her mum and her dad were having some kind of shared breakdown, which had spanned years. Then there was the simple fact that she could see and hear her mum's ghost. It all, strangely, made sense.

Picking the second notebook up and opening it, Jen glanced at the date on the first page.

'*21st June 1922.*'

'That's odd.' She then reopened the first notebook and looked at its last dated entry.

'*16th November 1915.*'

Jen found the time gap peculiar, as Elizabeth had written in her notebooks every week, it seemed, even if it was only a few short sentences. It was as if a whole book was missing between the two she had. She wondered if her mum had ever noticed.

With a huge sigh, she put the notebooks back in their box and closed the lid; the mystery would have to wait for another time. The day had begun; it didn't need her permission. Jacqui's funeral started at 11am.

Mark was in the kitchen making a coffee when Jen came down. She was wearing a knitted dress she'd bought with Laura on one of their previous shopping trips—a bold pink—accompanied by the earrings her parents had bought for her 30th birthday, which she never tired of.

'You look handsome, Dad.'

Mark had picked a navy suit, light blue shirt and Jacqui's favourite tie. 'Just about fits still.' he said jokingly, holding his stomach in.

The doorbell went, and Jen answered to find Laura standing there, resplendent in green, an homage to Jacqui's favourite colour.

'How are you doing?' Laura said, giving Jen a warm hug.

'Bearing up, just be glad to get this bit out of the way, you know?'

'Krish is waiting to take us, when you're ready.'

Mark had come into the hallway to put his shoes on. 'Thanks so much for driving us, Laura. It's very kind of you,' he said, tying his laces.

'Anything for you two.'

Jen could see Laura welling up. 'Please, don't start yet, otherwise you'll set me off too.'

The two of them looked at each other, a supportive look that said one would hold the other up today and for long as she needed her to, and that the other would always be there to return the kindness.

***

The sun was shining, and the sky was clear of clouds—an endless blue from the hill where the crematorium was. The view of the people coming in was just as spectacular. A riot of colour filled the ceremony room, and when Jen and Mark both stood to speak, they could feel the vibrancy emanating from their friends and family, the colours transmitting the love they had for the one they had lost.

Once the ceremony was over, Jen and Mark milled about with the guests for a bit, accepting condolences, until it was time to move on—there was another funeral to be held, and their mourners began arriving, such was the constantly turning wheel of life and death. Mark had booked a private space at Jacqui's favourite pub, where those who wanted to could enjoy some time remembering her.

Laura and Krish waited for Jen and her dad in the car to give them a little time together before meeting the crowd again.

'Well, for a funeral, I don't think it could have gone any better,' Mark said. 'Did you see how many colours everyone was wearing? Your mum would have loved it, assuming she didn't see it herself?'

Jen was holding her dad's hand and arm, leaning into him. 'I didn't see her here. I wondered if she might appear. Maybe she can't leave the house? I have no idea how it all works.'

Jen quietly worried that her mum wouldn't be back at all. It was possible that telling the story about the Ouija board was the main thing she'd held on for. If there was nothing else to explain, would she reappear? Jen didn't want to think about it; it would mean having to completely let go. She knew that should have started the day her mum died, but most people didn't have their loved ones manifesting as ghosts, or the ability to see them.

'Dad, if you want to, it's okay for you to go back to yours tomorrow. I'll be okay. You can't stay on the sofa forever.'

Mark would be lying to say he wasn't relieved. Staying in the house gave him the yips. Also, it had long been agreed that if anything happened to either him or Jacqui, their properties could be used by Jen. So, her living there on her own for the foreseeable future seemed only right.

'Only if you're sure, Jen. I can be there as long as you need me.'

'Honestly, I need to get used to it, and I feel okay about being there on my own. I still expect you round for dinner on a regular basis though!'

***

It was well into the evening when Krish delivered Mark and Jen back home.

The gathering at the pub had been more enjoyable than Jen had expected. The stories she heard about her mum—some she'd never been told before—made her laugh and cry in equal measure. Some friends had brought their own photo albums: Jacqui on a trip to Venice at nineteen; Jacqui at a table with friends at a wedding.

She and her dad had been bought far too many drinks, and by the time the pub called time, both of them were ready for bed.

Mark headed straight for the sofa, only bothering to take his shoes off.

At the top of the stairs, Jen was sure she could hear the chairs moving around in the dining room then a soft padding sound coming up behind her. She let her hand drop to her side, hoping to feel the fur on Bailey's back as he came past, but there was nothing.

Downstairs, Jacqui was sitting at one of the dining chairs. She'd been sitting there all day. She'd tried to follow Jen when they left for the funeral, but it hadn't worked. Every time she'd tried to walk through the front door—or the back door, for that matter—she'd found herself in the house somewhere: the lounge, the landing, the kitchen, but never outside. She'd tried to will herself to the place where the funeral was; that hadn't worked either.

Maybe she was confined to the house. Knowing the rules to her existence was impossible, same as when she was on the other side of the fence.

Bailey had laid under the table beside her the whole time. She'd known he was still in the house when she was alive, but since dying, she could actually see him for herself. With his big, brown eyes and soft golden fur framing his cheery face, he was a dog that always looked like he was smiling. It really was a wonder she had not expected.

She watched as he shoved the dining chairs out of place and followed Jen up the stairs, his tail wagging as he went out the door. Some things had changed, but some, thankfully, had not.

CHAPTER 12

Mark was at the door with his holdall in his hand. 'Are you sure you'll be okay? I really can stay for longer.' He didn't want to leave Jen on her own, but he had to be truthful to himself—he was glad to be getting out of that house.

Jen gave her dad a reassuring cuddle. 'I need to know that I can do this. I think I'll be fine. If I'm not, I know where you are, don't I?'

She could see the dark circles under his eyes and knew he was downplaying how tired he was. It was time for him to go home.

'Yes, you do. Okay, well, text me later.'

Jen waved as her dad's car pulled out of the driveway, then she closed the front door.

Looking at her phone, she saw a message from Laura:

'Just call if you need me, I'll drop whatever I'm doing. Otherwise, I'll leave you to it xxx'

Jen sent some kisses back, then looked down the hallway to the kitchen and then up the stairs. She walked into the lounge and through into the dining room. For the first time, she was taking the house in without either of her parents there. This was where she lived now, on her own—for the time being.

A sadness came over her; she knew she had people to lean on if needed, but at that precise moment, Jen felt utterly alone. She wondered what it might have been like if she had still been with Tom while all this happened. But the more she thought about it, the more she was comfortable that she was dealing with it without him. She'd grieved the loss of her marriage before she made the final decision to leave. Having him around, it just didn't fit now; it wasn't his support she needed anymore.

What worried her more than anything was the uncertainty around when her mum might reappear. What if she didn't come back? Jen felt like the loss of her mum and the associated grief were—just about—being held back, like they were behind a closed door. She knew the door had to be opened at some point, but if there was still time she could spend with her mum, she wanted to hold the tidal wave back as long as possible.

Perhaps this is really it, Jen wondered, ambling back to the kitchen and absent-mindedly opening the fridge to distract herself from her own thoughts. It was pretty much empty, as was the freezer.

Suddenly, a new resolve took hold. Jen located her keys, grabbed some bags and headed to her car. She was going shopping.

***

Having spent the best part of a cathartic hour browsing the shelves, Jen emerged from the supermarket very pleased with herself. She had plans to cook what she considered a healthy meal, with good intentions of improving her eating habits over the next week. Recent events had called for comfort food, but she couldn't keep relying on toast, batch-cooking from Laura and frozen meals. If her mum's heart condition was hereditary, it was essential that she looked after herself. Her one indulgence had been a packet of her and her mum's favourite biscuits—everything in moderation was okay, otherwise life would be pretty dull.

Between turning away to roll the trolley into its place and turning back to her car, a slender woman had appeared, standing next to her car—in fact, it looked like she was leaning on her boot, smoking. Jen had to look twice. Yes, there really was a woman leaning on her car smoking a cigarette.

'What the...?' Jen muttered as she marched across the car park, ready to have a few words. What a cheek, propping yourself up on someone else's car!

But as Jen got closer, the woman stood up straight, dropped her cigarette and stubbed it out on the ground with the pointed toe of her burgundy stiletto boot, and came to meet Jen a few metres from the car.

'Darling, you have been ages,' the woman said. 'I've been waiting to speak with you, and we don't have much time.'

'I'm sorry, do I know you?' Jen was taken aback by the woman's brashness. She guessed she was in her late sixties or maybe seventies, but she couldn't entirely tell as her face was fully made up with blush, eyeshadow, heavy mascara and lipstick, alongside flamboyant silver jewellery and clearly dyed hair, which was tied back in a ponytail. She looked quite fabulous.

'Certainly not, darling, we've never met. But I need you to speak to my niece, darling, it's quite urgent. She's getting rid of my shoes, and she hasn't even tried one pair on!'

Jen just stood there, staring. The first day in ages she'd decided to pop out, on her own, into the big wide world, and she comes across this one. What on earth was this woman on about?

The woman held her hand up to Jen's face and clicked twice in front of her eyes. 'My dear, can you hear me?'

'Ok, wow, you need to stop doing that,' Jen said, backing away from the woman and wondering how she could get around her quickly and into the car.

'She's just over there.' The woman pointed.

Jen didn't bother to follow the direction of the woman's hand. 'Well, if she's over there, why don't you speak to her yourself?' she said, raising her voice. She was getting frustrated now, she just wanted to go home.

'Because I'm dead, darling. She's not going to hear a word I am saying. That's what I need you for.'

Jen's stomach dropped and her palms went clammy. Even though her brain was a few seconds behind, her primal instincts kicked in and she now realised what was going on. Jen looked on the ground; there was no cigarette stubbed out by her car. She looked around the car park; people were walking to and from the supermarket entrance, throwing concerned or bemused looks in her direction.

'Oh, bloody hell!' Jen realised she'd been standing in the middle of the car park seemingly talking to thin air.

She looked back at the woman, who was now staring at her impatiently.

'Over there! Honestly, dear, you seemed a bit more sprightly than this.'

Jen now turned in the direction of her hand. Another woman, younger than Jen, had a few bags of shopping in her trolley and was moving a number of boxes around in the boot of her car, trying to find room for her new purchases. Her blonde hair was splayed out across the back of her red coat. A black woolly hat topped her head, the bobble bouncing this way and that as she shoved boxes left and right like she was trying to solve some kind of logic puzzle.

Jen's feet had already started walking towards her as her brain caught up. *What am I doing? What am going to say to her? This is your first proper ghost, Jen, think on your feet.*

'That's right, dear, that's my niece in the red coat.'

'So, you're her auntie then? What's your name?'

'Aunt, darling, not auntie. Joan Davidstone. You may have heard of me.' It was a statement not a question.

Jen had not heard of her but felt she clearly ought to have done. She was only a few metres from Joan's niece who, thankfully, hadn't yet turned round.

'So,' Jen said, 'you want me to tell her to try your shoes on?'

'Oh my God, darling, no. But if she had, I probably wouldn't need your help.'

Jen remembered what her mum told her about having to decipher what some of her visitors were saying. Many spoke in riddles or didn't even speak at all. It wasn't often that someone just came straight out with what they wanted.

Jen tried to hold her patience, but it wasn't happening; she felt exposed amongst the other people in the car park. 'Could you at least try to be clear about what it is you want me to say to her, please? You keep going on about your shoes and how urgent it is, but I'm not really understanding what's so urgent about your niece and your shoes. This is going to be difficult enough without you being all cryptic about it!'

Joan stared at Jen for a few seconds. She was not used to being spoken to like this; usually, she was the one dishing out the forthrightness. Then, a smile crept across her face. 'You're right, dear. Get to the point, Joan…'

As Joan got to the point, Jen listened, whilst realising that the niece was now looking at her in bewilderment. Awkward didn't really cover it.

'Excuse me, can I help you?' the niece asked.

'Yes, well, it's the other way round actually,' Jen said. She didn't know this woman's name but, realising that she ought to just get to the point herself, felt it was surplus to requirements. Taking a deep breath, she dived in headfirst, hoping she'd find her way back to the surface. 'The shoes in your car that belonged to your Aunt Joan, you're about to take them to the charity shop, but she expected you to try them on so that you would discover that some of them are stuffed with cash, so check them all before you drop them off.'

The woman just stood there, her mouth slightly open.

Joan looked back and forth between her niece and Jen. 'Oh, darling, tell Rebecca to close her mouth. It's so ungainly. Then get her to open the larger grey box, gold round the edge, top left corner. It has dark brown, calf-high, leather boots inside. She'd look divine in them, but I know she'll never wear them. Always in trainers, this one.'

Jen couldn't help glancing at the blonde woman's feet. Despite Joan's remarks, they were a very cool pair of trainers.

She cleared her throat. 'Rebecca, just humour me and try a box. The grey one with the gold going round the edge. There's brown leather boots in there.' She wasn't going to mention her mouth or the trainers—not the time.

Rebecca still said nothing, which Jen was thankful for. At least she wasn't hurling abuse or calling the police about the madwoman in the car park allegedly talking to her dead aunt. Not yet, anyway. She quietly turned and scanned the boxes.

'Top left corner,' Jen said.

Rebecca slid the box out and turned to sit on the edge of the boot. *Who is this woman and how does she know about Aunt Joan? How does she know my name?* Her curiosity had been piqued, but once she'd checked the box to find nothing special, she could tell the crazy lady to go away or speak to security in the shop.

Jen watched intently as Rebecca took the lid off to reveal some well-worn but still lively brown boots. She felt herself relax slightly; the boots Joan had described were in the box as she'd said they would be.

Joan gazed at the boots as if a stash of precious jewels had been uncovered. 'Made to measure these, darling. I looked amazing in them.'

Clearly, Joan had been a lover of all things footwear. Jen counted at least twenty shoeboxes in the boot and could see the overflow on the back seat.

Rebecca took the left boot in one hand and slid the other hand in, expecting nothing, which is exactly what she found. Picking up the right boot and sliding her hand in, she stared straight at Jen, ready for a few choice words.

But this boot was not empty. There was something packed into the toe. Squeezing her fingers further down, Rebecca managed to get her hand round the obstruction and pull it out. A roll of tightly banded twenty-pound notes. There looked to be at least five hundred pounds, if not more, in her hand. Her eyes widened. She didn't know what she was more surprised about, the amount of money in her hand or the fact that a stranger had found it for her.

Jen couldn't hide the beam on her face. It worked. Joan had been spot on, and she herself had passed the message to Rebecca.

Joan stood, clapping her hands, her eyes sparkling. 'There's more! Check all the right boots.'

'There's more,' Jen relayed. 'All in the boots, the right boots.'

Popping the bundle of money into her coat pocket, Rebecca pulled out another one of the bigger boxes. This time, it was a pair of dark green, suede, knee-high boots. And in the right one, another roll of twenty-pound notes.

Rebecca let out a laugh and shook her head. 'It had to be the right boots. As Aunt Joan always said, "I'm never wrong, I'm always right." And to be fair, she usually was. She was quite formidable but so wonderful. What a way to get me to find the money. She always had a flair for the extravagant, a bit of drama; she was a stage actress most of her life.' Rebecca held the green boot in her hands. 'Funny, I wanted to believe you. I was hoping she was there. I do miss her, my Aunt Joan. Can you tell her that for me, please? Sorry, I don't know your name.'

'It's Jen, and you just told her,' Jen replied.

Aunt Joan had somehow lit another cigarette from out of nowhere and was standing, quite smugly, looking at them both. 'Tell Rebecca that's all for her wedding. Whatever my darling girl wants. I'm all for charity, but that would be ridiculous, wouldn't it, dear?'

Jen passed on Joan's thoughts, at which all three women laughed.

'I best take these all home before I visit the charity shop, hadn't I? There's another twenty-odd boxes piled up in my hallway. My fiancé is not going to believe a word of it. I can't quite believe it myself! Thank you, Jen. What you can do… you have something very special there. You've definitely made my day!' Rebecca motioned to give Jen a hug.

Jen accepted, feeling that a good deed had been well done.

'Is Aunt Joan still here?' Rebecca asked before getting into her car.

Jen looked round. 'No, she's gone. But having spent just a few minutes with her, I don't expect there's a force on earth or in heaven that will stop her popping back if she needs to.'

Rebecca smiled. 'That's Aunt Joan.'

Jen drove back home, feeling a mellowness inside her. Joan had been her first proper visitor since her mum, and it had happened outside, not in the house as she had expected. Would it be the same every time? Did this mean her visitors could be anywhere?

She felt a tinge of excitement in her chest. It was all true, everything her mum had said. Then a heaviness descended. She wanted to tell her mum about it all, to see her face as she described the cash wedged inside the boots. But she didn't know if her mum was going to be at home anymore, if the last time she appeared had been the final time.

It dawned on her that every woman in the family who inherited the gift couldn't tell their predecessor about their first time, couldn't ask for advice, couldn't share in the amazement of the experience. It wasn't clear from the diaries if Harriet had presented herself to Elizabeth after she died, or if Elizabeth had tried to contact Violet. Jacqui, too, hadn't mentioned anything about seeing or hearing Nan after she had gone—apart from the photo frames being moved. Jen realised it was probably quite a lonely gift to have at times.

***

Jen cooked and ate the meal she'd planned, still buzzing from meeting Aunt Joan and Rebecca. Afterwards, she took a biscuit and headed into the lounge to open her laptop, then doubled back to grab the whole packet—one biscuit was not going to be enough.

A blank page stared back at her, its cursor blinking as if eager to get started. Jen began to type her first notes, starting with her name and the date, just like Harriet, Elizabeth, her nan and her mum. On the next line, she titled it: *'Joan Davidstone's Boots'*.

Jen became lost in her writing, forgetting the once-bitten biscuit perched on the cushion next to her. A few crumbs made an escape.

'You should have got a plate for that.'

Jen's laptop jumped along with her, and she looked up from the screen to see Jacqui sitting next to her. 'How long have you been there?'

'I didn't want to interrupt; you looked deep in concentration.'

Jen was elated. Her mum had returned. She launched into the day's events, promising to grab the hand vacuum for the crumbs once she'd finished.

'It was the most satisfying thing I have ever been involved with, Mum. To pass the message on and for every detail to be right. For Rebecca to believe me, it made me feel—how do I describe it?—sort of humble, to have been able to connect them for a few minutes.'

Jacqui listened intently and nodded at everything Jen said. 'When it goes like that, Jen, it really is wonderful. They're not all plain sailing, but for your first one, you got a good one.'

Jacqui reached to run her hand through Jen's hair, like she used to, then remembered that it wouldn't work. No more feeling her arms round Jen, no more kisses to her cheeks. Her face became downcast as she looked at her daughter.

'Hey, it's okay. I know. I know,' Jen said, trying to break the sadness between them, her own eyes welling up. 'You're here right now. Okay, we can't hug or anything anymore. But this, it's more than anyone usually gets, isn't it?'

Jacqui forced a smile despite how she felt. It was indeed more than anyone else got, but it still felt unfair. She was beginning to understand how her visitors had felt, the ones that had found her, needing their messages understood, their frustration and anguish at not being alive anymore but not completely gone.

Jen got up to find the hand vacuum for the crumbs. After tidying up her mess, she sat back down next to Jacqui.

'I've not stopped to ask how you're feeling, Mum, about being, well, dead.'

'Oh, Jen, that's the least you should be worrying about.'

'I still worry about how you are, Mum. You weren't expecting to be a ghost so soon, if at all. You must have been in as much shock as I was. A few sentences I never thought I would be saying!'

Jacqui had to smile then. She hadn't actually given it much thought.

'When I was alive, and knowing what I know, I wasn't worried about dying. Finding out I could talk to the dead, it gave me some solace that it's not the complete end. So, in myself, I knew I'd be okay, that there's some other space to occupy somewhere—not that I have quite worked out what or where that is yet; I keep going there but then coming back here. What I worried about was how you and Dad would cope, assuming I went first. I wouldn't be there to hold you or wipe your tears. That upset me the most. So, when I'm not here, I'm not thinking about much at all, but when I come back, I feel upset that I can't console you, Jen. That's how I'm feeling at the moment.'

'I get how frustrating it must be for you, being pulled back here but not being able to be fully present. Do you remember when you first told me about the notebooks, that you were about to tell me about three remarkable women? I think you got the story wrong. The story is about four remarkable women. I think you should count yourself in their company, Mum.'

As Jen went off to put the vacuum away, Jacqui began to wonder why she was back. Jen had the notebooks, she knew why her dad had moved out, she had helped her first ghost. Jacqui knew from her own experience that there was always something that pulled people back. It was usually one of three things: a message, an apology or a confession. She had thought the Ouija board incident was her message.

Why am I still here?

CHAPTER 13

Jen had not had the best night's sleep, waking up a few times and not being able to clear her mind entirely. She knew it was going to take a bit of time to get used to being in the house and her mum not being there, so she was trying to accept that she had to let the process take its course.

Her dad had been round all morning and was making good headway with the household paperwork. Jacqui had been very organised, leaving extensive notes, which was making it simple for Mark to know who to contact. Jen was being added to everything, which would make things easier for her to manage, and she was sitting with her dad, keeping a log of everything on her laptop. She had told him all about Aunt Joan, and he seemed genuinely relieved that her first encounter, aside from her mum, had been a pleasant one.

Jen's boss had checked in with her the day before, suggesting she take another full week off before they organise a return-to-work plan. He knew from his own experience to take things carefully, having underestimated his own grief when his mum died, despite his wife pleading with him to take more time off. He regretted how quickly he'd thrown himself back into work and normal life, as it caught up with him a few months later. Jen appreciated that he'd shared that with her and was glad for the extra time away.

'When should we start looking at Mum's stuff?' Jen asked her dad. 'Is it too soon? Should I leave it longer? Are there things you are better going through than me?'

Mark put down the bill he was looking at on his phone. 'There's never a right or wrong time, Jen. Just whenever you feel ready. You might start and then find it's too much and stop for a bit. Or end up getting through a lot with no trouble. My mum and I had no issue going through Dad's clothes; we got that done pretty quickly. But when it came to his books and his football memorabilia, I just couldn't do it. I didn't want to have to decide whether to let some of it go or keep it. Mum and I just packed it all in a box and waited until we could face it. I think I waited five years before looking at it all again.'

'I might ask Laura to help me. Pick one thing and see what we can do. Maybe clothes? Mum would say there's no point in them all gathering dust up in the wardrobe when someone else could be making good use of them. You know she hated having stuff hanging around and not being useful.'

'You start wherever you like. I think Laura would be a good choice for that job, better than me! I learnt a lot from that box of my dad's. One or two keepsakes stayed with me, but the rest I gave away. All you have to remember is that, in the end, the most important things we leave behind are our memories with each other. All the things—the clothes, the ornaments, the jewellery, the objects—they might help you recall those times but they don't hold the past within them. All those recollections are in us. So, you're not going to forget things if you choose to part with some of your mum's belongings. Time moves on, and the physical things we own, they move on, too. But the memories, they stay with us.'

Jen gave her dad's hand a little rub, and he got back on with the task at hand. Then, she messaged Laura to see if she was free that evening. A bit of dinner and some wine might make the task less arduous, and it would be good to spend some time together after everything that had happened.

Laura was more than happy to oblige and agreed to be round after Olivia was back from her drama club.

The rest of the day was meant to be spent going through the garage, not for Jacqui's things, just because Mark hadn't had a good clear out in there for a number of years, but he and Jen had become happily distracted with the bookshelves. Whilst Jacqui had been militant about decluttering, her one weakness was her fondness of books; she had taken pride in having an eclectic collection on display in the lounge.

Most of the books hadn't been read in years; the ones on the topmost shelf had thick layers of dust on them. Jen felt books should be enjoyed, as if they had feelings and were sad if no one was looking at them. So, with much satisfaction, she took the ladder from the garage—having convinced her dad it was far too cold to be doing a garage clear-out—and had him help lift the books from the shelves. They both amused themselves, stopping to look at cookbooks from the seventies and the cheesy romance novels Jacqui had become obsessed with when Jen was little. Mark spent ages leafing through a couple of atlases—pristine, as they had never been used.

As well as a gift for chatting to the dead, Jen had also inherited her mum's enjoyment for tidying and organising; it felt good for her soul to get things sorted. 'Do you think Mum will be okay with us going through some of this stuff already? Is it not a bit soon? She might think it's a bit of a check!'

'Your mum wasn't much of a hoarder, and once something had gone past being useful it was moved on. How these books escaped her laser focus, I am not too sure. But it's the living who are left behind with the objects and things to make decisions about. Do you feel okay doing it now? That's the main thing, Jen. If you're comfortable, then I am sure your mum will be fine with it. How slow or quickly it all gets done, that's up to you.'

Jen liked the way her dad explained it. If it felt like they were going through things too quickly, she could slow it down.

By the time they were done, they had four full boxes of books for the second-hand bookshop in town. Mark left, as it was getting dark, so Jen began to prepare dinner.

Laura arrived not long after, and the two of them opened a bottle of wine as they waited for the lasagne to cook.

'I was going to ask how you've been, but it feels like such a naff question when someone has died,' Laura said, opening the pack of garlic bread to put onto a tray.

'It's not a naff question, I know you care. I'm doing okay. That first day I was here on my own, I'll admit, I was lonely for a bit. I've been here on my own before, but that was when Mum and Dad went on holiday; it felt different this time. But it's something I have to get used to,' Jen said, knowing that wasn't all she had to get used to.

'I do worry about you here on your own. I don't know why. You would have been living on your own eventually, wouldn't you? Just not like this. Anyway, enough of this morbid chat, I have gossip to share!'

Jen was glad for the change in tone and took great pleasure in hearing Laura's news about a friend they used to go to school with.

After they had finished off a substantial amount of the lasagne, Laura filled both their glasses.

'Shall we give this a go then?' she asked, motioning towards the staircase. 'Or, we don't have to; we can do it another day.'

'No, let's go,' Jen said with resolve, getting up from the table.

Laura let Jen go first, but as they got to the landing, Jen hesitated for a moment. She wondered if her mum would pop up and how she would react, what with Laura being there. She desperately wanted to tell Laura what was happening but she wasn't sure how Laura would take it. The afterlife, ghosts—they weren't things they'd really had a big discussion on.

Laura could feel her friend's hesitation and wanted to break the tension. 'I brought two coasters up. I can't imagine Jacqui would want red wine rings on her dressing table.'

Jen scoffed. 'Absolutely right there.'

Her mum's bedroom door was open; Jen hadn't wanted to keep it shut all the time. She and Laura entered together. Laura took a seat on the dressing table stool and let Jen lead. Jen opened one of the wardrobes and stood for a moment, looking at her mum's clothes. Some she knew her mum had worn often; some she was sure she hadn't seen. Jumpers, tops, skirts, dresses, trousers—it all looked a bit overwhelming.

'How about we start with jeans? Something fairly mundane and simple,' Laura suggested.

Jen liked that idea. She had no attachment to her mum's jeans; they were all basically the same.

After a while, they had a pile forming, ready for charity, and a smaller pile for recycling, which was mainly made up of ones Jacqui had used for gardening or decorating.

Jen took a sip of wine. 'That wasn't as painful as I expected, but I think the blow was softened by you being here, Laura.'

She found herself able to let go of most of her mum's clothes, realising that they held no great comfort to her. Then they came to the emerald-green top with the grey flowers, which stopped Jen in her tracks.

'You okay, Jen?' Laura asked, helping Jen sit on the edge of the bed.

A tear dropped from Jen's eyes as she caressed the material. 'I'd like to keep this one.'

'Then keep it you will.'

Jen felt quite floored by the top. She knew it was because her mum kept appearing in it, which made it somehow even stranger to see it hanging up in the cupboard. Jen's brain couldn't entirely compute how it could be in two places at once. She and Laura just sat on the bed for a bit, arms around each other, until Jen felt like carrying on.

Most of the other clothes found their place in a pile. Laura stopped on a coral jumper, still with its label on.

'You should keep this, Jen, and wear it. It's so your colour.'

Laura held it up to Jen's body so she could see in the mirror, and Jen agreed. But she'd been increasingly distracted since looking at her mum's green top. She took a deep breath in; she wanted to tell Laura about the notebooks.

'Do you believe in ghosts, Laura?'

'Do I believe in ghosts?' Laura repeated the question to give it some thought, pushing some coat hangers along to get to a few jackets right in the corner of the wardrobe. 'Do you know what? I don't know. I never really thought about all that stuff, but after having Olivia, I do think about death and what happens afterwards more than I used to. Sometimes, I think about it too much and get myself in a bit of a state. Do you know what I mean?' Laura had grabbed four jackets and was laying them out on the bed.

Jen knew what she meant.

'Why? Do you believe in ghosts?' Laura asked. 'With everything that's happened I'm not surprised it's something you've been thinking about.'

Jen wanted to say she'd been doing more than thinking about it. 'What would you say if someone told you that they'd seen one?' She avoided eye contact with Laura by looking over the jackets.

'I'd probably say that if they believe that's what they saw then that's good enough for me,' Laura said, wondering where this was going.

Jen decided to tell Laura everything—the gift, her ancestors, Aunt Joan—when her fingers brushed up against a carefully folded piece of paper. Without realising it, she'd been going through her mum's jacket pockets. She'd pulled out a two-pence piece from one coat, and her hand was now in the pocket of a black leather jacket. She removed the paper from the pocket and opened it up to find it was cut out from a newspaper, half a page.

'*Sussex woman still missing after four weeks*' read the headline. It was a national newspaper article, and Jen recognised the picture of the woman from the TV a few weeks ago. She had what looked like permed brown hair, and you could tell she'd been cropped out of a family photo.

'What have you found?' Laura asked as she came over to take a look.

'It's about the woman who went missing thirty years ago round here. She's been on the news lately as the anniversary is coming up.'

'Yes, I know the one. They're going to do a reconstruction next week, see if it jogs anyone's memory. They're hoping someone might come forward, given all the time that has passed. Maybe a relative or friend that had suspicions but was worried about saying anything at the time. I think her son and daughter are going to speak, too.'

Jen read the article out loud as Laura looked over her shoulder. It was dated 16th December 1992.

'Police have had no new leads in the case of a missing mother of two from Horsham, Sussex, who disappeared on Wednesday fourth November. Helen Swift was reported missing by her mother at around eight pm that evening, having not returned from a dog walk in nearby Corsley Woods. Helen is described as being twenty-seven years old, around five foot ten tall with brown, curly hair and blue eyes. She was wearing blue jeans; a brown, roll-neck jumper; a large, blue fleece jacket; and brown walking boots. The Swifts' dog was discovered unharmed, but there has been no trace of Mrs Swift since.

'Police have declined to respond regarding a possible connection to an attempted abduction in the same area two months previously. Police have asked for anyone with any information, however insignificant, to contact them immediately on nine-nine-nine.'

'Why would your mum have this in her coat pocket?'

It was an excellent question. Jen had no idea.

CHAPTER 14

Laura had gone home just after midnight. Both she and Jen felt very satisfied for having sorted out most of Jacqui's large wardrobe, which just left Jen to deliver each pile to its destination. Jen kept a few chosen pieces in her own wardrobe, along with the emerald-green top, and she'd suggested that Laura try on Jacqui's leather jacket, which they had agreed looked amazing on her, so she went home with it.

Despite the late night, Jen had got up early, and was at her laptop in the dining room with a cup of tea and the newspaper clipping. Jacqui hadn't reappeared since Jen had told her about Aunt Joan, but she felt sure she'd be back. She was keen to ask her mum about the article and had to suffice with the internet for the time being. Typing Helen's name had brought up a multitude of stories, some dated recently, some going years back.

Jen scrolled through the headlines, then hovered over one in particular, written the week before by a national TV channel, which got to her.

'*Son and daughter of missing Sussex mum still believe they can find out what happened 30 years on*'

She clicked on it, and a different picture of Helen appeared. She had a relaxed smile on her face, compared to the formality of the photo in the newspaper. Jen could see a Christmas tree and gold tinsel in the background. Helen looked bright and happy.

'Sussex Police are hoping that a fresh focus on the thirty-year-old case of missing mother of two Helen Swift will encourage new witnesses to come forward. Swift went missing on Wednesday 4th November 1992, whilst out walking her dog in Corsley Woods near her home. Her case was featured in June this year on the popular true crime podcast Missing Without Answers.

Helen had two children, a son Matthew and daughter Emily. We spoke to Matthew Swift about how his family has coped over the last thirty years with their mother's disappearance.

"We're not delusional. We're not expecting Mum to come walking back through the door; we know something has happened to her. We just need to know where she is so we can bring her home, so she can be laid to rest next to our gran. Emily and I now have children who Mum will never get to see. But we can't tell them what happened to their own gran. We just need some answers."

Detectives will be staging a reconstruction in Corsley Woods, Swift's last known whereabouts, around the anniversary of her disappearance, on Wednesday 2nd November at 4:45pm. Detective Inspector Tola Obederin of Surrey and Sussex Major Crime Team said:

"Helen's disappearance drew widespread coverage across the media and continues to do so. We believe that someone knows what happened to Helen that evening. She had no history of mental health issues, she was a dedicated and loving mother, and we do not believe she would have gone missing of her own accord. We appeal to anyone who was living or walking regularly in the Corsley Woods area in November 1992 to think again about anything or anyone suspicious they saw at the time. Perhaps you were not in a position to give information back then, but things may have changed.

"Unfortunately, we were unable to give Helen's mother the closure she needed before she died. But together, along with Helen's children Matthew and Emily, we hope this renewed appeal will *jog memories and bring us closer to finding out what happened. We need to get answers for her family. She has never been forgotten.'"*

The article continued with how to contact the police with information and details of a substantial reward from Crimestoppers.

Jen sighed. She'd watched enough missing persons programmes to be very surprised if someone came forward after all this time with enough information to find Helen. Unless the killer gave themselves up—she was convinced Helen had been murdered and expected most people thought the same.

It was a tragedy all round and it was making Jen feel miserable, so she decided to get on with the day, starting with getting dressed. She only had a few more days before returning to work, so she knew she needed to get back into the flow of things. Getting up and dressed at a sensible time of the morning was first on the list.

Pulling on a jumper, Jen smelled the faint waft of lavender and rosemary and had the now-familiar feeling of not being alone. With an arm only partially in its sleeve, she came out onto the landing and peeked round the doorframe of her mum's room to find Jacqui looking out the window.

'When did next door take that tree down?' Jacqui asked, seemingly disgruntled at the tree's absence.

'Oh that, two weeks ago, I think. They did knock to say there'd be some noise. They reckoned it was a risk in the high winds.' Jen was glad to see her mum again. She wondered if Jacqui had realised her clothes were in piles.

'He never liked that tree; finally got his way, I suppose,' Jacqui replied, clearly suspecting foul play at the tree's demise. 'I see you've sorted my clothes. Glad to see you're getting on with things. No point in them all sitting in the wardrobe when someone could be making better use of them!'

Jen was relieved she'd guessed her mum's view on sorting her clothes correctly. She didn't need them to remember her by but she also didn't want her mum to be offended. Thinking about it, Jen realised she was in the unique position of knowing either way.

'I hoped you wouldn't mind; you always did move things on if they weren't serving a purpose. Laura helped me. I said it was okay for her to have your leather jacket; it really does look great on her.'

'That's completely fine, I hope she enjoys wearing it.'

'Talking about that, I did find something I want to ask you about. It's downstairs.'

Jen went back to her room to fetch some socks and was surprised to see her mum following her. She hadn't actually seen her walk anywhere since she died, she usually just appeared and stayed put.

'You okay, Jen? You look like you've seen a ghost.' Jacqui giggled to herself, pleased with her joke.

Jen burst out laughing. 'Yes, very good, well done. Seriously though, it was just odd seeing you walk out of your room. Like normal. Usually, you appear and then stay where you popped up.'

'I seem to be mastering my new form. Thought it might be a bit less weird if I just followed you down the stairs instead of disappearing and reappearing?'

Jen nodded, not sure if seeing the ghost of her mum wandering around like normal was any less weird than her just materialising. She'd have to think about that one.

Downstairs, Jen grabbed the article and held it up for Jacqui. 'Found this in your leather jacket pocket, which shows how long it had been since you last wore it! Why did you cut it out?'

Jacqui stood quietly. She hadn't seen the article for ages, had forgotten that she even still had it. She was trying to think quickly but could tell Jen was sensing a delay in her answer, which would only lead to more questions.

'I got a bit obsessed with it, if I'm honest, which is embarrassing,' Jacqui lied, hoping she sounded convincing enough.

Jen narrowed her eyes. 'Why were you so interested in Helen Swift going missing? Did you know something? Did you speak to the police?'

Jen's head was whirring. They lived a fair distance from Horsham, but maybe her mum knew something about what had happened somehow? Surely she would have contacted the police if she did? She could tell her mum was holding something back.

Jacqui was finding this line of inquiry uncomfortable. She did feel embarrassed, but not for the reason she'd tried to make out.

The stand-off in the dining room was getting increasingly awkward, when Jen heard a voice coming from the kitchen. Jacqui was standing right in front of her, and there was no one else in the house. It was a female voice, soft but clear, and it was singing. Jen had to listen intently for a few moments before recognising the song.

'You are my sunshines, my only sunshines,
You make me happy when skies are grey.
You'll never know, dears, how much I love you,
So please don't take my sunshines away.'

The sound of the words elicited an emotional response from Jen and brought tears to her eyes. It was meant to sound happy but it was so forlorn, so sorrowful.

Jacqui's reaction was very different. *Dear God, no*, she thought as Jen walked past her into the kitchen.

The song had started over, and Jen was taken aback as she reached its source. Standing, slightly taller than her, with curly brown hair and distinct blue eyes, was, unmistakably, Helen Swift.

CHAPTER 15

Jen turned to her mum, absolutely dumbfounded. 'It's Helen Swift! In our kitchen, Mum!' She tried not to sound like someone who had just spotted a famous person. She knew it wasn't the right way to react, but she couldn't believe the missing woman was right in front of her.

Jen waited for her mum to say something, but Jacqui looked less than happy about the situation.

'This is amazing right?' Jen continued. 'We might be able to help her. We might be able to get her home. Isn't this what it's all about, having this gift of ours?' She was feeling ever more puzzled by her mum's reaction.

Jacqui rubbed her face in disbelief and a thought began to dawn on her. *A message, an apology, a confession.* 'This can't be it, seriously, not again,' she said despairingly.

Jen's arms dropped to her side, her mum's words deflating her like a balloon. 'What do you mean, "again"?' she demanded.

Helen began her third rendition of 'You Are My Sunshine'.

Jen turned to look at her. Why was she singing it over and over? She had a glazed expression in her eyes, as if she didn't realise where she was or that Jen was there at all.

'She's going to keep singing that song. She won't stop,' Jacqui finally replied.

'How do you know that?' Jen asked, a split second before her brain caught up and answered the question for her. 'You've seen her before! Haven't you?'

Jacqui readied her confession. 'Yes, she's been here before.'

'Well, that's good, isn't it? You tried to help her before but obviously couldn't get anywhere, so she's come back. Maybe because it's me this time?'

Jacqui shook her head, she felt like she ought to hang it in shame. 'I… we, well, I didn't try to help her the first time. I…'

Jen could feel herself getting agitated. 'You what?'

'We decided, after what happened with the Ouija board, it was too much of a risk. Something very bad had obviously happened to her, Jen. I couldn't take the chance of inviting anything else in.'

Jen slammed the article down in front of Jacqui on the kitchen counter.

'You are my sunshines…'

'Go in the hallway,' Jen barked at Jacqui, then mouthed 'sorry' to Helen as she closed the kitchen door behind them.

Fourth time round, and the song was beginning to grate.

'Are you telling me that Helen has been here once before, and you… turned her away? And what do you mean *we*? Did Dad know about this?'

'Of course he did, I didn't hide any of it from him. Certainly not after what happened that night. You weren't there, Jen, it was the scariest moment in our entire lives. We had to protect our home and you. I couldn't get us involved in something dark and horrible. What was I meant to do anyway? Call nine-nine-nine and say I had the ghost of Helen Swift in my living room? They wouldn't have believed me. I couldn't get a word of sense out of her anyway.'

Jen was furious. More than that, she was disappointed. She'd expected every visitor that came to her mum would get the same help. She hadn't expected her to pick and choose. Who else had she ignored? Had her nan done the same thing? What about Harriet and Elizabeth? This was yet another side to their gift she hadn't considered.

'But she was your age. She had kids! Didn't you feel any empathy towards her?'

Jacqui was now getting cross herself. 'Of course I did,' she snapped back. 'The whole thing was on the TV, in the newspapers; it was everywhere you looked. How could anyone's heart not break knowing that a woman had been snatched away from her children? God knows what was done to her. But we had to protect our own family. Something had spelt all our names out, Jen. Something awful. We couldn't take the chance of anything happening to you.'

Both women stood staring at each other. Jen's feelings on the matter were becoming blurred. She knew her mum would always have helped where she could, for the living and the dead, and her parents had looked so frightened when they told her about the entity. But she was also disappointed in them both. What if they could have found who had taken Helen? What if that person has done it again? She pushed those thoughts away; she could 'what if?' herself into a rabbit hole otherwise.

Jacqui looked pleadingly at her. Now the apology. 'I'm sorry, I know you expected more of me. I expected more of myself, in all honesty.'

'It's not me you need to apologise to, is it?' Jen said, then immediately regretted her tone. She didn't want to make her mum feel any worse than she already did. What mattered was what they did now. 'What's done is done, Mum. I sort of get why you didn't do anything the first time. Perhaps this is why you're sticking around. We're pretty much done with all the notebooks.' She wished she could remedy the moment with a hug or an arm around a shoulder.

Jacqui relaxed a little but remained apprehensive. 'You're going to try and help Helen this time?'

'Yes! Don't you get it, Mum? You are here to do what you could have done last time. Maybe between us, we can find her.' Jen couldn't believe her mum was considering anything else.

'Jen, I'm worried—'

Jen put both hands up to stop her mum from continuing. 'I know you're scared that whatever it was will return. And I know it's wild to think we could solve a thirty-year-old mystery. But she's here. And we're here together. Think of us like a modern-day Randall and Hopkirk, sort of.' She raised a smile, trying to put her mum at ease. They'd loved watching repeats of the old detective show together.

Jacqui knew she had no choice; Jen would not be swayed. 'Okay, but I am telling you, I barely got anything out of her last time.'

Jen did a little fist pump and headed back towards the kitchen.

The singing had stopped. She wondered if Helen had gone; maybe they'd taken too long.

Jen was about to open the kitchen door when Jacqui spoke. 'Helen isn't going to be like Aunt Joan, or me for that matter. She's going to be more difficult to communicate with.'

Jen released her hand from the door handle and turned back to her mum.

'If you think about what she could have gone through, at the end…' Jacqui continued. 'Any living person that might have survived it would have been recommended counselling. But she died; there was no one to help her through it, no one to comfort her, no one to make any sense of it for her. You'll need to be very patient with her, Jen.'

Jen nodded in agreement. This wasn't someone needing a message passed on about shoes. Helen was a victim. Jen had never talked to anyone who had been through anything remotely traumatic, let alone someone who had been most likely abducted and killed. She wasn't a trained therapist, and she didn't want to get it wrong or make things worse for Helen. Her mum was right: patience was required here.

She thought it would be a good idea to grab her laptop to make notes. If Helen was struggling to communicate, it would be handy to have something to go back to later.

Ready with her laptop in one hand, Jen opened the kitchen door with the other.

Helen was still standing there, in the exact same spot as before. She'd stopped singing, and although she was directly facing Jen and Jacqui, she seemed to be staring past them.

'Hello, Helen, can you hear me?' Jen asked, gently putting the laptop on the counter and opening it up.

'Who's there?' Helen asked as her eyes darted from left to right.

'Don't be frightened,' Jen said, immediately regretting her choice of words. Helen couldn't help being frightened, and rightly so. 'I mean, you don't need to be frightened of me. My name is Jen. I'm here with my mum, Jacqui.' She motioned for Jacqui to speak.

'Hi, Helen, this is Jacqui.'

Helen's face changed slightly for a moment, as if recalling something. 'I've heard your voice before.'

Jacqui felt a guilty pang in her stomach. 'Yes, we spoke a while ago, Helen. I'm sorry I didn't help last time, but you've found me again. We're here now and we're going to do our best.'

Jen had been watching Helen whilst Jacqui spoke. She was looking around as if searching for where the voices were coming from.

'Do you know where you are, Helen?' Jen enquired.

'It's too dark, I cannot see you. Have you found me? Can I go home now?'

Jen's heart sank. 'We'll try to find you, Helen. But we're not where you are. You're talking to us, in our house. You've found us.'

Helen's face conveyed her bewilderment. 'That doesn't make any sense. How have I moved?'

'I know, Helen, it must sound very confusing.' Jen paused, wondering if her next question was going to be too much. 'Do you remember what happened to you, Helen?'

Helen's face contorted as if she were experiencing physical pain.

'Helen, are you okay?' Jen knew she had gone too far.

Helen began to sob an uncontrollable, despairing sob. Through that sob, she began to sing.

'You… are… my… sunshines, My… only… sunshines…'

Jacqui shook her head. 'It's the same as before. Asking her to remember anything about what happened sends her back into this song. It's like a safe place to retreat to.'

Jen tapped out some notes.

'Did you hear her say "it's too dark"? I think that's why she can't see us, but she can hear us. It's as if her line of sight is blocked or she's somewhere pitch black.' *Somewhere pitch black.* The thought made Jen shudder. The poor woman could be hidden anywhere. 'And don't you find it amazing that she remembers your voice? Time must have little relevance for her. Plus, you're a ghost too now, and she can still hear you. How does that work?'

Jacqui hadn't even thought about that. Ghosts chatting to ghosts. 'No rules', as Elizabeth had said.

Helen continued singing.

'How long does she do this for?' Jen asked, watching the woman in the middle of their kitchen, singing, oblivious to anything else.

'One day, she was here for near on four hours. I couldn't break her out of the trance she had gotten herself in. I remember it clearly, as I brought the usual weekly clean forward two days just so I could have the vacuum on. Other times, she was completely silent. But, back then, I wasn't trying to talk to her,' Jacqui said sheepishly.

'So, she doesn't disappear and come back? She's just going to stay here?'

Jacqui squinted as the song started over. 'If it goes the same as last time, she will eventually vanish. Then she'll be back. Three days she came and went. But this time, I don't know. She did stay for longer on each visit, as if she was getting stronger at holding herself in place.'

Jen attempted to break the spell. 'Helen, can you still hear me?'

Helen continued singing, not breaking once from the tune when Jen spoke. If she could hear Jen, she showed no sign of it.

'I think we just leave her for now,' Jen decided. 'When we walked away before, she did stop. I think she might do the same if we leave her be, but I'll opt for my headphones instead of the vacuum.' She turned back to Helen. 'We're going to be in the next room, Helen, and we'll come back once you're… more calm. You're not on your own; we're still here.'

Jacqui and Jen left Helen in the kitchen. Jen now fully understood that getting any clear information from her was going to be difficult. But while they bided their time, there was something useful they could do.

'What we should do for now,' Jen said, 'is plot out what we do know. Then hope that whatever gaps we have left can be filled by Helen.'

Jacqui looked back at the kitchen. The tune was seeping out under the door but was thankfully muffled with it closed. She watched as Jen looked up a map of Horsham and noted down dates from an article she had found.

Sitting next to her, Jacqui felt a renewed sense of purpose. 'Maybe, this time, we can do it.'

CHAPTER 16

'I'm not wholly sure about you getting involved in all this, Jen,' Mark said. 'In fact, I'm not keen on it at all.' He stuck his head into the loft. Jen stood at the bottom of the steps, waiting to receive the empty boxes she needed.

'Well, maybe if you'd both helped Helen in the first place, we wouldn't be doing it now. But you made your decision for a good reason; I get it. We need to do it, Dad. Imagine if we found her!'

Mark hauled himself through the hatch and started handing folded boxes down. 'It felt like the best thing to do at the time. And yes, it would be amazing if we could find her, but I wouldn't get too excited about that. She's been missing for thirty years; no one saw anything of her after she entered those woods. She's not exactly in a position to be giving you a precise location or even a description of where she is—she might have no idea where she is. She could have been taken out of the county.'

Mark stopped as he narrowly dodged one of the eaves. 'But my main concern is what else it might lead to. What if something nasty tries to come through, piggybacking on Helen's trauma? What if the murderer is dead and ends up in this house with you? It's okay helping people out with boots full of money, but kidnap, a murdered woman, it's another level. It's too dark and too dangerous.'

Jen could feel her dad's anxiety from the bottom of the loft ladder, but she wasn't being deterred. 'I'm not getting carried away. We just need to try this time and try really hard. Between the three of us, we could come up with something. Plus, Mum will be here as my back-up if anything weird does happen, which I am sure it won't. You were playing with a Ouija board, you know? You were actively stirring up trouble. I would never touch anything like that.'

Mark sighed. 'True, true. I know I'm not going to convince you otherwise; I've said my piece.' He knew he wasn't going to change Jen's mind, but there was no way he was going to hang around as and when Helen did appear. 'There's about four boxes left of your nan's bits up here. Did you want me to get them down to have a look through?'

Jen's first reaction was yes; she wondered what nostalgic items she'd find. But then the thought of having to go through her nan's things as well as sorting her mum's was a bit too much. 'Leave them for now, Dad. Let's get done with more of Mum's and then I can have a look at what we have left from Nan. I thought Mum had done it all?'

'She did a great job at the time, but as with me, there were some things she just wasn't ready to let go of. A job for another day then.' Mark climbed back down the ladder and closed the hatch.

'I'm astounded at how many glasses and cups Mum has!' Jen said as they shuffled the boxes downstairs.

'To be fair, we did accumulate most of these between us. There's no way we've used them all. Some might have been wedding presents. Maybe they're worth selling?' Mark pondered.

As Jen rounded the corner into the dining room, her eyes wandered to the kitchen door. After her first visit, Helen had disappeared after about thirty minutes of continuous singing. She hadn't been back since, and that was three days ago. Jacqui had also not been back, but had been able to stay long enough to work with Jen through the timeline of Helen's disappearance and piece together what they could from the internet. A lot of the detail they found came from the recent podcast.

Apparently, the last eyewitness saw Helen at around 5:15pm, entering the woods with her dog, Pip. Pip was a Jack Russell, and regular dog walkers remembered seeing Helen and Pip most days at about that time. Some had had brief chats with her before, the kinds of things dog walkers say to each other, nothing in depth. Pip had actually been found by Helen's brother, who had come out to look for her after their mum had called the police. Pip had tried to make his way home on his own and was apparently fine, but there had been no trace of Helen. She'd walked to the woods, as she normally did, so her car was still parked outside her house. Over time, the police checked for proof of life, in an attempt to determine whether Helen had left of her own accord or some harm had come to her. The latter seemed to be the case. She did not use her bank accounts after going missing; mobile phones had only really just come out, and she hadn't had one; her passport was left at home; her driver's licence had been in her bag, which was with her when she disappeared, but there were no records of anyone hiring a car in Helen's name anywhere in the UK. There had been no contact at her GP surgery for her records, and her name did not match anyone admitted to hospital in the days and weeks after her disappearance. By all accounts, Helen Swift had vanished.

Jen had felt a bit dejected after all their research. There really wasn't much to go on. The only chance of finding Helen was to know what she knew. Jen had to find a way of getting through to her.

After much deliberation about glassware, Jen's stomach was rumbling. 'Why don't I shift some of these boxes to the charity shop and grab us a sandwich on the way back?'

'Sounds like an excellent plan. Can you get me one of those tiger rolls, any filling? I'll help you get some of these in the car,' Mark replied, his stomach also signalling that it was time for a break. 'I've left those posh wine glasses on the table in their boxes. I think they're worth selling—unless you think you and your mates can work your way through and use each one.' He laughed.

Jen rolled her eyes. 'Rude, but yes, perhaps we can!'

Together, they put the boxes in the car.

Mark looked back at the house with a grimace he hoped Jen didn't notice. 'I'll pop to the tip while you're out, get some of the actual rubbish out of the way.' He was wary of being in the house on his own. He didn't fancy entertaining Helen if she popped back; not that he'd know she was there, but the thought she might be was off-putting enough.

As Jen pulled out of the driveway, she mulled over Helen's case again. Her mind unconsciously drifted to how horrible her death must have been to leave her in such a broken state in her afterlife. Jen's heart ached for her.

Sitting at a red light, she glanced up at her rearview mirror to check the traffic behind her. Out of the corner of her eye, she noticed the light move to amber—then needed to check the mirror again. She let out a high-pitched shriek and, in sheer panic, pushed down hard on the accelerator, screeching the tyres but going nowhere.

She twisted round. 'What the—!?'

Looking directly at her, and sitting in the middle of the back seat, was a man.

She turned back to the front, not believing what she had seen. But he was still in her rearview mirror. *Don't panic. You're in traffic. He can't do anything with all these people around. Just find somewhere to stop that's still in the open.*

Jen was on her second go at trying to move on the green light. The car behind beeped, so she indicated, intending to pull over on the side road.

How did he get in here? Did I leave the car unlocked last night? Was he lying down when I got in? All this was carrying on in her head, and trying to keep an eye on the man in the back and look where she was going was only making her anxiety worse.

In the meantime, Jen's passenger had said nothing and was casually looking out of the window.

She stopped the car on the side of a road that looked relatively busy and opened her door, getting out as quickly as she could. She gave herself a few moments, while her guest seemingly ignored what was going on.

I can't just stand here all day. Plucking up her courage, Jen opened the driver's side back door and stood well back.

'Can you get out of my car please? How long have you been in there? Have you been sleeping here? You didn't even put your seat belt on.' Jen listed off everything she wanted answers to, knowing it was probably a bit much all at once.

The man gaped at her, surprised at her outburst. 'Why have you stopped? I need you to take me to my house.'

'I'm not Uber, mate. Now come on, get out of my car or I'll have to call the police. Maybe they can take you where you need to go.' She was less worried now that he might be a danger to her and more concerned that he needed some professional help; he seemed a little vacant and completely unaware of how odd it was to be in the back of a random person's car without permission.

Jen reached in to pull him out. Placing her hand on the sleeve of his jumper, she recoiled. 'That's sopping wet.' She looked at her hand, but there was no moisture on it. She could have sworn his jumper felt like it was soaked.

'I really need to get home. My family, they think I did it deliberately. I need to explain.'

Jen's nostrils now detected a dank smell coming from inside the car. She scrutinised the man's appearance more closely. His jumper hung heavily to his body, and she could see dampness outlining his hands on the car seat. His skin was pale and he had droplets of water on his forehead. His short, blond hair was stuck round the edges of his face and the closer she got to him, the more he smelled like mud and wet wood. If it weren't for the bright sunshine, she'd have been sure he'd been caught out in a heavy rain.

Then, just as it had been with Aunt Joan, Jen's stomach dropped and her hands went clammy. But was this really another ghost? She had managed to touch him.

'I'm really sorry to be blunt about this but, are you…' Jen paused for a moment, worried she would get a Helen-type reaction. 'Are you dead?' The questions she was asking these days, even she had to laugh a little to herself. It was incredible.

The man hung his head a bit. 'Yes, I am,' he replied, not wanting to look at her.

'Hey, it's okay, I didn't realise. You just gave me a fright, just appearing like that in my car.' Jen wondered if her back seat was going to need drying out. 'I'm new at all this; it's not your fault.' She reached out again, her curiosity knowing no bounds. She could feel the wool from his sleeve under her fingers, almost see the water caught in the fibres.

The man looked down at Jen's hand then back at her. 'Fifty-six Brookefield Road.'

Jen took her hand back, realising she was being intrusive. *Personal space, Jen, dead or alive*, she reminded herself. *May as well see how near it is*. She pulled her phone out to check for directions, while wondering what she was going to say to her dad if it delayed her sandwich shop visit too much.

As the map came up, she saw that the man's requested destination was only a three-minute detour. 'That's not far. Looks like we're going to Brookefield Road then.' Jen didn't want to speak the rest out loud: *But what am I going to find when I get there?* Although her confidence was still high off the back of Aunt Joan's visit. 'No harm in taking you there,' she said reassuringly.

The man went back to saying nothing. He just looked out the window; he seemed content with seeing the world go by. Jen asked him his name, but he didn't reply. She wondered if he had been a man of such few words in life as well.

As they pulled into Brookefield Road, he pointed to the side of the street with the even numbers on. Jen stopped outside number fifty-six and once again turned the engine off. They sat in silence for a minute. Jen waited for some information to be volunteered, but it wasn't forthcoming.

'Okay, we're here. What do you need me to do?' she said, looking at him in the rearview mirror.

A car drove past them. The man said nothing and continued to look out the window.

'Okay, mate, this isn't going to work if you don't provide me with some information. Your name would be a start. I can't just go knocking on someone's door without, at the very least, your name.'

Jen turned to face him now. He looked shy, uncomfortable. He was very young, probably not much older than twenty. If he had been alive, he would have been freezing in the wet clothes he had on. He looked in need of a blanket and a warm drink. Most of all, a hug. He lowered his head and looked at his feet.

'You have nothing to be ashamed or scared of.' Jen tried to encourage him.

The man lifted his head and looked sheepishly at her. 'It's David. My name is David.'

'Hi, David. I'm Jen. Now, what do you need me to tell your parents?'

Jen listened carefully to what David told her, realising quickly that her confidence from her first experience may have been a bit misplaced. This was a much more difficult message to pass on, there was no cash prize at the end of this for David's loved ones.

She texted her dad to say she'd got a bit delayed and would explain over the sandwiches.

'I'll do my best for you, David.' Jen got out of the car and opened the gate to the house.

Two hanging baskets, with winter pansies bursting out, framed the front door. There was no doorbell, so Jen used the knocker, which sounded really loud and obtrusive.

Not the subtle introduction I was hoping for.

She hadn't planned what she was going to say; she'd think of that once the door was opened. *They might not even be in*, she thought.

Then she heard a door chain slide and the click of the lock turn. Her heart was pounding.

'Who is it?' a woman's voice hollered from down the hallway. 'If it's not a delivery, tell them to go away.'

A young man stood, smiling at Jen. Unsurprisingly, he looked very much like David, or rather, David looked like him. Jen presumed it must be his dad—then, clocking his age, guessed an older brother instead.

'Sorry,' he said. 'She's not a fan of answering the door to people.'

'That's no problem. I was wondering if I could speak with your mum though, Patricia, please? That is your mum, yes?'

'Err, well, what's it about? Does she know you?' the man asked, suspiciously.

'No, we don't know each other. I am guessing you are Daniel?' Jen said, trying not to freak him out too early. But she needed to move things along.

The man looked a bit floored. Who was this woman on their doorstep who knew both their names? Had to be from some mailing company or something; probably had a list of the neighbours' names and addresses.

'She's not interested in whatever you're selling. Me neither, unfortunately, but thank you,' he said, trying to be polite as he closed the door.

Jen felt she had no choice but to be bold and put her hand on it to resist. 'I'm not selling anything. I need to pass a message on. I know you're probably going to think this is all a load of nonsense, but your brother David needs to explain what happened to him.'

Daniel was now staring at her, very much like David had when she had asked him to get out of her car. She was about to ask again to come in but could hear footsteps coming down the uncarpeted floor of the hallway.

The front door flung open, nearly catching Daniel in the face.

'He said we don't want any. Now GO AWAY!' the woman shouted, then abruptly shut the door.

'This has not gone as well as I had hoped. I can't make them let me in, so what am I meant to do?' Jen walked back down the path to the gate, but stopped, looking at David sitting on her back seat. He'd been watching the whole time through the window. *He's not going to leave, is he?* The message had to be passed on; she had to find a way of doing it.

Jen turned, walked back up the path and knocked on the door again with renewed vigour.

The door opened, but before she could get one utterance out of her mouth, a barrage of words was directed at her from Patricia.

'How dare you come here and start talking about my David! Who the hell are you? Upsetting my Daniel and me with your rubbish about a message. Have you got any idea how much heartache you have dredged up for us? DO YOU? Get away from us and our house or I am calling the police.' The door slammed shut, pushing warm air from the house into Jen's cold face.

She walked back down the path again, shut the gate behind her and got into her car. She didn't feel embarrassed—she had never been worried about what people thought about her—she felt frustrated. How could she get them to listen?

After a couple of minutes, she had gathered her thoughts. 'Has your mum always been like that, David?'

David let out a snort, which Jen found amusing; the first bit of expression he had really shown. 'Mum's form of defence is attack. You've upset her, probably not Daniel that much, but to her that means you get both barrels. If anyone upset me or Daniel, that was it. She's pretty fierce, but that's part of what makes her a great mum.'

'I can't knock on the door again. I think she might give me a slap if I tried. But maybe it's not your mum I need to get through to.'

Jen pulled her phone out of her pocket to see a message from her dad. All it contained was a ghost emoji and a question mark. It made her smile. She could do this.

'Does Daniel have an email address?'

***

Daniel was sitting in his room, listening to his mum ranting to her friend on the phone.

'It's unbelievable, isn't it? On the doorstep, the brazen rudeness of it all. She's sitting out there right now in her car. If she's not gone in five minutes, I will call them, no doubt about that.'

Patricia had not yet calmed down, and Daniel felt it best to stay out the way.

The thought of a message from his brother had buoyed him, even if it sounded completely unlikely. It had been eight months since they lost him. Their dad had left some time before that; he'd said he couldn't cope with David's mental health challenges, but that was probably because it meant he had to face up to his own. He walked out one evening and didn't return.

That left Daniel and his mum to help David as best they could. Daniel had thought that they were seeing the light at the end of the tunnel, but then David didn't come home after a night round a friend's house. His body was found in the local river. They hadn't been able to reach him as much as they'd believed.

Daniel checked out the window of his bedroom, which was at the front of the house. The woman's car was just pulling away.

'That's that then,' he mumbled.

He scrolled absent-mindedly on his phone, then noticed a new email. He didn't recognise the sender and was going to junk it, but then noticed the title:

'I'm sorry I ruined your favourite jumper.'

Daniel's breath caught in his throat and his thumb tapped the email to open it.

'Dear Daniel,

My name is Jen and I am helping David write this message to you and your mum. Please read it all before deciding whether to bin it or not. The rest of the message is from David verbatim. I hope this brings you both some comfort and I am sorry if I caused you any upset today.

Daniel. I did not jump into the river. I did not kill myself. I know most people think that, including you and Mum, but it isn't true. You and Mum had helped me so much, and it was really working; I felt loved and I felt safe with you both. We talked about it a lot, and I know you didn't want Dad to go, though you do know it was better after he left. He had his own problems and he had no interest in helping himself. We were all doing better; there is no way I wanted to leave you both. I know he's been calling Mum, trying to see if she'll take him back. Neither of you need him, not at home anyway. Try and convince her to let him go.

It was so stupid. I was walking home from Liam's, the same way I always go. I stopped at the bridge to have a look over the side, the same place I always did. But this time, I leant too far and I fell in. It was so cold, and you know how bad I am at swimming. That was it. I didn't jump; I fell. I needed you both to know that. I was on my way home to you.

And I'm sorry about ruining your favourite jumper. I borrowed it without asking before going to Liam's. Make sure Mum gets you a new one at Christmas, and tell her it's from me.

I love you both,

David.'

Daniel's face was wet with tears. 'You are so right about Dad, you always were,' he said, rubbing his eyes as the screen became blurred. 'I so hoped it was really you. No one knows about that jumper.'

David walked downstairs to find his mum sitting in an armchair.

'You've been crying, son. I've got a good mind to find out who that woman is, look at how much she has upset you.'

Daniel sat on the floor next to the armchair by his mum's feet. He lent his head against her legs and passed her the phone. He believed the email and he wanted his mum to believe it too.

'Just for me, Mum, read this in full before you say anything else.'

***

Jen had restarted her journey to the charity shop. David was still in the back of her car. *How will I know if my email has been read? What if Daniel just deleted it? What if David never leaves my back seat? That's going to make giving lifts a tad awkward.* Thoughts tumbled around Jen's head.

She parked off the high street and apprehensively checked her emails. Thankfully, there was no reply from Daniel or his mum. She'd taken a chance sending an email; they could contact her if they wanted, or give it to the police and say she was harassing them. All she wanted was for them to read the message and know that David had not meant to die that night. She didn't need a reply. Doing her bit was important to her; it felt like a responsibility.

'I'm dropping the stuff in the boot to the shop then getting some sandwiches. I suppose you'll just stay here then?'

David shrugged. 'I've been stuck hanging around for a while now. I guess here is as good as any place.'

Jen thought any place might be better than the back of her car, but there wasn't much she could do about it at the moment. Maybe she could try again in a few days if David remained there, let the dust settle.

She took one box out, hoping someone in the shop might walk back with her for the rest. Closing the boot, she realised David's head was no longer visible. She walked round to the side, and he was gone.

'Blimey, maybe it worked,' she said, a sense of relief and satisfaction flowing through her.

She hoped it had. There was no way of knowing without a reply, but that was okay. Three people had been brought a little bit of peace, perhaps. But she knew that if she didn't get back soon with her dad's sandwich, there'd be little peace for her for the rest of the afternoon.

CHAPTER 17

Jen unlocked the front door and pulled her boots off, steadying herself on the end of the banister. She was shattered. It had been her first day in the office since her mum had died, and she felt like she'd been on the go for all of it. She was sure everyone in the company had come over to speak to her, to see if she was okay or if she needed anything. She'd been in lots of meetings to get up to speed with goings-on. When it was time to get off the train, Jen realised just how overwhelmed she was and ended up having a little cry in the car. She knew it wouldn't be like this every time, but was glad that the day was over.

Jen had noticed that that time of year had come round again: dark when she left the house and dark when she returned. The heating had been on for a while before she got home, making the house feel like it had rolled out a warm, cosy welcome. With her favourite loungewear on, she warmed up some homemade soup—which she was very proud of having made over the weekend—along with a crusty roll. She'd sent her dad home with a few tubs; he'd seemed less enthusiastic, but grateful.

She was keen to sit down and peruse the internet for any new information about Helen's disappearance. The reconstruction had taken place that evening, while Jen was travelling home. She doubted any new leads would be announced so quickly, but nonetheless, she wanted to keep up to date with it as much as possible.

Jen settled onto the sofa with her soup and first had a quick reread of her notes about David. She still couldn't wrap her head around the fact that she had felt him—his jumper, at least. Her mum hadn't said anything about being able to touch any of her visitors and she couldn't touch anyone as a ghost either, although they both wished that wasn't the case. But then, Jacqui sometimes did feel like Bailey was brushing past her, so maybe that was on the same level. Jen had no idea what the rules were; maybe there really weren't any at all, as Elizabeth had alluded to in her notebooks.

Jen then clicked through the major news pages for the day. There were articles from earlier that she had already read, but nothing new. There was nothing new at home either; neither Helen nor Jacqui had reappeared.

She didn't know if it was the warmth of the soup or the heating, but Jen could barely keep her eyes open after eating. She placed her laptop on the floor and curled up, her head on a cushion. She was so tired, and it wasn't long before she had nodded off completely.

***

'Jen. Jen. Wake up.' Jacqui was standing over her daughter. She'd attempted to shake her, forgetting that wasn't going to have any effect, and was now left with trying to rouse her with voice alone. 'Jen! Wake up! Helen's back!'

Jen stirred and partially opened her eyes. Her mum's face came into view, and for a moment she forgot about ghosts and her mum having died. Then, in a flash, it flooded back into her mind.

'I'm awake, I'm awake. What time is it?'

'It's only twenty past nine, in the evening. Helen's been here a while. I think we're on her seventh rendition of that song. It's sending me a bit mad.' Jacqui covered her ears, although it made little to no difference.

Jen leapt up, then wished she hadn't; she'd made herself dizzy. She had been sound asleep.

'Has she done anything else but sing?' she asked, whilst grabbing her laptop and walking to the kitchen.

'No, same old routine. I did try talking to her myself, since she heard me last time. But nothing; it's like I'm not here,' Jacqui said, ignoring the irony.

Jen went into the kitchen to find Helen Swift standing in the same spot as before and singing the same tune as before.

'You are my sunshines, my only sunshines…'

'She's in a complete state of trauma, isn't she?' Jen said. 'That song is all she can manage. She may have had it going round in her head to distract herself from what was happening.' She shook her head as if trying to shake off the grim thoughts. She had to admit, though, she was at a bit of a loss of what to do next.

'I had a thought while you were asleep,' Jacqui said. 'I noticed she's singing it slightly wrong. I'm sure it's "sunshine" not "sunshines".'

'Are you sure?' Jen asked, opening up her music app and finding the song. She saw her mum was right as soon as she looked at the title. It was 'sunshine', singular not plural.

A nursery rhyme version of the song began playing from her laptop. Jen had pressed play by accident and was about to pause it when she noticed Helen had stopped singing. Not only had she stopped singing, but she was facing Jen, almost looking straight at her, presumably trying to work out where the music was coming from. Jen moved her hand away from the laptop and let the tune play on until it finished.

Helen stayed quiet.

Jen took her chance. 'Helen, it's me again, Jen. Do you remember me?'

Both Jen and Jacqui stood quietly, eagerly anticipating any response from Helen that wasn't song based.

'Yes, I remember your voice. Have you come back to get me?' Helen asked, searching the darkness for the source of the voice.

Jen decided on a different tack from last time. 'Yes, we've come back to get you. My mum is here again, too. We just need a bit of help from you so we can take you home.'

'Okay, what do you need me to do? I hope it doesn't take long; I really would like to leave now.'

Jen and Jacqui looked at each other, both trying to think of a question that wasn't going to send Helen back into her singing frenzy.

This time, Jacqui decided to go for it. 'Helen, can you tell us how you left the woods, please? It will help us.' She felt as if she was having to verbally tiptoe.

Helen hesitated for what seemed like a long time, as if she was building up the courage to say something. Jacqui and Jen braced themselves as she began to speak.

'I was looking for Pip. He... had run off. I couldn't find him. There was a man. He told me he had seen Pip. He was going to take me to get Pip.'

Jen couldn't believe it. This was something no one knew, she was sure of it. There had been a man, and he had claimed to know where Pip was. Maybe this was the man who took Helen.

Jacqui realised her mouth had been open the whole time while listening. 'Thank you, Helen, that's really important information that will help us. Did you find Pip?' she asked.

'Yes, he was in the man's car. But… it was all wrong. I…' Helen became increasingly agitated, shaking her head.

'It's okay, Helen, we're here with you,' Jen said. 'He can't hurt you now. Try to stay calm.' She felt they were going to lose her again.

'Pip was barking… He was scared. My head… The man… I don't want to… Stop… NO!'

It was as if Helen was hyperventilating, and she couldn't get her words out. She became hysterical; cries became screams.

Jen wanted to hold her tight and console her, but it was impossible. She couldn't bear to watch Helen in so much anguish, so she played the nursery rhyme again, hoping it would soothe her. They couldn't ask her any more right now. It wasn't fair, and neither of them really knew what they were doing. Jen felt like they were hurting Helen more than helping.

Seeing Helen was becoming quieter and beginning to sing her song again—to herself through her sobs—Jen motioned to Jacqui to go out of the kitchen.

'We can't do this to her anymore, not this way,' Jen said as she pulled the kitchen door slightly closed.

Jacqui nodded.

'She has been through so much; she's too disturbed to tell us everything. It's completely understandable. We know about this man now, but it's still not enough to find her.'

'So, what do we do?' Jacqui said, noticing that the song on the laptop had finished and she couldn't hear Helen.

'I don't know yet. I need to have a think. But I can't keep pushing her; it's cruel and we're no professionals. If she were a living person, she'd be speaking to a qualified counsellor. Or—' Jen suddenly had an idea.

'What? You've just thought of something haven't you?' Jacqui could tell by the look on Jen's face.

'I have, but it could majorly backfire. And I'd look pretty stupid. But neither are good enough reasons not to try.'

Jen had also noticed that the kitchen was quiet and nudged the door open. Helen was gone. 'I hope she feels she can return, otherwise what I have in mind will definitely not work.' Jen retrieved her laptop from the kitchen and went to sit back down in the lounge, typing out what Helen had told them as word perfect as possible.

She heard Jacqui tutting. 'What have you been eating in here? There's crumbs everywhere.' Never had Jacqui been more desperate to have a solid body again; she really needed to get the handheld vacuum out and clean up. 'Did you not have a plate?'

'Oh, Mum, give it a rest. I'd been out all day and had my tea on the sofa. I'll clean it up.' Jen swept the bits of bread roll off the sofa and onto the floor.

Jacqui was beside herself.

'Stop worrying about the crumbs and think about this. We need someone who is trained to speak to people who have been through something as serious as Helen. Someone who can get the right information that will hopefully lead to where she is.'

'So, what, we need to find a psychic therapist?' Jacqui said, looking confused.

Jen stared at her screen for a moment. It was a wild idea. It was a considerable jump from what they were doing, but she couldn't think of anything else that might work. Notwithstanding, neither of them knew how long they could keep Helen coming back for.

'No, we need her,' Jen said, turning round her laptop to show Jacqui an article headlined *'Police hope reconstruction will help solve the 30-year-old disappearance of Helen Swift'*, underneath which was a picture of Detective Inspector Tola Obederin.

Jen listened to Jacqui laugh a lot, then patiently waited while she reeled off all the reasons why going directly to the detective in charge of Helen's case was a mistake. Jen didn't interrupt, because she knew her mum couldn't sway her and she needed Jacqui to run out of steam before she could say anything else.

'… and even if she does believe you, which is highly unlikely, how will you make sure she's here when Helen appears? We don't know when she's going to come back. I just can't see how it's going to work. What if they arrest you for, I don't know, wasting police time or for just being a nuisance? Your dad is going to have a field day with this.' Jacqui was glad she no longer needed to use up precious time drawing breath in between points.

'Have you finished?' Jen asked calmly.

'Well, yes, probably,' Jacqui replied indignantly. She couldn't believe that Jen was actually going to speak to the police. 'There's no way they will take you seriously.'

'What other choice is there? You tried, albeit not extensively, to speak to her the first time round. This time, okay, we've got some new information, but we could ask one too many of the wrong questions and she completely vanishes or never speaks properly again. I don't know how to get her to focus. Do you? I think this is the only way forward, and if I look like an idiot in the process, then, whatever,' Jen said resolutely.

'But it's the actual police, Jen! They are not going to take it lightly if they think you're making it up. They could charge you with hampering an inquiry or something!'

'Ugh, don't be ridiculous. They don't have time to charge every person who gives them rubbish information. They must have had loads of odd people over the years telling them tales; they won't all have been thrown in prison,' Jen defiantly replied, hands on hips, unrelenting.

Jacqui knew her daughter and knew there was no point arguing. She hoped Mark might be able to change her mind, but from experience, she knew that was unlikely too. Rolling her eyes, she conceded. 'Well, just make sure your dad goes with you if he can. I'd rather you not go to a police station on your own.'

Jen smiled. 'It's going to be fine.'

'Yes, well, let's hope so. Have you spoken to Laura since she was last here?' A much-needed change of subject was in order to lighten the mood, Jacqui thought.

Jen winced a little bit. There were two messages on her phone from Laura that she hadn't replied to. 'No. Well, she messaged me, but I haven't had a chance to go back to her yet.' Jen had had plenty of chances, but those chances had been spent writing

her notes about David or looking up more information about Helen.

'Try not to shut her out, Jen. She'll be wondering
what's going on, probably worrying about you.'

'I know, I know. I just don't know what to say to her
at the moment. I usually tell her everything, but how
do I tell her about this? Did you tell anyone other than
Dad?' Jen was hoping for a yes.

'No, I didn't feel like I could tell any of my friends.
I was worried they'd stop wanting to see me. I don't
think Nan told anyone either, apart from the budgie.'
Jacqui could see that wasn't the answer Jen was looking
for. 'But you and Laura, well, you're different to me and
your nan. You two aren't fazed by anything. I'm sure
she'll understand once you start explaining to her. And
it's not just you that knows all about it, your dad is here
too. She'd believe both of you, surely?'

Jen was looking at her lap, picking a thread in her
jeans. 'Maybe. What if she doesn't believe me, though?
Or it freaks her out and she's scared of me? She might
just think I've totally lost it. But the alternative—not
telling her—it's kind of like I'm being dishonest. I'm
not lying to her about anything but I'm missing a big
chunk out of what's happening to me at the moment. It
doesn't sit well with me. I need to think about it more.'

Jen waited for her mum to reply, but when she
looked up, Jacqui had departed.

'Gone again.' Jen began to wonder if Helen's visits
were connected to when her mum showed up, or vice
versa. She hoped not and shoved the thought out of
her mind.

She found her phone, scrolled to Laura's last message and started writing a much-delayed reply.

CHAPTER 18

The next morning, Jen called her dad to explain what she was going to do.

'I'm sure your mum would not be happy about this,' was Mark's opening line; a similar reaction to Jacqui's, as Jen had expected. But he abided by Jen's choice on how to proceed.

Jen had convinced her parents that this was the best thing to do, but she still had a niggle that it could be a nightmare for her if it went wrong. Ignoring the niggle before it stopped her in her tracks, she dialled the number from the appeal page online, and waited.

A woman answered and introduced herself as being part of the Major Incident Team at Sussex Police.

'Hi, I would like to speak to the detective in charge of the Helen Swift case, please?' Jen said.

'Is that Operation Firecrest?'

Jen scanned the page on the internet and saw the name 'Operation Firecrest' as a reference by the phone number. 'Yes, that's the one. Helen Swift's disappearance.'

'Any information you have you can share with me now, and I'll make sure it is passed to the team handling the case. You can do this anonymously, if you'd prefer.'

'I would really rather speak to the detective in charge, please. Tola Obederin, I think it is.'

The lady on the phone sighed. Jen wondered how many calls they had received since the reconstruction. Had any of them been of any use?

'I will need to take your details so that someone can call you back.'

'Yes, that's totally fine.' At least it wasn't a point-blank no.

Jen relayed her information and was promised a call from someone within the investigating team that day.

The rest of the morning was filled with work meetings. Jen feigned as much interest as possible but spent most of the time checking her phone for missed calls—even though there wasn't any way she could miss a call; her phone was not on silent and the volume was up to maximum, plus she barely took her eyes off of it.

While Jen was making a sandwich for lunch, still keeping one eye on her phone in case her ears weren't fully functioning, she went over all the ways to explain about Helen—none of them sounded great. A tiny part of her hoped the call back never came, but then the phone rang.

It was Detective Inspector Tola Obederin herself. 'I understand you want to speak to me directly, Mrs Hattley?' She sounded authoritative on the phone.

'It's Miss Hattley. And yes, though it would be better if I can speak to you in person. It would be easier for me to explain everything.' Jen had her fingers crossed. She felt Tola Obederin was considering if this was worth her time. 'I think I have new information about someone Helen spoke to when she left the woods.'

'And you can't tell me over the phone?' Detective Obederin asked.

It was a fair question. If it was key information, you'd want to pass it on as quickly as possible. Jen knew it would be way more difficult if she had to explain it over the phone; a phone call could simply be stopped, disconnected. Actually having to walk away from a conversation would be trickier.

In the time Jen had spent debating her answer in her head, Detective Obederin had made her own mind up. 'Okay, I can see you later today at four-fifteen pm. Is it okay for me to speak to you at your home?'

Jen hadn't expected a visit to her house, then remembered that the first woman she'd spoken to did take her address as well as other contact details. Tola knew she wasn't local to the case. At least it would be safe ground for Jen if the conversation took a negative turn.

'Yes, that will be fine.'

'Okay, I'll be there at four-fifteen, and we will speak then. Goodbye, Miss Hattley.'

'Succinct and to the point. Blimey.'

Jen had amazed herself; it was actually happening. She called her dad to tell him and ask if he could be in the house with her. If the detective didn't believe Jen on her own, she might believe two of them. She just hoped her dad was up for it.

'I don't think this is what your mum had in mind when she said I should go with you. I'm sure she meant for me to just sit in the car outside wherever you were going to relay the information.' Mark was clearly unconvinced about the role Jen had in mind for him.

'Detective Obederin is going to think it's odd that my dad is sitting in his car on the driveway while she comes in to talk to me, isn't she? And it will be way more believable if my own dad can actually say it's all real. Pleeaase. I'm only going to get one shot at this.'

Mark made a whiney sound; he was giving in. 'If it's going to help, then fine. But I'll hang around in the kitchen and you can just call me in if you need me. Not that I'll know what to say, apart from that I'm sure you're not having a breakdown or hallucinating or something. She might assume we're both a bit loopy.'

He felt out of his depth speaking to an actual police officer, but it was for his daughter. This was a big deal to her, and she'd had enough to cope with recently. Plus, at the end of it all, there was a family missing their mum. Wimping out wasn't an option, so he was all in.

'Thanks, Dad, this means a lot. Mum will be relieved to know you're here with me. She might even drop in herself.' Jen hoped that she would. But then, what if Helen appeared, too? With the detective there as well as her dad, it could be chaos. Maybe best if there were no extra visitors when Tola arrived.

***

Tola Obederin got into her car and told the satnav where she wanted to go. It was a longer drive than she'd been used to in recent weeks—most cases kept her local, so it made a pleasant change to get out and take in some different scenery.

'Why this woman needs to speak to me in person… but every bit of information has to be run down, Tola,' she muttered to herself as her seat belt clicked into place. Years in the job had taught her to never assume anything and to exhaust every lead, every time. 'You never know, this could be what you've been waiting for.' She really wanted this case solved, so she would go anywhere if it meant getting new information.

She thought back to when she'd first become involved in Helen Swift's disappearance. As a senior detective and newcomer to Sussex, a number of cold cases had landed on her desk as well as the day-to-day live ones—Helen's case had been open for about fifteen years by the time Tola took over the investigation.

It was a real mystery. No suspects like a jealous lover or violent husband; no witnesses who could verify seeing anyone suspicious or any unknown vehicles at the entrance to the woods. Many people, mainly women, had disappeared without trace over her career, but there was usually a suspect that they just couldn't pin down, or a shred of evidence, or they had found the body at the very least. With Helen, it was as if she had been spirited away.

When Tola had read the file in full for the first time, her own son was the same age as Helen's son was when she went missing. Tola always remembered the anger she felt for the injustice of Helen's little boy and girl losing all that future with their mum. That anger drove her to make sure Helen was never forgotten during case reviews. It drove her to pull out Helen's file on each anniversary and scrutinise every witness statement, every photo, every map all over again, just in case she'd missed something the last time she looked. She felt duty bound to find her.

Which was why she had driven out of Sussex for the best part of an hour.

Pulling up outside the address for Jennifer Hattley, Tola hoped that this time she was going to hear something that would change everything.

CHAPTER 19

'Oh my God, she's here,' Jen said to her dad.

He gave her two thumbs up, then pushed the kitchen door half shut so he could hide but still listen in.

She was feeling sweaty and really nervous. She might have sounded completely confident to her mum and dad earlier, when convincing them of her idea, but it was real now. The fear of messing up the opportunity to find Helen, it made her feel sick. Looking like a complete weirdo would be an unfortunate consequence, but she'd get over it.

She'd practised what she was going to say with her dad and now it was time to get on with it. Opening the door, Jen found the detective there, ready with her ID.

'Good afternoon, Miss Hattley. May I come in?' Tola believed in politeness and courtesy with whomever she met.

'Yes, of course, please. Would you like a drink before we sit down?' Jen felt the need for pleasantries.

'No, I'm fine, thank you.'

'Okay then, just through here. Oh, by the way, my dad is here. He's pottering around in the kitchen. He's just here for a bit of support, I hope that's okay?'

'That's no problem at all,' Tola replied as she sat down in an armchair and took out her laptop. 'Have you given a statement before, Jen?'

'Thankfully, no.'

'Okay. I'll be taking notes as we speak. Once you've explained your information to me, it may feel like I ask a lot of questions. Apologies in advance, but it's so that I can really understand the facts. But to begin with, I'd just like to hear everything you have to say without interrupting.'

Tola liked to be upfront about how many questions she would ask. An initial, full statement from a witness meant she could take some notes; she could then delve deeper and work out any inconsistencies or something the person hadn't realised themselves and think about if it matched statements from other people or other information she knew from the file. But mainly, her first job was to listen.

While Tola was giving her introduction, Jen observed her fully. She'd only really seen one or two photos of her on the internet. Sitting there in person, Tola Obederin looked quite the force of nature. She gave off an air of confidence, someone who was highly capable. Jen felt immediately that she could trust her to at least hear her out. She couldn't work out how old she was, but given her position and the way she carried herself, Jen expected she was closer to her mum's age than her own.

'Are you okay to begin, Miss Hattley?'

Tola observed Jen with equal measure. She had been surprised by her age; Tola was not sure how she would have information about a thirty-year-old missing persons investigation when she was probably only a young child at the time. But she'd insisted on speaking to her in person. Maybe she knew something about an older relative.

Jen swallowed hard. *Get straight to the point*, she thought. *No dilly-dallying, as Mum would say*. 'Right. Helen was approached by a man while she was looking for Pip the dog. He said he knew where Pip was. Helen went with the man, and when she found Pip, he was scared and barking.'

Having now said it out loud, Jen thought it sounded like a pitiful amount of information.

Tola typed rapidly, then looked up, wondering if Jen had paused or finished. Feeling that she was waiting for a question, Tola obliged. 'Okay. That's very interesting. Do you know what time this was on the day she disappeared?'

'No, sorry. I don't.'

'Can you tell me anything about the appearance of the man that Helen spoke to? Hair colour, skin colour, what he was wearing?'

'No, nothing on that either.' Jen stuck her hands under her legs and squirmed in the chair. She felt like a child at school who had done something naughty and was about to be found out. She knew she'd done nothing wrong, but the feeling wouldn't subside.

'Do you know his name?'

Jen shook her head.

Tola rested her hands on her laptop keyboard. Jen's face and body language suggested she was being genuine, that what she had just explained was truthful, that Jen, at least, believed what she was saying. She was clearly nervous, but Tola and her colleagues had that effect on a lot of people.

'Miss Hattley, how do you know this? How do you know that Helen went with a man to look for her dog?'

There it was. The million-dollar question.

'Please, it's Jen. Miss Hattley reminds me I used to be married.' Jen laughed, trying to take some tension out of the situation for herself. 'You know how you said you'd listen without interrupting? Which you did, thank you. Would you mind just doing that again for me, while I explain this next bit.' Jen had to get this caveat in before she continued.

'Of course, Miss—sorry—Jen. I'm here for you to tell me what you know, uninterrupted.'

Unbeknownst to either of them, Jen's dad was also listening to what was being said. Mark couldn't hear properly from the kitchen—blaming the door rather than his ageing ears—so, stealthily (he thought), he had tiptoed down the hall to get closer. He thought Jen was handling it well so far, but this was the crunch point. He hadn't realised he'd been holding his breath while waiting for Jen to speak again, and nearly gave his position away, breathing out quite loudly.

Jen turned her head towards the lounge door; she could have sworn she'd heard someone gasp. *Please, not another visitor now*, she thought as she turned back to Tola.

She'd jumped in with both feet; now she'd see if she would sink or swim. 'I know all of this because Helen told me. I've inherited a gift—an ability, you could call it. Dead people come to me with messages or information they need me to pass on. My mum could do the same, but she died recently. The ability passes between the women in my family on death, hence why I can do it now.

'Helen came to my mum soon after she disappeared, but for reasons I won't go into, my mum couldn't help. I believe that due to the thirty-year anniversary, or perhaps because I'm new in the job, so to speak, Helen has appeared again. She's been here twice, and the second time, we managed to get that information from her.

'Helen's the only one who knows what happened and where she finally ended up, but she's not in a good way; she's confused and scared. She keeps singing the same song over and over, and I thought the best thing would be to get a professional to speak to her. So, I called you because you must know how to speak to people who are frightened, who have been through huge trauma.' Jen inhaled and exhaled deeply. 'And that's it.'

There was total silence from Detective Inspector Tola Obederin. She had stopped typing after she'd heard the words 'dead people come to me with messages' and just listened out of pure astonishment.

Jen waited, rooted in her chair. Mark waited with his back to the hallway wall, trying to stay as quiet as possible.

Tola closed her laptop, and Jen knew it was game over.

'Miss Hattley. Thank you for contacting me about this case. I appreciate your time, but I feel it would be best for both of us if I get on my way.' She put her laptop away and began to get up from the armchair.

Jen knew she had little time left to convince Tola to help. 'I did not expect you to believe me straight away, Detective Obederin. It's quite an outrageous claim, saying I can talk to the dead. But I can, and Helen has more to tell us. Other visitors I've had so far, they have been more articulate, or I was at least able to get the information I needed from them fairly quickly. With Helen, it's going to take skills I don't have. I need you to help us.'

Tola wanted to be respectful. She'd met many different people over the years—different cultures, different beliefs; she'd had apparent psychics contact her before, even on Helen's case, claiming they could find her, that they knew where she was. In earlier days, she'd listened to them, because what if one of them actually held the answer? But in the end, none of them had. Tola had come to believe that the dead could not talk, and their secrets would remain known only to them.

'I understand that you want to help,' Tola said. 'It's an upsetting situation for the public. But I cannot take a statement based on what the ghost of Helen Swift has told you. I appreciate your efforts, I feel they are coming from a good place. But this is where it stops, Miss Hattley.'

Jen wasn't giving up and raised her voice in frustration. 'But she can tell us everything! After all this time, isn't any lead worth pursuing, even if it's not from a conventional source? Do you really have the luxury of turning my help down?'

Tola Obederin's face became stern. This woman had overstepped the mark. 'Miss Hattley. This is a serious investigation with far-reaching consequences for Helen Swift's two children, her remaining family and friends. Do not presume to tell me how I should be doing my job and what lines of inquiry the police should be taking to find the truth. Your claim that Helen Swift has visited you is ludicrous. It's an insult to her and her children that you have told me this story about her dog and this man in the woods. Making up information like this wastes our time and slows down the investigation. I have spoken to enough people like you, trying to make a name for themselves and become famous on the internet for five minutes. I will not stand for it, Miss Hattley. Now, I would prefer you not to contact me again unless you can provide me with facts from a *living* person.'

Jen hated how Tola had emphasised the word 'living'. She knew she was burning a bridge right there and then, but she wasn't stopping; it was too important.

'I'm not interested in fame or people knowing I helped. Say someone anonymous called in, I don't care! What matters is getting the message to where it needs to be heard. I think you might be the only one who can get Helen to open up. It's you who needs to hear what she has to say, through me. We need to get Helen home.'

Tola shook her head; she'd had enough of Jennifer Hattley. As she went to leave the lounge, she was surprised to find her path blocked by a man.

Mark had heard the whole confrontation and had his own point to say. 'Now look here, Detective Obederin, my daughter is telling you the truth. I won't have you suggesting that she's up to no good and wasting your time for her own gain. My late wife had the same gift; it runs in the family.' Mark had to ignore the lump in his throat as he said the word 'late'. 'And yes, it all sounds completely mad. But whether you personally believe in this stuff or not, quite frankly, is irrelevant. I have seen how it works with my own eyes; what we need you to do is suspend your disbelief and help Jen find the information that you need. You haven't found her, have you? It's been thirty years. Surely this cannot do any harm?'

Mark had surprised himself with his outburst and did not realise that he was preventing their guest from leaving.

'Dad, move out the way!' Jen had to intervene. Stopping Tola from exiting was not aiding their cause, but she loved that her dad was trying to rescue the situation for her.

'Oh dear, I am very sorry, Detective. Blame my over enthusiasm,' Mark said, stepping aside and giving Tola some space.

'That's quite alright, Mr Hattley. It's admirable to hear you defending your daughter, and I apologise if I said anything out of turn, but the answer is still no.' Tola was resolute.

'It's okay, Dad, thanks for trying; it was always unlikely that I'd be believed. The detective has a long journey back in the rush hour traffic, we should let her go home.' Jen turned to Tola and held her hand out. 'I am sorry if you feel this has been a waste of time for you.'

Tola shook her hand. 'Thank you for understanding my decision, Jen. And I am sorry to hear about your mum. My condolences.' Tola may have not believed the story, but she had been listening intently. She knew grief could be complicated; maybe this was a way for the family to cope with what had happened. She would probably never know.

Jen was opening the door to let Tola leave when she recalled her mum's thought the last time Helen visited: *'She's singing it slightly wrong. I'm sure it's 'sunshine' not 'sunshines.'* Then, Tola reprimanding her: *'It's an insult to her and her children.'* Suddenly, the penny dropped.

'Please, just one more thing,' Jen said. 'Then you can drive away and forget you ever spoke to me. Please?'

Tola could never curb her curiosity, and since Jen had let the issue go amicably, she decided to entertain this final bit. 'Okay, Miss Hattley, go on.'

'Helen is traumatised and she sings this song to herself over and over. And I mean on constant repeat. I can rarely get her to focus. But she sings it wrong.' Jen cleared her throat and sang. '*You are my sunshines, my only sunshines…*'

She paused for a moment to see if the detective would notice the error. When Tola didn't speak, Jen continued.

'Can you hear? The song should be "my sunshine", not "my sunshines". I think she used to sing it to her children, and she changed the song so it included both of them. Ask them, see if they remember. There is no way I could know this unless I heard it from Helen.'

It was all Jen had left. She could do no more.

'Thank you, Miss Hattley. I'll take it into consideration.' Tola walked to her car, rolling her eyes to the sky out of Jen's sight.

Jen closed the front door and looked at her dad. 'My God, that was intense. I couldn't have done any more. I don't know where we go from here with Helen.' She felt so downbeat; she had failed.

Mark gave her a huge hug. 'Your mum would have loved that, Jen. She'd be as proud of you as I am. You really stood up for what you believe in.'

'Thanks. And you didn't do bad yourself, Dad! I hope, somewhere, Mum got to see how much effort we both put in.'

Mark led his daughter down the hallway to the kitchen and pulled a bottle of wine from the rack. 'I think we deserve a glass of something. We did our best for Helen, and that is all that matters.'

CHAPTER 20

Tola was trying to shake off her discussion with Jennifer Hattley on the drive home, disappointed that it had been a waste of time. She'd leave the notes as they were—it was always important to keep any information she had gathered—but they were not going to be of any help.

She didn't want to walk in her front door in the mood she was currently in, so offered to pick up a takeaway after a quick call with her husband. An extra twenty minutes, waiting in her local Chinese, might be enough to lighten her outlook.

The extra twenty minutes became nearer forty. After arriving at the Chinese, Tola realised they were having a refurb, so she diverted to their second choice, slightly farther away, which she knew how to get to without needing the satnav; the name of the place always escaped her.

After placing her order, Tola sat and stared at the television high in the corner of the restaurant. The sound wasn't very high, so she mainly watched the pictures, guessing at what was going on. It looked like a soap, and some high drama was unfolding—based on the agitated looks of the characters.

Tola's internal monologue was on its own soapbox. She imagined trying to tell her bosses that the latest lead she'd discovered had come from the ghost of Helen Swift. She'd spent most of her working life building her reputation, gaining respect and challenging people to take her seriously; it was her toughest achievement, getting to where she was in the job she had always wanted to do. There was no way she was going to unpick all that effort because Jennifer Hattley believed she had messages from beyond the grave. She'd been right to stop the interview.

A lady walked down from the kitchen and handed Tola her order. This had been a good idea; she felt more at ease and ready to go home.

She tried very hard not to take the remnants of her day back into her house; it wasn't fair on her husband. He worked hard too, and both of them needed some simple peace and quiet at the end of a long day. Tola's home was her sanctuary away from the stresses of work and the depravity of human behaviour; it was always to be protected.

Her stomach rumbled as the waft of spring rolls filled the car. The food would certainly go some way to cheering her up, she was sure.

The takeaway bag was sitting on the passenger seat, and as she pushed it further back to stop it potentially falling off, she noticed the menu stapled to it. On the menu was the restaurant's logo and name in bold red lettering: *'Sunshine Valley'*.

She sighed and shook her head. It was just a coincidence.

***

After her dad left to meet some friends, Jen put her pyjamas on and curled up with a packet of biscuits and another glass of wine. She was tremendously fed up. Maybe she'd given herself a false sense of confidence with Aunt Joan and David; both of them had gone comparatively well. David's message had been more challenging to deliver, but she'd pulled it off. With Helen, it felt like the message itself was going to be elusive, let alone telling the police about it.

Suddenly, the doorbell rang. Jen wasn't expecting anyone, so had a quick look on the camera to check who it was—she was not answering the door to any randoms at this time of the evening.

To her surprise, she saw Laura waving at the doorbell camera.

'Brrr, get me inside. It's really dropped in temperature out there,' Laura said, walking straight down the hallway and into the kitchen.

Jen closed the door, feeling the evening chill round her bare ankles where her pyjamas weren't quite long enough. 'Is everything alright?' she asked as she joined Laura in the kitchen.

Laura gave her a puzzled look. 'Yeah, I messaged earlier to say I'd pop round while Olivia is at Scouts.'

Jen hadn't checked her phone since Tola arrived. 'Sorry, I've been distracted this afternoon, I missed it. But you're here now, so all good.' Jen was pleased to see Laura but wasn't sure if she had any energy left to engage in conversation.

'I've only got about half an hour,' Laura said. 'But I haven't seen you since we sorted your mum's clothes out, so I thought it would be good to grab some time together.'

Jen nodded and raised a smile. There was so much she wanted to tell Laura, but she couldn't right now. She just wanted to finish her wine, go to bed and forget all about Helen Swift for a bit, which made her feel awful.

Laura could tell something was off. The two of them always had something to talk about whenever they got together. But Jen was unusually quiet; she looked tired and disheartened. It was a rarity, but it felt awkward between them. Laura didn't like it. But she didn't want to keep asking Jen how she was feeling about her mum—it was as if there was nothing else to talk about.

'So,' she started, 'anything been going on? How's work been since you went back?'

'Same old, same old really. Nothing much happening,' Jen replied. She knew she was being rubbish company.

Laura wasn't being put off though. 'I know, it's a weird time. Some days you'll feel fine, others you probably would rather go back to bed. It's going to be like that for a while, I expect, as you get used to your mum not being here.'

'It's not that,' Jen said. More abruptly than she had intended, she could tell by Laura's face.

Silence hung between them for a moment. Laura searched her brain, looking for the right words to explain how she was feeling. But none seemed quite right. Losing her mum had changed Jen; something was different. She felt like she'd lost Jen somewhere, or that she herself was getting left behind from something. She couldn't quite put her finger on it.

'Then, what is it, Jen? You're clearly not one hundred percent, which is completely normal given what's happened, but you're not talking to me either. You don't reply to my messages; you're struggling to put a few sentences together for me right now. I don't even think I've seen you cry that much. Not that it means anything, how much you cry, I suppose. You must believe me: I'm here for you, whatever you need. But I feel like you're shutting me out of something. And it's weird.' These weren't the exact words Laura had hoped to say, but it was the best she could manage.

Jen looked at her best friend. Laura's face was pleading with her to tell her what was going on. Maybe she could get a little way there, for now, just enough to make them both feel better and that their friendship wasn't going south.

'There is some other stuff going on,' she said. 'But I need time to work out how to explain it to you. I do want you to know. I'm sorry if I am being obtuse. I promise I will tell you, just not yet. There's too much going on.' Jen looked at Laura intently, wondering if that had just made it worse.

A promise was a promise though. She'd committed and she would tell Laura. Not today though.

Laura held Jen's eyes for a few moments. It was enough for now. 'Okay, well, if time is what you need, then I can be patient. A promise is a promise, though, and I'll hold you to it. Whenever you're ready, you know I will always be here, whatever it is you have to tell me. Just don't leave it too long and get yourself in a muddle.' Laura checked the time on her watch. 'I need to shoot to pick Her Ladyship up. Teenagers, different breed! Look after yourself, and please, just reply to my messages so I at least have some idea of how you are, yeah?'

'Yes, I will do better. Sorry.' Jen was relieved to have made Laura a little happier. Their friendship meant everything to her; she didn't want to see it dwindle and change.

***

Tola sat contentedly on the sofa with her husband, Samuel, watching their favourite quiz show. The food had done the trick, and she was forgetting about her encounter with the Hattleys. She would move on to the other leads she had received, although none of them looked particularly promising.

'I visited your mum this afternoon,' Samuel commented as the ad break started. 'They're repainting the foyer and the corridors. It's looking real smart, much brighter as you walk in.'

Tola's mum was in a home for patients with dementia. They had both cared for her from home for a number of years, before her symptoms worsened considerably during Covid. Accepting that they could no longer give her the best care, they chose a nearby home for her. It had been heartbreaking to let her go, but Tola knew it was the only way for her mum to receive the care she needed.

The home had worked out well, and Tola couldn't have asked for any better peace of mind. Or a better husband to support her. Samuel always visited her mum twice a week whilst running his errands. It filled her heart with joy to know he was keeping an eye on things for her so she could concentrate on her work. Tola would visit between shifts, so between them, they saw her as much as they could.

'Yes,' Tola replied, 'there was an email saying about the improvements. I'm looking forward to seeing it all when I pop down there tomorrow. How was Mum?'

'Very much the same. She didn't recognise me but mentioned her dad a lot, like she always does. I read the weekend's sports results out; she seems to like it when I do that.'

Tola gave him a kiss on his cheek. 'You're a good man; I am lucky to have you.'

'Yes, you are.' He smirked and got up to make them another cup of tea. 'Oh, and they're going to put some wall art up at the main entrance. They've bought those wall stickers, the nurses were showing me. Massive, they are. And in the middle, there'll be these huge rays of sunshine coming out. It's going to look quite impressive, I think.'

Rays of sunshine. There it was again. That word. Like it was following her about since leaving the Hattleys'.

She wasn't having any of it. *It's just a coincidence, Tola, your brain is making patterns up that aren't really there.*

CHAPTER 21

Tola was up and about with enthusiasm. On her days off, she liked to be as productive as possible. She had a visit to her mum planned, lunch with two close friends, then a trip to the shops for the meal she would cook later. Her work didn't allow her as much time as she'd like to conjure up her culinary masterpieces, so this was another reason her days off were valuable to her. Any chance to cook something new was taken every time. Samuel looked forward to her days off as much as Tola did as he knew he'd get fed very well that evening.

With her list in her bag and keys in her hand, Tola got into her car to drive the short distance to her mum's care home. She was usually one of the earliest visitors they had in the mornings, and as the car radio came on, the weather forecast was being read out.

'After a slow start, we expect lots of sunshine today and clear skies. A day for winter coats and sunglasses.'

Tola tutted. It was hardly a surprise. The skies were already clear, hardly any clouds. But hearing the word 'sunshine' yet again, it was as if someone was trying to poke at her.

Just a coincidence, Tola. It was probably sunny yesterday, too, but you didn't notice.

Arriving at her mum's residence, she greeted the receptionist and some of the nurses she recognised. One particular nurse always said the same thing: 'Are you here to see Grace? Ah, she'll be pleased that you've come again.' She said it even though her mum, Grace, might not know she was there at all. It was a comforting thing to say, though, and was always meant well.

Tola noticed the wall art Samuel mentioned hadn't gone up yet, so that was one less sunshine to be reminded about.

She made her way to her mum's room and knocked lightly on the door, calling out so as not to startle her. 'Mum, it's me, Tola, your daughter. Is it okay to come in?'

Grace was sitting in a high-backed chair, looking out of the window; the home was in a built-up area, but she had a pleasing view over the residents' garden. She was out of her nightwear and dressed. On the table beside her were some toast crusts on a plate, along with an empty cup of tea. Tola was pleased to see her mum had eaten some breakfast; it wasn't always the case these days.

Grace didn't turn round as Tola walked in, and only noticed her once she sat on the bed opposite.

'Hi, Mum. It's Tola. I've come to see you.' Tola reached out and held her mum's hand.

Every visit, Tola's heart leapt at the thought that this time, maybe, her mum might remember her, that the deterioration would have stopped and, miraculously, it might have even reversed. But that was never to be. It was a dream to think that it could. The reality was that Tola and the rest of her family had slowly lost their mum. Little pieces here and there had gone missing, never to be found again. It was a cruel journey to be part of.

Grace looked at her daughter unknowingly, her watery eyes searching for something she couldn't place. The lady in front of her looked nice enough, so Grace patted her hand in return, a signal that it was okay for Tola to stay and keep her company.

Tola smiled and shook her sadness off to focus on her visit. She tried hard not to be upset or cry while with her mum; she wanted it to be as positive as it could be, for both of them.

Tola took out the book she'd been reading for the past few days. It was a tale of romance and intrigue, set during the Second World War. Not the sort of story Tola liked reading, but her mum used to love them, and there was a particular author she had always liked, so Tola had bought a few to bring on her visits. As she began on the page where she'd left off, her mum seemed to settle into her chair as if she were ready for the rest of the story.

***

Jen had slept relatively well, despite still being dissatisfied with the outcome of the meeting with Tola the day before. She'd gone from wanting Helen to come back as quickly as possible to dreading the moment she returned, if she did at all. Her mum had not been back since either, which was preying on her mind. If Jacqui being around was connected to Helen, then what would happen if she was found? Not that it was likely now.

Laura had said not to get in a muddle, and Jen was trying very hard to follow that advice. She decided to focus on one thing: getting on with some work. If Helen showed up, then she'd handle it when it happened.

Jen prepared for her next meeting and had a quick scoot through her phone. She was determined to be quicker off the mark when Laura next messaged. There was nothing so far today, but then, their fairly serious conversation the night before was probably enough for a couple of days. She'd hoped, too, that Detective Obederin might have had a change of heart and maybe sent an email or tried to call, but no such luck. Jen felt that ship had definitely sailed.

Seeing the time, she logged into her meeting and made small talk as the rest of her team appeared, one by one, on the screen in front of her. She had had to set herself up a mini-office in the spare room. There was a good view out of the front window, overlooking the street, and she had managed to organise her workspace into something resembling functional. A few old books she used to read as a teenager were on the shelves, along with some ornaments she used to have in her bedroom. She was happy to keep them around; they gave the room a sense of nostalgia.

A couple of minutes passed as she waited for the final few people to settle themselves, then the meeting started. It was a quarterly catch-up, so Jen was fully prepared for a long stint at her laptop. She knew that she had at least twenty minutes of figures to survive before anything remotely interesting got discussed.

Various slides appeared in front of her from someone's shared screen. Whilst trying to digest the latest numbers, from behind her, through the open door and travelling up the stairs as if on some invisible wind, Jen began to hear a faint but familiar tune.

Oh, not now, surely? she thought, seeing her own face on the screen and trying to keep it straight.

'You are my sunshines, my only sunshines…' Helen's sorrowful voice was unmistakable.

What am I going to do? She knew she really ought to stay in the meeting, and anyway, she had no idea what she was going to say to Helen now—there was no help coming from Tola. If her mum had also arrived, then she'd need time to explain what had happened when the detective had visited.

'Oh, you're in one of those meetings. Helen's downstairs.'

Jacqui had appeared next to Jen and made her jump. Thankfully, none of Jen's colleagues had noticed as their eyes were on the slides. Jen checked she was on mute, then turned her camera off; she hadn't seen her mum on the screen, so the camera clearly didn't know she was there, but seeing Jen talking to an empty space might grab someone's attention away from the monotonous deck they were all having to read.

'Blimey, Mum, any chance of a warning next time?' Jen pushed her chair back from the desk.

'Sorry, dear, you know I can't always decide where I come in. You know she's down there again, singing?'

'Yes, I heard her before you got here. But I can't just leave this call, I need to get back up to speed with everything. There's also loads I need to catch you up on, but the long and short of it is: Detective Obederin didn't believe me whatsoever; we're on our own.' Jen couldn't hide her disappointment.

'Oh, Jen, I'm sure you did your best. You always do. How about you stay here and finish your meeting? I'll try to keep Helen here for as long as possible.' Jacqui sounded positive despite what Jen had told her.

'But what more can we do, Mum? I don't think we'll get anything more out of her without extra help.'

Jacqui was surprised to see her daughter so defeated. 'Now, that's not the attitude. We'll think of something, I am sure of it.'

Jen was wholly unconvinced but had no argument against her mum keeping Helen occupied for a bit.

As Jacqui left the room, Jen pushed the door shut a bit more to drown out the noise. She put her video back on but left herself on mute, just in case, somehow, people thought she had nursery rhymes on in the background.

***

Tola had been reading for nearly an hour, with intermittent breaks to talk about something in the garden or to recall where Grace's dad used to live. Grace always talked about her dad, a single point in a history she had otherwise all but forgotten. She had his address written down on bits of paper in her room; she asked regularly if Tola had ever been to his house, which she hadn't, and if she had met him, which she also hadn't as he had died before Tola had been born. The questions Grace asked were always the same, and the answers Tola gave were always the same. It was a routine that both of them performed on most visits, one knowing the steps and the other not realising it had all happened before.

As Tola was nearing the end of another chapter, there was a knock on the door.

'Good morning, Grace. How are you today? It's just me, Louise.' Grace's carer motioned a wave to Tola with her gloved hand. 'I see you have a visitor, which is always special.' She moved round the room calmly, plumping up Grace's pillows and tidying her sheets. She took the empty cup and plate out to a trolley in the corridor then came back in to check for anything else that might be out of its place. 'The singing group is about to start, Grace. Would you like to join it today?' she asked.

'Yes, I think so,' Grace replied quickly.

Tola was surprised to hear her mum respond at all, let alone as fast as she did.

Louise held her arm out to help Grace lift herself from her chair. 'Let me help you there, Grace.' Then, turning to Tola, she explained, 'They've all been enjoying it, sitting together and singing some of their favourite tunes. Sorry, I should have asked if you were done with your book first.'

Tola had already marked the page and popped the book back into her bag; she was glad her mum had other things to occupy her time. She knew there were activities happening every day, but to know her mum participated in at least this one made her a little happier.

'I was pretty much done anyway,' Tola said. 'And I'd rather she was enjoying herself out of her room for a bit.'

'You're welcome to stay and join in if you have time,' Louise said as she guided Grace into the corridor towards the seating area in the conservatory.

Tola checked the time on her phone; she had enough time before she needed to leave for lunch, so followed Louise and her mum to where more residents were getting seated and took a seat herself. One of the care assistants turned on a speaker and queued some music up on her phone.

As the first notes sounded out from 'Somewhere Over the Rainbow', Tola found herself swaying side to side. It turned out that it was musicals that morning.

Having become lost for a little while in the song and enjoyed the twinkle it brought to the eyes of the residents involved, Tola excused herself and went over to say goodbye to her mum. She gave her a kiss on the cheek and said she'd be back in soon.

At that moment, Grace took hold of Tola's arm and beckoned for her to come closer. This was very unusual; Grace normally barely acknowledged when Tola or her husband left.

Her voice had become much softer in recent months, so Tola needed to lean in to hear what she was saying over the hubbub of the other residents. Grace's whispered words were unexpected, to say the least.

Tola gave her mum a tender hug and made her way out to the car. She sat there for a few moments, pretending that she was waiting for the heating to warm up, but really trying to understand what her mum had just said and how it was at all possible.

'Helen has been singing on her own for too long; she wants to go home.'

CHAPTER 22

Jen's meeting overran by fifteen minutes and it was evident on the faces of all her colleagues that it was fifteen minutes too many. Logging off, she listened out for any sounds but could hear nothing from downstairs.

Hoping that Helen was gone, Jen went down into the kitchen. To her dismay, she was still there. At least her mum was also still around.

'You could look a bit more happy, Jen; I'm pretty pleased with myself.' Jacqui was standing by the back door, looking content for having managed to keep Helen there on her own for all that time.

Jen poured herself some juice from the fridge. 'It's impressive, Mum, sorry. I just don't know what we can say to her anymore that's going to be of any help. How did you get her to be quiet?'

'I just hummed the tune along with her for a bit then, when she stopped, I told her a few stories from when you were small. Like that time you kept looking down the garden hose, and we told you so many times not to touch it, so your dad turned it on and you got soaked. Then the one where you and your dad got stuck on those rocks in Cornwall, and the tide was coming in, and I'd told him not to take you out so far.

'She seems to have liked listening to me. It's been nice, a bit like having a friend to chat to again. A quiet one, mind you. She replied once or twice, but more to check I was still here, I think.'

Jen hadn't thought about her mum not having anyone else to talk to anymore. It was just Jen. Helen was the only other person who could hear Jacqui, and it must have made a pleasant change of late to have someone listen to her just recall old stories.

Jen put her glass down in the sink, and the noise made Helen turn her head.

'Is there someone there?'

'It's okay, Helen. It's Jen. I've just come in.'

'I want to go now. It's so dark here,' Helen said hopefully.

Jen sighed heavily. She had to be honest with her. 'Helen, unless you can explain to us what happened to you, we're…' She stopped. It was horrible, having to break this to her.

'We're not going to be able to find you.' Jacqui completed the sentence for her daughter.

'But… I don't understand. You're here, I can hear you. I just can't work out where you are.' Helen was utterly confused.

Jen rubbed her face in frustration and tried to exercise the much-needed patience the situation required. She was struggling, and her mum could see it.

Jacqui took control. 'Helen, I'm sorry if this comes as a shock but, after you left with the man to look for Pip, you didn't come back.'

Jen had got herself into a bit of a cul-de-sac with it all and needed her mum to take the lead. Jacqui knew she should have done more the first time Helen came to her; now she had another chance. Although, she didn't know how long either she or Helen had left to try—neither of them had time to skirt round the elephant in the room anymore.

'Helen,' Jacqui continued, 'we're certain you died. Probably were killed. And no one knows where you currently are. You have been missing, presumed dead, for thirty years. Your children still have hope of finding you, and the police have recently launched an appeal for new information. We think the timing of it is why you're back here with us. I'm very, very sorry this had to happen to you, but this is how it is.' Jacqui crossed her arms.

It was harsh but it was the truth. Jacqui knew what it was like to die suddenly. Unexpectedly. To be taken away from the ones you love intensely. Different circumstances—a far more shocking experience for Helen—but Jacqui felt she had to know the truth. Avoiding the reality was doing her no good.

Jen had been watching Helen as Jacqui spoke. Her expression went from confused to anguished, then to abject horror, as if something was trying to push its way into the forefront of her mind. Then a stillness rested upon her face.

Jen and Jacqui's eyes met, waiting.

***

Tola thoroughly enjoyed her lunch with her friends, despite having her mum's parting words bouncing around in her head. Was it another coincidence or was something—she didn't know what—trying to get her attention?

Her mind was providing argument and counterargument. *It has to be a coincidence. Over the years, Mum must have read about Helen's case in the news and knew I was working on it. Her brain was misfiring and plucked Helen's name from the recesses of her memory…*

But she's never mentioned Helen before, and we have no relatives called Helen that I know of. There are not even any nurses called Helen that I've met or who've looked after her…

And why mention Helen singing on her own? The only person who has mentioned anything about Helen singing is Jennifer Hattley. There's no way Mum could have known that…

It's just another pattern your brain is creating that isn't really there. They'd just finished a song in the singing group, so singing was obviously on Mum's mind. Couple that with a name plucked from the obscurity of her memory, and you have a random sentence…

But the whole sentence has context. Helen was allegedly singing on her own and, in all likelihood, did want to come home. How could Mum's memories have conjured that up?

The debate continued churning around Tola's head in the supermarket, and later as she cooked.

Sitting down to eat, Samuel knew that his wife had something on her mind; he could always tell. 'You've been quiet since you came home. Was everything okay today with your mum?' he asked between mouthfuls. His wife always had something to chat about, especially when she'd been with her friends, so it was odd that she hadn't said much.

Tola placed her fork down and took a sip of water. She never discussed work at home, let alone over the dinner table. It was an unwritten rule she'd created for them both. But she needed his help and didn't know many other people who gave better advice.

'Mum's fine,' she said. 'I sat in on their singing group today; it was lovely to see her joining in and enjoying the music. I don't think I've seen her smile like that for some time, you know.'

'Good, good. And lunch? The girls are all doing well?' He was working through the day's events; maybe one of the girls had had bad news to tell.

'They're all very well. Diane has another cruise booked for near Christmas.'

Samuel nearly choked on his food. 'That's her third one this year, isn't it? I'll never know where they get all their money from.'

Tola had to laugh.

'So, if the day went so well, where have you been—in here?' Samuel pointed to his temple. 'There seems to have been some deep thinking going on while this was being made—it's very good, by the way.'

Tola laid it all out: her visit to Jennifer Hattley, the way she'd dismissed what she said, how strongly her father had spoken up for her and Jennifer's last attempt to change her mind, telling her about the song Helen was always singing. Then, the visit with her mum and those words that had been haunting her since.

'So,' she continued, 'I am now left with a decision. Do I actually ask the Swift children about this song? I mean, they're grown adults now, they might not even remember. And how do I justify asking about something I ought to know nothing about? It's not professional. I could seriously compromise all the work we've done so far. What if I upset the family? It's just nonsense, isn't it? But what if their mum did sing them this song? Would that mean Jennifer is really talking to the spirit of Helen Swift? It's too incredible to believe, surely?'

Samuel listened to all of it with his hands clasped and elbows on the table. He didn't interrupt, not even to continue eating, until Tola had finished. He made a noise, signifying that he was considering everything she had said, and allowing him time to clear his plate.

Cutlery down, he reached across the table and took her hand. 'You'll do the right thing; you always do, Tola. Whatever you choose to do, it's going to work out, because you'll make sure it does. I believe in you, I always have. Anyway, I think you've already decided what you're going to do. You'll do it with care—you don't know any other way.' With that, he collected the plates up and went to wash up.

Tola sat there, relieved. He was right. She'd decided after her mum had spoken to her what she was going to do; she'd just needed to sound it out with someone.

'And if you're going to ask them,' Samuel called from the kitchen, 'do it before you go to bed, Tola. You know you won't sleep otherwise.'

Tola smiled. He knew her so well.

'I won't take long.'

She went upstairs to the study and looked up Matthew Swift's phone number; she'd try him first. Both of the Swift children had been in her phone for years. She always hoped that one day, wherever she was, she could make the call telling them what they had been waiting for. She checked the time; hopefully it wasn't too late.

Mathew answered, and she could hear excited children in the background.

'Hi, Matthew, it's Detective Obederin. Nothing new, I am afraid. I hope it's okay to speak, though?' She always let Helen's children know straight away if there was no new news; she didn't want to lead them on.

'Oh, hi, Tola. Sorry for the noise. It's my nephew's eleventh birthday. It's all got a bit crazy!' Matthew spoke to her like an old friend; they had known each other for well over a decade.

'Wish him a happy birthday from me. Does that mean Emily is there with you? I just wanted to ask you both something. It's nothing important and can wait if you're busy. Just something I want to tie up from a witness statement.'

'Yes, she's here. Em! It's the detective on the phone. Come here and I'll put us on loudspeaker.'

Tola couldn't believe her luck that both siblings were together.

Matthew moved into another room and the din from the children subsided.

'Hi, Tola, I'm away from the madhouse,' Emily said.

They both sounded so happy, Tola didn't want to spoil the mood, but she had to get this question out the way. 'So, as I said, nothing new to report. I just wanted to check something that a witness mentioned, if that's okay? It doesn't tell us anything about what happened, but it will help me corroborate the statement.'

Both Emily and Matthew agreed it was fine, so Tola continued.

'Okay, an odd question, I know, but was there a song that your mum used to sing to you both? Something she might have hummed or sung to herself when out walking, perhaps?'

All Tola could hear was the muffled sound of boys playing.

'Erm, nothing is springing to mind,' Matthew said. 'Did someone say they heard Mum singing in the woods?'

'Well, humming or singing was what they said.' Tola crossed her fingers for the fib. She felt a bit bad, making the witness up, but there was no other reason to be asking about it—although she could argue that Jennifer was the witness, but she'd rather avoid that.

Emily had been quiet, and Tola heard Matthew ask her if she was okay.

'Sorry, Tola, I went a bit funny there,' Emily said. 'I'd forgotten all about it until you just said. Matthew is a bit crap at remembering things like this, but Mum did sing a song to us both, ever since we were really small. Gran told me she would sing it to Matthew when it was just him, then she changed it after I came along. I can't believe you don't remember, Matthew—especially at bathtimes, she was always singing it.

'Oh, wait, yes. We'd be singing it, too, by the time we got into bed. How did it go?'

Matthew started to attempt the tune, but Emily beat him to it. 'It was, hang on, let me get it right. *You are my sunshines, my only sunshines, you make me happy, when skies are grey.* That one. Oh, that's made me quite teary, sorry.'

'Oh, Emily,' Tola said. 'I hope I haven't upset you on your son's birthday.'

'No, no, it's a lovely thing to remember, thank you. Was that all it was, Tola?'

Tola assured them that was all she needed and apologised for the call during the celebrations. She ended the call and looked at her phone for a moment, astounded by what she'd just heard.

Downstairs, she sat next to Samuel on the sofa.

'So, did you get the answer you needed?' he asked.

'I think I did.'

CHAPTER 23

Jen and Jacqui had retreated to the lounge; Helen had retreated into her song, having ignored everything Jacqui had said to her. Helen was in complete denial of the situation, which Jen felt was fair enough given what likely happened to her, but it didn't help them get any further forward, and they didn't know how to break her out of it.

Jacqui could feel her daughter's enthusiasm for her new abilities had waned. 'This is probably the hardest visitor you'll ever have, Jen. Please don't think they are all going to be like this. It's extraordinary what you can do and, even more so, what you are trying to do for Helen.'

'It's not enough, though, is it? I can't get her back to her family, and the person who did this is just living life somewhere—not having to answer for their crime, not having to face any consequences for what they did to her or the grief they put onto her kids. It's not fair that they get away with it; it's not fair that Helen is stuck out there, in the dark, on her own. What's the point of me being able to see these people if I can't help her?' Jen started to cry. She was upset for Helen and angry at the injustice of it all, but she was also crying for herself. It was all finally beginning to come out. 'It isn't fair that you died already. It isn't fair that I can't see you when I want to anymore, or give you a hug, or cuddle into you when I watch television. Nothing about any of this is fair, and I hate it, Mum. I hate it.'

Jacqui sat right next to Jen. It was as close as she could get, and she wished Jen could feel her warmth like she used to.

'You're so much braver than me,' Jacqui said. 'You know that? And your nan. We both kept all this as under wraps as we could. Confined it to our homes, made sure no one saw anything—except your dad, of course. But you? Straight away you're talking to Aunt Joan in a supermarket car park, you're driving to a stranger's house to deliver a message, then you tell a detective on one of the country's longest missing-persons cases that you're talking to their victim's ghost. All because you feel it's your responsibility to do it. You've not stopped to worry about how it makes you look to the outside world. You're like Elizabeth, wanting to experience it all and explore. You're fearless, Jen. I am so proud of you.'

Jen took a breath and wiped the tears from her face. 'I don't feel brave right now. And I'm not fearless, I think I'm just scared of different things. Like, I was scared that David's family wouldn't listen to me for *his* sake, not that they would think I was a weirdo. I'm scared that I have failed Helen and her kids because I can't get her to communicate with me. I'm a little scared that Laura will look at me differently when I tell her about all of this.

'But you're brave, too. You avoided Helen before to protect all of us; this time you've put that fear aside and you've been brilliant. Look at you in there, telling her what she needed to know. I'm proud of you, too.'

'We're both pretty great, I think,' Jacqui said. 'I think they know that you're open to them, Jen. The ghosts. Your visitors, it feels like they know you can be approached, that you won't dismiss or ignore them, that you'll try to assist them as best you can. I never had anyone appear to me outside, like you have. I think you're going to be a bit busier than I was.'

Jen wasn't sure how she felt about that. She'd help anyone she came across, that she knew. But juggling it with normal life? She was going to have to work that one out. She had visions of visitors popping into work meetings or on packed commuter trains on the way home.

'I hadn't thought of it like that,' Jen said. 'Are ghosts telling other ghosts about me? What if loads of them start turning up?'

Jacqui had to laugh. 'What, like they're leaving a review of you somewhere for other ghosts to look at? I have no idea. I certainly haven't been chatting with other ghosts; I just hear from you and Helen.'

Jacqui wondered if somehow word was getting around about her daughter. Like Jen's skills were being advertised somewhere, or if the fact she was so open meant they could find her more easily to ask for her help. It really was a mystery.

'Talking of Helen, I can't hear anything.' Jen got up from the sofa to look in the kitchen and came back downcast, her heart quickly filling with dread. What did this mean for her mum? 'Have you noticed that you're only appearing when Helen is here? What if we've pushed her too far and she doesn't come back? Will you not be back anymore either?'

Jacqui hadn't wanted to bring the subject up, but the connection hadn't been lost on her.
'I haven't really wanted to think about it, Jen. I don't know which time is going to be the last time, but then, that's not much different from actual life, is it?'

Jen could feel herself getting upset again. Her grief had been on hold—her mum's visits had kept it at bay, under the surface, like a monster hiding in the deep, waiting to unleash itself when the moment demanded it. She knew it would be all-consuming, and she could feel it starting to seep up through the cracks. Her mum had said she was fearless, but the idea of finally losing her entirely scared Jen completely.

'Look, I can't promise when I will be here. But whatever borrowed time we have left, Jen, let's just make the most of it, as the cliché goes. We were pretty good at doing that when I was alive, weren't we? No need to change now.

'All this talk about dead people, it's too morbid anyway,' Jacqui continued, trying to lift Jen's mood. 'Tell me about something else that's been happening. I'll stay for as long as I can, I can promise you that.'

Jen inhaled deeply and pushed the monster back down into the depths. Her dad had suggested some new paint colours for the dining room and lounge, a topic she knew her mum would have an opinion on.

***

Jacqui stayed through it getting dark, through cooking dinner and watching TV. Jen felt herself getting tired but she willed her eyes to stay open. If she fell asleep, her mum would be gone, and that could be it. Forever. She felt sure of it.

But she couldn't stay awake, despite her desperate attempts.

'Jen, time for bed, come on.'

Jen began to lose control again as she walked up the stairs and got changed. Feelings she'd had when her nan died, that realisation that she could never see her again—it felt like that, but much worse.

'Can you stay until I've gone to sleep, please, Mum.' Jen couldn't control her tears. 'Oh God, I don't want to go to sleep. I don't want to wake up and you be totally gone.'

Jacqui motioned for Jen to get into bed and pull the covers over herself. She couldn't bear to see her daughter suffering like this. 'I understand now why we're not meant to stay,' Jacqui whispered. 'Watching you like this, it's breaking my heart, and there's nothing I can do about it.' She'd known heartache when she lost her own mum, but this was so much more excruciating. Nothing made this part of life easy. It just had to be endured. 'I'll stay here until you fall asleep. I love you so much, Jen. I always will and nothing will ever be able to change that. Shhh, now. You are so tired. I'm here.'

Jen sobbed with her eyes closed, frightened to open them in case her mum had already gone. After not too long, her tears subsided and she became quiet, her breathing softening and slowing as she drifted into sleep.

Jacqui sat on the bed, keeping watch over her daughter for as long as she was able to. She was sure she could hear soft paws, padding up the stairs, then the slump of a tired dog, resting on the landing.

Then Jacqui was gone.

CHAPTER 24

Tola pulled her coat on and picked up a few files. She had thought about calling ahead, but something in her wanted to give as little warning as she could when visiting Jennifer Hattley again. She still couldn't quite believe she was taking this all seriously, but the facts were clear: the Swift children had been sung the same song that Jennifer claimed Helen was singing, and Tola had no idea how Jennifer could possibly have known it. If it was all made up, then she wanted to catch Jennifer out, see how she did it, like discovering how a magician pulled off her trick.

'Interviewing a ghost, eh? This is a new one for Detective Obederin,' Samuel said as he handed Tola's bag to her.

'Oh, stop it. It's probably still a load of nonsense.'

'If you truly believed that, you wouldn't be going back.'

Tola tutted and gave her husband a kiss goodbye. 'I will call you when I'm done, then head back to the office.'

She scraped the morning frost from the windows as the car warmed up, her fingertips becoming numb before she'd got all the way round. It made sending a message to Jennifer a bit more challenging. She wrote a short sentence to say she was going to stop by before trekking back to the office, keeping it as vague as possible.

***

Jen was sure she could feel a warm body on her feet as she woke up. It felt just the same as when she still lived with her mum and dad, when Bailey would sneak into her room if he was cold and nestle around her legs.

It had been a brief respite from how she now felt. Her eyes were sore from the tears she'd cried before going to sleep and tears she'd cried after waking up. She felt utterly alone. She knew she wasn't—she had her dad, Laura and her other family and friends—but the feeling remained.

Getting up felt like a waste of time, she was completely unmotivated to do anything. She reached over to the bedside table for her phone but then remembered she'd left it downstairs. She couldn't even be bothered to go and get it at that moment.

The house was too quiet, and she didn't like it. It made it all worse. She lay there just concentrating on not crying; it was all she could do. The monster had risen from its deep slumber; the grief she'd suppressed was taking over.

From out of the soundlessness, Jen heard footsteps, which seemed to be approaching her front door. She waited for the postman to drop the post through the letterbox—then had the fright of her life when the doorbell rang. She hadn't ordered anything lately that needed a signature or was too big to be posted.

She didn't want to talk to anyone. They could come back another time.

Jen closed her eyes.

***

After a minute, Tola began to wonder if Jen was in. But the car on the driveway and the closed curtains suggested she must be.

She rang the doorbell again. She had to speak with Jen. She didn't want to wait and come back later.

***

On the second ring, Jen got straight out of bed, not stopping for her dressing gown. Whoever it was needed to leave her alone; she was in no mood for chit-chat.

'Why can't the parcel just be left on the doorstep, like they normally do?' she muttered as she unlocked the door to find Detective Obederin looking at her.

'Oh, I do apologise, Miss Hattley. Have I woken you up?' Tola said, thinking it wasn't that early, but not everyone got up at the same time she did.

Jen looked dishevelled. Her eyes were puffy and she was in her pyjamas. She was also in shock, as Tola was the last person she'd expected to see at her front door.

She began to panic. 'Am I in trouble about the other day? Or is my dad? He really didn't mean to be rude—'

'No, no, Miss Hattley. I've come to see you because, well, I've had cause to change my opinion about what you told me. May I come in?'

Jen was floored. She stepped aside so Tola could come in, and closed the door.

'Shall I go into the lounge again?' Tola asked.

'Yes, sorry, you've caught me off guard. I don't normally answer the door like this.' Jen crossed her arms, feeling exposed. 'I should go and get dressed quickly. Are you okay here for a moment?'

Tola nodded and started to unpack her laptop.

Jen ran up the stairs two at a time, brushed her teeth quickly and threw on the first pair of jeans and jumper she came across.

As she walked back down, she paused by the picture of her, her mum and her nan. 'I wish you could all be here to help me,' she whispered. Jen was ecstatic that Tola had returned, but it was too late. Helen wasn't coming back.

'Right, sorry about that. Can I get you a drink? I definitely need one.' Jen was parched, her face particularly felt like it was lacking in moisture.

'Yes, a glass of water will be fine. I'll come out with you.'

Tola followed Jen into the kitchen and waited while she put the kettle on.

'I think I owe you an apology, Miss Hattley. You were right, Helen Swift used to sing 'You Are My Sunshines' to her children. Often. Her daughter remembered it quite clearly. If you were right about that then I have to ask myself what else you might be right about. So, I have no other choice—at the moment—but to believe you.'

Jen felt vindicated; the truth had found its way out. Her dad would be over the moon when she told him. But the thrill of being believed was trodden over—they'd scared Helen away and the detective was too late.

The kettle clicked, but Jen did not move to make herself a drink. Her teardrops fell onto the countertop. How she had any left, she'd never know.

She turned to face Tola. 'I am really sorry, but they're gone. They're both gone, and I don't think they're coming back.'

Tola was used to witnesses becoming upset, but she hadn't expected Jen to be this distraught.

'My dear, what on earth has happened? It's going to be okay, whatever it is.'

Tola could see Jen was bereft. Normally she'd give someone a pat on the back or, at most, an arm round the shoulder, but a mother's instinct kicked in and she put both her arms around Jen in a strong, reassuring cuddle.

Jen thought her legs might fall from underneath her. It felt so good to be held like that. She hadn't known how much she needed it.

'We tried to talk to Helen again yesterday, but we messed it up. We thought she needed to know she was dead, that it might jolt her into telling us more. But she just ignored us and escaped back into her song.'

'Is this you and your dad?' Tola kept hold of Jen, she could tell she wanted the comfort.

Jen sniffed. She didn't want to tell lies. 'You're going to think I've lost it. It was my mum and I.' Jen released her hold on Tola and stepped back. 'My mum comes back when Helen does. It's a long story… Mum saw her before, when she was alive and had the gift.'

Tola was in unchartered territory. *There's more than one ghost involved? Should I call them ghosts?* She couldn't think of a better word.

She decided hitting the reset button on their conversation might help both of them. 'Okay. How about you finish making yourself that tea and we go sit down? Then, you can start from wherever the beginning really is. I also think we might need some biscuits, if you have them.'

Jen agreed and brought their drinks into the lounge along with a packet of biscuits.

She handed a plate to Tola. 'Mum hates crumbs. Hat*ed* crumbs. You know what I mean.'

Tola took the plate and a biscuit from the packet. Her laptop was currently on the floor next to her chair; she reckoned that settling in to listen to Jen's entire story first, before taking any notes, might be wise. She'd have to consider what to commit to record and what to omit.

Jen took a sip of her tea and placed the cup between her hands on her lap.

'In your own time, Miss Hattley—sorry, Jen.'

Jen decided that she had to go all the way back. For some reason, telling everything to Tola felt like the right thing to do, and it felt good to explain it to someone other than her dad. She got the notebooks to show the detective; she described the moment she realised her mum had died and how she'd then begun to see the spirits of dead people; she talked about Aunt Joan and David, then brought Tola up to speed with what had happened with Helen. She laid all of it out bare to be scrutinised by this relative stranger. It made her wonder why she had ever worried about telling Laura. Laura was more likely to believe this crazy tale than anyone else she knew, because Laura would believe Jen was telling her the truth no matter what.

Tola had paid attention throughout. Jen's account of what had happened to her over the past few weeks was, by any measure, impossible. She must be having a mental health breakdown due to losing her mother; there was no other explanation. Except, there was:

that everything Jen had just said was the absolute truth.

Tola knew when she was being lied to; it was her job to know. She could recognise deceit in a face, a mannerism, a tone of voice. She couldn't see or hear any of it in Jen.

'Firstly,' Tola said, 'if I didn't believe you, I'd be recommending you for professional help, Jen. You have to know that what you have just told me is beyond belief?'

Jen felt an uneasiness in her stomach; she wasn't sure which way this was going.

'But—and it goes against so much of how I have lived my life up until now—I do believe everything you have told me. You have been through so much, Jen; more than anyone else who loses a parent. You've taken on board so much in a short space of time. I am now not surprised by how upset you've been since I got here. I'd be petrified if it was happening to me.'

Jen visibly breathed a sigh of relief. 'I cannot tell you how amazing it feels to know you believe me and that you get what I am saying. I thought I was coping with it all okay, but clearly not. I've been silly and not told my best friend; she probably could have helped me deal with it better. You came round just at the right time; I needed to tell someone. Thank you.' Jen paused so Tola could absorb just how grateful she was for her visit. 'As for Helen, I think you're too late. She's been coming and going for about two weeks now. I don't know if she has a time limit, but considering the condition she was in yesterday… I'm so disappointed. I think you really could have made a difference. I wouldn't bet on her being back.'

'It's a good job you were never much of a gambler then, isn't it?'

Jen's head spun round to the lounge doorway. Tola could sense something had shifted around them but could see nothing where Jen was staring.

Jacqui smiled. 'We never know which time is going to be the last time, but it wasn't last night.'

CHAPTER 25

Jen leapt up and headed straight to the kitchen to find Helen standing still, as always, but quiet for the time being. She then looked back at her mum and returned her smile.

'Tola, they're back. My mum and Helen.'

Tola came into the kitchen to see nothing different from when she'd left it. It was her and Jen; she couldn't see or hear anyone else.

'Is this who I think it is?' Jacqui said, surprised, watching Tola looking around the kitchen. 'Why did she come back?'

'She had a change of mind, Mum, thankfully. Tola's going to help us.' Jen realised another introduction was needed; she didn't want Helen getting spooked. 'Helen, it's Jen and Jacqui. Thanks for coming back to us. We have another lady here to help. Her name is Detective Tola Obederin.' Jen signalled to Tola to say hello.

'Hello, Helen.' Tola tried to sound less ridiculous than she felt.

Jen could feel it though. 'Sorry, Tola, you've only got my word for it that they're even here. Are you really okay with all this?'

'I'll have to be! What else can we do?' Tola shrugged.

Tola believed Jen, but standing in the kitchen with Jen's deceased mum and the woman she'd been searching for for years was taking more than a few minutes to get her head round. She did feel a bit awkward; there was nothing in the police handbook for a situation like this. But it could be her chance to finally find Helen.

Jen looked to her mum, then back at Helen, who seemed to be listening but not ready to respond, then back to Tola. 'Oh blimey,' Jen said. 'I'm going to be playing go-between here. You can't hear Mum or Helen, can you? I hadn't thought of that until now.'

Tola put her professional hat on and went back into the lounge for her laptop. 'This is no different to when I have someone in for an interview who cannot speak English. I have an interpreter, and I have no choice but to trust that what they are telling me is verbatim. That means that you'll need to relay everything Helen is telling you to me, word for word. It sounds easier than it is, Jen. You can't paraphrase or miss anything; it needs to be her words exactly. Can you do it?'

A strange excitement began to take hold of Tola. Fifteen years she had been on this case. Could she really be on the edge of finding out something new, something crucial that could lead her to a victim she had been searching so long for?

Jen's heart was pumping faster. Moments ago, all seemed lost, yet here they all were, four women together, trying to solve the mystery. 'I can do it. But the minute we start asking anything, she'll get upset. Mum and I have tried a few times.'

'Can Helen hear me?' Tola asked, already considering how she could best handle this unique eyewitness interview.

Jen looked to Helen. 'Helen, can you hear Detective Obederin? It's important that we know you can hear her okay.'

Helen's head turned toward Jen. 'Yes, I can hear her.'

Having checked with Jen where Helen was supposedly standing, Tola took up a position by one of the kitchen counters.

She considered her words for a moment.

'Helen, as you know, I'm a detective. I work for Sussex Police, and for the last fifteen years, I've been looking after your case. You went missing around thirty years ago. I know Jacqui has explained this to you before and, understandably, you're struggling to accept what has happened. Today, I'd like you to go back for me and explain how you went missing. Hopefully, we'll be able to work out where you are and bring you home.'

'I don't know. I don't want to remember…' Helen's face turned pensive.

Jen looked over at Tola, trying to warn her that this could be the start of Helen drawing back again, but Tola remained focused.

'Helen, I know it's frightening, but now is the time to face what was done to you. Jen, Jacqui and I are here, and we won't leave you. You are safe with us; no one can harm you now. It's a memory, a painful one, but without this information, I cannot get you back to Emily and Matthew.'

Jen noticed a spark in Helen's eyes, a recollection of something happy and full of light. Nothing like the darkness and fear she had been lost within.

'My babies… I have missed them so much. I couldn't get away. I couldn't get back to them.'

'They have missed you too, Helen. I speak to them regularly; they are wonderful people. You should be so very proud of them.'

Tola felt her eyes might well-up at the thought of Emily and Matthew. She felt duty-bound to them; she had since the start. She could not help the sadness she felt knowing how long they had yearned to know what happened to their mother. She swallowed the emotions down; she had to stay calm and level.

Jacqui looked at Jen and felt Helen's pain, wishing she could get back to her daughter. But it wasn't to be.

Helen was motionless for what seemed like an age.

This could go either way, Jen thought to herself.

Just as she began to think Helen would be lost to them forever, the ghost of the missing mother brought her hands in front of her and clasped them together.

Then, a resolute look came over her face. 'Okay, I will try.'

Tola's words seemed to have gotten through. Jen hadn't realised she'd been holding her breath, and on hearing Helen say she'd give it a go, breathed out louder than expected. Jacqui shot her a look, worried any interruption could derail Helen.

'That's good.' Tola opened a fresh page for her notes. 'We will go slowly, and if you need to stop for a moment, you just say. Helen, are you ready?'

Helen began to cast her mind back to the day she went missing, and Jen repeated her words to Tola:

'I took Pip for his usual walk around four o'clock, before it started to get dark. The kids stayed with my mum; it could be tricky taking them all out together, the kids and the dog, so I'd wait until she came home from work.

'I'd been walking for about twenty minutes when I noticed Pip wasn't behind me. I looked around for a while, called his name a lot, but he didn't come. I started to worry in case he'd gone down a badger or rabbit hole, like terriers do.

'A man approached me. He asked if I was looking for my dog and said he had found one running in the fields behind the woods. He told me he'd managed to catch it and shut it in his car, and he'd come back to the woods to see if he could find the owner. It was getting quite dark, but I could just make out his face. He looked familiar. I was sure I'd seen him round the woods before. I was so relieved he'd found Pip; the kids would have been so upset if I'd lost him. It wasn't until later that I remembered I had seen him walking in the woods before, but he'd never seemed to have a dog nearby.

'I followed him out of the back of the woods and across the field. I didn't usually walk up there; I always came in the front entrance, which most other dog walkers used. It had become much darker, and I wouldn't normally still be out walking, but I had to get Pip. The man had a torch and walked in front of me. I could see a car parked up ahead, where the field ended and met the road.

'Pip started barking when he saw the torch. He was going nuts. Scrabbling at the back window, he was frantic. The man stopped and held up the light for me… I walked past him to the car… I didn't think…' Helen's words started to fail her.

Jen could see her hands were clenched in fists, her nails digging into the skin of her palms, not that Helen would feel it. Jen looked at Tola and shook her head, Helen was getting close to panicking.

Tola held her hand up to Jen, a signal to pause. 'Helen,' Tola said. 'It's okay. Let's stop for a moment so you can gather your thoughts. We have lots of time.

There's no rush. You are doing so well. You are being incredibly brave. When you are ready, carry on telling Jen what happened.'

Jacqui had been quiet the whole time. She didn't want to interrupt and break the connectivity that Tola had created, so she observed silently, her arms folded across her stomach, thinking to herself, *Are we really going to get what we need out of this?*

Jen took the opportunity to get a glass of water for herself and Tola, as well as break out some paracetamol. The tension across her forehead was building, and she needed to maintain her concentration. She knew the worst bit was to come and was apprehensive about what she would have to repeat.

Glancing at Helen, Jen noticed she was about to resume:

'I felt a sharp pull… he had my hair in his hand and he… he… smacked my head down onto the roof's edge of the car. That's when I knew: this is all wrong. I couldn't open my eyes fully. I heard the car door open and Pip scrabbling out. He was snarling and growling, then I heard a yelp. My poor Pip.' Helen shook her head.

'Pip was okay, Helen,' Tola said to reassure her. 'Your brother found him. Your mum had called him to go look in the woods for you, when you didn't return home as planned.'

'Oh, I am so glad. The kids would have missed him so much.'

Jen watched Helen regain some composure, then gave a thumbs up to Tola.

'I felt his hands on me, pushing me into the car. I just couldn't fight him off, my head was hurting so much.

I felt blood on my face. I could tell he was tying my hands… my ankles. I knew I had to get back for Emily and Matthew, but I couldn't move. I tried to scream, and he slapped me. He said I had to stay lying down and be quiet, that he would let me go if I was quiet. I didn't believe him. He wasn't going to let me go.'

Tola paused her typing. 'Helen, stop there for now. No need to go further yet. Stay with us. Can you go back a little for me, before he hurt you? When the man let you walk in front of him, can you remember what colour the car was? I know it was probably dark by then, but he shone the light for you. Anything you can remember about that car would be extremely helpful. Really concentrate, Helen, please.'

Jen took a quick sip of water, anticipating when Helen might speak.

'The car was red. Pip was in the back… I was going to let him out… It had four doors, not a hatchback. There was a black trim round the side, in the middle of the doors. That's all I saw.'

'That's great, Helen. And what about the man? Can you tell us what he looked like or sounded like?'

'I couldn't make out much; it was dark. He was clean-shaven, he had a black hat on and his coat was done right up to his neck. He sounded posh, well spoken. He just seemed normal. I was so stupid to go with him.'

'You are not stupid, Helen,' Tola said. 'It sounds like he deliberately took Pip to make sure you followed him back to his car. None of this is your fault. Remember that, Helen. Okay, so you're in the car and you cannot get out. Can you tell us what happened next?'

'He drove us away from the woods. I was too scared to try and sit up, so I stayed down like he had told me to.

It didn't feel like we were in the car that long before he stopped.

'He opened the door nearest my feet. He dragged me out, then pushed me against the car to stand me up. I tried to scream again, and he punched me in the stomach—I don't want to do any more… please.'

'Helen, it's okay. Stop there for a moment. Stay by the car for me. What can you see?'

Helen's hands remained clasped in front of her; she was really trying to concentrate.

'It was very dark, there was only one streetlight on. There were no lights on in the houses, which I thought was odd as it wasn't really that late. Terraced houses, all in a row, like workers' cottages. I could tell there was no one inside any of them, no one who could help me. It was eerily deserted. I stood there, on the pavement, and could see at the other end of the road a postbox, and by that, a phone box.

'I couldn't believe it, he untied my feet, and I thought, if I can just kick him and run to that phone box and dial nine-nine-nine, I'll be safe! But I didn't realise until then that he had a knife. He saw me looking at the phone box and he said he'd hurt me if I screamed or didn't go where he wanted.

'He started making me move towards the house at the very end—I, I want to stop now… I can't.'

Jen and Jacqui knew what was coming; Helen didn't want to go any further. Her eyes had glazed over and her hands were dropping to her side. She began to hum, ever so faintly.

'Tola, I think we've lost her,' Jen said. 'She's started to go back to her song.'

Jacqui had been on the sidelines the whole time. They had found out so much. They couldn't start all over again, not now. And she was feeling something else… She was becoming angry, enraged even. Listening to how Helen had been duped into following this man, how he had been so violent—and what was to come? They had to find her and, hopefully, find who did this to her—and make him pay.

'What was it that made Tola come back?' Jacqui asked Jen, who passed the question on.

Tola duly answered as though she were talking to Jacqui herself. 'It was the song. I asked Emily and Matthew about it, and their mum did sing it to them, the way you described: 'My only sunshines', changed to include both of them. It was a good way to get them in the bath and changed for bed. Amazing, isn't it? I had no idea how you could have made it up, so I had to believe you.'

Helen was two lines into the song, her hands by her sides. She was part singing, part sobbing, trying to forget what was so desperately needed to be remembered.

Jacqui stepped forward. She didn't know if it would work, or what compelled her to do it, but she stood beside Helen and slid her fingers into her hand, grasping it as tightly as she could. To her astonishment, she could feel Helen's hand in hers, could feel Helen squeezing back just as tightly.

Helen stopped singing and turned, knowing someone was there that she couldn't see.

'You used to sing that to your babies, Helen, didn't you?' Jacqui said. 'You used to get them ready for bed, all clean and ready for their pyjamas. And you would sing that to them, and they would feel safe and loved.

Can you see them?' Jacqui moved to face Helen and took her other hand. 'You hold that picture of them in your mind. You stay with them, warm and protected. Take us through the remaining part of what happened, Helen. Say the words to us, but in your mind, stay with them. Then, once it's over, you will never have to remember him or what he did ever again. You will only need to think of Emily and Matthew, your sunshines.'

Jen watched her mum in awe. She couldn't believe what she was seeing—which was saying something given the last couple of months. A ghost holding another ghost's hand, to comfort them and help them feel less alone. No rules.

'What's happening, Jen?' Tola was in the dark as to what was going on but could see that it was important based on Jen's face.

'I think Mum might be getting us over the final hurdle.'

'Helen,' Jacqui continued. 'Think of your sunshines and tell us how you died. We're all here and we will keep you from any more harm.'

Jacqui squeezed both of Helen's hands this time, and as if a switch had been flicked, Helen's eyes met with Jacqui's for the first time.

'Oh my God, I can see you,' Helen said, as shocked as any of them.

'Then you know that I won't leave you. Finish your story, Helen. It's time to come out of the dark and go home.'

Jen signalled to Tola to be ready. She felt this was going to be their last shot, somehow.

Helen focused on Jacqui for a moment, then closed her eyes. She was back at home, chasing Matthew up the stairs with Emily in her arms. She had the bath taps running, and bubbles were growing up from the water; she could hear the sound of the water splashing and gurgling as she closed the stair gate and put Emily down. She began to sing, and her children joined in with the bathtime chorus. She pulled them both in for a cuddle inside their towels. She could smell the tea tree oil she used to keep away the nits, and feel their soft skin against her cheeks. She would never leave this place with them; she would always be there.

'He pushed me towards the last house on the terrace and went to take me in through the front, but then seemed to change his mind. It had a blue, metal gate and a path that led up to the same blue front door, a brass door knocker. But no number. He marched me past the front window, down a side entrance. It was so quiet; there were no other cars.

'He had keys. He unlocked the back door and pushed me into the house. I tripped and hit my head on the floor as I couldn't put my hands out. Then, it was like he'd turned into a rabid animal. He was in a frenzy. I knew what he was going to do. I couldn't move with him on top of me. I couldn't fight him off. My ears were ringing and my head was pounding.

'Then, when he was finished, I couldn't breathe. His hands were over my face then round my neck. I desperately wanted to be back at home with the kids. But I knew there was no longer any hope and I was going to die in that house. No one was coming to save me. Then, there was nothing. Just the dark.'

With that, Helen opened her eyes and saw Jacqui smiling back at her.

Jacqui put her arms around Helen and held her close. 'You have been so brave. You can stop now. You don't have to think about him ever, ever again.'

Jen wiped tears from her cheeks and saw Tola do the same. They had both followed Helen into her harrowing final moments, and it had been draining. A calmness resonated around all four of them, as if the memory of what had happened to Helen had been expelled.

'I feel… changed,' Helen said. 'I feel like, maybe, I can leave now.' A look of contentment settled on her face for the first time since Jen had seen her. 'I'm glad I got to see you, Jacqui. I loved hearing about when Jen was little, and your stories. It was kind of you to stay and keep me company.'

Her grip on Jacqui's hands loosened. Jen watched them both and could see that Helen was not as solid as she was before. She was beginning to fade.

'Tola, Helen's disappearing,' Jen said. 'It's like we've freed her from wherever she was.'

Tola shut her laptop and came over to stand by Jen, putting an arm around her shoulders. 'Then we have done everything we can for her. All we have left is to find where she rests, if we're able. Thank you, Helen!' Tola said, feeling overwhelmed by what she had just witnessed, even though she hadn't actually seen anything at all. But she had felt it; it had been real.

'Goodbye, Helen.' Jen was sad that Helen had to leave, but she deserved to be at peace somewhere bright and with the memories of her children. Jen wondered if this was how her mum would finally depart, just fading away in front of her. And she wondered how much time they really had left together. She didn't expect it to be long.

Jacqui let go of Helen and stood back. 'Safe trip,' she whispered as Helen's image grew faint in front of her eyes. Then, she vanished completely.

Everyone stood still for a few moments, then Jacqui turned to Jen. 'So did anything she told us give us a lead on where she might be?'

'I don't know, Mum. Tola, did we get anything you can use?'

Tola motioned to go and sit in the lounge. It had been an exhausting morning.

Jen slumped back into the armchair, her headache fighting against the tablets she'd taken.

'I need to go back over what Helen said and cross-reference it with the other witness statements, see if anything corresponds,' Tola said. 'But I've read those files hundreds of times, and this man, he is new. His car, the terraced houses, it's all new. I should be able to plot her exit from the woods on older maps, the newer ones show a housing estate that was built behind the woods about a decade after Helen went missing, so the land-scape is very different now.

'But I need to set your expectations. I have no names, no car make or registration; I don't know the road name she was taken to or really how long she was in the car; I don't have the man's name or much of a description of his appearance. If I can find her, it's cer-tainly not going to be much easier than it was before.'

'We made her go through all that, and it still might not be enough? It's just not fair, is it?' Jen was not hap-py, but she wasn't surprised. She'd been able to tell, as Tola had been taking her notes and by what Helen was saying, that there were no specifics. There was no single detail that pointed in one direction or another.

'But we have achieved one thing,' Jacqui interjected. 'Helen is free. She isn't trapped in the darkness anymore; she isn't waiting for us to find her. That's something.'

Jen shared Jacqui's thoughts and added her own. 'But her children, they are still waiting for her to be found. We've got to give them the closure they deserve.'

Tola began to pack her laptop away. 'The quicker I can get back to the office and start looking at it, the better. It could take me some time, with the other cases I have. But, like I said, keep your expectations low on this one. Nothing Helen said is screaming out at me, but you never know.

'I've sent you my contact details just in case Helen returns with any new information, but I'm guessing she won't. And, of course, if you want anyone to talk to, Jen—what you can do, it's really very special, but I expect it can also be very lonely. I'm here if you ever need someone who believes you.'

Jen let Tola out and watched as she pulled out of the driveway. After shutting the door, she walked back into the lounge to find Jacqui had gone. The house was quiet apart from the hum of the boiler as it worked away at keeping the rooms warm.

Feeling at a bit of a loss with what to do with herself, and not wanting to imagine that that was the last visit from her mum, Jen called her dad to tell him all about Helen's final visit.

CHAPTER 26

Jen scrolled up and down her work emails mindlessly. There was nothing she felt compelled to get on with. All her current jobs were either a bit of admin or something equally mundane, which she could do quickly but had no motivation to start. She'd not heard from Tola for nearly a week. She'd not seen her mum again either.

Maybe I should get out of the house, get myself something for lunch, she thought. As she contemplated getting her coat on, a voice message appeared from Laura. Hearing her voice was a welcome distraction.

'Hey! I was hoping you might be free tomorrow afternoon. I've bought a new bed for Olivia off someone online and need a hand collecting it. It'll be a bit of a road trip, but I'm sure we can amuse ourselves. Krish will be with Olivia at those hockey trials all day, so I really could do with an extra pair of hands, if possible. Let me know!'

Jen was glad to have something to do out of the house so replied to Laura straight away.

The rest of the day plodded along uneventfully, and the following morning, Jen woke up with purpose. She was going to tell Laura what had been going on; it was a good opportunity with the trip planned. If she could explain it all to Tola, then she just needed to do the same with Laura. It sounded simple, but she still worried that Laura might recoil from what she had to say.

***

Tola had been mulling over Helen's information in between her day-to-day work. It hadn't yielded any new leads, and she was left downhearted. Without realising it, she'd pinned a lot of expectation on what Jen had told her, but the reality was that nothing tied up with anything any other witness had seen, and she had nothing she could run against any databases.

On her screen, she had the final thing she wanted to check. Helen had said that it didn't feel like she was in the car very long before it stopped and that the man had taken her out on a road with some terraced houses. The map she was looking at was dated *'1992'*, the year Helen went missing.

Tola placed her finger on a road that ran along a field: a field that backed onto the woods. She felt this was the place Helen described. The road either went east or west. Her finger traced left, following the road until it split at a junction, into three. *Too many options*, she thought as she went back and followed the road right. This time, it split into two, but Tola could already see a residential area ahead along one of them. It was small; not a lot of houses, in a line, with gardens parallel to each other. They looked like terraces, so she checked a current map in the hope they might still be there.

'Well, there you are,' Tola said to herself, seeing the houses were still there on the latest map. Looking at her schedule, she still had a number of meetings and appointments but resolved to drive past the road on the way home. *Got to be worth a look at the very least*, she thought as a slight flicker of excitement skittered across her stomach.

***

Jen and Laura arrived at a very well-maintained detached property with a 'Sold' sign in the front border, to find an older couple in the middle of trying to downsize.

'I cannot believe you only paid fifty pounds for this, Laura. It's mint; I doubt anyone has actually slept in it.'

Jen helped dismantle the bed and place it into Laura's estate car. She had wimped out of telling Laura about her new abilities on the way there, convincing herself that the conversation was best left for the way back—if it went wrong, at least she'd have a quick exit strategy.

'I know, it's an absolute bargain,' Laura said. 'They clearly just want to get stuff out of the house. We should have got Olivia a new one ages ago, after she broke a few of the slats on her other one, jumping about. But the patch-up seemed to work, so we never got round to it. But she's much bigger now and its starting to look a right state. She'll have this just in time for Christmas, which will be good.'

Christmas! Jen thought. It had snuck up on her like a thief. She had lost track of what was going on in the living world and hadn't bought any presents or sent any cards. She wondered if people were expecting much from her this year as she'd lost her mum, but resolved to get straight online when she arrived home and rectify the matter, regardless.

'Where will you be for Christmas?' Laura asked. 'At your dad's?'

Jen hadn't given any thought to that either. 'It's completely passed me by, Laura. I need to speak to Dad; I don't think either of us have realised Christmas is nearly here.'

'That's understandable. Well, you're both welcome round ours on the big day. We're at home this year, and my sister is entertaining my parents. They'll be down for New Year's. Olivia loves it when you stay over.'

New Year's, another hurdle to get over. Jen didn't want to think about it and shuffled parts of the bed round in the back of the car, even though they fit in just fine.

Having paid the couple and wished them a Merry Christmas, Laura started the car and set the satnav for home. 'Looks like some traffic has built up or there's been an accident,' she said. 'We're going back a different way to earlier. Oh well, a little scenic drive in the country won't hurt. We can spot all the festive lights.'

Jen was enjoying the drive. It had been a while since she and Laura had chatted about normal things that didn't involve her mum or how she was feeling. She didn't want to spoil the moment with talk of ghosts and a missing woman.

'Olivia is doing so well with her hockey, Jen, it's almost unbelievable. She's trying out for county level next month. I think she gets her sporting streak from me, Krish can't bear anything that involves the remotest bit of exercise, unless he's watching it on TV.

'And we're thinking of moving next year. Need a bit more room. Another lounge or snug-type space would be great, then Olivia can have her friends over without Krish and me having to go hide in our bedroom. Not far though, I still need to be near you.' Laura gave Jen's arm a little squeeze.

Jen was content, happy taking in all the things Laura was saying, and she realised that she'd missed her a lot.

Glancing at the satnav, she watched the arrow weave its way along the road they were following. Then she noticed a blocked-out green area, to the right of the arrow on the map, called 'Corsley Woods'. A cold shiver shot up her spine in spite of the heated seat she was sitting in. She looked around. There were trees lining one side of the road and detached houses on the other. Then there were trees on both sides and, up ahead, Jen could see more houses.

'You okay?' Laura asked. 'You seem to be a bit twitchy all of sudden.'

Jen pointed at the satnav. 'You see that wooded area there that we're just moving away from? That's Corsley Woods, where Helen Swift disappeared from. You remember the newspaper article in Mum's jacket pocket? I've been in such a daydream; I hadn't noticed we were in Sussex.'

'Yes, I remember. We're right next to it, are we? Did you see if anything came of the appeal they did a few weeks ago?'

Jen was about to answer when her eyes widened and fixated on a red object up ahead. 'It can't be…' She leant forward, up to the windscreen, as if that was going to give her a better view. The car approached the start of a row of terraced houses, and on the pavement at the other end stood a postbox.

'Laura, can you pull over here, please? Anywhere.'

'What? Why?' Laura asked, pulling over but utterly surprised by the request.

The car stopped a good few metres away from the postbox.

Jen undid her seat belt and turned to Laura. 'I will explain everything to you, I promise. But right now, I need you to stay in the car. Do not get out, and don't come and see where I've gone.'

'Am I heck! Where are you going?' Laura also undid her seat belt. Jen was not making much sense, but she certainly wasn't going to stay in the car whilst she went off wandering.

'Please, Laura, it's probably nothing, but I just need to go and take a look at the postbox. I'll have my phone on me, see?' Jen waved the device in front of Laura. 'I know I said that I would tell you about some stuff that's been going on. Well, it's about time I explained—after I've checked this out. Please. Stay here, you can be my lookout.'

'Lookout for what? I don't like this, Jen. It's getting dark soon.'

'Honestly, five minutes tops.' Jen already had the door open and was halfway onto the pavement.

Laura tutted. She waited for Jen to shut the door, then locked the car. She shuffled in her seat and watched Jen walk towards the postbox.

'These must all still be empty, the state they are in,' Jen said to herself, looking at the houses as she walked past. The Victorian houses all had their bay windows and doors covered with metal shutters. Every front garden was full of shrubs and bushes that had long since been left unattended and uncared for. Distinctive brown cones of lobelia were rife, exerting their dominance anywhere they could find space. There were no bins or other signs of human life going on; only the plants and wildlife were thriving.

Jen knew that Helen had seen a postbox and phone box next to each other. There was no phone box now. What remained was a rectangular patch of concrete, which didn't match the rest of the pavement surface. *It was here,* Jen thought. Then she turned, knowing that she needed to be at the other end of the road. 'I've got to check, since I'm here,' she muttered. 'But this can't possibly be it… That would be ridiculous.'

She walked back past Laura and pointed to the other end of the road, signalling where she was going.

Laura watched her in the rearview mirror, the one streetlight casting shadows in the dusk.

Jen's heart was beating hard. She reached the last house in the row and found the front door was replaced with a metal shutter, the same as all the other houses. But the front gate remained. Jen shone her phone light over it, crouching to run her hands over the flaking paint. Blue flecks dotted her fingers.

Keeping the light on, she pushed the gate open and walked up the path to see it wind round the front bay window and disappear to the side.

This is it. This has to be it. Jen couldn't believe it.

Without a second thought, she followed the path down the side of the house, tucking her hands into her sleeves to avoid the marauding weeds and nettles.

Laura watched Jen disappear up the path of the last house in the road then vanish completely.

'Where are you going? You are testing my patience, Jennifer Hattley,' she muttered as she started the car, put it into reverse and backed up the road so she could position herself right outside the house Jen was looking at, ready to follow, if needed.

Meanwhile, Jen had made it to the back garden, which was equally as unkempt as the front, and found herself staring at where the back door should have been. It and all the back windows were covered in the same shutters as the rest of the road. It was more or less silent, save for the last of the day's chirps from some nearby birds; dusk had begun to fall. If there was anywhere she expected to see a ghost, it was here; it was the spookiest place she'd ever been.

She knew the best thing to do was to go back to the car and call Tola, leave it to her to check out, but she took a couple of steps towards the house, regardless.

'Helen might not even be in there,' Jen told herself. 'He might have taken her somewhere else. Or he might have buried her in the garden.'

She moved closer to the shutter covering the back door. She had no way of seeing inside; there were no slots or gaps in the covering. Holding her light up to the edges, she could see that someone had tried to remove it before; some old scrapes on the metal and a few missing screws gave the game away. So, it wasn't entirely secure.

Jen put her phone down, and with her fingers wrapped in her cuffs, she gave a light tug. After looking around to see if anyone was watching her—highly unlikely, but she felt she ought to check nonetheless—she gave it another, heftier tug. Two more screws fell out from the edge closest to her.

I should leave it. Tola will be furious. It's a crime scene. What am I doing? Her mind was urging her to stop, but she had to at least look inside.

With one last pull, the metal shutter gave way and clattered to the floor, revealing the back door. It was so loud; Jen heard some birds take flight from a neighbouring tree.

Cringing at herself, she stood back and shone her light in through one of the gaps where a pane of glass was missing, perhaps damaged when the shutters were installed. She tried the handle and, of course, it was locked.

It's an old, weathered, wood-framed door. How much of a shove would it need to open it? Whilst Jen contemplated how they broke doors down on TV, she continued to peer into what looked like a kitchen, and shuddered. Once Helen had reached here, it was the beginning of her end. Jen shut her eyes, trying to block out the images her mind was putting together.

The stillness around her was disturbed by a loud noise she was sure came from within the house. Her eyes opened abruptly and tried to adjust to the darkness again. Her light created a short path into the kitchen, and she could see the start of another room.

As she began to look away, something passed through the faded beam of light. Fear shot through her. Surely, no one was in there? The place looked deserted. Perhaps someone had managed to move one of the shutters, like she had?

Jen was beginning to regret being so bold when something moved across the light again—but this time, it stopped.

'Helen?' she asked, then realised: this wasn't Helen.

Jen got as close to the opening in the window as possible. She could see no discernible shape and its edges were undefined, as if it was coming out of the gloom. It had glided across into the light, not stepped into it; whatever it was seemed to move unnaturally. She couldn't see any eyes, but she knew it was watching her, studying her. It was curious. This was nothing like Aunt Joan or David; this was something else.

Suddenly, a wave of rage came over her, emanating out from the being. Wave after wave, it came at her. It was disturbing and terrifying, heightening her fear to levels she'd never known.

Jen's phone rang, causing her to drop it.

'Oh, come on,' she said, fumbling to find it on the ground. It had landed torch down, but luckily the light hadn't gone off.

'Where are you?' It was Laura.

'I'm just at the back of the house.'

'I'm coming round. Someone else is here.'

'What? No! Stay in the—' Jen gave up; Laura had put the phone down, and she heard the car door slam round the front. She then heard Laura shuffling her way down the side entrance, a few expletives muttered at the overgrown plants.

Laura's phone light emerged ahead of her.

'You were meant to be staying in the car,' Jen said, knowing full well that if the shoe was on the other foot, she'd be standing exactly where Laura was now.

'Yeah, as if I was going to do that for long. Anyway, someone else is here. They walked to the same spot you did by the postbox and now I'm sure they're heading up here. I jumped out of the car to come warn you.' Laura was looking the house up and down. 'What is this place?'

Jen looked back inside to find the dark mass had gone. The rage had passed. She recognised the anger; she'd felt it herself at times, but this time was like nothing she had ever experienced before.

'Jen, why are we here?' Laura asked, waiting for some kind of answer.

Jen leant back against the wall. There was no point in making anything up, but telling Laura all about what was happening was not going exactly as she had hoped.

'It's a very long story, but the short version is: I think this is where Helen Swift was taken to and, sadly, never returned from.'

'How could you possibly know anything about it? Is this what you wanted to tell me? Oh my God, did your mum know something about it? Is that why she had the newspaper article in her pocket?' Laura started to hop from one foot to the other, partly due to her adrenaline kicking in and partly because she felt anxious about standing outside a strange house in the dark, talking about a long-disappeared woman.

'No, Mum didn't have anything to do with it. Well, not like that. As I said, it's a long story and, to be fair, I am well overdue telling you about it. I'm sorry. You must think I've completely lost it.'

'Well, it did cross my mind. So, what are we waiting for? Can we go?'

'Not yet. I need to call the police—actually, a detective I've met.'

'You've met a detective?! What else has been happening that I don't know about?' Laura was barely able to disguise how put out she felt about not being in on whatever was going on.

Jen didn't want to answer. Quite a lot had been happening.

For a moment, there was quiet between them. Then a noise came from inside the house, interrupting the silence; a distinct thud on what sounded like wood.

Jen and Laura turned their lights simultaneously towards the doorway.

'What was that?' Laura asked, moving closer to Jen.

'I am not entirely sure,' Jen replied, trying the handle again, hoping the door would miraculously open this time.

'Don't you dare go in there, Jennifer Hattley!'

Jen leapt out of her skin to find Tola Obederin shining her larger, brighter torch in her and Laura's faces.

CHAPTER 27

Jen and Laura put their hands up to shield their eyes.

'Tola? How did you know I was here?' Jen said.

'I didn't. I wasn't getting anywhere with what we were told; the last thing I could do was check out the old maps. This row of houses looked like they were worth checking out, so I thought I'd do it on the way home today. How did you end up here?' Tola wanted to ask if Helen had been back with more information but thought it best not to with another person there. 'And who's this?' she asked with an authoritative voice.

'Sorry, this is Laura.' Jen pointed to her friend.

What has Jen got me into? Laura thought, sheepishly waving at Tola.

'Laura and I were picking a bed up for Olivia, Laura's daughter, and by sheer chance, passed this road. I had to stop. You saw the postbox?'

'Yes, I saw it, and the spot where the phone box was. It's likely this is it.' Tola took in her surroundings and noticed the discarded shutter on the ground. 'Like that when you got here, was it?'

Jen grinned apologetically. 'I haven't gone in.'

Tola rolled her eyes. She was surprised to find Jen there, but finding Laura too was a cause for concern. What were they thinking, traipsing around a potential crime scene? 'As pleasant as this is, ladies, I need you both to get back in your car, please, and go home. I can't have two members of the public wandering around, as you can probably appreciate.' Tola shone the light back and forth between Laura and Jen.

'I'm not leaving, Tola,' Jen insisted.

'You most certainly are, Jen. I can't have you here. You've already been through the front garden and this back area. I don't want to have to explain why you were here.'

'There is something in there,' Jen said, pointing inside.

Tola swung her light into the house through the doorway. 'Did you see someone in there?'

'No, not some*one*, some*thing*. It's not…' Jen paused, knowing her next words were only going to confuse Laura even more. 'It's not a person and it's not Helen. It's something else. You need someone with you who can see it; it could be dangerous. Like, my-mum-and-dad-with-the-Ouija-board dangerous.'

A look of realisation came over Tola's face. Utter bewilderment reigned over Laura's.

'Laura,' Jen said. 'I really need you to go back into the car and wait for me. You can't go in there; I don't think it's safe.'

Laura knew that, whether she understood what was going on or not, she couldn't follow Jen into the house. The detective would never let her—plus, she didn't want to. If a missing woman from thirty years ago was in there, she certainly did not want to see.

'When we leave here, you are telling me everything, Jen. And I mean everything. I don't care how bonkers it is. I trust you to tell me, you understand?' Laura was bordering on her cross tone, something usually reserved for Olivia or Krish.

Jen stepped towards Laura and gave her a hug. 'I promise.'

Laura's tone warmed a little. 'Fine, I'll go back to the car. But if I don't hear from you in the next fifteen minutes, I am coming back in.' Laura reluctantly let go of her friend and disappeared back down the side of the house.

Both Tola and Jen listened for the car door opening and closing before continuing.

Tola shuffled about in one of her pockets and produced a pair of gloves and shoe covers for each of them. 'I always have spares wherever I go, force of habit. Put these on. But they don't mean you can touch anything. Just keep yourself to yourself as much as possible.'

Jen took the gloves and covers from Tola. 'How are you getting us in there? The door is locked.'

'There's a reason they put the shutters up.' Tola stood by the door, checking the frame. Then, with one solid, flat foot, she kicked the door. It didn't relent. She gave it another kick, and a crack could be heard around the door handle. 'One more should do it.' And with that, Tola gave the door one final kick. The area near the door handle splintered, and the door opened.

Jen shook her head in awe. 'Shouldn't you be waiting for backup or something?'

'I wasn't expecting us to have company in there, certainly not the kind you're describing, but a discreet colleague knows where I am. And I always make sure Samuel knows, too. You and I are quite alike, Jen. We can't help letting our curiosity get the better of us. I'll tidy this up with my boss later. In the meantime, of course, I'm going for a look. No point wasting anyone's time if there's nothing to see, is there?'

It was a traditional Victorian terrace, with the kitchen to the back. It was devoid of the usual culinary clutter; no knife block or pots of utensils. It had clearly been empty for decades.

Tola searched the walls for a light switch and, on finding one, gave it a few flicks. Nothing happened.

It smelled musty and damp, and as both women moved their torches side to side, they could see heavy dust, stains and rodent excrement dotting the work surfaces. Gloves or no gloves, Jen had no intention of touching anything after seeing the state of this room.

They moved slowly into what could have been a dining room; it was as empty as the kitchen. Just four walls, an understairs cupboard and no furniture. Tola led them through another doorway into the lounge. The carpet was still intact but filthy, in a similar condition to the kitchen worktops.

Jen coughed. It felt like the atmosphere was thick and cloying, the fresh air not having made its way into the room for some time. As she turned to look up the stairs, she was certain that something moved from the doorway into the dining room. A shape even darker than the pitch black around it so that, peculiarly, it stood out in the murk. A wave of anger washed through Jen's mind. She pushed it aside.

Suddenly, Tola's phone began to ring, and Jen yelped.

'Yes, it's Tola, what did you find out? ... Okay. ... Really? ... Not surprising, I suppose. And is that as far back as you have gotten so far? ... Great work, keep me posted.'

'Who was that?' Jen asked, glad for the distraction from whatever was hiding in the next room.

'I messaged my very discreet colleague after looking at the postbox. She has been checking who owns this house for me. In fact, the same organisation owns all the houses. It's the local council, bought under a compulsory purchase order six months before Helen went missing. They had plans for a development but hit a roadblock with greenbelt regulations. Typical of a local authority, they've been backwards and forwards on it with no resolution, and these houses have been left empty and unused ever since. It's a complete waste; the amount of homeless we have in this county, and these are just sitting here waiting for a load of red tape to be navigated.'

'But Helen said the man had keys. So, it's someone from the council?'

'Or the previous owner. My colleague is still digging. Have you seen any more of this "something"? I'm not going to get possessed or anything, am I?' Tola asked light-heartedly but was mildly concerned at how likely it was after hearing what had happened to Jen's parents.

As she finished her question, both women heard a muffled but unmistakable thump. Their ears were drawn to the staircase.

'Did that come from upstairs?' Tola asked, moving to the bottom step and shining her torch to the top. Another thump. This time it was easier to identify where from.

'No, it's under the stairs.' Jen pointed with her phone. 'The cupboard.'

She remembered that Laura had heard the noise when they were outside, and Tola could hear the activity from inside. Whatever was residing in the property, it wanted their attention, and it was making no secret about it. It was not interested in discretion.

Tola moved back into the dining room and walked towards the cupboard door. It had a small, tarnished latch handle. With the light firmly fixed on the door, Tola stood arm's-length away, flicked the latch and pulled the door open.

Immediately, the smell of ammonia hit her, taking her breath away and making her step back.

The waft punched Jen in the nose, and she covered her face. 'What is that smell?'

'That is the unmistakable aroma of a well-established family of rats or mice. I've had the pleasure before,' Tola said, lowering her light and finding the bottom of the cupboard taken up with a rolled-up duvet. It spanned the length of the base of the staircase.

Tola crouched herself down, being careful not to touch it. There were all manner of stains all over the duvet, along with nibble marks and evidence of rodent activity. She flooded the area with light and followed the length of the duvet down as far as she could see. Poking out the end of the dirtied fabric was a brown walking boot. It wasn't entirely visible, but Tola recognised it immediately. She had a replica of the exact same boots in evidence storage.

'Lord, have mercy.' Tola exhaled. 'The day is finally here.' She unfurled her legs and sat for a moment, not caring about the decrepit carpet. Her back leant against the dining room wall.

'What is it, Tola?' Jen couldn't bear it.

'You've been here all this time, you poor girl.' Tola lent forward and gently placed her hand on the edge of the duvet nearest her. 'I'm here now, Helen. I'm sorry I took so long.' She lowered her head for a moment before turning to face Jen. 'I think we have found Helen.'

Jen gasped. She'd thought it was likely that Helen would be in the house, but now they had actually found her, it was quite a shock.

'She's been left in this cold, dark house, all alone, for thirty years. I can't think of anything more sad,' Tola said.

Jen nodded solemnly, but then something began to speak inside her head, replacing the sadness. It was not her own voice. This one whispered with intent.

'Discarded like she was nothing. Left there to rot. Left there to be forgotten.'

Jen could see events playing over in her mind, as if she had been there herself, but distorted through the eyes of the 'something' this voice belonged to. It had watched the man shut the cupboard, lock the back door and walk away—as if he was just leaving the house to go to work.

'He's out there, free, without care, without remorse. Where is his punishment? Why is he not being made to suffer like Helen did?' The whisper was no longer in Jen's head. It was outside, around her, in the room.

She looked at Tola, but the detective was focused on the body in the cupboard. She clearly couldn't hear the disembodied voice.

Jen then felt an icy breath on her left ear, and electricity ran right through her.

'He should be made to suffer.'

Jen was snapped back into the moment by Tola. 'Don't come forward, Jen. I've seen enough in my career that I wish I could unsee. You don't need this imprinted in your memory. You must leave now. Go home with Laura. I am going to call this in immediately.'

'I don't think I should leave you here on your own, Tola.' Jen wasn't sure what she was dealing with. She certainly didn't want to see Helen in the state she was in. And she didn't want to hear any more from whatever was in the house with them, but she wasn't totally sure of its intentions. On the one hand, it had seemingly led them to Helen; on the other, it was making her feel uneasy and nervous.

'You can't be here when the team arrives. I cannot explain your presence, not plausibly. What is it? What have you seen?'

'I've not really seen anything concrete, but I've heard things. Then there's the feeling it's giving off. It wanted us to find Helen, I think, but it's not finished. I just don't know if it can hurt you.'

Tola had heard the noises herself. She had been in plenty of frightening scenarios before. This, however, was a threat she couldn't see and therefore couldn't defend herself from.

'We don't have a choice, Jen. You have to leave, and I have to wait on my own.'

Jen knew Tola was right but was wholly uncomfortable about it. There was one thing she could do, for what it was worth. She stood, firm-footed in the middle of the room, and spoke loudly: 'I don't know who or what you are. I do know you wanted us to find Helen, and we have. This lady here is going to make sure she gets home. So, you leave her alone, do you hear me? Tola is here to help. Don't you go near her. No more noises, no more whispering. That's enough.' Jen wasn't sure if it was going to listen, but she felt being assertive with it was the best course of action.

She turned and reluctantly bid Tola goodbye, but as she walked through the kitchen to the back door, she found her path was blocked. The thing moved like smoke. There was a malevolence about it that, even though it wasn't directed at her, she didn't want it getting into her head again. She looked behind her and saw Tola was already on the phone.

Jen ideally didn't want to engage with it, but she couldn't get out. 'You need to let me go,' she whispered. 'I'm not totally sure what you want but, whatever it is, I cannot give it to you.'

It observed Jen as she spoke. A glimpse of what looked like a woman's face emerged from the smoke, which surrounded it like swirling, inky-black hair. Deep ebony eyes formed and stared at Jen. Its form was not constant, moving in and out of focus, as if it couldn't quite maintain itself.

Jen kept her voice low. She knew she had to leave, but intrigue was getting the better of her again. 'What are you? You're not like the other ghosts I have spoken to.'

'I am something… different.'

'I really don't need cryptic answers right now,' Jen retorted, her voice slightly raised.

This seemed to amuse the 'woman'. *'Very well. I was once vibrant with life, like you—a very, very long time ago. I died in terror at the hands of a man, and I rose again to take my revenge. Now, I exist in this form, looking for those that need retribution. I've been given many names, but they all mean the same thing.'*

Jen wasn't sure what all that meant; the woman was still not speaking very clearly. But Jen needed to get to the point. 'Why are you here?'

'I heard Helen's cries. I watched as she took her last breath. I come back here from time to time, waiting for someone to find her. I want what is deserved.'

This was new. Not a ghost of a person, but an entity of some description. But Jen knew she had no time left to chat with whatever it was in front of her. 'You need to let me pass. I cannot be here when the police come. Leave Tola alone, she is here to help. You hear me?'

The woman stared back at Jen, motionless, and seemed to take notice. Its image began to break down, but Jen was sure she could see it smiling at her. Then, the kitchen was empty and Jen's path was clear.

She looked back to see Tola unmoved since her call. She couldn't have heard anything.

Jen ran out of the back door and didn't stop until she reached Laura's car. She almost leapt into the passenger seat and slammed the door. There was something about this one, it had frightened her right to the core.

'I was about to come looking for you. What happened in there?'

Jen put on her seat belt and looked back at the house. She could see blinks of light through the shutter as Tola moved around. 'Just drive, Laura. I will tell you everything. But we need to get going now.'

Laura didn't need asking twice, and before long, they were back on familiar roads.

Tola stood alone, guarding the cupboard door and Helen's body. Helen had been found. That part of the journey was over, and a new one was about to begin. Tola's adrenaline was pumping; not just because of the creepiness of the house and the warning of something otherworldly being there with her, but because the chase had been reignited. Finding Helen's body meant the case would be fully reopened and more resources would be allocated to find who had done this to her.

Tola relished the impending hunt. After looking unlikely for so long, justice might be served after all.

As she attempted to slow her racing heart, she noticed everything around her was still. She would have preferred Jen to stay, but it just wasn't possible. She ran her fingers over the gold chain round her neck and down to the cross that hung from it. It was the only comfort she could think of while she waited for her colleagues to arrive.

CHAPTER 28

Laura pulled up to her house and cut the engine. She'd listened to Jen for the whole journey home, not interrupting and not asking any questions. She now sat quietly looking out the driver's side window.

Jen had not seen Laura this contemplative before; she always had an opinion or a comment for everything. Jen worried that this was a step too far for their friendship. She desperately hoped it wasn't.

Laura turned to face her. 'Well, I wasn't expecting any of that.'

'I'm not surprised. I wasn't expecting any of it either,' Jen said.

'So, your dad will say that everything you've just told me is true?'

'Yes, every word of it.'

'And these notebooks, I can take a look at them if I want to?'

'Yes, totally. In fact, I would love you to. There's no secret with them; you can read them no problem.'

Laura took Jen's face in both her hands and gave her a kiss on the forehead. 'You really could have told me all this before, you know? It's mental, I'll give you that, but I would have believed you. I do believe you. You're my best friend in the whole universe. I thought you were going to tell me you were dying or something. That would have been horrendous. Ghost-hunting crime fighter? Totally okay with me.'

Jen couldn't keep it in any longer. She leant her head on Laura's shoulder and sobbed. A relieved, long-needed sob. 'I've been holding it all in and I just wanted to talk to you about it.'

'That's not all you've been holding in though, is it? Your mum never really left, so how you've been able to grieve her properly, I have no idea. You should have just told me as soon as it all started happening; you didn't have to deal with all this on your own. Okay, your dad knows, and that detective seems nice, but you've been looking for Helen and helping these other ghosts—who's been helping you? It should have been me. You never have to hide anything from me.'

Both women sat in the car for a while, just being together and quiet, knowing that there was nothing that needed to be hidden between them and nothing that couldn't be overcome.

'I am so sorry.' Jen wiped her face with her coat cuff. 'Full disclosure from now on. Promise. And I'm no ghost hunter or crime fighter. I'm just the messenger, I suppose.'

'You're never *just* anything, Jen. But what you can *just* do now is help me take this bed inside; then you can *just* help me order some food and then *just* help me open a bottle of wine. And you can just stay here tonight, if you want. We must talk about this more, but I do need this bed put up before Olivia needs to sleep on it.'

Jen was more than happy to oblige on all accounts.

'I have so many questions Jen, honestly. Like, do you think your mum could pick something up if she tried? And how do they know what clothes to appear in? Why do only some people come back and some don't? Imagine if you had a queue of them in your house!' Laura was back to her usual inquisitive self, and Jen was very glad—even if she had few answers to offer.

Getting out of the car, she thought about Tola in the empty house with her team, busy surveying every inch of the property for clues. Her inquisitive self wished she could be there.

***

Tola stood outside and watched her breath dissipate into the evening air. Various vehicles were now parked at the front of the house, blue lights illuminating the otherwise dark street. If there had been neighbours, they would surely have been twitching their curtains.

Tola was letting the last hour or so sink in when she noticed a woman striding purposefully up the pavement towards her with her hands in the pockets of the long coat she was wearing.

'The big guns have arrived,' Tola said to herself.

She'd known someone senior would appear sooner rather than later, but she hadn't expected it to be the chief superintendent. But Helen's disappearance was one of the county's biggest missing persons cases, so it naturally attracted national attention. It was no less than Helen deserved.

Tola ran over her rehearsed lines one more time in her head.

'Good evening, Tola. This is a surprise turn of events, isn't it?'

'Good evening, ma'am. Indeed.'

'So, how did you come to find our victim here? It's quite an unlikely location to check, based on what we already know.'

'We had an anonymous tip. No name given and we couldn't trace the number. They just gave this address. Perhaps the appeal jogged someone's conscience. Whatever the reason, it's a welcome result.'

'What do we know so far?'

'Helen was found in the understairs cupboard of this house here. She was wrapped in a duvet, but there was no real attempt to conceal her. These houses are all owned by the council, and were purchased six months before Helen Swift disappeared. We'll know more once the team has been in and swept the place.'

'Very good. And the family, have you contacted them yet?'

'No, I felt I should wait until I had spoken to you, ma'am.' Tola had wanted to call the Swifts the minute she had found their mum, but protocol meant she had to bide her time.

'Well, I don't want them finding out via any other media, so make the call and let me know once you have spoken to them. I'll then make arrangements to give a statement to the press. I don't need some halfwit journalist getting the facts wrong here; we still have a way to go.

'This is great work, Tola. Your perseverance has paid off. You know as well as I do, we don't find many of these victims. We can bring this one home at least.' With that, the chief superintendent patted Tola on the back and went off to grill another officer.

It didn't feel like much of a win to Tola, not like some cases did. It just felt like an end to the first part of the mystery. Helen had been found and could now be laid to rest in the proper place; her children could stop wondering where she was. But they didn't yet know who had put her there. Tola hoped there was enough evidence in the house to bring him to justice.

Taking her phone from her pocket, she found Matthew Swift's number, and with a deep breath, she made the call she'd wanted—but not wanted—to make for years.

***

Krish and Olivia had returned home a while after Laura and Jen got back, full of excitement at Olivia's success at the trials. The takeaway had turned into a celebration meal, and Jen revelled in being part of it all. She'd missed this bit of her life, seeing Laura with her family and sharing in their news. Olivia took Jen upstairs to show her the new colours on her bedroom walls and her latest wardrobe additions. Jen pretended she hadn't already seen it, having put the bed together with Laura earlier. Olivia had wanted Jen to tuck her into her new bed, so they chatted for a bit before a day's worth of fresh air and running around finally saw Olivia fall asleep.

Jen tiptoed out of her room and headed back downstairs.

Krish was tidying up from dinner and putting the leftovers in the fridge. 'I assume you two are going to be up for a while. I'm going to catch up on some TV in the comfort of my bed. I am knackered.'

'You'll be asleep in ten minutes, I reckon.' Laura laughed.

'I don't doubt it. Goodnight!' Krish gave his wife a kiss and Jen a wave, then ascended the stairs.

While Laura poured some more wine for both of them, Jen noticed a message on her phone. It was from Tola.

'Hey, check this out,' Jen said, showing Laura the phone.

'We've made a statement to the press about Helen. No specifics but to confirm a body has been found. I've said the lead came from an anonymous tip-off.'

There was also a link to a brief news article.

'Police in Sussex have confirmed the discovery of a body this evening in a house in the west of the county. It is believed to be that of Helen Swift, who disappeared on 4th November 1992. Her family have been informed, and the investigation is ongoing.

Sussex Police appeal to anyone who has information relating to this incident to contact them immediately via 999 or 111.'

'So, what now for you and Helen? Is that it?' Laura asked.

'Well, I suppose my part in this is over. I can't get involved. No one can know how Tola really found her. There's nothing more for me to do.'

'But don't you want to know who did it? It's making me furious just thinking about it. Goes on all the time, doesn't it? Women being attacked, disappearing, never to be found. You know, I watch those missing persons programmes, the same as you—I shouldn't because it just winds me up—there's just so many of them. I don't know what I would do if anything happened to Olivia, or you, or any one of our friends. It's like someone just being plucked out of existence.'

Jen was listening, but her mind had wandered back to the creature in the house. Furious. But not on a level Jen had ever experienced. She hoped that it had moved on from the house and left Tola and her colleagues in peace.

'Well,' Jen said. 'I have only known Tola for a short time, but she'll get him. I know she will.'

***

Tola was tired but wired at the same time. She knew the investigation in the house was going to take a few more hours, and felt she ought to stay with the team, but what she really wanted to do was get into her pyjamas and lie in her own bed. She wanted to forget about Helen, just for a little while, but she also wanted to be the first to know about anything new. So, she was staying put.

She was sitting in her car with the heating on when she saw her husband pulling up ahead of her. He had a lunchbox in his hand, and a flask.

'You sweet man, you didn't have to come out with this for me.' Tola gave him a hug.

'I know you'll be here a while, and you must be hungry. How's it going?'

'It's going to take a while. The property has been vacant for decades, but there's been a lot of animal and insect disturbance. The victim is in a bad state; the team needs to take their time to have the best chance of collecting as much evidence as possible.'

'It's a sad end. Expected, but no less sad,' Samuel said. 'Well, you know where I'll be if you need anything else.'

'I do, now get back home, old man; it's too cold for you to be out at this time!' Tola joked.

'I'm three years younger than you!'

Samuel walked back to his car, and Tola smiled as she listened to him chuckling. She opened the lunchbox and found it full of her favourite snacks. 'Such a good man.'

As she tucked into her surprise, her phone rang.

'Tola here.'

'Hey, it's Vanessa. I've managed to check the records, and I have a name for the previous owner, before the council. It was a Mrs Doris Strickland, but she died a year before the council took it over. So, I checked again and there's an elder son who seems to have taken ownership of the property. I'll need to review title records and utilities in the morning, but I found a record of her last will online. He definitely inherited it. She had other children, but he got the most of everything, it looks like.'

'What's his name?'

'Russell Strickland.'

'Why is that name ringing a bell?'

'Because you have read the case notes more than anyone else! It sounded familiar to me, too. He was interviewed after Helen's disappearance at Corsley Woods. It's the same guy; I have double-checked. I couldn't believe it.'

Tola slid her lunchbox onto the passenger seat and got out of her car for some much-needed air, despite how chilly it had become.

'You still there?'

'Yes, sorry. I'm just a bit stunned.'

'Yeah, I can imagine. I've got his address, when you're ready. I expect you'll be wanting to speak to him.'

'Thanks, Vanessa, this is amazing work.'

Tola looked back at the house. She didn't want to jump to conclusions, but this wasn't sitting right at all. The house was near the woods but not that close. Yes, it was owned by the council when Helen disappeared, and technically anyone could have had access to the keys, but to have been interviewed as a witness at the time *and* be the original owner of the house Helen was found in—it couldn't be coincidence. Tola felt a little sick. If this man had taken Helen, he'd had the audacity and the arrogance to return and speak to the police. He'd pretended to be a helpful member of the public; he likely wanted the attention, or thought he was being clever.

'The press statement…' Tola looked round to check if the chief superintendent's car was still there, which it was. She rushed back towards the house. If he hadn't seen it already, it wouldn't take long for Russell Strickland to notice the headlines.

CHAPTER 29

Jen woke up contentedly in Laura's spare room. Despite the craziness of the previous day, she felt at peace within herself. Helen had been found and was going to be returned to her family. There was nothing more Jen needed to do for her. And Laura knew about the ghosts, so no more hiding either.

She could hear Olivia singing to herself in her bedroom, and decided to get up.

She knocked on Olivia's doorframe and asked to come in. 'How was the new bed? I thought you'd still be asleep after all the energy you used up yesterday!'

'It is nearly eleven, you know? And the bed was cool,' Olivia replied, happily enough but with slight teenage sarcasm. Laura had said it was beginning to creep in.

'Wow, that's late. Are your mum and dad up?

'Unlikely.'

Jen gave Olivia a little squeeze and headed downstairs. She was familiar with Laura's kitchen and thought getting the coffee machine up and running might entice another adult from their slumber.

After a few minutes, Laura emerged at the bottom of the stairs. 'Good morning. We really slept in, didn't we?'

'Yes, we did. Busy day all round yesterday. I slept really well. Thanks for letting me stay.'

'Never a chore. What plans do you have today?'

'I need to get myself sorted for Christmas; I've done nothing. A bit of online shopping and a tidy round the house is in order. Can you send me a few ideas for Olivia, please? I don't want to be getting that wrong!'

Laura took a cup of coffee from Jen and held it in her hands for warmth. 'Sure, I'll add a few bits for me, too.' Laura smiled.

***

On the drive back home, Jen saw the decorations adorning people's houses and shopfronts. They had all gone up without her noticing.

She picked up some leaflets off the doormat as she got in, then went into the kitchen. She had been enthusiastic to get on with some present buying, but now the moment had passed. The house looked bare and lonely compared to the festivities going on outside. Jen knew where their decorations were, but didn't have the inclination to put them up—it wasn't like she had another person to appreciate them with. She certainly didn't want her husband back—he wouldn't have coped at all with her new-found abilities—but there was no one to sit on the sofa wrapping presents with, no one to help string the lights up. She supposed she could ask her dad, but she wondered how enthused he was about it all this year. With her mum no longer around, Jen felt the joy had been taken out of 'the most wonderful time of year' and she was full of sorrow.

She wondered how people got themselves through after just losing someone. She thought about how much Jacqui had always loved Christmas and made a big deal of still putting the tree up, even after Jen moved out. Every year since Jen could remember, without fail, her mum would hang a pack of twelve chocolate toy soldiers on the branches. They would all be for Jen, and they had spent many years trying to stop Bailey from pinching them when he thought no one was looking.

Jen's mind started to speculate if her mum was going to reappear again. She'd avoided thinking about it at Laura's, as she had plenty of distractions there, but it was not to be abated this time. Helen's body had been discovered, her ghost had no need to return, the task was complete. There was no reason for Jacqui to come back either.

Stop it. Stop thinking about it.

The same primal fear as before took hold of her; the fear of facing something unavoidable, something that cannot be stopped or undone. She shook her head, as if trying to shake the thoughts out, and began to feel overwhelmed.

Seeing her laptop, she snatched it up and curled up in the armchair. A few tears splashed onto her jumper as she started to look up the items that Laura had suggested for Olivia's presents.

After half an hour or so of jumping from one website to another, Jen felt a bit better about her Christmas prep, and the tears had dried. She'd managed to find most of the things Laura had suggested, plus a few surprises. Although, she wondered if the teenager could be surprised these days.

Before she finished, she searched for chocolate tree decorations and added a packet of toy soldiers to her basket. She wasn't sure if she'd put them up or not, but buying them was a start.

Jen's fingers hovered over the keyboard as other thoughts began to whirl in her mind.

Her memories of her time in the house where Helen was found pushed their way forward. *What would I type? Ghost lady with dark hair?* Jen thought. *No, that's not enough. What was she talking about? Retribution, that was it.* Jen started to tap out words to search.

'ghost lady wanting retribution' went into the search engine, and Jen felt herself wince as she pressed 'Enter'. 'That's just going to show me a load of nonsense, surely.'

Images of ethereal women appeared instantaneously, alongside popular commercial images of ghostly figures with long, black hair, sketches and anime art. Article upon article streamed down the page.

Jen rubbed her forehead. *There's too much here*, she thought.

Scrolling down and back up, none of the links were looking particularly useful. But then, she didn't really know what she was looking for. There were religious sites, book suggestions and tips on how to hunt ghosts.

After a third pass, one caught her eye*: 'Is your haunting a ghost or a demon?'*

She'd known straight away that it wasn't the ghost of a dead person she was interacting with, but she hadn't considered what else it could be. She didn't know what all the options were.

Her fingers hovered again over the keyboard, but this time with more uncertainty. *Do I really want to be searching about demons?* She imagined her mum's reaction: 'If you start typing about them, then you're just encouraging them to come here.'

Jen shook her head as if it might dispel the worries. 'Just get on with it,' she said out loud to herself and changed her search slightly.

'demon woman revenge'

This time, there were more forums and chatrooms, and fewer official-looking links. It looked like other people had been talking about a similar thing for years—Jen wasn't sure whether to be pleased about this or not. But again, there were too many to choose from.

Scanning the list, one caught her eye. The conversation thread was sampled in the link:

'… she appeared as if like smoke in front of me…'

The link took her to a fairly rudimentary site, draped in black with unoriginal images of headstones and ghostly apparitions. With a quick scan, Jen realised it was a forum for people to discuss their own paranormal experiences.

Technically, these are my kind of people. But really? This site needs work, Jen thought, contemplating a quick exit before her eyes settled on the excerpt from the link. It was an old thread between members about something one of them had seen.

'11th July 2004

scare1287: Can anyone help me identify the entity I experienced last night in my home? She appeared as if like smoke in front of me. Long, flowing hair. Eyes like coal. I have never seen her before, and she doesn't look like anyone I know who has died in my family.

ghosthunter666: Hey! Long time, no speak. Need more deets, but def sounds creepy.

scare1287: She didn't say anything, but ever since I saw her, I've had this voice in my head. It's not nice, she's saying things about my father. How he should get what he deserves. He's in prison now, so I don't get what she's talking about.

amylovescake1986: Bad, bad, bad. Get someone to cleanse the house ASAP!!!!

ghosthunter666: Yeah, this could be one of them vengeance demons. There's a few names for them. Different countries have their own ones. The Japanese call theirs onryō. *These are badass and you should avoid them at all costs.'*

'15th July 2004

scare1287: She's talking to me during the day. She won't stop. She's driving me mad. She wants my permission to give dad what he deserves. She won't leave me alone.

amylovescake1986: You need to go to your local church, get yourself blessed. You've got an attachment!!!!!

ghosthunter666: Sorry dude, this def sounds like a demon. I feel for you big time. You need to get rid of it. What's she going to do to your dad?

scare1287: She's going to kill him.

ghosthunter666: Shit!

amylovescake1986 has removed herself from this thread.'

'17th July 2004

ghosthunter666: Hey, @scare1287. You OK out there? Getting a bit worried about you.'

'21st July 2004

ghosthunter666: You out there, @scare1287?

scare1287: Sorry man, been a mental week. She's out of my head. Gone. I sent a letter to my dad like she asked. Got a call from the prison yesterday afternoon. Dad was found dead in his cell. I'd like to say I was bothered, but I'm not. Just had to go down there to do some admin. Thanks for the check-in.'

Jen couldn't quite believe what she was reading.

Is this even true? Do people really just casually chat about this stuff online? she thought, then scoffed at her own words, considering the other depraved things people do where they think no one is looking.

Jen went to close her laptop but paused. She searched for one more word:

'*Onryō*'

The definition, on what looked like another homemade webpage, made her shudder.

'*These spirits are considered some of the most vengeful and ruthless across the paranormal world. Over centuries, they have become heartless and cruel. In some eyewitness accounts, they appear completely deranged.*'

Feeling it best to leave thoughts of the onryō behind, Jen shut her laptop with conviction and placed it on the sofa. *Hopefully she stayed put in that house or has floated off somewhere else.*

She needed something more wholesome to fill her head and decided a trip into the loft, even for the smallest bit of tinsel, was worth it, even if her mum wasn't there to enjoy it.

CHAPTER 30

Tola hadn't had as much sleep as she would have liked, but the investigation would not wait for her energy levels to get back up to maximum. Having got into the office ahead of most other people, she'd grabbed a coffee and searched the internet for anything about Russell Strickland.

There was plenty to find. He owned three businesses in the county, all successful on the face of it; his social media was full of clips of him at talks and forums, shaking hands with upstanding members of the local community and even a local MP. Interestingly, there wasn't one obvious bit of negative press; everything seemed to point to Russell Strickland being a valuable member of society.

Despite having no evidence to the contrary, Tola wasn't buying it. Seeing her colleagues had arrived, she sat down with them to run through initial findings. It wasn't good news. They had two scenarios to work. One involved an unknown council worker or contractor who happened to be connected to the house purchases and knew the houses were empty, and who randomly selected that particular house to hide Helen. The other was that Russell Strickland killed her.

Either one had used the property, expecting it to be levelled in the foreseeable future. The destruction of the house would have made it virtually impossible to investigate the crime scene, making it easier for the perpetrator to get away with it. But the demolition never happened. Both scenarios had to be on the table, but one was looking more likely to everyone.

They had several challenges, though. Russell Strickland's DNA would naturally be all over the property; even a junior lawyer would be able to talk that issue away. He also hadn't owned it at the time and would argue that anyone else could have entered it and dumped Helen's body there.

Tola hated knowing something the others didn't, because she couldn't use it. She knew whoever it was had driven Helen to her final destination and unlocked the back door with a key.

After much deliberation, the next course of action was agreed upon.

'It has to be early,' Tola said to the team. 'If we turn up after seven, I think he'll already be out doing whatever it is he does. Networking. He seems to be here, there and everywhere, based on his social media accounts. This guy likes to be out and about, promoting himself and his brands. As much as embarrassing him in front of his peers or the public seems appealing, I think it could easily backfire; we might have the wrong person. Better we pick him up from home and bring him here.'

Her colleagues nodded in unison before dispersing. Tola just had to be patient a little while longer; the chief had to give the plan the go ahead.

***

Russell Strickland had been smiling constantly for over a minute and his jaw was aching. The photographer wanted him in every single picture, and it was beginning to grate. He motioned his head at his PA to come over during a rare break from posing.

'How long do I have to do this for, Kaylee? I've got to be online in forty minutes.' He was disgruntled but maintained his grin.

'Just another ten minutes and you can be out of here. I can wrap up the rest,' Kaylee replied, not looking up from her phone, which was always perched in her hand.

'You didn't tell me there would be this many kids here.'

'It's a youth centre, Russell. Not a nursing home.'

'Russell, can we have you back, big man?' the photographer called.

Russell obliged, joking with the youth centre volunteers as the photos were being taken.

'Now one with the cheque?'

Three of the youth centre's volunteers, in their yellow branded T-shirts, paid for by one of Russell's companies, walked forward holding an oversized cheque for £25,000.

The leader of the youth centre settled himself next to Russell. 'We really cannot thank you enough, Mr Strickland. This money will enable us to keep running some of our most important clubs. You've done so much for these children.'

Russell maintained his gaze at the photographer for a couple more flashes, then turned and took the team leader's hand and shook it vigorously. 'It's an absolute pleasure of mine, Tony. Local businessmen like me, we need to be doing more for the areas we grew up in. It's only right that we should.'

***

Kaylee looked up from her phone and watched Russell with the volunteers. She couldn't bear to look at him these days, preferring to pretend that there was always something important she needed to keep tabs on via her phone.

Another performance, she thought, walking away to the back of the hall where fewer people were. She sat down and rubbed her ankles. 'Why am I wearing these anyway?' she said, looking at the three-inch heels she had on. Trainers would have been a far better option on the shiny wooden floor.

She flicked through the email she had been writing one more time, tapped 'Send', then threw her phone into her handbag.

They did warn me, but no, I had to show I could deal with it. But when it actually happened, I didn't know what to do, did I? If I'd said anything at the time, he would have just made out I was overreacting. Maybe I gave him signals that it was okay to try what he did. These thoughts had been repeating in Kaylee's head, over and over, since telling her plan to a close friend, who had also helped her tidy up her CV.

She breathed a big sigh, one that brought with it blissful relief.

***

Russell spent another five minutes saying goodbye to everyone, then waiting until the three cheers in his honour were completed. He didn't say goodbye to Kaylee, instead heading straight for his car.

Once inside with the door shut, he leant back on the leather seat and enjoyed the silence. 'People get on my bloody nerves.'

He opened his messages and emails to quickly scan for anything important before his next meeting. Kaylee's email titled *'Resignation'* jumped out immediately.

He read it quickly. It was no surprise, but it annoyed him that she had beaten him to it. She'd been a great PA back when he hired her ten months ago—a cinched waist in her pencil skirts and tailored tops. He'd thought she was game for some fun as she'd never rebuked him for an arm round her waist, or a squeeze of her bum or thigh when at the bar with colleagues. She smelled amazing whenever he got close to her; he could never work out if it was her perfume or her moisturiser, or a combination of the two.

Her reaction when he tried to kiss her in his car a few months back was not so much of a surprise; he'd had it before. But the pepper spray was. She'd sprayed directly at his face but hadn't realised it would instantly fill the whole car up. Knowing he couldn't stay inside the vehicle for any length of time, he'd relented and unlocked all the doors. Both of them fell out, choking and their eyes streaming. She was screaming at him, threatening to call HR. He'd shouted back at her that everyone in the office thought they were having sex anyway, so who was going to believe her? He had no idea if that's what anyone thought, but he didn't need another whining woman going to HR about him—not that anyone had done anything about the previous complaints.

Russell nonchalantly forwarded the resignation to HR to deal with, not bothering to reply, then started the engine and made his way out of the youth centre carpark. He already had someone in mind to replace Kaylee.

He rang his head of marketing as he pulled onto the dual carriageway.

'Hey, Russell.'

'Hey, that new girl who started. What's her name? Tammy? Teresa?'

'It's Marie.'

'Yeah, her. I'll need her to work with me from next week. She'll be taking over from Kaylee. Advertise for a replacement for her in your team.'

There was an audible huff and a tut at the other end of the phone. 'Sure thing, Russell.'

Without pleasantries, Russell ended the call. 'On to the next one.'

CHAPTER 31

At 6:30am, Tola arrived outside Russell Strickland's home, along with two uniformed officers. It was a detached building, surrounded by a large lawn and established shrubs, with a majestic willow tree on the right of the entrance. Two cars were parked on the driveway, an SUV and a convertible, both with the latest-issue number plates. Three proud, leaping stags were positioned across the grass, ready to light up after dark, and Tola spotted a Christmas tree, heaving with baubles, through the spacious lounge window.

The house gave the impression that its owner was successful, an achiever. Tola saw nothing but an ego on display. But she was trying to keep an open mind—this man might have nothing to do with Helen's disappearance; it's innocent until proven guilty—despite everything telling her that she was right.

Tola rang the doorbell, knowing the occupants could see her and the other officers on the camera. She heard at least two small dogs yapping. Standing back, she waited as the lock turned.

In front of her stood a woman of average height, with blonde hair tied back and impeccable make-up for the time of the morning. Two small, white bichons, looking very like clouds on legs, danced around her feet, barking at their unexpected visitors.

'Good morning. My name is Detective Inspector Obederin. I need to speak with Russell Strickland. Is he in, please?'

The woman looked startled. 'Yes, he's here. He's just on the phone. Would you like to come in?'

'Thank you, and you are?'

'Emma Strickland, Russell's wife.'

Tola entered the house while the two officers waited outside. Emma closed the door and went into the kitchen; her two miniature bodyguards followed closely on her heels. It was a spacious entrance with room for a large armchair. An ornate mirror covered one wall, and a brightly coloured abstract artwork the other. Tola could see Emma speaking with a man, who had his hand over his phone while he listened to her. He looked markedly older than Emma, by at least ten to fifteen years. He made eye contact with Tola, then continued with his phone call.

Happy to keep us waiting, Tola thought to herself. Her ability to keep an open mind was waning.

Emma came scuttling back towards her, scooping the dogs up and putting them into the front lounge. 'Sorry about those two, they're very cheeky; Coco and Bella are typical bichons. Russell won't be a moment. Can I get you anything?'

'No, I'm fine, thank you, Mrs Strickland. It's a beautiful house. Have you lived here long?'

Tola noticed Emma look back at the kitchen, checking if she was being watched. She was perfectly presented. Her clothes were well thought out, her hair styled with care. But there was something missing behind her eyes. A lack of spirit. It was as if she was haunted. Tola had seen that look many times in her career.

'Thank you. We moved in about seven years ago.'

'Lovely, and have you been married long? I was just admiring your rings.' Tola couldn't miss the gems on Emma's hands. More statement pieces.

Emma pulled her sleeves down as if to hide her hands. 'Yes, they are beautiful. We've been married four yea—' She suddenly stopped as she saw her husband walking down the hallway.

Russell Strickland walked behind his wife, placed his hands on her shoulders and gave them a tight squeeze. He was smartly dressed, his shirt tucked into his jeans. His face was clean-shaven, and his brown hair styled but slightly thinning at the front. Tola wondered if he plucked his eyebrows.

'Detective Obederin,' he said. 'I understand you wish to speak to me. Russell Strickland.' He held his hand out, and Tola obliged with a firm handshake. He seemed completely unfazed by her visit, almost as if he had been expecting her. He returned his hands to his wife's shoulders.

'Good morning, Mr Strickland. I have some questions about an ongoing case. It concerns a property you inherited from your late mother, which you owned up until early 1992. We'd like you to accompany us to the station, if you could, please. It shouldn't take long.'

'Am I under arrest, Detective Obederin?'

'No, Mr Strickland, you would just be helping us with our inquiries. But these kinds of discussions are usually easier and quicker at the station.' Tola glanced at Emma then back at Russell.

He seemed to take the hint. 'Of course. Emma, can you get my coat and keys for me, darling.' It was less of a question and more of an order. He released his grip on her shoulders, and Emma went off to run her errand.

'I assume I will be driven to the station. I'll ask my lawyer to meet us there, shall I?'

Tola was unmoved by his request. 'You can, Mr Strickland, as is your right.'

As she led him out of the house, she saw Emma looking bewildered and the bichons up at the window, watching the show.

CHAPTER 32

Russell sat casually in the chair, with his hands in front of him on the table. He didn't seem to be anxious or concerned about being in the police station; he held a placid yet disingenuous smile on his face. His lawyer had been waiting for him when he arrived, and they both sat calmly opposite Tola in the interview room.

After taking care of formalities, Tola opened the dialogue. 'You inherited your late mother's home in 1991, the terraced house in Paternoster Lane, correct?'

'Yes.'

'The council purchased it and the other properties on the road the following year, I understand.'

'Yes, that's correct.'

'The reason we are here, Mr Strickland, is that we discovered a body last night, in the house you owned previously. It's believed to be that of Helen Swift, who went missing in November 1992.' Tola looked directly at Russell as she spoke.

There was no change of expression on his face and his hands remained where he had put them. But he couldn't hide his eyes. He had striking, blue eyes, and his pupils widened as Tola said Helen's name. Adrenaline had begun coursing through his body.

Tola continued. 'We know you didn't own the house by then but, as you'd expect, we need to speak to you about anything you might remember about Helen's disappearance. You were good enough to speak to us at the time, Mr Strickland. We have a witness statement from you, taken outside the entrance to Corsley Woods by one of our officers. Do you remember?'

Russell leant back slightly. 'Yes, how could I forget such a terrible local incident. I regularly walk in the woods, as do many dog owners, so I gave a statement along with everyone else. It's taken so long for you to find her? I really feel for her family.'

Tola ignored the dig. She'd played this game many times. 'Can you remember what you said in your statement, Mr Strickland?'

'Yes, detective, but I'm not sure why it's relevant as I didn't own the property that the body was found in. It was off my hands about six months before, which I think you probably know from your records already.'

Tola wondered why he needed his lawyer there if he was going to be this talkative. 'All correct, but it's important, as I'm sure you understand, that I check over every detail again, given that it's an extraordinary co-incidence that you gave us a statement at the time and then Helen was found in a house that you previously owned.'

Tola paused and waited for Russell to make his next move. She detected the slightest of smirks from the corner of his mouth. He was enjoying this.

'Very well, detective. I took our dog for a walk at about three-thirty pm, then returned home to my wife and stayed in all evening. I didn't see the missing woman, although, based on a photo I was shown, I did recall seeing her on my walks.'

'I can see your wife corroborated this for you at the time. I assume she'll be able to do it again? Although, I am guessing that wasn't Emma, since you've only been married for four years and, well, the age difference is noticeable.' Tola decided she'd get her own dig in if that's how this was going to go.

The lawyer raised his eyebrows but said nothing. Russell moved his hands to his knees, and his congenial smile wavered a little. It was there, a slight chink. He was getting old, and a man so worried about his appearance would not like hearing about it. Then there was information Tola had, however small, that he hadn't been able to control. Tola wondered if it might cause Emma problems later.

'My first wife, Anne, sadly passed away, so no, she will not be able to confirm that for you.'

'I'm sorry to hear that, Mr Strickland. How did she die, if you don't mind me asking?'

'Anne committed suicide. A tragedy, she was a beautiful woman. I'll never forget how I found her. It left a hole in my heart; I thought I might not recover from the loss.' There was no emotion behind Russell's words. They sounded rehearsed, a verse he likely said when asked about Anne to maintain some sympathy.

'My condolences to you. So, how do you suppose Helen's body came to be in your house, Mr Strickland?'

The lawyer held a hand up and whispered something to Russell before confirming he could answer.

'As I have said, the house was not in my ownership when the woman went missing. So, I couldn't possibly know how she came to be in there, could I?'

There was a knock at the door, and a colleague asked if Tola could step out for five minutes, so she excused herself.

'What is it?' Tola hated to be interrupted during interviews, but she knew there was a lot of activity going on in the background.

'Initial results back are inconclusive for cause of death. The victim is, well, not in a state that the pathologist has much to work with, and there are no obvious injuries on the bones based on an initial review. But the full post-mortem is yet to be done. And, as we expected, there are a number of male DNA samples around the house, also on the duvet and the cupboard door handle. We're expecting one to be a match to Strickland when we take his sample, not that it gets us anywhere. Overall, we have nothing.' Tola's colleague looked as downtrodden as she felt.

'Was that why you interrupted me?'

'No, one bit of good news. The search warrant has been granted—exceptionally, given the case and the circumstances. The team is heading to his house now. Thought you might like to let him know.'

Tola smiled as her colleague handed her a copy of the warrant.

'Well, let me know if they find anything.'

Tola re-entered the interview room and sat down. Leafing through her paperwork, she deliberately sat quietly for over a minute before speaking.

'Just so you are aware, we have a warrant to search your property.' She handed the copy to Strickland and his lawyer to review. 'Our team is on their way. We'll make sure your wife is disturbed as little as possible.'

Tola watched Strickland as his lawyer looked over the details. His forehead started to perspire ever so slightly. There was something in the house he didn't want them to find, she could tell. But whether it could be found was another question.

'This seems excessive but nothing we can challenge,' the lawyer said. 'Did you have anything else you wished to discuss?' The lawyer clearly thought it was time to leave.

Tola wanted to keep them both in the interview room as long as possible. She didn't believe that Strickland would confess or give himself away, but she had one tactic left that might rattle him a little, and she felt like going for broke. 'We were considering how someone might have gotten Helen's body into your old house, weren't we? I know, from having checked with the council, that the security shutters were not installed until the following year, when it was clear the development was in jeopardy. There were notes made by the contractors that a clear attempt had been made to break into one of the houses at the other end of the street, but no other damage was reported to any of the others, including the one you owned, Mr Strickland. No broken windows, no forced doors. It's as if whoever put Helen in there had keys to get in.

'I imagine Helen was driven to the house—the woods were not quite close enough, and trying to walk her all that way without incident, it's unlikely—then, maybe, taken in through the back door. Yes, it would have been more discreet, and even further away from the phone box that used to be there. That must have been tempting for her, if she'd seen it. She would have still been alive, able to walk herself round past the front door—under duress, of course. What woman would willingly go into a deserted house with a complete stranger?'

The lawyer went to interrupt, but Tola shot him a glance. It was a big risk but, thankfully, he backed down. She doubted she'd get any more chances.

'It would have been dark, and the road was uninhabited; no one would have heard her screams from the kitchen, where I expect she fell. Where I expect unspeakable things were done to her. No one would have heard her body being moved about. No one would have heard the back door being locked and Helen's assailant driving away. What car did you have at the time, Mr Strickland?'

For the first time, Strickland looked surprised and taken off guard. Tola could see he hadn't just been listening to her, he had been remembering and wondering how she knew what he knew. He went to answer her question, then checked himself. He looked at his lawyer, who nodded that it was okay to respond. The records could be checked anyway.

'I drove a Peugeot 405 back then.'

Tola knew that, when she looked it up, it would be red and have four doors with black trim around the middle.

The lawyer now found his voice and was in no further mood for his client to cooperate. 'Detective Obederin, do you have anything you wish to charge my client with?'

Tola sighed heavily. 'No, I do not. I would like to take a DNA sample so we can eliminate him from our inquiries, though. Would you have an issue with that, Mr Strickland?' Tola directed the question to him, ignoring the lawyer.

The serene smile had returned to his face. She felt sick to her stomach because she had no choice but to allow him to walk straight out of the door, and he knew it.

'That's no problem at all.' Russell and his lawyer stood up to leave. 'I hope you can find whoever did it. It's awful to think they are still out there, isn't it?'

Tola returned to her desk feeling beaten. Russell had given his DNA sample and left the station straight afterwards; she'd watched him get into a car with his lawyer and drive away. Inquiries were still being run down at the council, but Tola did not expect anything fruitful from it. She knew who had killed Helen. She now had to wait to see if anything turned up at the house.

It was infuriating. She had all the pieces; she knew how Helen had been kidnapped, she knew how she was killed, and now she knew by whom. But no one was going to believe the witness statement of the victim herself.

CHAPTER 33

The discovery of Helen's body made the local and national news, maintaining coverage for a few days before the next big story took over. Tola had worked overtime, trying to find something, anything that would tie Russell Strickland to the murder, but nothing. Even the search warrant had come up blank. It wasn't the outcome they were hoping for; they wanted more for Helen and her children.

Tola had seen cases like this before, where they knew who had done the crime but couldn't make a case for the CPS. These cases ended unresolved, and made her feel like she had gone ten rounds and lost. She didn't like being made to feel that way, especially by someone like Strickland. The bin under her desk in the office, with its dents and kick marks, bore testament to how she felt about the whole situation.

***

With Christmas fast approaching, Jen resolved to break out of her slump by getting her dad over to help with a few decorations. They agreed that Jen would stay at Mark's on Christmas Eve so they could be together on Christmas morning, open some presents and have breakfast. Then it would be off to Jacqui's brother's house for lunch.

Jen always enjoyed seeing her cousins, even if it wasn't that often. She loved to reminisce about times they spent at their nan's playing hide and seek, as her house had seemed so much bigger and more mysterious than theirs. Her uncle was looking forward to having them there; it seemed he needed the distraction from losing Jacqui as much as they did.

Then, Mark was going to spend a few days with his own brother, dropping Jen at Laura's on the way. They had it all planned out. No time to be sat on their own. No space for miserable thoughts to creep in.

Jacqui had not returned, and Jen had not heard from Tola. She'd not seen anything online about an arrest and wondered if everything was going okay with the investigation. She'd nearly called or messaged Tola a couple of times, but decided it was best to leave her alone. If Tola needed help, she was sure she would contact her. Jen didn't want to be a nuisance, but it was frustrating not knowing what was happening.

She'd had only one spiritual visitor since Helen, a lady called Sally who seemed very distressed as her children mistakenly thought she had died without making a will. The truth was, she had made a will but she'd hidden it so well and forgotten to tell them where to find it. After getting some names from Sally, and a quick social media search, Jen was able to track down the family and tell them where the will was via a message. One of the children actually replied to say they had found it—no questions about how Jen could possibly have known where it was, just a thank you and a Merry Christmas. Jen had been more than pleased with that.

Jen pottered around her kitchen, waiting for the oven to finish cooking some sausage rolls. The smell always reminded her of parties.

She was popping round to her uncle's house later, just for drinks and nibbles. She and her dad had been invited, along with some other friends and family that had known Jacqui. Jen hadn't thought she'd be too enthused to go, but was actually looking forward to it. She could tell how much people wanted to look after both her and her dad, and it felt good to let them.

She went into the lounge to draw the curtains across the patio doors. Despite it being only mid-afternoon, it was already getting dark. Plus, it was starting to rain. The place felt cosier with the curtains closed.

The doorbell sounded, and Jen went to see who it was, expecting to find the parcels she was waiting for. To her surprise, it was Tola.

'Sorry I didn't call first. Is it okay to come in? Oh, and these were on your doorstep.'

Jen ushered Tola inside and took some mildly soggy packages from her. 'Wow, I ordered more than I thought,' she said, trying to keep all the parcels from toppling out of her arms. 'I wasn't expecting to see you. Is everything alright?'

Tola took her coat off and hung it on the banister. 'No, everything is not alright—'

Tola was cut off by the oven timer.

'Go sit in the lounge, I'll only be a second.' Jen got the sausage rolls out and, feeling like Tola needed a pick-me-up, popped a few onto a plate, burning her fingertips as she plucked them off the tray. 'I should have asked if you're vegetarian. Just be careful, they're hot out of the oven. So, what's happened?'

'Well, that's the problem. Nothing has happened!' Tola grabbed a sausage roll and ate it in one. The heat didn't seem to bother her. With her mouth still partially full, she continued. 'I'm sorry to just barge round here. I've been back and forth about whether I should come, but no one else will understand. No one else knows what we know. That's what makes it all even more annoying. I know who murdered Helen. I've interviewed him. It's definitely him. But I can't get him. I can't arrest him.'

Jen was taken aback. 'Why the hell not!?'

'I can't arrest him based on the evidence we have. We don't have enough to prove it's him and not a random council person who could have taken Helen and left her in the house. We found nothing when we searched his home that connects him to Helen. He can argue that of course his DNA would be all over his mother's house. There's other male DNA in the house, and we can't test everyone in the world.

'I only know it was him because Helen told us he had keys and she gave us the description of the car he was driving. No one else knows she was even taken by car. It's just so excruciating. I feel like I have been screaming in my own head for days.' She leant forward and put her head in her hands.

Jen got up and put an arm round her. 'So, there's nothing that can be done? He can't be made to pay for what he did?'

'No, I can't charge him based on what we have, let alone get a prosecution out of it. His lawyer would run rings round us. And what's even worse is that he knows it. He knows we can't touch him. He's just laughing at me, at Helen, at her family. He's an utter creep, twisted. It's a game to him. He wasn't worried that we'd found

Helen; he basically enjoyed the fact. The years I have spent trying to find him and get Helen justice. He's just out of my reach.'

Jen sat back down in her seat, grabbing a sausage roll on the way. 'It's not fair, is it? She went through all that: being taken, dying the way she did, then coming back to us to tell her story.' Jen was thoroughly hacked off. This was not the ending she wanted.

The two of them sat there in silence, listening to the rain outside hitting the bifold door windows. Defeat hung in the air.

Tap. Tap. Tap.

Tola glanced over at the curtains.

Tap. Tap. Tap.

Jen now looked over. The sound was coming from the window.

Tap. Tap. Tap.

They looked at each other. It wasn't the rain, they could still hear that in the background. The tapping was a sound of its own. Three, slow, deliberate taps. Jen recognised the sound because she made it herself sometimes when she saw the neighbour's cat in the garden, stalking birds.

Tap. Tap. Tap. A fingernail on the glass to get their attention.

Jen stood up and slowly made her way over to the curtains. She stood still, her ear up to the fabric, hardly breathing.

THUMP.

Jen jumped back, expecting the glass to have shattered, but the window remained intact. She could see the security light had come on, its light seeping in round the edges of the curtain.

'Someone is in your garden,' Tola said, now standing up and alert. 'I can go out and check.'

'No, don't. We'll be safer here.' Jen didn't want Tola going outside. If it was another visitor, a not-so-friendly one, they would be protected by the additions her parents had made to the walls all those years ago.

Tola moved beside Jen as she gripped the edge of the curtain and slowly pulled it across to reveal the dark of the evening. The raindrops' pattern on the glass made it hard to single out anything.

The security light went off. They couldn't see anyone there.

'Maybe it was just a bird? Or a bat?' Tola surmised.

Jen stared past the glass, trying to spot any movement, but there was only stillness. And rain.

As she reached to pull the curtain back across, the security light stuttered, and there, in the moment the patio was illuminated, she saw a figure.

'Bloody hell!' Jen said. 'There is someone out there.'

The security light flickered again as if it was being drained of its power. With every blaze it managed to make, the figure moved closer towards them. Until the light was forced to give up, leaving an abyss.

Jen felt her heart beating fast. Then, in her head, a familiar voice spoke. And it was still angry.

'Where is the justice for the wrongs he has done?'

'Who is that speaking?' Tola now had her hands around Jen's arm.

'You heard that?' Jen said.

'Yes, didn't you!?' Tola exclaimed.

The voice was not just for Jen anymore. It was out in the open.

Two palms suddenly appeared against the glass, violently and with purpose. The fingers were bent so the long, ragged nails all touched the window, as if they were clawing to get in. The skin looked devoid of life, blackened in places; there was no blood pumping within those hands.

Alarm bells were going off in Jen's head. Everything her mum had worried about was happening. She'd dismissed the concern that a malevolent force could be enticed into their home by simply helping Helen, but it had happened; it was here, and Jen wasn't sure what to do.

She wondered how long the protections in the walls would keep it out. Then, as if just by thinking about it, the scent of rosemary and lavender filled the air, and an instant calm came over Jen.

Turning her back to the window, she found Jacqui standing behind her.

Confused as to why Jen was no longer paying attention to the ominous creature outside, Tola also turned. 'Oh my God, is that your mum?' she said with a high pitch to her voice and pointing directly at Jacqui. She'd recognised her from the photos around the house.

'Mum, you're back!' An overwhelming relief washed through Jen.

'It seems that way, doesn't it?'

Tola was beside herself. 'Oh my God, I can hear her as well! What is happening?'

Jen's mind was a whirr. Tola could see Jacqui and the thing outside. What was going on?

'What is that out there!?' Jacqui alerted them to an image now appearing in the glass behind them.

Jen and Tola reverted to the window and Jacqui came to stand beside them. They all watched as a woman's face emerged from the blackness as if floating to the surface of a pond. Lifeless, pale skin was pulled taught over the cheekbones, and the eye sockets were sunken. Her thin lips bent into a smile, and as they did, her eyes shone like black pearls. Her features were surrounded by cascading, inky hair, which framed her face and seemed to merge with the nighttime background.

Despite her frightening appearance, there was a beguiling beauty about her. Jen looked into those eyes, and they reminded her of the brooch on Elizabeth's cloak, gifted to her by Annabelle Fitzroy-Lawson. The unending emptiness in them was almost hypnotic.

'You followed me back from the house, didn't you?' Jen asked.

'I go where I am needed.' Her voice was no longer a whisper. It had confidence and volume. Despite being outside, it sounded like the creature was in the room with them.

'We don't need you here. Please leave.'

'Oh, I think you do, Jennifer. I think you all need me.'

'What does she mean, Jen? Who is she?' Tola couldn't believe what was happening. She'd seen a lot of awful things in her time, but that was usually human beings doing awful things to other human beings. Now she could see and hear ghosts—or whatever it was outside in the garden. It was amazing and terrifying all in one.

'Jen, I don't like this,' Jacqui said, starting to panic. 'I told you something bad would come through.'

The smile on the dead woman's face grew wider. 'Now that we are all here, we can decide.'

CHAPTER 34

Jen had a lot going through her head, and her questions were piling up. But before she could ask anything, Jacqui jumped in with her own.

'How did this get here, Jen? Has it been in the house? What does it want? Maybe you should call your dad. No, don't call him. Not after last time.'

'Mum, just stop! It only appeared a few minutes before you did, and I only saw it once before that. It's not the same as the thing you encountered. And it can't get in the house. I'm pretty certain of that.'

Tola was just watching them in awe. There she was, Jacqui Hattley, dead a few months yet conversing in front of her, seemingly as real as Tola herself.

Everyone's attention was drawn back to the window as the security light burst back on. They could now see the creature completely. She was fully formed, no longer like smoke as when Jen had seen her before. Her whole body was shrouded in a grey gown, but it was torn and ripped in places, as if time itself had taken its toll on the fabric. Tresses of hair flowed downwards, touching the ground then splaying out, as if anchoring her. She looked at each one of them in turn, waiting patiently for the inevitable questions.

Jacqui was not pleased to see this unwanted guest but couldn't help getting closer to the window to observe her. There was something about her that pulled

Jacqui in. 'Where did you see her before, Jen?' she asked as the creature mirrored her stare.

'It was in the house where we found Helen. But she wasn't as fully formed back then.'

'You found Helen? Oh that's, well, wonderful is the wrong word. I'm glad her family has some peace.'

Tola stepped forward so she was only a few inches from Jacqui. The two women looked at each other.

'I cannot believe it. You're standing right here, just like I am. I'm Tola Obederin. It really is a pleasure to meet you.'

'I know who you are.' Jacqui gave Tola a warm smile. 'You couldn't see me, but I could see you. Yet, you can now… How is all this possible, Jen?'

"No rules, remember, Mum? But I think this…' Jen tried to find the right word; she wanted to be polite. 'This *woman*, she can tell us for sure. Can't you?'

The woman behind the glass never stopped looking at all of them. Jen noticed she never blinked.

'What would you like to know from me?'

'You're an onryō, or like one, aren't you?'

'Names are of no matter. I mean the same everywhere.'

'Where did you come from?'

'I have always been. As long as men do the despicable things they do, I will always be.'

Jen rolled her eyes. 'Can we not go down the speaking in riddles route again, please? Just talk to us normally. You can do that, can't you? You spoke to me normally in the house where Helen died.'

The woman opened her mouth a little too wide, and laughed. She liked Jen's forthrightness. *I could feel you were brave when you found me, Jennifer. I will speak as plainly as I can for you.*

'My husband wanted me gone so he could marry his new bride. He beat me savagely and left me for dead in the forest, where the animals could hide his deed. I had only one last breath, and with it I screamed for justice.

'In that moment, he was revealed to me and gave me a choice.'

'He?' Jen was trying her best to follow.

'He came from within the trees. He promised me complete and utter revenge on my husband—to begin with—then the ability to exact justice on any man for his crimes. My soul was of little use to me by then, so I willingly agreed.

'But he had his own tricks. Men are never to be trusted.'

'Hang on. You did a deal with something in the forest, to turn you into this, so you could get back at your husband?'

'Yes.'

'Doesn't look to be working out so well,' Jacqui couldn't help saying.

Jen shot her a look. 'So, you were originally a person, but now you're a demon of some kind?'

'Some might say so. Some might call me an angel.'

Tola let out a tut and received a similar look from Jen.

'What do you want from us?' Jen asked. 'You said we needed you, but I don't think that's quite true. I think you need us.'

'I heard Helen's cries. I watched as she took her last breath. I have been returning to where she lay, waiting. When you came and took Helen away, I had to follow you. Such power you have, Jennifer. The things you can see that others can't. You can help me fulfil my purpose.'

Jen asked the next question already knowing where it was heading. 'And what is that purpose?'

'Oh, come now. Surely you know. He hasn't paid for what he has done, has he? Tell them what choice they have. Tell them what I can do that you all cannot.'

Jen had an inkling, and it made her massively uncomfortable. She wanted to change the subject, change direction. 'But how can Tola see and hear you and my mum? How are you doing that?'

'I'm not doing that, Jennifer. You are—or rather, you all are.

'I've not seen one like you before, with this much… power. I can see you have inherited this from your mother and she from her mother. A little kink in the chain, but the gift has always moved from one to the next. Generations of women like you, and these abilities have been growing, child after child after child.

'Then there is your collective passion.' She looked specifically at Tola. *'Your want to find Helen, your anger at the injustice. You have all made me whole.*

'And you, Jennifer, you have so much… potential. Look at what you can do. The dead and the living can see each other.'

Jen wondered what was meant by 'potential'. How could she have enabled Tola to see her mum? What else might she be capable of doing?

Tola and Jacqui had been listening, and both were trying to keep up.

'Jen, what is she talking about? What choice?' Jacqui's face was full of concern again.

Jen sat down on the sofa and leant her head back; she just needed a moment. Tola and Jacqui came over to her, leaving the creature by the window.

'She's followed me here because… I think she wants to make Russell Strickland pay for what he did to Helen. She knows he's going to get away with it.'

'Sorry, you say the man who killed Helen is going to get away with it? How can this be the case?' Jacqui blurted out. She was trying to stay focused on the demon, but Helen's killer not being brought to account threw in a curveball.

Tola explained where the investigation had got to, and by the time she'd finished, Jacqui was boiling over.

'But this is a joke, surely? Is there nothing you can do, Tola? He abducted Helen, raped her and then killed her. He hid her body in his own mother's house. She couldn't even be mourned by her family properly because of how she was hidden. It's all wrong!'

They both looked at Jen, waiting for a response.

Jen had been listening but all the while kept her eyes locked on the creature outside. It wasn't its rage she had inside her head anymore; it was her own. They were all now seething about Russell Strickland getting away with what he had done.

But Jen didn't like being made to feel like this, so closed her eyes, concentrating on pushing the negative emotions away. 'He can be made to pay for what he has done. Just not the way we were all expecting,' Jen said, then wished she hadn't.

'What do you mean?' Tola asked.

'It's what she was created to do.' Jen tipped her head towards the woman outside. 'Enact revenge.'

Tola sat down next to Jen, the penny dropping. 'So, she's some kind of angel of vengeance?'

'Something like that. She's asking us to unleash her.'

Even as Jen said it, she couldn't quite believe it. The demon wanted them to take the law into their own hands. Not even the law; it was more like making moral judgement and issuing punishment—judge, jury and executioner all rolled into one.

'But, what would she do to him?' Tola asked.

'I would make him suffer the way he has made the women in his life suffer.'

'Women? Are you saying he's done this before?' Jacqui said.

'There was one he tormented so much that she could not bear to be alive anymore. And there is another, she lives day to day in constant fear. She'll leave one day the same way.'

'My God, his first wife, Anne, died of suicide,' Tola said. 'He told me himself. Then there's his second wife, Emma. I could tell there was something nervous about her, she looked worried that we were there at his house. I had wondered if he'd gone on to kill others that we didn't know about; instead, he just found a new game to play and new toys. I've seen it time and time again, a constant cycle of abuse until the victim leaves, one way or another.'

Jen had to know the answer to one more question. 'What exactly are you going to do to make him suffer?'

The demon's face lit up. *'How do you say it? An eye for an eye?'*

A hush came over all of them.

Tola started to shake her head. 'No, no, no. This isn't how we do things. We have laws and rules we must abide by. It's just bad luck that I can't use them to make Strickland accountable for what he has done. It's the way things go sometimes in cases like this. I'm as upset about it as anyone else, but that doesn't give us the right to exact retribution. We're not vigilantes.'

Jen looked at Jacqui. 'Mum, are you okay?'

'No, I am not okay! It's like the Ouija board all over again. This thing is dangerous. We shouldn't even be talking to it. We need to force it to leave.'

The demon, having been patient for a time, now became irritated. She smacked her rotten hands against the window, startling all three women. *'You cannot make me leave.'*

'Well, you can't get in, can you? We're not doing it, so you may as well go,' Jacqui replied.

The demon thought for a moment. *'Helen would have wanted her killer brought to justice. You would be doing this for her.'*

Tola flew straight in. 'You have no idea what Helen would or would not have wanted. You might have waited with her all those years, but she was dead. You didn't know her in life. I spent over fifteen years on her case; I got to know her children, her grandchildren. Yes, Helen would have wanted justice, but the way her children talk about her, the way she lived tells me that she would have wanted it the right way or not at all. So don't you dare try using her memory now to get us to do what you want.'

The demon's mouth started to screw up as if she was about to have an almighty tantrum about not getting her own way. Her head bent back, further than it should have been able to do, and as it returned to its original position, her mouth opened, and she screamed. A shrill, ear-piercing scream. If sound were solid, it would have filled every inch of space around the three women, suffocating them.

Jen and Tola felt their ears throbbing in pain.

It did not seem to affect Jacqui. 'Stop doing that, you're hurting them!' she pleaded, seeing the distress the other two were in.

As quickly as it had started, the screaming stopped. Tola dropped to the arm of the chair in relief, while Jen rubbed her ears.

'You think your little plants will keep me out here for long? I have endless time to wait.' The demon paused. She was

considering something else as she looked at Jen and then her mum. *'Someone is looking for you.'*

'What?' Jen snapped back, confused. 'Who?'

'She let them in before with her game of numbers and letters.' The demon was now pointing accusingly at Jacqui. *'They have been looking for a long time.'*

Jacqui started to panic. 'Jen, the Ouija board. The names. It spelt out all our names: ours, Nan's, Elizabeth's. It can't be, can it?'

Jen desperately wanted to hold her mum, to ease her worry. 'What do you know about it?' she asked the creature.

'They are still looking. The longer I am here, the more likely it is they will find you. Every time you use your gift, Jennifer, it's like sending out a beacon. You can be seen.' The demon went quiet again, then seemed highly amused at the prospect of what she was about to say. *'Or, perhaps I could follow one of you from here instead. I followed Jennifer, didn't I? I could have chosen to stay with your friend instead—and her little girl…'* As the demon spoke, her image morphed into that of Olivia. *'I might not be able to get in there with you, but you can't stay inside forever.'*

Jen was up off the sofa in a flash, her face right up against the glass, her hands balled into fists. 'You stop that! You are never to go near them!'

'Or perhaps I could visit the old woman who no longer knows who she is.' Olivia changed into Tola's mother Grace.

'Oh my God, Mum. No! Stop this!' Tola couldn't bear to think of this creature anywhere near her mum.

'Or lead the one who is looking for you right here.' The demon changed into her final costume, reflecting Jen's image back at her.

'You leave my daughter alone!' Jacqui was beside herself.

The demon was content with the reactions she was getting; she was enjoying herself. *'It's either you'*—her decrepit finger pointed to each of them—*'or him.'*

Jen was angry. This creature had threatened them all, tried to hurt them. She had the advantage.

Jen's hands were still tightly clenched when Tola came and held one of them. 'Jen, what do we do? I don't understand why she needs us to give her permission. Why can't she just go off and do it?'

Jen looked up at the mirror image staring back at her from behind the patio glass. But unlike Jen, her doppelganger was devoid of any compassion or rational thought. That had ebbed away over time, leaving only a drive for violent, deranged revenge.

Directing her voice to the glass, Jen had another question. 'You said the forest-being had his own tricks. What happened? What was in the deal that you didn't know about?'

The creature's face dropped slightly. *'I was not told the conditions of my revenge.'*

'Go on. Get to the details.' Jen was growing ever more impatient.

'I must gain permission and be delivered willingly to the perpetrator. I cannot freely do what I want.'

Jen had to laugh. 'So, for all your words about getting justice for what a man did to you, you let another man trick you into a trap! Doing his bidding for all eternity!'

'Do not mock me,' she warned.

Tola squeezed Jen's hand. 'Know when to back off, Jen. Don't anger her.'

Jen took a breath and tried to change her tone. 'So, it's not about protecting women or providing justice. It's purely about you getting someone to allow you to do what you want—which is to cause someone else considerable pain and suffering because you think they deserve it.'

The demon said nothing. Her face returned to a serene smile, and she continued to stare at them all.

Jen turned her attention to Jacqui and Tola. 'If we don't let her do what she wants to Strickland, she'll do something to someone we care about. We've got no way of stopping her. Look what she's just done to us. Imagine what she might do, roaming round your mum's care home, or at Laura's.' Jen felt completely backed into a corner. 'But if we agree to it, what on earth do I tell Dad? He would completely freak out about this demon being here, after last time, and that's before telling him I sent it to kill someone. And Laura, how do I explain this to her? She's okay with all of this at the moment, almost excited by it, but this isn't passing a message on to make someone's life better or helping someone find something. This is terrifying. It could completely change the way she sees me. I don't want to be carrying another secret.' Jen had her head in her hands.

'You're not on your own in this, Jen. We make this decision together,' Tola said, rubbing Jen's back, while Jacqui longed to be reminded of what it felt like to comfort her daughter.

Tola continued. 'Samuel always says to me, when I run something past him, that I already know what I am going to do. That I'll always do it with thought and care. He trusts me and how I make my decisions. I don't know what he'll make of this one or what he may think of me afterwards, but when I tell him what happened, I'll do it knowing I did what I thought was right. We're here now. We're the ones facing this demon, this dilemma. So we decide together and hope that what we have done is for the best.'

Jen looked at Tola and sensed that her decision was already made. 'Are you saying we just allow it to kill him?'

'I can't do anything about the investigation. My hands are tied. I cannot have it anywhere near my mum or anyone else. I have my own children; there's Samuel. I know it's not right, Jen, it goes against all my principles, but it can't leave here unless it's going to just one place.' Tola was visibly wrestling with her conscience, but she was resolute.

Jen felt cold, struggling to comprehend what was happening. 'Mum? We can't do it, surely?'

'Let it do what it wants,' Jacqui said reluctantly.

Jen couldn't believe it. After everything to do with the Ouija board and a life spent avoiding anything sinister or remotely dangerous, her mum was agreeing to a deal with a demon.

'I know, Jen. After everything I've said. But if it's you or him, it has to be him. The decision is not difficult for me to make. There are things beyond this living world that are dangerous, and this is one of them. We have to get rid of it by any means necessary. I know you are worried about what your dad and Laura will think of you. They will understand. They know you are a good person and will understand that you did what you thought was right.' Jacqui wasn't sure if this was true, but she hoped very much that it was.

'Bloody hell. What are we doing? How has this happened?' Jen crossed her arms in front of herself, chewed a fingernail and paced the room.

They were going to let a demon kill a man. This was a million miles away from where she'd expected her new abilities to take her. She knew this wasn't how things were supposed to be resolved—if people did this kind of thing all the time, the world would be in chaos—but the demon was threatening Olivia, Tola's mum, Jennifer herself. She knew she couldn't take the risk of the demon attaching itself to one of them, someone innocent, and wreaking havoc upon them. This was a decision being forced upon them, and she hated that fact.

Then there was a very small part of her—a part that she didn't want to admit existed to Tola or her mum—that believed Strickland should suffer. She knew revenge just encouraged retaliation, that sending in this assassin could literally come back to haunt her later— she imagined Russell's ghost could torment her for the rest of her life—but she wanted him to pay.

'Are you both sure?'

The other two women nodded reluctantly.

'The choice has been made.' The demon returned to her original form. She clapped her decaying hands with excitement, like some demented child.

'Stop celebrating. We're not doing this willingly; you're basically blackmailing us. You are no better than Russell Strickland in the end. Different methods but the same evil, the pair of you!' Jen didn't want her revelling in their decision.

The demon ignored her; she had no capacity for sentiment. *'Now you must get me to him, Jennifer.'*

Jen looked back at the demon, confused, then realised what she meant, recalling the chatroom and the letter to the father in prison. 'Ah, I get it now. This is why you need us. You can't get to him on your own, can you? I suppose you would have done that already if you could. I need to physically take you to him. How am I supposed to do that?'

'Take me to him and I'll do what needs to be done.'

Jen pondered for a moment, then her eyes landed on the parcels Tola had brought in, piled up in the corner of the lounge. She remembered the chatroom thread and the mention of a letter.

It was unprofessional to ask, but she expected Tola would have little resistance. 'If Tola can tell me his address, I can do it.'

'Why does it have to be you?' Jacqui asked, concerned.

'Tola can't do it; he knows who she is. And Mum, well, you can't leave the house, be seen by anyone or touch anything. So that counts you out.'

'What are you going to do?' Tola asked.

'If she just needs to get near him, I'll take a dummy parcel to his house and, when he answers the door, presumably she can attach herself to him? I can do it today and then it is done. Is that how it works?'

The demon nodded.

Jacqui walked over to the demon and stood firm in front of the glass separating them.

The demon regarded her with curiosity. *'You shouldn't be here, Jacqueline Hattley.'*

Jacqui looked behind her at Jen. Jen and Tola could clearly hear what the demon was saying.

'I know that.'

'You will have to leave her soon. You have borrowed too much time.'

'I don't need you reminding me of that either. If Jen gets you to him, that's it. You leave her alone, you never come back here, you leave Tola alone. All of them.'

'Agreed.'

Jacqui leant in closer as she spoke, trying to make sure that neither Tola nor Jen could hear her. Despite the moral quandary, a significant part of her also wanted Russell Strickland to pay. 'One more thing. You make sure that, at the end, he knows there is no longer any hope, that he knows he's going to die and no one is coming to save him.'

The demon nodded. It was a deal.

CHAPTER 35

Jen finished taping up the box and printed an address label. Jacqui, Tola and the demon at the window watched on as she stuck it to the top of the box. It looked much the same as any other parcel.

'Do you really think this is going to work?' Jacqui asked.

Tola pointed to the demon still staring in at them. She was giving her the creeps, how she just kept watching them, making sure they were doing what she wanted. 'She seems to be happy with the idea, so, I guess so. What else can we do?'

'Okay, so I'm just going to pull up outside, ring the doorbell, hand over the parcel and leave. They must have loads of deliveries this time of year; this should all go unnoticed.' Jen had checked: she could drive to Strickland's house and still be back in time for her uncle's get-together. She didn't want her dad asking questions about what she had been doing, so needed to stay on schedule.

Tola felt like she needed to leave. Technically, there was no more she could do to help. She couldn't go with Jen. But she also just wanted to get out of the house and away from the creature outside. The reality of what was happening was starting to sink in, and now she was just plain frightened. 'I think it's best that I get home. I told Samuel I'd get something for dinner on the way back, and I need to get myself together before I see him. It's not going to follow me, is it?'

'No, Tola, it's going to stay with me now. It knows I will take it to Strickland.' Jen spoke convincingly. She could tell Tola was frightened and didn't want to make it any worse by sounding unsure.

Tola started to put her coat on and turned to face Jacqui. 'Even though this whole thing has been less than pleasant, it has been an absolute pleasure meeting you, Jacqui. I wish we could have a bit more time together. I think you and I would have gotten on nicely, you know?' She barely knew Jacqui, but they had shared an experience that was truly unique; it felt irrelevant that only one of them was still alive.

'If there's only one good thing to have come out of today,' Jacqui replied, 'it's having been able to talk to you, Tola. I'm glad Jen met you. Thank you for believing in her. It means everything to me.'

Tola buttoned her coat up and turned back to Jen. 'I don't know what to make of everything I have seen today, Jen. It's going to take some time for me to understand it all. Maybe it's not to be understood.'

'I'm sorry you had to go through it all. This isn't how I expected it to go. Will you be okay?' Jen hadn't stopped to think how it all might be affecting Tola. 'Ghosts have become something normal to me, and I forget that it's abnormal to everyone else.'

'I'll be okay, I just need to clear my head.' Tola went to leave, but turned round before she stepped out into the night air. 'This gift of yours, Jen, it truly is amazing. But it comes with its own dangers. Remember that and protect yourself. I do in my job; you need to think about how you can do it in yours.'

Tola waved goodbye and headed for her car with haste. Jen shut the door, wondering how she could do what Tola had suggested. But for now, there was a task at hand.

'Will you be able to stay here while I do this, Mum?'

'I'll be here, Jen. I'm not done yet. I wish I could go with you. I'm not sure what I hate the most: you delivering this demon on your own or you speaking to the man who killed Helen. It's all so horrible.'

'I'll barely have to say anything to him, and I won't be hanging about.'

Jen went back to the lounge to find the demon had gone from the window. Grabbing the box, she looked at it, wondering if some miniature version of the horrific woman was now inside.

She went back into the hallway to put her shoes and coat on, pausing to think about what she was about to do. 'She's going to kill him, Mum. Are we sure we can do this? I could just tell Tola that I did what we said. She's gone now so the demon can't follow her and attack her mum. You were so against this sort of thing before… look at what it did to you and Dad.'

'We've been left with no choice. I can't allow her to harm you, and you wouldn't be able to forgive yourself if she did something to Laura or Olivia.'

Jen finished putting on her shoes and stood up to face her mum. 'I know. She forced our hand and it's so frustrating. Okay, I'll be as quick as I can. Hang on for me.'

Jen hoped her mum could wait. She didn't want that to be their last moment together, but the quicker she could get this demon away from them the better.

***

Jen arrived outside Strickland's house with butter-flies doing tricks in her stomach. She felt physically sick. She had convinced herself that it was all pretty straightforward before, but now, sitting outside and knowing what she was about to deliver, she felt wretched.

'It's not me who's going to do anything to him. It's the demon. And she gave us no other option,' Jen said out loud, trying to absolve herself, her mum and Tola of blame.

Picking the box up, she walked past the sweeping lawn. The reindeer decorations were dazzling, and the willow tree was underlit with a light that slowly changed colour. Jen found the whole display quite impressive, despite who lived there.

As she approached the door, Jen spotted the door-bell, which was lit up in the darkness. She could hear the dogs inside had already detected her presence. Her finger hovered inches from the button for a few seconds before she pressed it, announcing her arrival.

Emma shushed the dogs and opened the front door to see a delivery person, standing there open-mouthed. Neither of them spoke.

Emma broke the awkward silence. 'Hello. Is that for us?' She looked down at the box in Jen's hands.

Jen was flummoxed. It hadn't crossed her mind that anyone else would answer the door; she'd completely overlooked Russell's wife being there. She didn't know what to do. Would the demon harm her too? Or would she use the wife to jump to Russell?

She didn't have enough time to decide on another course of action and found herself moving the parcel in Emma's direction.

Emma took it from her, said thank you and shut the door. That was it.

Jen stood there, wondering what awful fate she may have just unleashed onto the wrong person, then realised she should be leaving. She headed back down the driveway to her car at a sprint.

***

'What a strange person,' Emma said, looking at the parcel and noticing it was addressed to Russell. She took it into the kitchen and placed it on the island. 'There's a delivery for you,' she called.

Coco and Bella were going crazy. 'What's the matter with you two?' Emma said. 'I've never seen you so agitated. Even the squirrels don't drive you this mad!'

The bichons were snarling, teeth bared and spitting. Emma reached down to pet them, but they both backed away, their little paws skating over the kitchen tiles as they tried to find reverse. They were usually her unflinching shadows, but at the moment they didn't want her anywhere near them.

Russell came into the kitchen and shooed the dogs out the way. He had little time for them. 'Hopefully it's the wine we've been waiting for, otherwise I'm going to have to go to the shop and pick some up.' Russell took hold of his wife and looked at her. 'You look dreadful, darling. Go and spruce yourself up before dinner. Put some effort in for your husband.'

'Of course, dear, I was just about to.' Emma knew from experience there was no advantage in fighting back.

Coco and Bella had stopped barking and watched suspiciously as Emma walked past them and headed upstairs. They looked at Russell and sniffed the air, then, with a yelp, rushed as quickly as they could in Emma's direction. They had no interest in staying in the kitchen.

Russell looked disapprovingly at the parcel. 'This doesn't look big enough to hold twelve bottles of red.'

After opening a drawer to retrieve a knife, he sliced through the packing tape and opened the box to reveal a pile of shredded paper. Bewildered, he reached inside and searched around to find the box completely empty. He checked the label for a return address, but found nothing of use.

Swearing under his breath about the incompetence of delivery companies, he collapsed the box and placed it in the recycling bin, baffled by the whole thing.

Out of the corner of his eye, he thought he saw something move, just beyond his line of vision. He assumed it was one of the dogs, but they were both nestled next to Emma in the bedroom, staying as far away from their unwelcome visitor as possible.

***

Jen returned home and straight away searched the house for her mum. 'Mum! Mum! Are you here?'

'In here, Jen.'

Jen breathed a huge sigh of relief to find Jacqui in the lounge, looking out of the bifold window. She'd been looking out there since Jen had left to be doubly sure the demon was gone.

'How did it go? Have we completely got rid of her?'

Jen collapsed onto the sofa. 'Oh, Mum, his wife answered the door. She took me by surprise. I just handed the box over and left. What if the demon scares her, or worse, hurts her too? What have I done?'

'She saw her as a victim, so hopefully she'll leave her be. That was the point, wasn't it? For him to pay for what he has done, not just to Helen but his wives as well. I'm sure she knows who to focus her attention on. You were brave to go and do it, Jen. We all made the decision, but you're the one who had to get the job done. There's no different way this could have played out.' Jacqui tried to sound her most convincing. She didn't trust the demon by any stretch of the imagination, but she didn't want Jen feeling any more guilty than she already did. She hoped her daughter would not beat herself up about it for long—she knew she wouldn't be around to keep her from doing so.

'How will I explain this to Dad? I have no idea.'

'Do you have to tell him?' Jacqui asked.

'I can't have secrets, Mum, it's exhausting.'

'Yes. That they are. Give yourself time, Jen. You'll find a way to explain it. He'll understand it threatened you and you had no choice. Make sure he knows that.'

Jen got up and stood by her mum. 'The demon, she said you shouldn't be here anymore. What did she mean?'

Jacqui turned to Jen, wishing for just one last brush of her daughter's cheek. 'Oh, my beautiful girl, it's time for me to go. I can tell that I'm not meant to stay. This isn't how things should be.'

'But why can't you stay? It's not affecting anyone. You could stay here with me. There's probably loads more you need to tell me about the ghosts and how to talk to them. I need you to help me.' Jen's face streamed with tears.

'It is affecting someone, Jen. It's affecting you, and you are the last person I want suffering because I haven't moved on. When someone dies, it's final. There's no reversing it. It's an inevitability we all have to face, as frightening and life-shattering as it is. Grief has to be felt and worked through. It takes time; me staying is stopping you from starting that process. You can't grieve me if I am still here. It's not fair on you.'

Jen knew what her mum was saying was right, and she hated it. They had been granted this temporary stay of execution, but their time was up. She had worked out a while back that her mum still being around was holding her grief in check. It couldn't flow as it was meant to; it wasn't lessening, it was just waiting to be fully felt.

'Mum, how do I say goodbye to you? I'm not sure I can do it.'

'None of us think we can do it, but we must. I remember at your nan's funeral, waiting with your dad and you while everyone filed out, knowing I had to make my final farewell. That once I walked out of that room with my back to her coffin, having to leave her there, that would be it. It was one of the hardest things I have ever had to do. But we all have to say goodbye eventually. Everyone has their end, Jen.'

Jen could do nothing but sob. There was no argument she could make to counter her mum's words.

'It doesn't matter which way you look at it, Jen. At some point you might have had to watch me in a hospital bed for days as my body slowly gave up on me, or visit me in a home where I slowly forgot you and Dad and then everything entirely. If you didn't have this gift, you would have just found me in my bedroom, and then your goodbye would have been at my funeral. It is inescapable. But because of your gift, we get this moment. I don't know anyone else who gets this privilege. Isn't it wonderful?'

It didn't feel wonderful to Jen. It felt like a kick in the guts. Her heart was breaking into pieces. But then, it would have broken no matter how her mum had passed. It was always going to hurt this badly; she was as sure of that as she was of the sun rising each day. 'I don't want you to go.'

'I know. And I don't want to leave you, I have to leave you. I'll pop back in my own little ways, making sure you use a plate when you have a biscuit, or nudging you to get the vacuum out.' Jacqui was hoping to get a smile out of Jen, but it didn't work, not this time. 'But I can't stay here like this anymore. You have to let me go, Jen.'

'Mum, I'm so scared. I'll be on my own.'

'You'll have Dad and Laura, and all the other people in your life that will look after you. You are not going to be alone. It's time, Jen. Let me go.'

'I can't. I don't want to.'

'You have to.'

Jen felt like there wasn't enough air in her lungs and she couldn't breathe. Her head was pounding. The walls of the room were getting too close; she was being suffocated. She wanted to reach out and grab hold of her mum, hold on to her so tightly that no force in heaven or earth could take her away.

Just when she thought she might pass out, the comforting aroma of lavender and rosemary filled the air and she breathed it in deeply. The walls receded, and her breathing calmed.

'Let me go, Jen.'

Jen looked into her mum's eyes. There was nothing she could do to stop this. It was out of her control, save for one last thing she had to do, for her and for her mum.

Jacqui couldn't leave unless Jen was ready.

'I love you, Mum.'

'I love you too, Jen, forever and always.'

Jen closed her eyes and took one long breath in, then forced the words out. 'It's okay, Mum, you can go. Goodbye.'

She opened her tear-filled eyes to find that Jacqui was gone. Another wave of sadness crashed over her and she collapsed onto the carpet with her back against the sofa, her head in her hands and cries pouring out. She was all the way back in her mum's bedroom, having just found her; it was time for the grief to start its journey outwards.

***

Jen wasn't sure how long she had been sitting there when a wet nose touched her hand, seeking out a scratch on the head. Bleary eyed, Jen looked down to see a golden-coloured snout, then large, brown eyes looking at her.

'Bailey?'

Jen's hand ran through fur, and before she knew it, Bailey was up licking her face and had her pinned.

She tried to stand up. 'Hey, boy, time out! How are you here? Am I asleep?'

If she was, it was a wonderful dream that she didn't want to wake up from. Bailey wagged his tail with the same enthusiasm he'd had when he was alive. Jen's eyes were wide. She reached out again, expecting to feel nothing. But there it was, that warm, amber fur through her fingers and Bailey's body wiggling with all the excitement.

'Not a fan of rules either, eh, boy? You didn't go with Mum, then? I'm glad you stayed with me, you big lump. Not left on my own.'

Jen laughed through her tears as she fussed over Bailey's smiley face. 'And this time, there'll be no dog hairs on my clothes.' It felt good to laugh.

Jen wiped her face and looked round the room. 'Just you and me now, Bailey. Maybe it is a kind of wonderful.'

She couldn't help but keep touching her dog's head, and Bailey was in no rush to move. A peacefulness came over her, and a calm replaced her solemn mood. The sadness was still there but she could bear it for now.

'Come on, boy. I need to get changed for this party. I can't miss it, it's important that I'm there for Dad and everyone else. I'm not the only one that misses Mum.'

Bailey bounded past Jen up the stairs, beating her to the top like he always had.

***

'Jen! Come in, come in.' Jen's aunt answered the door and ushered her niece in, expertly removing her coat in a well-practiced move. 'Let's get you a drink. Your dad's here already.'

Jen made her way into the living room to see her dad in conversation with her uncle, who was over in a flash with one of his famous bear hugs.

'Jen, how are you? We are so happy you're here. Your dad says you're thinking of doing a bit of redecorating, colours I think Jacqui would approve of. You don't want her coming back to haunt the place because of the decor, do you!'

Jen just stared at him and for a moment, Mike wondered if it was too early for jokes. Then Jen smiled and let out an uncontainable laugh. It was funny because it was true; if her mum got the chance, she would definitely be back to comment on the choice of paint.

'It's bad enough trying to keep on top of any crumbs,' Jen said. 'I have visions of the vacuum coming to life all on its own when Mum isn't happy with my cleaning!'

Mike looked massively relieved.

Jen's aunt came in with a glass and handed it to her. 'Thought we'd start with these.'

It was a glass of Baileys, Jacqui's favourite drink.

Jen noticed everyone had one, even those who she knew hated the stuff. 'Brilliant, I love it, Mandy.'

Mike chinked his glass to get everyone's attention, and Jen moved over to where her dad was standing.

'Now we have everyone here,' Mike began, 'I know it's still early but I need to get this out of the way now, before the drinks make it harder to hold the tears back. It's been a tough few months. Losing Jacqui was a shock for all of us, none more so than Jen and Mark. But she would hate us to be moping about and being miserable, especially at one of her favourite times of year. So, let's raise a glass. To my sister, Jacqui.'

'To Jacqui.' Everyone in the room had their glasses raised, then people started to 'cheers' each other. The sound of clinking glass cascaded around Jen. She saw a few tissues deployed to dab wet cheeks. Some people pretended they just had something in their eye.

'How's your day been, Jen?' Mark asked.

Jen took a sip of her drink and contemplated her answer. After checking how close anyone was to them, she leant in as she replied, 'Mum left for good today, Dad. She won't be back this time.'

Mark wasn't sure how to respond. He'd already begun his journey of letting go of Jacqui, but he knew that Jen's unique gift meant she was a little behind him on that road.

Jen's eyes welled up a little, but the flood that she expected didn't come. The deluge had passed for now. She was sure it might come back at times, but for now she could manage. 'I'll be okay, Dad. I just need time to adjust now. I'll get there.'

Mark put an arm round his daughter and kissed her head. 'You will, and in your own time.'

Jen overheard one of their family friends recalling a time when Jacqui tried to cook moussaka for a dinner party and it went horribly wrong, resulting in a takeaway being ordered; she saw her aunt laughing as she showed a friend a family album that Jen recognised. She noticed her cousins, sitting on the sofa keeping a casual eye on their children. They all looked over and gave a little wave but seemed unsure on how to approach her. Jen remembered that they hadn't really known what to say to her at the funeral.

She walked over and sat herself down between two of them. 'I can't promise I won't cry at some point, but you can talk to me. I won't break into a million pieces, I promise! So, what's been going on?'

Just for a little while, thoughts of the box delivered to the Stricklands were far from Jen's mind.

CHAPTER 36

After disposing of the peculiar parcel, Russell went back to his home office. But every time he started to get into a flow of work, something would move behind him, just out of view. It irritated him and he couldn't concentrate.

'Those bloody dogs.' Russell got up from his chair and marched to the bottom of the stairs. 'Emma,' he shouted up. 'I have told you to keep those stupid rats of yours out of my office.'

Emma looked at the two little puffball faces staring back at her from the comfort of the duvet. They looked as confused as she did.

'They're both up here, Russell. But yes, I'll make sure they don't disturb you,' Emma replied politely, shrugging her shoulders.

Coco and Bella wouldn't dare go into his office anyway. Last time they did, Russell kicked Bella so hard that Emma thought he'd done the little lady permanent damage.

Shutting the door behind him, Russell sat back down to continue his work. He was keen to get a few more jobs done before dinner. The office was Russell's shrine to himself. Framed pictures of him with business colleagues at various dinners and talks adorned the walls. There were none of him and Emma; they were in the lounge, just for guests to see. A couple of industry awards were displayed on a shelf above the desk, which you could see from the kitchen if the door was open, which it always was if guests were round, so he could show them as part of his tour. His aftershave wafted through the whole room, which Emma detested whenever she had to go in there to clean.

The office had a patio door leading out onto some decking, which connected to the well-manicured lawn and the rest of the large garden. Russell was in the zone, tapping away a response to one of his emails, when one of the security lights came on in the garden. He ignored it; it was standard for the lights to come on occasionally. The light went off after ten seconds, as it was programmed to do.

After a minute or so, a different light went on, about two or three metres away from the last one. Russell now stopped what he was doing. It was early evening and already dark. Perhaps a cat was setting the lights off. He watched, waiting for the light to go off, then waited some more to see if another came on. Nothing happened, so he went back to his email.

As he typed the next word, all the outdoor lights came on at once, and standing in the centre of them was a woman.

Russell jumped up from his chair. 'Who the hell is that in my garden?' He was out the patio door in a flash and charging up the lawn to see who the intruder was.

'Oi, what do you think you're doing here?' he shouted as he approached the figure.

She stood perfectly still—unnaturally so.

'I said, what are you doing here? Answer me!' He couldn't believe her audacity.

The closer Russell got, the more he began to feel something he had not experienced before. It was a heavy feeling, so much so that it was making him walk more slowly, like he was dragging his feet through thick mud. He couldn't fathom what was going on; it was taking all his effort to get near the woman.

She hadn't replied or moved since he'd left the office, she just kept staring at him.

He was within a few strides of her and, with the bright lights on, which inexplicably had not gone off as they should have done, he could now make out her face. It was similar to a face he had in his memories, the face he liked to think about when he wanted to remember his power, the face with his hands around her throat.

'What? How? How can you be—?'

Helen Swift was standing in his garden. But she didn't look like the scared, defenceless woman he had killed. There was something off about the face looking back at him. It held him in a predatory glare, its eyes transfixed.

She opened her mouth, and in a whisper that seemed impossibly close to Russell's ears, she said one word. *'Run.'*

A feeling that Russell couldn't quite articulate was now completely taking him over. It was in the pit of his stomach; it was in the tightness of his chest.

It was absolute dread.

He started to back away, not sure of what he was seeing. He spun and headed back at a run to the sanctuary of his house, but tripped, just managing to get his hands out in front of him before hitting the rain-saturated grass. He scrambled his way back to standing, soil and grass finding a home under his well-looked-after nails, then he fell back into his office, pushing the door shut with such force that the frame shook.

The lights had now gone off, and he had no idea where the woman was. Out of breath, he looked out into blackness, trying to surmise if she was still out there.

I must have imagined it, he thought. All the news and the renewed investigation into Helen's disappearance must have got to him more than he'd thought.

Still keeping an eye on the window, he suddenly felt that someone was behind him, like he was being watched. He didn't want to see her face again, but he also didn't want to go back into the garden. Whatever was behind him was blocking his way out.

He turned quickly, grabbing a stapler off his desk, ready to attack—to find Emma looking at him, bewildered and with her arms up to defend herself.

'What were you doing out there, Russell? What happened to you?'

Russell looked down at himself. His chinos were muddied at the knees, his hands were dirty, and his face was sweaty. He looked far from his customary well-turned-out self. Slowly, he lowered his arm, trying to regain his composure. He couldn't bear that Emma was seeing him like this, vulnerable and scared.

'Get out of my way!' he said rudely, pushing past her to head for the shower.

Emma was used to Russell treating her like dirt but not looking like it. Coco and Bella stayed behind her as he went past, curling their lips up and showing their teeth.

Emma went back to preparing dinner, listening for the shower turning on upstairs. That gave her at least forty minutes peace; Russell usually spent ages there.

***

Dinner was a quiet affair. Russell would usually talk about the latest deal he had on the go and why the outfit Emma had on didn't suit her or how her make-up was making her look old. But he was subdued, preoccupied with something. He had barely touched his food; the bichons were hoping the leftovers were coming their way.

Emma was quite content with the silence between them. She didn't often get time to just sit and eat without being talked at. But even though it was pleasant, she could tell something was wrong, and this was making her increasingly nervous. When something was wrong, Russell always seemed to find a way of blaming her, and that brought its own consequences.

Emma finished her meal and stood up to clear the table.

'Where do you think you're going?'

Emma froze to the spot. 'I was going to clear the table.'

'Sit back down.' Russell's voice was full of spite.

Emma slid back into her seat. She sipped some of her water as her mouth had become dry. It was coming.

'I don't know what game you think you are playing, but it's not going to work,' Russell said.

Emma had no idea what he was talking about but refrained from saying anything. It never did any good.

'How did you make her appear on the lawn? That, I have to admit, was clever. But you're not clever, are you, Emma? You're far from it. Did you think it was going to frighten me? My chinos are ruined; that's your fault.'

Emma looked down at the table. She really did not know what Russell was alluding to. Make who appear on the lawn? Did he see something in the garden?

'Are you going to answer me, Emma?'

When she looked up from the table, Emma saw madness in Russell's eyes. He was angry.

'I-I don't know what you're talking about, Russell. I haven't done anything in the garden.'

'DON'T LIE TO ME, YOU STUPID BITCH! You think you can fuck with my head, make me see that Swift woman? Do you honestly think I'd feel guilty after all this time? I couldn't give a fuck, Emma. You've really pissed me off with your little charade… Maybe I'll show you how Helen died first-hand.'

Emma's adrenaline was in overload. It was no surprise to her that he had actually killed Helen Swift—she'd known since the police had turned up—but fight or flight, it never mattered. If she fought, he always won; he was stronger than her and more vicious. If she hid or tried to run, he always found or caught her, or threatened to hurt Coco and Bella, so she'd come out anyway.

She resigned herself to what was about to happen. She was tired. Deliberately, she stood up, ignoring what she was told to do. She piled the dishes ready to take to the kitchen, and as she walked past Russell, her hands full with cutlery and china, he punched her clean in the stomach. The pain caused her to let go of her cargo, allowing the plates to crash, one on top of the other, to the wooden floorboards. Cutlery clattered and food spattered the walls and floor.

Emma lay amongst the disarray, clutching her stomach and trying to catch her breath.

'Look at the mess you've made, you stupid woman. How much is this going to cost me to clean up, you clumsy idiot?'

She wondered if it would be her end this time. Something was different; Russell was incandescent with rage. She closed her eyes and waited for the inevitable kicks and punches. She heard Coco and Bella lapping at the dinner spilt around her then begin to bark.

But after a few seconds of tensing up, ready to take the hits, there was nothing save some muffled, gurgling sound she didn't recognise. No nasty words or physical attack.

Waiting a few more seconds, in case her wishful thinking had got the better of her, she opened her eyes and sat up as best she could while still holding her side.

Russell was no longer in his chair at the table where he had struck her from. He was about five feet up the dining room wall, pinned by a hand that was covering his mouth. His shoe heels banged against the wall as he struggled to take in air, making scuff marks along the pristine paintwork. He looked utterly terrified, and Emma could see why.

The hand, grey and dead against Russell's pink face, belonged to an arm that was clothed in grey rags, torn and ruined. The arm extended abnormally from a body dressed in the same cloth, the body of the woman positioned in the dining room with them. A woman with black, empty eyes and wild, untameable, black locks of hair, which were floating and weaving across the ceiling and doorway into the kitchen.

Emma had no idea where she had come from. The two bichons ceased their barking and scuttled out of the other dining room door, which led to the hallway, and waited at the bottom of the stairs, hoping their mistress would join them in safety.

But Emma did not run. Slowly, she stood and supported herself on a chair.

The grey woman regarded her respectfully, her grip still firm around Russell's face. *'You can leave. I will not harm you.'* She spoke in a calm voice.

Emma wondered if she was hallucinating. Maybe Russell had beaten her so badly she had passed out, her imagination conjuring up this protector in front of her. But she could tell she was neither unconscious nor seeing something that wasn't there—it really was there, and it was causing Russell an immense amount of distress.

She didn't mind seeing him in this position and took a moment to really look at the fear that was in his eyes. The fear he always put into her.

He was trying to say something to her. The woman released her hold, and he fell to the floor like a rag doll in a heap.

'EMMA! Don't leave me, help me, please.' He was visibly crying and trying to crawl round the table towards her.

At least that confirmed that she wasn't seeing things, unless they had both gone mad. Emma backed away from him, closer to the exit into the hallway.

The grey woman stretched her arm out to an impossible length and took hold of Russell's ankle, pulling him back so he was flat to the floor. His fingernails scratched at the wooden boards, but he could make no purchase.

'Emma, do something! Please, I beg you. I'll be better. I'll never hurt you again. I love you.'

Emma looked at Russell writhing around on the floor amongst the spilt food, like a pig, begging for her help. Then she looked up at the woman, who seemed to be waiting for her to respond.

'You choose, Emma.'

Emma didn't take long. 'Fuck you, Russell.'

The grey woman grinned and began to laugh, a satisfied laugh of unadulterated enjoyment.

Emma turned her back on Russell, grabbed her handbag and car keys, and let herself and the bichons out of the front door.

As it closed behind them, Russell screamed. 'Come back here, Emma, you bitch! You can't leave me! You need me!'

He felt a tug on his leg as the grey woman reeled him in like a fish ready to be gutted.

'Oh, but she doesn't need you, Russell. No one does. You're staying with me now.'

Both doors to the dining room slammed shut, as did every other door in the house. The locks on the front and back doors turned of their own volition, sealing the house from the inside.

As Emma drove down the driveway, she looked back at the house that had been her prison. Coco and Bella snuggled down into their baskets on the back seat.

Russell's screams couldn't be heard over the car radio, but Emma wouldn't have cared if she'd heard them anyway.

CHAPTER 37

Christmas arrived, as it always did, and Jen took her time with it. She'd prepared for not knowing how she was going to feel, so put no pressure on herself to feel any sort of way. Christmas without her mum was never going to be the same, she knew that. She was just going to take it all as it came and allow others around her to hold her hand.

Christmas morning felt very special, despite the gloom. Jen and her dad sat quietly over breakfast and didn't hold back their tears. They swapped presents, keeping their family tradition of opening stockings first, and without the other realising, had both bought a little something for Jacqui, which sat under the tree unwrapped.

There was less quiet and more activity over at Laura's, and Jen was glad to be part of it. Olivia was proudly wearing her new hockey gear when Jen arrived and even sat down to eat dinner with it still on. Although there were times when Jen felt sad and a bit out of place, Laura and Krish were there with a cuddle and a smile.

Jen had worried she would feel less loved with her mum gone, but the opposite was abundantly true. She'd never felt more loved by those she held most dear.

The relative calm of the week between Christmas and New Year's brought with it an opportunity to rest for Jen. The day after Boxing Day, she went home and pottered about, tidying here and there, and making plans for the next few months. She went to bed relatively early and slept so soundly that she didn't wake up until the afternoon of the following day.

Having managed to get herself out of bed but not bothering to get dressed, Jen sorted herself out some toast and noticed two messages from her dad and two missed calls from Laura. A shot of panic cut through her, and hoping something bad hadn't happened, she phoned her back immediately.

'Hey, it's me, saw your calls. Is everything okay? Sorry, I've had the phone on silent most of the time.'

'Yes, everything is fine here. I was checking if you'd seen it?' Laura said, expecting Jen to know what she was talking about.

'Seen what? I've only just got up.'

'Blimey, you must have been tired! Hang on, I'm sending you a link. It's on all the major news pages; it was even on the telly earlier.'

Jen put Laura on loudspeaker and clicked on the link to a news article.

'Sussex businessman found dead on Boxing Day.

Russell Strickland, 57, was found on Boxing Day by a neighbour in the early hours of the morning. The police have confirmed that Mr Strickland left a letter confirming that he was responsible for the abduction, rape and murder of Helen Swift, who went missing in November 1992. Her body was recently discovered in a house in Sussex.

Police are not seeking anyone else in connection with his death.'

Russell Strickland was dead. Jen had been trying to push all thoughts of what might have happened to him from her mind, but there it was in black and white. The demon had killed him, just as she had said she would. Or rather, had pushed him to the point where taking his own life was the better option.

A cold chill came over Jen. She had assisted in Russell's demise; in that she felt there was no question. She took no pleasure in it. Now was not the time to confess, however.

'Jen, did you read it?' Laura asked impatiently.

'Yes, wow. Well, that's it then, isn't it. Case closed.' Jen wanted to keep the chatting to a minimum, but she was out of luck.

'Did you know it was him? Did Helen tell you? How does it feel, Jen, to have helped bring her home and find out who did it? What an amazing thing to be involved in! Okay, it's a shame he committed suicide and wasn't made to go through a trial and everything, but at least he's not hurting anyone else.'

Laura's words cut deep. Jen knew the case would never have gone to trial; Russell Strickland would not have been made to answer for what he did in a court of law.

She was squirming inside. She'd finally managed to tell Laura everything, but she was now back to square one, having to hide something again.

Avoiding Laura's questions, Jen tried to reply as plainly as she could. 'Yes, his suicide is unfortunate, but, as you say, one less horrible person in the world. What else has been going on then?'

Jen managed to swerve Laura onto Olivia's hockey endeavours quite quickly. After spending another ten or so minutes on the phone, she ended her call with Laura, already knowing what the messages from her dad would be about.

'Give me a call when you get five mins.'

Two minutes later.

'I assume you're not up yet, check the news out.'

Jen reluctantly called her dad.

'Morning sleepy, have a good lie in?'

'Yes, I definitely needed it. And yes, I have seen the news. Laura was ahead of you.'

'Had you heard of him from Helen?' Mark enquired.

'No, she didn't know who the man was.' Technically that wasn't a lie, Jen told herself.

'I wonder if he was already on the police's radar. Had Tola told you anything? Maybe that's why he opted for suicide. Although, a man who could do something like that, I doubt he felt guilty enough to kill himself. He would have done it sooner, surely?'

Jen didn't want to speak in case she tied herself up in knots. Lying was not her forte; she was rubbish at it. She really wanted to tell her dad what really happened—between him and Laura, Jen felt he would get it the most—but she just couldn't do it, not yet.

'No, not heard from Tola recently.' Another technical truth. 'Suppose we'll never know now what he was thinking and why he killed himself.'

'Very true—probably best not to know, he was clearly a nasty piece of work. Presumably that's the end of it then? No more visits from Helen?'

'No, I'm not expecting to see Helen again.'

'Quite right, she deserves some peace. As do you, until the next one turns up. Hopefully someone with a much simpler message that needs passing on. Anyway, what's on the agenda? Anything you need help with at the house?'

Jen breathed a quiet sigh of relief as her dad moved on from Russell Strickland.

***

Jen spent the next few days wondering how Tola was feeling and if she now regretted their choice. Then, on New Year's Eve came the phone call. Tola asked if she could meet Jen, somewhere between them both.

They arrived at a café within a few minutes of each other, and after exchanging pleasantries, they sat down with drinks in their hands.

Neither one spoke for what seemed an eternity.

Jen broke the silence. 'It's funny, but I don't really know what to say to you. Which is silly really, considering all we've been through. How was Christmas anyway?'

'It was lovely, lots of time with family, which is what it's all about. Oh, sorry, I forgot about your mum.' Tola winced at her error.

'It's okay, please don't worry. To be honest, I wondered if I would hear from you again. I thought you might be too scared of me after what happened.'

'I'm not scared of you, Jen. I am scared, but more of what may want to talk to you. And on that subject, I have some information you need to hear—but it's not pleasant, I warn you.'

Jen motioned for Tola to continue.

'The press was asked to hold off publishing any more details until Russell's confession could be fully verified, which it now has. They've also not been told some of the major details. I wasn't first on the scene, but I can tell you, it was one of the most bizarre I have ever seen.'

Tola recounted the statements the police had received.

'Emma explained that Russell had been acting strangely the day before Christmas Eve. He was saying peculiar things; she said it was as if he was having a complete mental breakdown. She admitted that she saw it as her chance to get out of the house without him. Russell rarely allowed her to go anywhere on her own and she hadn't been allowed to spend any time with her family since marrying him. She took the dogs and didn't bother packing. She went to her parents that evening, where she stayed until the police contacted her. She said that she hadn't felt compelled to contact Russell, assuming he would call her if he needed anything.'

Jen felt her chest physically relax. She had been worrying herself into a rabbit hole about Strickland's wife and was thankful that she had come to no harm.

Tola continued. 'A neighbour had tried to call Russell several times late on Christmas Day, because the large reindeers on the lawn were flashing continuously, making it difficult for them to get to sleep. He said that he and Russell had never really got on, that he found Strickland to be exceptionally arrogant and, in his own words, "a bit of a creep". The reindeer usually went off on a timer, but that evening, they were flashing in various patterns and there seemed to be no stopping them.

'In the end, frustrated with a lack of response on the phone, the neighbour went over to the Stricklands' around one-thirty am and pulled the power lead out of the socket himself. On turning to leave, he looked up at the willow tree, still lit up in various colours as that light had a battery, and saw what he thought looked like a figure hanging from one of the higher branches, a ladder toppled on the ground underneath. He got closer to be sure; I am sure he regrets that now.'

'He was hanging from the tree in the front garden?' Jen said, astonished, remembering the statuesque feature taking up much of the frontage. 'I just assumed he was found inside his house somewhere.'

'It seems our dangerous visitor wanted a spectacle made of Russell Strickland. When our team arrived, they found he was indeed hanging from a branch of his own tree. His smart shirt was smeared with blood and half undone; he had no shoes or socks on; the front door was unlocked. But this is where it starts getting really crazy: one of the officers who entered the property said it was as if the house was telling them its own tale of a man driven mad by his own guilt.'

'That's an eloquent description,' Jen noted.

'She's quite the reader. Anyway, three letters were found on the kitchen island. One addressed to us, the police, with a set of door keys on top, containing the confession to Helen's murder. Strickland described how he had watched Helen for months in the woods and how he had kept a set of keys when his mother's house was sold to the council. He gave details about what Helen's dog Pip looked like and how he had snatched him to lure Helen to follow him to his car. He recounted how he hit Helen's head to daze her before driving her away, eventually raping and killing her in his mother's old house. He described how he wrapped her in a duvet that he had brought in the car and dragged her into the downstairs cupboard. At the end of the letter, he begged for forgiveness from Helen's children.'

Jen sat back in her chair. 'Wow, more or less exactly as Helen told us.'

'I know, that's astounding in itself, isn't it? The second letter was addressed to Anne's sister, you know, his late wife. Strickland admitted that he knowingly pushed her to take her own life and that he used her history of depression to cover up his own actions—a depression only caused by years of physical and mental abuse, all of his own doing. He confessed to how evil he was to Anne, saying that she was worthless, that no one else could possibly love her. He called her ugly, disgusting, overweight and gross. He made her think that no one would believe what he was doing to her and that she was truly alone. At the end of the letter, he begged for forgiveness from Anne's family.'

'Well, I wonder if he'll ever be granted that,' Jen said, sipping the rest of her coffee.

'I think forgiveness was quite far from Anne's sister's mind when she read the letter. Apparently, she was so angry she threw a glass across the kitchen while our officers were still there. It must still hurt deeply, what happened.

'Finally, the third letter was addressed to Emma. He admitted to starting the cycle of abuse all over again, knowing that her youth and inexperience kept her submissive and unlikely to leave. He described how he alienated her from her parents, siblings and friends to make sure she had no one to turn to apart from him. At the end, he begged for Emma's forgiveness.'

'So, do you think the demon forced him to write all these before she made him hang himself?' Jen asked.

'I think she made him do a lot more than that before he went outside with the rope. As our investigators made their way methodically through the house, Russell's mental state, during the days between Emma leaving and his death, was evident for all to see.

'The three letters seem to have been written before he had completely lost his mind. The envelopes and paper were pristine and the writing neat and clear.

But there were other notes scattered throughout the downstairs of the house, torn bits of paper with words scrawled and blood smudged across them. *"She won't stop"* and *"I am the devil"* were some of the easier ones to read.

'Bloody fingerprints were found across the walls in every room, on the sofa and on the kitchen surfaces. Chairs had been knocked over, cushions thrown to the floor, books and ornaments pulled from their shelves; pictures were askew on the walls or thrown to the floor, and one door looked like it had been kicked down from the inside. It was as if Russell had been running from something; the police presumed it was himself.'

Jen sat rooted to her chair, saying nothing. She was imagining the terror ripping through Strickland as he moved through his house. Tola had paused for a drink. She seemed to need a boost before continuing.

'A pair of tweezers were found in the downstairs toilet basin, along with fine hairs, flecking the porcelain. It was the pathologist who made the gruesome observation during the initial review of the body, that Russell had no eyelashes. It seems that Russell Strickland stood in front of the mirror and plucked out every single one of his own eyelashes. Have you got any idea how painful it is to deliberately pull out just one eyelash?'

'Oh, I do know. I had a stye once and thought it would be sensible to pull the infected lash out myself. The pain was incredible. Makes me feel a bit sick thinking about it.'

'Then you'll appreciate how insane he must have been to pull every single one out. And that's not all. Bloodied finger and toenails were found in a pile on the kitchen floor next to a pair of pliers. Our guys later established that no one else had entered the house, and based on how they were extracted, Russell had to have done it to himself.'

'Jeez, she really put him through absolute torture. No less than he deserved, though.' Jen instantly wondered if that was too harsh given the circumstances; she wondered if she should be revelling in any of Russell's demise.

'This demon, woman, whatever she is, was unrelenting. We checked the doorbell camera and watched Russell going out into the front garden at twelve forty-three am with a ladder and a rope. He was easy to see in the glow of the light under the tree. We watched him climb the ladder and tie the rope. He then put his head through the noose and kicked the ladder out from underneath himself. He didn't struggle, it was as if he had given up completely, resigned to his fate.

'The last thing we saw on the footage was a dark shape moving across the camera. When the shadow moved away and the video adjusted focus, Russell was no longer moving. All we could see was the flashing Christmas lights, highlighting where he was, on and off.

'There was one final note found in his trouser pocket:

'"I have been found guilty of my crimes and now I must pay. I took hope from all the women I hurt. I know I am going to die, and I know there is nothing that can save me."

'It didn't take us long to rule out any third parties as having anything to do with Russell Strickland's death, so, pending the paperwork, it's considered a clear suicide.'

Tola sat back, relieved to have finished what she had come to say.

'I have to admit, I am shocked at the lengths she went to. I thought she would—well, I didn't know what I thought she would do, really. But this is far worse than I imagined. She had him trapped for, what, nearly three days? Jesus. She really tormented every last second of his life, didn't she?'

'Jesus was certainly not there to help him,' Tola said. 'Neither should He have been.'

'Do you think he deserved all of it then?' Jen wasn't totally sure herself.

Tola breathed in deeply and exhaled slowly, giving her answer much thought. 'We had no right to sentence a man to that end. Even if we thought that getting away with what he did to Helen was completely unacceptable. I'm not sure where I sit on it all at the moment, but it was him or someone we loved. We were threatened with an impossible decision. And given that as the choice, there was no choice. I can absolve myself of a little guilt with that fact alone. I won't torment myself with regret for something we were forced to do, so I recommend that you don't either. Maybe one day there'll be a judgement upon me, but for now, I'll have to live with what has happened.'

Jen considered Tola's response while looking out the window at some people crossing the road. 'Part of me absolutely believes he deserves everything he got. Then the other part makes me feel bad for even thinking that way. Then there was my mum—I couldn't believe after all her warnings that she agreed to it.'

'She did that to protect you. I was protecting my mum, you did it to protect your friend's family. That is the bargain we were made to make.'

'I suppose. I'm not sure how my dad is going to take it. And I can't even begin to work out how to explain it to Laura. I was hoping to go the rest of the way with no more secrets, but I'm back to where I started.'

'I understand. Maybe soon I'll tell Samuel about it; he really won't be expecting this story! But not yet. As for secrets, the sooner you can find a way to tell them, the better. You mustn't have this weighing on you for too long.'

'I feel like I've been used, but like you said, we had no choice. I do feel guilty, but there's a part of me that can't feel sorry for him. Not after what he did to Helen, how he treated his wives. He was never going to stop.'

The awkward silence from the beginning of their meeting returned, and Jen sensed Tola was not completely finished. 'Was there anything else you wanted to ask me, Tola?'

Tola shifted in her chair and looked around to see if anyone was close enough to hear her. 'Are there other things like her, Jen? Demons, I mean. She talked about when your parents called something into the house.'

'My honest answer is that I don't know, but perhaps. How she knew about that, I have no idea—maybe there's some kind of social media or noticeboard on that side they're all looking at. Could you imagine? I know that's probably not what you wanted to hear, but it's my honest answer.'

Tola made an agreeable noise and shook her head. 'I'll never complain about an honest answer. Well, let's hope that is the end of it. It got what it wanted from us.'

Jen hoped, too, that it was over. But a sense of foreboding was forming. Who was the someone looking for them? She was not keen on being seen as a beacon every time she used her gift. She desperately wanted to avoid attracting the wrong attention.

***

Jen had trouble getting to sleep that night. She fidgeted in bed until she gave up and walked across the landing, hoping a reset might help.

She put the bathroom light on and looked at her face in the mirror. On the windowsill, next to her toothbrush were her tweezers. She picked them up calmly and hovered them close to her eye. Deftly, she took hold of one eyelash between the metal tips and lightly tugged, feeling the lash taut within her eyelid. She stared at herself intently and pulled, watching as her face screwed up in pain. Then she took hold of a clump of eyelashes with the tweezers and yanked.

Looking back in the mirror, she could see bruises forming and blood seeping around her eye. As she blinked, the face in the mirror switched. Russell Strickland stared back at her, with his own bloody eyes.

'I can find you anytime, Jennifer. I know what you did.'

Jen started to scream, a desperate, fearful scream. But her mouth wouldn't open, and the only sound she could make was a muffled whimper.

She awoke, sweating and breathing fast, and leapt out of bed as if she had something crawling on her that needed to be shaken off. Was this what absolute guilt felt like?

She ran out onto the landing, scared to get back into bed and not wanting to go in the bathroom. As her breathing calmed, she noticed Bailey, sitting up and looking at her.

'I don't want to go back to sleep, boy,' Jen said, lying on the floor next to her faithful friend. She stroked his fur and tried to convince herself that Russell was just in her subconscious.

He's not really here. He's not really here.

CHAPTER 38

New Year's for Jen was a bit of a mixed affair compared to Christmas. Whilst the festive period held some cheer and happiness for her, the new year brought with it sombre beginnings, not the usual, eagerly anticipated ones. She was leaving one year, in which she had lost her mum, and had no option but to start a new one without her. There was no escaping it.

At midnight, as Laura and Krish kissed and Olivia gave Jen a New Year's hug, Jen felt that she was letting go of her mum all over again. Maybe every year was going to feel like this; she had no idea.

Laura clocked Jen's sadness, and they both ventured out into the garden, watching the neighbour's fireworks going off above their heads.

'It's not always going to feel like this, Jen,' Laura said in an attempt to console her best friend. 'Every day it will sting a little less. It won't go away completely, but it will feel like you can cope more.'

'I am tired of being okay one minute then so upset the next. I just need something constant for a bit, something to help me ground myself.'

'I imagine having ghosts popping up doesn't help much. Although, it must be lovely to have Bailey there. It really is amazing, Jen; in that way, you are so lucky with your gift. If I could give Captain Smuggins another tummy tickle, I would love that.'

Jen smiled at the thought of Laura's old cat. He had been black and white, inherited from Laura's nan after she died. He'd lived to a ripe old age and died peacefully in his basket, back when Laura and Jen still lived with their parents.

'Ah, the Captain. Well, if I ever see him wandering around, I will definitely let you know.'

***

Tola spent New Year's with Samuel, her children and grandchildren. It was the first one where she no longer needed to wonder if this would be the year she would find Helen. She raised a glass to all the Swift family as the clock struck midnight, hoping that wherever Helen was, she was enjoying bathtime.

***

Helen's memorial service was in the first week of the year. Hundreds of local people turned out to welcome her home, lining the road that led to where she would eventually be laid to rest. The service itself was private, but the family passed a statement onto the local news media to thank everyone for their kindness. They said they could literally feel everyone's love as they drove past and that their mum would have wondered what all the fuss was about.

Russell Strickland was cremated at the same venue two weeks later. His brother attended the funeral out of duty, and acknowledged Emma at the end, who had stood at the back of the room during the whole of the short service.

She had only attended to check that Russell was really dead. She had admitted to her parents what she had seen at the house, worried they might dismiss it, knowing what she had been through, but they didn't. They were beyond glad to have her home with them. Both of them were sure, without doubt, that an angel had come to save their daughter, and Emma was happy for them to think that.

If the woman had been an angel for her, she certainly hadn't been for Russell. At the end of the service, Emma walked up the aisle, stood by the casket and placed a card next to it. Inside, she had written: *'Not forgiven, but you will be forgotten.'* She knew he'd hate that.

***

Jen dreamt about her face in the bathroom mirror and the tweezers every so often. She'd convinced herself it was a way for her brain to process what had happened, and that's what dreams were for. She refused to entertain the notion that Russell Strickland could reach her beyond the grave, despite her own evidence to the contrary.

With January underway, Jen felt that getting the Christmas decorations back into the loft was well overdue, so she called her dad over for some help in exchange for lunch.

'You look tired, Jen. Are you getting enough sleep?' Mark asked as Jen climbed into the loft.

'I'm fine, just getting used to everything. It was bound to keep me awake some nights.' She did not feel compelled to go through the whole story with him at that moment. 'How many more?' she shouted down the hatch, changing the subject.

'That's it. We didn't put that much up. We'll have to go mad next time to make up for this one.'

Jen shuffled the boxes her dad had passed up back into their annual resting place. She was about to descend the ladder when she saw a couple more with *'Mum's Bits'* written on them in Jacqui's handwriting.

'Can you help me bring these ones down?'

Mark grabbed the boxes as they appeared through the hatch one after the other. 'Ah, these are the ones I was talking about when I said some of your nan's stuff was still upstairs.'

'I thought it might be nice to see some of her old things. I wonder what Mum kept.'

They brought the boxes downstairs and put them on the dining room table. Jen opened the first one and found some egg-shaped ornaments wrapped in newspaper. She recognised them from her nan's glass cabinet. She had always wanted to play with them, as they were made in two halves and could be opened, but her nan had thought better than to let an eight-year-old play tea parties with her delicate china.

Mark opened another box. 'It's clothes. Your mum must have wanted to keep these ones. Looks like a couple of jumpers and a blouse.'

'I remember Nan in that.' Jen placed the eggs carefully back in their paper, and picking up a mint-green jumper, she brought it up to her nose. It had a tinge of loft mustiness, but behind that it still smelled of her nan. 'I think I can do something with these. Laura told me about a lady she knows who makes bears out of any material you give her. Like a memory bear. That would be lovely, wouldn't it?'

'Excellent idea, Jen. It's not like you're going to wear any of it. I'll pop these eggs out of the way; we don't want them getting broken.' Mark took the box of ornaments back upstairs to the spare room as Jen opened the last box.

Inside, she found a large, wooden jewellery box wrapped in a few sheets of tissue paper and secured with an elastic band, and some smaller ring-sized boxes. 'Oh my God, have you been up there all this time?' Jen was surprised to find her nan's favourite rings, all stored safely inside.

She expected her mum had intended to pass them on but never got the chance. Jacqui wasn't much of a ring wearer herself, and her nan had not been able to wear them in the latter part of her life.

'What do we have here?' As Jen went to remove the elastic band from around the large box, it disintegrated, having deteriorated over time.

The piece of paper had three words on it in capitals. Jen could tell it was her nan's handwriting.

'BROKEN. DON'T USE.'

The wooden box was beautifully crafted and decorated with a floral design on the top.

'Shame you have been sitting in the loft all these years,' Jen said to herself.

The lid opened to reveal one completely empty compartment lined with red felt.

'Doesn't look broken to me. Maybe she meant the hinges?' Jen turned the box this way and that to discover what might be wrong with it. 'What's this?' She felt something moving within the box as she turned it.

She tipped it more slowly from side to side. 'There's definitely something in here.' Looking underneath, she could see some of the wood was chipped, as if the base had been prised open before. Looking back inside, it seemed the bottom was false.

'What are you doing with that? That's really not the right tool for the job,' Mark said, bemused to find Jen performing surgery on the box with a butter knife from the kitchen.

'There's something in here,' Jen said.

Suddenly, the bottom of the box popped off to reveal its secret. A book, a piece of paper and a smaller black box fell out. The book she had seen before, or at least ones like it. It had a blue leather cover and gold embossed flower on the spine. Jen knew whose words would be inside without having to open it.

She ran her fingers over the small, black box; its velvet exterior felt expensive. Her hands were tingling in anticipation of what might be inside.

'Oh my, look at you,' Jen said as she opened it.

For a moment, the demon's eyes filled her mind, but in a blink, Jen dismissed them. In their place, right in front of her, was the onyx-black oval stone from the old photographs of Elizabeth and Annabelle. Jen turned it over to inspect the tarnished gold back, its pin and clasp still in place ready to be worn once more.

'What is it?' Mark asked.

'It looks like another of Elizabeth's notebooks and her brooch, plus a note. They have been hidden here for who knows how long. Why do you suppose anyone would do that?'

The End

ACKNOWLEDGEMENTS

Thanks to all the team at Rowanvale Books for making my dream a reality. I found you by chance, searching the internet one day. But maybe some things aren't chance. You have all been fantastic.

To Sally, my first early reader. Thank you for your enthusiasm and truthful feedback. All of it was appreciated immensely.

To Sarah, you may have been too scared to read the book yourself, but you've been such an absolute cheerleader for me all the way.

To Rachel, for always listening, usually over a tableful of Italian food. You never doubted my ambition. And I am proud of you, too.

To Caroline, for your photo expertise.

Thanks to anyone who listened to me blithering on about my book. The school mum gang, Funmi, my Kent girls, my work colleagues and random people I'd just met. To talk about it made it real and made me believe it was something I could actually do.

Thank you, Mum and Dad, for supporting me and allowing me to follow whatever path I chose. I love you both very much.

Thanks to my husband for allowing me to pursue my dream, no matter how off-piste it may have originally seemed. I love you.

Finally, to my beautiful daughter. Thanks for not being a complete pre-teen and showing some interest in what Mummy was writing, even if I haven't let you read it yet. I'd like very much to come back as a ghost for you one day and make sure you're using a plate for your biscuits. I love you more than I have words for.

AUTHOR PROFILE

Claire Bamford is the mum to a daughter and a dog, and lives with her husband in Surrey. She loves cooking, puzzling and all things paranormal.

This is Claire's first novel, and she hopes to complete her next one in between working and being a taxi mum.

What Did You Think of *The Messenger*?

A big thank you for purchasing this book. It means a lot that you chose this book specifically from such a wide range on offer. I do hope you enjoyed it.

Book reviews are incredibly important for an author. All feedback helps them improve their writing for future projects and for developing this edition. If you are able to spare a few minutes to post a review on Amazon, that would be much appreciated.

Publisher Information

Rowanvale Books provides publishing services to independent authors, writers and poets all over the globe. We deliver a personal, honest and efficient service that allows authors to see their work published, while remaining in control of the process and retaining their creativity. By making publishing services available to authors in a cost-effective and ethical way, we at Rowanvale Books hope to ensure that the local, national and international community benefits from a steady stream of good quality literature.

For more information about us, our authors or our publications, please get in touch.

www.rowanvalebooks.com
info@rowanvalebooks.com

Printed in Dunstable, United Kingdom